The Other Story

The Other Story

Tatiana de Rosnay

St. Martin's Press ♏ New York

THE OTHER STORY. Copyright © 2013 by Éditions Héloise d'Ormesson, Paris. All rights reserved. Printed in the United States of America. For information, address St. Martin's Press, 175 Fifth Avenue, New York, N.Y. 10010.

www.stmartins.com

Library of Congress Cataloging-in-Publication Data

Rosnay, Tatiana de, 1961–
    The other story / Tatiana de Rosnay.—First U.S. Edition.
        p. cm.
    ISBN 978-1-250-04513-3 (hardcover)
    ISBN 978-1-4668-4353-0 (e-book)
    1. Authorship—Fiction.   2. Family secrets—Fiction.   I. Title.
    PR9105.9.R66O88 2014
    823'.914—dc23

                                            2013046591

St. Martin's Press books may be purchased for educational, business, or promotional use. For information on bulk purchases, please contact Macmillan Corporate and Premium Sales Department at 1-800-221-7945, extension 5442, or write special markets@macmillan.com.

First published in France under the title À L'encre russe by Éditions Héloise d'Ormesson in 2013

First U.S. Edition: April 2014

10 9 8 7 6 5 4 3 2 1

This book is for Héloïse and Gilles (they know why).

And for Sarah Hirsch (she knows why, as well).

IN MEMORIAM

❧

*My grandmother Natacha Koltchine de Rosnay
(Saint Petersburg, 1914–Sens, 2005)*

*My uncle, Arnaud de Rosnay
(Paris, 1946–Formosa Strait, 1984)*

❧

Forget the books you want to write.
Think only of the book you are writing.

—HENRY MILLER

You don't write because you want to say something;
you write because you have something to say.

—F. SCOTT FITZGERALD

Friday
July 15, 2011

All is vanity. Nothing is fair.
—WILLIAM THACKERAY

WHEN NICOLAS ARRIVED AT the Gallo Nero, he felt as if this was not a hotel, but someone's home, a long ocher house with a dark red roof and green shutters. Lamborghinis, Ferraris, Porsches, and Jaguars were parked farther off. Up a couple of steps, then the door opened. A svelte woman in a black suit uttered his name as if it were the most enchanting sound in the world. Malvina and he were shown through a lobby which looked nothing like a hotel lobby, more like the entrance to a friend's welcoming abode: tiled floors, beamed ceilings, a stone fireplace with a painting of a rooster hanging above it, comfortable white sofas, bright-colored cushions, plants, low tables, stacks of books and magazines. Through the open bay windows, he could see out to the candlelit terrace and hear the murmur of voices, laughter, the click of ice cubes, the tinkle of a piano playing "The Girl from Ipanema." The Gallo Nero smelled of cinnamon and sunshine, lemon and lavender, but also, most important, of pleasure and money.

Two weeks ago, in Paris, on a sweltering day at the beginning of July, a blue-eyed journalist from a glossy magazine, Frédérique, a pretty girl with a toothy smile, had murmured over lunch at the Cigale Récamier, "Nicolas, you must go to the Gallo Nero." She mentioned it as being the ideal place for a luxurious getaway. Easy to remember. The Black Rooster. He looked it up. Exclusive. The kind of spot the happy few discreetly flocked to. The resort was situated on a tiny island off the Tuscan shore. It had a private rocky beach accessed by a James Bond–like elevator built into the cliff, a famous chef, tennis courts, and a kidney-shaped seawater pool. The prices were indecent. But this was tempting. He was longing to escape from the stuffy Parisian summer. And he had not been back to the Italian seaside since 2003, since that trip with François, his best friend. He called the Gallo Nero, and the condescending person who answered the phone announced, "I'm sorry, signor, there are no vacancies for that week. We are booked months in advance." Nicolas mumbled an apology, and this: "Can I leave my name and number in case you do have a vacancy? It's my girlfriend's birthday, and . . . well . . . ." A sigh on the other end of the line. He assumed the sigh meant a yes, so he muttered, "Nicolas Kolt." Before he could get started on his number, a stran-gled moan was heard. "Excuse me?" gasped the woman, as if someone were throttling her. "You said Nicolas Kolt." He was get-ting used to this, but it had not yet begun to weary him. "The writer? The author of *The Envelope*? Signor Kolt, you should have told me right away who you were; of course we have a room for you—in fact, one of our prettiest rooms, with a lovely view over the Monte Argentario. When would you be coming, Signor Kolt?"

They got in late Thursday evening, Malvina supine, after a long trip, a flight from Paris CDG over to Rome FCO, where a chauf-feur came to pick them up, and then the drive along the coast. This Friday morning, Malvina is still asleep in the large room, which is indeed lovely. Tasteful tones of sand and beige, aquarelles of Italian villages, creamy white curtains and bedcover. White roses, small bowls of figs and grapes. An envelope with a personal greeting from the hotel director, Dr. Otto Gheza. Nicolas rises

early, taking care not to wake Malvina, and peeks out from behind
the curtains to the balcony with its two deck chairs, square teak-
wood table, and potted bay trees. He slips his bathing suit on and
the fluffy bathrobe hanging on the bathroom door, and silently
makes his way outside to breakfast on the terrace, clasping a black
Moleskine notebook and a black Montblanc fountain pen.

Nicolas cannot help noticing that the entire staff, from the
housekeeper in charge of the room to the maid who brings bottled
water, seems to know his name. They know it and they pronounce
it properly, à la russe, with a round *o,* as if they are aware it has
been truncated from Koltchine. They smile at him, yet he feels no
hypocrisy in those smiles, no bowing and scraping. There are few
rooms here, he informed Malvina during the flight, only twenty or
so. The place closes down for the winter but is full from April to
September. He told Malvina what he read on the Web site, that
the Gallo Nero was imagined in the sixties by an American pilot
and a Roman heiress who fell in love and built this villa overlooking the sea. They had no children, so thirty years later, the estate
was sold to a rich Italian, who turned it into a hotel. Malvina found
this romantic, which Nicolas knew she would. Malvina was a firm
believer in romance, an aspect of her personality he was often
charmed by.

A breakfast buffet is set up beneath large square parasols. There
is little noise. Only the whizz of a sprinkler, the chirp of an invisi-
ble bird, the muffled roar of a plane high in the cloudless sky. Despite the early hour, several clients are already having their meal.
Nicolas is ushered to a table overlooking the view, and he sits down.
The sea shimmers, vast and turquoise, dotted here and there with
yachts, ferries, and cruise ships. He is asked whether he prefers
tea or coffee; he answers Lapsang souchong. It is brought to him
in a heavy teapot within five minutes. He waits a short while, then
pours out the Lapsang. A smart-looking man in a dark suit glides
by, nods his head, and mouths, "Have a nice day, Signor Kolt."
Nicolas nods back, wondering if this is the hotel director, Dr.

Gheza, and whether he should have said something, or should have gotten up. He has a sip of tea, reveling in its ashy tang, takes his notebook out of his pocket, and lays it on the table in front of him, opening it to the first page. He reads his last notes. Notes for the goddamn book he is pretending to be writing. Notes so that he can look the part, notes so that it can be said, in all earnestness, in all truth, Nicolas Kolt is writing his new novel, the one they are all waiting for, the follow-up—yes, that book. Notes so that Alice Dor (French publisher and agent) and Dita Dallard (publicist) feel relieved. Notes so that Emma Duhamel née Van der Vleuten (mother) feels relieved. Notes so that Malvina Voss (girlfriend) feels relieved. Notes so that Delphine Valette (ex-girlfriend) and Gaïa Garnier (her daughter) and Elvire Duhamel and Roxane Van der Vleuten (aunts) feel relieved. Notes so that Lara Martinvast (best female friend) feels relieved. Notes so that Isabelle Pinson (banker) and Corinne Beyer (tax expert) feel relieved. Notes so that Agneta Sandström (Swedish publisher), Carla Marsh (American publisher), Ursula Berg (German publisher), Lorenza Manfredi (Italian publisher), Marije Gert (Dutch publisher), Alina Vilallonga (Spanish publisher), and so on and so forth, so that all these worried women around him, in and out of the publishing world, feel relieved. Nicolas is writing his new novel. Look at him scribbling away, eyebrows turned down in a concentrated frown, pen feverishly scrawling. Little do they know, those anxious women, that his notebook is full of doodles and sentences that have no meaning, no structure, mere strings of words linked one to the other like beads on a necklace.

Nicolas thinks of the fluid writing process for *The Envelope* and feels guilty. He wrote that novel four years ago, on Delphine's rickety kitchen table, rue Pernety, with Gaïa babbling on one side, the kettle whistling on the other, Delphine on the phone with her mother or Gaïa's father. No one could prevent the words from tumbling out of him, spewing out with passion, anger, fear, and delectation. There was never a moment when his inspiration wavered. How many times had he told that story to journalists? They never seemed to tire of hearing it. "And did the idea for the novel really dawn on you when you had your passport renewed?" they asked, and still do ask. How could Nicolas ever tell them today that there is no new book because he cannot find the time, because what he likes best is flourishing in the media's constant attention, in his readers' steady adoration?

On Nicolas's left, a silent and serious couple. Nicolas observes them. He likes to look at people, their faces, their clothes, their watches. From an early age, he has noticed watches. But now, with his newfound fame, and the wealth that has accompanied it, he also notices brand names, logos, clothes, shoes, sunglasses, a trait that annoyed his ex, Delphine. During the painful moments of their breakup, she was fond of reminding him of how much he had changed. Of how vain he had become.

The man is reading; the woman is studying her nails. French, he'd say. In their fifties. He is trim, deep tan, thinning hair (which no doubt upsets him). A Bréguet watch. A navy blue shirt with a green crocodile. Madame has those highlights women favor when they get to that age. Menopausal blond. A pale green shirtdress. He wonders if they have had sex recently. With that kind of tightness around the mouth, she probably doesn't often come. And certainly not with her husband, judging by the way her body is turned away from him. Husband is munching cereal and sipping coffee. Wife is toying with a fruit salad. She has now stopped examining her nails and is looking out to the sea. A wistful expression floats over her face. She must have been pretty, once.

On his right, another couple. Younger. She is perhaps thirty. Mediterranean type, olive-skinned, round shoulders, unruly hair, the kind you cannot comb. Dark glasses, Italian brand. He is from the Middle East, plump, hairy, cigarette hanging from his lip. A black-coated Rolex Daytona. He has three phones lined up on the table like smoking guns. He picks one up, talks loudly, puffing at his cigarette. The girl rises to admire the view. Her legs are disappointingly short, stocky, with thickset ankles. She is wearing high platform heels with glittery straps. She probably keeps them by the bed, slips them on even to pee.

Nicolas chooses his breakfast. The profusion of food is mouth-watering. He picks Bircher muesli, melon, and yogurt. The French have gone. He hopes he will never end up that way, carrying around that bitterness. He thinks of Emma, his mother. Guilt takes over. He hasn't been to see her in a while. He makes a mental note to call her. As he scoops up the muesli, he imagines his mother in the apartment on the quiet, paved rue Rollin, where he grew up. The rows of books lining the hall, newspapers piling up in the study, the faraway roar of the busy rue Monge coming up through the open windows, literature and knowledge radiating from the walls. His mother bent over stacks of exam copies, wielding her red pen. Her swift, sure strokes over the paper. He will call her, to-day; he must call her today. They will talk for a little while, he will find time for a lunch date with her, sometime between the Singa-pore event and the Scandinavian tour, and he will take her to that Greek restaurant she likes on the rue Candolle. He will sit and listen to her woes, her complicated on-off relationship with Renaud, a woebegone divorcé, her difficulties with her philosophy students from the Collège Sevigné, and he will think, as ever, that she looks younger than her fifty-two years, lovely still, with misty gray eyes and pale skin that flushes red when she is upset, his mother, with the clear-cut Belgian accent she never lost in spite of over thirty years in Paris. His mother, who has been living alone since his father's death, eighteen years ago. Nicolas is their only child. There has been string of lovers and sometimes unfortunate boyfriends, but she is still alone, despite the fluctuating affair with Renaud. He knows that during the lunch, over a moussaka, she will gaze at him with those fog-filled eyes and she will ask, "I hope all this has not changed you too much?" And when she says, "all this," she will make those delicate, vague gestures in the air, tracing bubbles with her fingers. Nicolas knows she often sees his ex. Del-phine comes to lunch or tea with her daughter, Gaïa, now thirteen, the same little Gaïa he watched grow up for five years, and he knows they all sit in Emma's kitchen and talk about him. And they will say that he has changed. Yes, "all this" has changed him. And how could "all this" not have changed him?

Malvina makes an unexpected appearance at the breakfast table. Her face is puffy with sleep; she has sheet marks across her cheeks, creases in her skin that make her look older. She is strangely pale.

"Happy birthday," he says. "Twenty-two!"

She grins at him; he ruffles her hair. He asks her if she wants orange juice, tea, a muffin. She nods. He goes back to the buffet. The hairy man is still on the phone, making jabbing motions with a pudgy index finger. The short-legged brunette has disappeared. Nicolas and Malvina have their first breakfast at the Gallo Nero quietly. They do not talk, but they hold hands. Nicolas likes the way Malvina's eyes are the same color as the sea behind her. Her skin is soft under his. Fragile. The protective tenderness he feels for her makes him squeeze her wrist, grasping it the way acrobats clasp each other in midair.

Malvina's birthday present is up in the room, in his luggage. He will give it to her tonight, during dinner. A watch. It was tricky tracking down the one he wanted. He found it online, and met the vendor, a slick Serb, in the bar of the Grand Hotel Intercontinental, rue Scribe. "Why do you love watches?" He was now asked that question in nearly every interview. Yet it had been amusing answering it for the first time, two years ago. The journalist was a voluptuous blonde with a shrewd eye. In the Ambassade Hotel in Amsterdam, on Herengracht, he had an afternoon of interviews lined up one after the other: *De Telegraaf, Alegemeen Dagblad, de Volkskrant.* Marije, his publisher, opened the door to the private salon from time to time to check on how he was bearing up. *The Envelope* had scored unexpectedly high sale figures in the Netherlands, even before the movie had been released. The press was eager to find out more about the young French writer who had taken the publishing world by storm with a first novel about a taboo family secret.

"In all of your photographs, you wear a different watch," said the blonde. "And sometimes you wear one on each wrist. Why is this?" And so he had explained. His first watch, a Hamilton Khaki, had been offered by his father for his tenth birthday. It had a black face with dual dial markings, large Arabic numerals, one through twelve, and an inner ring of smaller numerals, one through twenty-four, a small date window at three o'clock, a dark leather band, a stainless-steel case, and an austere, no-nonsense military style. "Soldiers wore that watch in Vietnam," said his father as Nicolas opened the box with awe. His first watch. "You don't ever forget your first watch," he told the journalist. His father died soon after. The Hamilton Khaki became a relic. A talisman. Nicolas did not wear it, but he never let it out of his sight. When he traveled, he took it with him. He looked at it often, and just by staring at it, or cradling it in his palm, he could conjure, Aladdin-like, the image of Théodore Duhamel in his last year, thirty-three and glorious, standing tall by the fireplace on the rue Rollin, a customary cigar clamped between his long, thin fingers. His father had had an orange-faced Doxa Sub, which never left his wrist. Nicolas often thought about that watch, which was not found after Théodore Duhamel's death. "Sometimes I wear two because I can't choose. Every watch tells a story," Nicolas said to the blonde. "Who gave it to you, on what occasion, when. Or, if you bought it yourself, where and how. I'm not interested in fashionable models, although I admire them." (He thought of the Rolex he'd given his mother for her fiftieth birthday, a 1971 Oyster Perpetual, marked *Tiffany & Co.*, which he'd bought on the rue de Sèvres, from one of his favorite shops. But he did not mention it, as he had learned to be careful with the word *Rolex,* especially in front of a journalist wearing a Swatch.) "I prefer a rarer kind, one that is hard to find, one that has a little wear and tear, one that doesn't glitter, as if things have happened to it."

The blonde nodded. "I see," she said. "Like your heroine, Margaux Dansor? A woman who has been around, seen a lot, but still has something to discover?" Clever move, he noted, her linking his passion for vintage watches to his middle-aged heroine, Margaux. A twenty-six-year-old man creating a forty-eight-year-old housewife, and pulling it off. Making her credible. Shaping her into one of those quaint, serious yet zany, irresistible heroines. A daughter, a spouse, a sister, a mother, a girl next door. A fictional character who made him famous around the world, later brought to life on-screen by Robin Wright in Toby Bramfield's film adaptation, a performance that earned her an Oscar in 2010.

Will Malvina like her present? He studies her as she eats her muffin. Malvina is sallow-skinned, slender, perfectly proportioned. She has a mixed background: a Polish mother and a Welsh dad. She is not talkative. All her gestures are intense. They have been together for nine months. He met her in London, when he was there for an event at the French embassy in Knightsbridge. She was a promising student at the Royal College of Arts. She had attended his conference, and came to get her book signed. There was something serene, gentle, about her face, her smile. Nicolas was still dealing with the choppy aftermath of the end of his five-year relationship with Delphine. After a succession of faceless women, one fling after the other, this quiet, dark, blue-eyed creature entranced him. He persuaded her to have dinner with him, in a Chinese restaurant on Brompton Road. During the meal, she revealed a tongue-in-cheek humor he relished. He laughed outright, nearly choking on his spring rolls, and for the first time since Delphine, he felt a glimmer of hope, that somehow this lovely girl might be the one to help him forget Delphine, or at least to help him turn that page at last. He took her back to the Langham hotel on Regent Street. She hugged him so hard during sex, it moved him deeply. When she fell asleep in his arms, he had felt unexpectedly safe with her, safer than he had ever been with any woman since Delphine.

Nicolas likes the fact she doesn't talk much. She wouldn't be here with him now had she been a chatterbox. As Malvina pours herself another coffee, he reflects on what he is supposed to be doing here at the Gallo Nero. Writing the new book, of course, but also taking a break, a well-deserved one after the hectic year he's had. How many trips? He cannot count them. He'd have to check his calendar to make sure. Short trips around the country for book fairs, book signings, meeting classes, students, presiding at literary award ceremonies, and then the same schedule abroad, in a dozen different countries, for the international publications of *The Envelope,* and finally the added and recent excitement with the movie release, Robin Wright's Oscar, the press junkets in the United States, in Europe, and the movie tie-in editions, which had gone high on the best-seller lists. He had indulged in a series of whims his French publisher and agent, Alice Dor, had not approved of. Those glossy ads for a men's fragrance, shot off the coast of Naxos, where, half-naked, he languorously reclines in a yacht. The black-and-white commercial for a watch, which seemed to grace every magazine he opened. "Was that necessary?" barked Alice Dor. "Don't tell me you need more money." No, with thirty million copies sold around the world and an Oscar-winning movie, he did not need more money. In fact, Corinne Beyer, his financial adviser, was working on that. If the money kept rolling in as such, she announced, he'd have to think about living somewhere other than France, because of the taxes.

Malvina and he slip back to the room. She is a tender and sweet lover. So fervent, it sometimes brings tears to his eyes, although he fully knows he does not love her. At least not the way he loved Delphine. Malvina lies back on the bed and opens her tanned knees to him. Later, as they take a shower, Malvina's fragile shoulder blades bring him back to another shower, Delphine's milky skin, his hands on her hips, in the bathroom on the rue Pernety, and he wonders with dismay whether he will ever love another woman the way he loved Delphine. It has been two years. When will her name sound like any other woman's? When will he stop wondering if she takes showers with other guys, and who has been stroking that white skin? Coming to the Gallo Nero is also a way of keeping Delphine out of his mind. So what is he doing? "Come on, Malve, let's go have a swim," he says, shutting out Delphine and showers with Delphine.

They go down to the private beach, using the James Bond elevator. All the staff here wears black. A waiter says Nicolas's name and room number; then they are ushered over to another, who proffers deck chairs—"Signor Kolt, a parasol, a towel, in the shade, no shade, near the sea, up by the cliff?"—and lo and behold, yet another one appears—"Would you like a drink, something cold, maybe, a newspaper, an ashtray?" They choose near the sea, with one parasol, a Coke for Malvina, iced tea and *Libération* (yesterday's issue) for him.

This beach is not really a beach. No sand. It is a thick slab of concrete lining the bottom of the cliff, studded with parasols, deck chairs, pool ladders, and a diving board. More and more guests emerge from the elevator as the sun climbs into the clear July sky. Nicolas hears them talk and guesses where they are from. A Swiss couple, particularly fascinating. Impossible to determine their age. Anywhere between forty and sixty. He is as bald as a kneecap, tall, stooped, bony yet fit. She is even taller, firm flesh, wide shoulders, flat breasts, a true daddy longlegs. Short silver hair. He watches them as they meticulously arrange their clothes, towels, magazines, sun cream. They don't speak to each other, but he senses great companionship. The man has tight-fitting swim shorts; she, an Olympic-style bathing suit. Suddenly, they get up, like two large, skinny birds taking off. She squeezes a swimming cap onto her head; he adjusts plastic goggles over his eyes. They both slip flippers onto their feet and hobble to the edge of the concrete slab with a peculiar elegance, in perfect harmony, and Nicolas guesses this has been repeated over and over again for many years. They dive into the sea and break into an effortless crawl stroke. They swim without a pause, reaching the brown reef that must be half a mile away. When they return, they shower in the nearby changing cabins and reappear wearing dry bathing suits. As they pass near him, he notices the man's Girard-Perregaux Sea Hawk. They see Nicolas looking their way and they smile. They spend the next ten minutes rubbing sun cream over themselves and each other with precise movements and grim concentration.

A Belgian family now. Nicolas picks Belgians out easily, because of his mother. Father and son are stocky, ginger-haired, red-skinned. The son is Malvina's age and already running to fat. His nose is sunburned and freckled. He is wearing a fashionable French-brand bathing suit. Dad is an older version—same bathing suit (red) and a Blancpain Fifty Fathoms on his wrist. The mother is one of those lithe muscular types, with a green bikini she looks good in. She is reading a paperback. Nicolas strains his eyes, but he already knows. *De Envelop,* Flemish movie-tie-in edition, with Robin Wright on the cover. He is also getting used to that, being confronted with his readers wherever he goes. The daughter is pear-shaped but appealing. Earbuds clamped into her ears. Reading a magazine. Nails bitten to the quick. Not half as high-maintenance as her mom. The father dishes out twenty-euro bills to the waiters in black. His gestures are smooth and blasé. *"Grazie, prego."* Waves of a plump pink palm.

Nicolas lies back on his deck chair, his face turned up to the sky like an avid sunflower sucking in the golden light, flaring nostrils catching the particular scent of the wind, hot and dry, sprinkled with the perfume of cypress and pine trees, the tang of lemon and salt. Summer of 2003 is the last time he reveled in that fragrance, during his trip to Liguria with François. Nicolas has been back to Italy (Milan, Rome, Florence) since Hurricane Margaux overturned his life in 2008 (that was how he described the book to journalists). But he had never been back to the Italian shore. He remembers the dusty night train from Paris to Milan, then the smaller train from Milan to Camogli. They stayed at an unpretentious bed-and-breakfast run by a jovial Canadian couple in their fifties, Nancy and Bob. When they got to San Rocco, they discovered they had to walk to the house (no taxi, no car) and drag their suitcases along tiny paved paths.

Camogli was also where a disheveled Margaux Dansor, his heroine, arrived one morning, hot on the trail of her quest for the family secret that was about to disrupt her life. Margaux had also dragged her suitcase—bump, bump, bump—all the way to the white stone house. Nicolas smiles, thinking about how "tickled pink" Nancy and Bob were when they found out he had put them in *The Envelope.* He had changed their names to Sally and Jake, but they were easily recognizable, Bob with his jaunty ponytail and eye patch that gave him a Captain Jack Sparrow attitude, and Nancy's Hottentot Venus bottom, which sparked lewd sotto voce exchanges between François and him. In the book, Nicolas described Bob and Nancy's abode exactly as it was. The patchy walls, the tiled crooked terrace, where every evening he would knock back limoncello until mind-blasting migraines took over, transforming his brain to putty, blurring the astounding view of the bay. The small, high-ceilinged, cool bedrooms, painted blue and green, the faltering plumbing system, the kitchen and its aromas: fresh pasta, glistening pesto, mozzarella and tomatoes on a bed of arugula. The other guests were a beautician from L.A., emaciated and tanned like crisp toast, and her shy, overweight daughter, who read Emily Dickinson in the shade. In Toby Bramfield's movie, they all ended up looking exactly like how Nicolas had imagined them.

Nicolas suddenly wonders how François is. When was the last time they talked, sat down for a meal? He cannot even recall it. That is what comes with living this way, always on a train, on a plane, hours in waiting rooms, too many messages to respond to, too many e-mails piling up, too many invitations, propositions, solicitations. Not enough time to see friends, family, those who count. Again the pang of guilt. He should call François. They have been friends since their teens, when he was still Nicolas Duhamel, attending the prestigious Lycée Louis-le-Grand, then the grueling hypokhâgne and khâgne classes, specializing in humanities. Nicolas ended up being held back his second year, dubbed a "khûbe," as student jargon would have it. While François soared upward and onward, Nicolas fumbled and stumbled, to his mother's despair. Although he was aware of what he was letting himself in for, he had been overpowered from the start by the workload, the permanent stress level, the sarcasm of the teachers. This was part and parcel of the demanding legend of the prestigious literary preparatory courses his mother had brilliantly succeeded in during her youth. In addition to class time and homework, Nicolas spent several hours each week laboriously completing exams and *colles* (spelled khôlles to look like a Greek word, another "khâgneux" insider joke). But there was nothing remotely funny about the khôlles, which soon became a nightmare for Nicolas. One hour to prepare a short dissertation on a given topic. Then, in twenty excruciating minutes, he had to present his work orally to a scathing teacher. François excelled at the dreaded khôlles, and even the harshest teacher, with the keenest expectations, begrudgingly bowed down to such supremacy. François never showed any signs of discouragement or apathy, contrary to Nicolas, who lost weight, lost sleep, lost his spirits. Like a fighter pilot dodging missiles, François triumphantly angled toward the highly competitive national exam that awaited them, the holy grail of a *concours* that a tiny elite would pass. Nicolas knew, from early on, that he did not have that ambition within him. François did, and he was aware of being the nugget those schools hungered for, the breed that formed professors, teachers, future Nobel Prize winners. The first time Nicolas flubbed the final exam, not even scraping through to the no-man's-land of the *sous-admissible* category, the second-chance gang, François was already embarked on the firmament of the Ecole normale supérieure in Paris, nicknamed "Ulm," for its address on the street that bore the same name.

The trip to Italy had been their way of patching up, of getting their friendship back on track after the strain of the khâgne and Nicolas's failure. François earned a salary as a proud normalien, while Nicolas went on struggling halfheartedly, still living at his mother's place, barely making ends meet by giving philosophy lessons to reluctant students. François remained the one who had succeeded, the one for whom it all seemed easy. But that changed when Hurricane Margaux blew along five years later. Except for François and Lara, the only ones from the past who have remained part of his life, Nicolas's new friends are from the publishing world—writers, journalists, editors, publicists, booksellers. He sees them at literary events, on TV or radio shows, at cocktail parties, book launches, nightclubs. He has their e-mail addresses, their mobile-phone numbers; he is their friend on Facebook, their follower on Twitter. He hugs them, slaps them on the back, ruffles their hair, but very few of them are truly close. He gets drunk or high with them, occasionally has sex with one or two of the women, but what do they know about him, apart from what they may glean in the papers, or on Twitter? They know nothing. And he knows nothing about them, in return. He is fleetingly aware of the emptiness of his life, of the cruel fact that the entire world has learned his name but that he is, in truth, alone.

Every time Nicolas thinks of François, like at this very moment, as his eyes roam over the splendid sea, the guests basking in the sun, the servers bringing drinks and fruits, he is confronted with his own inadequacies as a friend. Did he not let François down? Did he not stop calling, meaning to call, always leaving it until the next day, and then simply forgetting to do it in the end? Yet François had been the brother he'd never had, the one he went to judo classes and tennis lessons with, the one he could confide in when girls became an obsession, the one who gave him support when his father died. François had a long, serious, bespectacled face, even as a kid, and adults trusted him. This had proved useful when they were children, indulging in devilish pranks. The "cheese incident," for example. Nicolas had been punished by their principal, the odious Monsieur Roqueton, for not handing his homework in yet again. During a lunch break, on a stifling summer day, François innocently found his way into Monsieur Roqueton's office, armed with a stinking Camembert. He deftly unscrewed the mouth-piece of the man's old-fashioned telephone and squashed bits of cheese into it before replacing the top. A few days later, the stench became unbearable. One could not use the telephone without retching. Nicolas grins, and nearly laughs out loud, remembering. They were never caught. It had been a triumph.

There is another memory Nicolas is fond of. Granville, Normandy, summer of 1999. Nicolas and François were seventeen. François's parents owned a half-timbered white-and-brown house, with a sloping garden giving on to the beach. Every summer, Nicolas went to spend two weeks in August with the Morin family. He felt like he was one of them. François had two younger sisters, Con-stance and Emmanuelle, and an older brother, Victor. His parents, Michel and Odile, gave a summer party each year while Nicolas was there. About a hundred people came. The girls wore their prettiest summer frocks. Odile went to the hairdresser. Michel showed off his tan in his favorite white jeans and a denim shirt opened to his navel. Victor, Nicolas, and François wore clean T-shirts and shorts. It poured one summer, and the party was held inside, an amusing squash. But that summer, the summer that Nicolas and François would never forget, Odile invited a new couple in town, Gérard and Véronique, who came with a Parisian friend of theirs, Nathalie. The women were in their early thirties; the husband was older. Véronique was plump and blond. Nathalie was tall, slender, and dark-haired, with the longest legs Nicolas had ever seen. They were wearing the same tight dress, but in different colors: black for Véronique and white for Nathalie. Gérard mingled with the older crowd, but Véronique and Nathalie took their drinks and crossed the garden, going out to the beach, daintily kicking off their high-heeled sandals. The sun was setting, staining the sea red. There was no one on the beach. The two young women waved, gesturing for Nicolas and François to join them. For a while, the four of them sat on the sand and chatted. When their glasses were empty, Nicolas rushed back to the house and smuggled a bottle of champagne under his T-shirt. The sun disappeared and the darkness drew inviting shadows around them. Nathalie, the long-legged brunette, puffed away on a cigarette, held delicately between two slim golden fingers. From where they were sitting, they could hear the music and laughter of the nearby party. Nathalie wanted to know if they had any girlfriends. This embarrassed François, who was less successful than Nicolas with girls. Véronique, the blonde, then asked, in a low, intimate voice, what they had already done with a girl sexually. Nicolas noticed how close the two women were, how Nathalie's tanned thigh brushed against his naked calf every time she moved. In the soft blue light, Véronique's cleavage was a deep, milky cleft. He told them, frankly, that all his girlfriends had been from the lycée, girls of his age. He had had sex with six of them so far, at parties, in a drunken stupor, in the bathroom or in someone's bed. Only one of them had been a pleasant surprise, willing to try everything with the fierce energy of a Stakhanovite. Once the novelty wore off, Nicolas found her exhausting. The two women on the beach with them that night were in another league. They exuded a mysterious, languorous sensuality. "Does your girlfriend kiss you like this?" murmured Véronique, and before François could respond, she glued her lips to his, while Nathalie's silken arm found its way around Nicolas's neck. Then she kissed him in a way that Nicolas had never been kissed before in his life. Could they be seen from the house? he wondered fleetingly, stroking the soft skin under her dress, enraptured. Suddenly, Véronique was in his arms, and Nathalie moved to kiss François. Nicolas gave in to the new mouth on his. He could not resist touching her breasts, and when she pulled his lips down to their fullness, he thought he was going to pass out from ecstasy. What would have happened, he often wondered, if Véronique's husband had not started to call her name from the garden? Had he seen them? They all got up quickly, brushing the sand off their clothes. The women patted their hair, giggling. Nicolas felt dizzy and nearly stumbled. François's face was white, his lips swollen and red. He seemed about to faint. The women nonchalantly picked up their glasses and their shoes and strolled back to the house arm in arm, shouting out gaily to Gérard that they were coming. François and Nicolas waited a while before joining the party. When they turned up, nervous and blushing, Gérard, Véronique, and Nathalie had already left. Nicolas never saw them again. But he knew he would never forget that night. For years, he had only to whisper "Granville" to François with a knowing smile, and the memories of that evening would flood back, intact.

Nicolas gets up now for his first swim. He will text François later. He glances down at Malvina, curled up under her parasol like a little animal, fast asleep. Her face still seems pale. He dives into the sea, and when he comes up for air, he finds himself gasping with a mixture of pleasure and joy, the pleasure of the velvety caress on his skin, the joy of coming back to the exact sensation he had missed since Camogli. The water here is deep immediately. It is absolutely transparent. Nicolas can stare all the way down to the seabed, paved with pale oval stones, and watch silvery fish flit past. He flings his arms and legs out like a starfish and floats on the surface. Underwater, his ears make out the tranquil putter of a nearby boat.

Three days. Three blissful days. Three days just for him. This beautiful, quiet haven. The blue of it. No one knows where he is. He did not even Tweet it, refrained from posting it on his Facebook wall. Should he be needed, his BlackBerry is there to do its job. "Have a good rest, signor," the beach attendant had said, beaming as she spread out a towel for Nicolas on the deck chair. Three days to pretend to be writing the book. Three days of laziness.

Malvina opens one eye as he is drying himself.

"You should have a swim," he says.

She shrugs. "I don't feel too good."

"Maybe something you ate?"

"Maybe."

She nestles back into her deck chair.

It is getting on toward noon. The sun pounds down. The frizzy brunette and the hairy guy arrive. He is still on the phone (is he ever off it?), and she totters on her glittery platform shoes. Once they have decided where to sit, once they have been handed the thick black-and-white towels stamped with the letters GN, she stands up. Slowly and tantalizingly, she takes off the top of her bathing suit, like Rita Hayworth removing that glove. Her breasts are round and pert, with dark pink nipples. Not fake bosoms, but glorious real ones that wobble ever so slightly and that Nicolas can imagine frantically cramming into his mouth. She starts to anoint them with sun oil, and Nicolas can hardly believe she is doing this, right here, right now, with such deliberate, slow movements. All the men are staring. The staff members seem transfixed, sweating under their black shirts. The Belgian goes pinker, the Swiss adjusts his dark glasses, and the French ogles to such an extent that his wife gives him a dig in the ribs. Only the boyfriend seems impervious to the scene. Nicolas neatly takes his eyes off her just before Malvina notices.

Nicolas has learned to be clever where Malvina is concerned. Her intensity harbors a powerful strain of silent jealousy. She picks up the remotest sign of what she imagines is danger—an over-admiring fan, a too-friendly reader, or simply a pretty girl. When Malvina left London two months ago, giving up her studies and all her friends there, to come to live with him in Paris on the rue du Laos, Nicolas discovered her unhealthy obsession with his past, with his relationship with Delphine. He found it impossible to make Malvina understand that Delphine and he have been friends for the past two years, since their breakup, and that he needs this special bond with his ex. Malvina cannot fathom how he can be "friends" with Delphine. She is convinced Nicolas and Delphine are still lovers. And any reasonably attractive woman is a threat to her relationship with Nicolas.

As a result, his BlackBerry never rings or even vibrates. He is too careful for that. He gave up his beloved iPhone when he started dating Malvina in 2010. The iPhone 3GS, he told a friendly male journalist in Oslo, is an unfortunate device if you are being spied upon by a jealous partner. Picture messages show right up on the screen, along with the name of the person sending them, as well as missed calls. A nightmare. "Switch to a BlackBerry if you have secrets to keep," he had said, chuckling. Malvina had not seen the Norwegian article with that exact caption and a picture of him brandishing his BlackBerry over a shot of Løiten Linie Akevitt. A small miracle, considering she spent hours keeping track of him online, checking every comment he posted on Facebook and Twitter, and, worse still, every comment posted by a female in response. He had 150,000 followers on Twitter and over 250,000 on his Facebook fan page, so Malvina was certainly busy.

His BlackBerry is protected by a code he changes constantly. The only sign of an incoming text or e-mail is the little red signal that blinks. The screen remains black. Nothing shows up on it. He knows how to look at the phone swiftly when Malvina is occupied with another matter. It is a risky daily battle. He knows how to smuggle the BlackBerry into the bathroom, tucked into his sleeve like a stash of drugs. In the privacy of the toilet, he knows how to hastily peruse his e-mails, his text messages, check his Facebook page, scroll through his Twitter feed. This morning, as Malvina visits the ladies' room (that will leave him four to five minutes), he sees there are new e-mails on his private account—one from Alice Dor, his French publisher; one from Dita Dallard, his publicist; one from Bertrand Chalais, a French journalist he is friendly with; another from a writer friend, Patrick Treboc, whom he parties with. And on his other e-mail account, the one used for his Web site, there are about fifty new messages from readers around the world. He used to answer them all in the beginning, when the book was just out, not yet on the charts or translated into all those languages. When he first started to receive the e-mails, they were a gratifying surprise. But when the messages poured in as the book gained recognition in more countries, on more charts and lists, and when the movie came out, he found he was swamped. "Hire an assistant who will answer them for you," suggested another writer friend, but Nicolas felt that wasn't right. "Just read them and don't reply," said another. And that was what he ended up doing.

This morning, the most important element on Nicolas's Black-Berry is the blue-spotted logo on the screen. A BBM. He knows it is from Sabina. He will not have time to answer right now, but he reads it fast (heart pumping) and erases it promptly. "I am wearing nothing, it is hot in my room, and I am thinking of you. Shall I tell you what I am doing right now, Nicolas?" He has to delete every single message from Sabina as soon as he reads it. There is no other way.

Last April. Berlin. A book signing at the Dussmann das Kultur Kaufhaus on Friedrichstrasse. She had stood in line patiently for a long while. She had handed him *Der Umschlag* (German edition, with the postcardlike sepia cover of Camogli in the fifties, a glimpse of sea, the village clustered by the cliff, the inky green cypress trees). He had said blandly, "Your name, please?" like he always did, and she had answered, "It's not for me; it's for my husband. His name is Hans." There was something about her eyes. An ash blonde wearing a trench coat. Fifteen years older than he was, he guessed. Fine catlike features, small smile. Reminiscent of Charlotte Rampling in *The Night Porter*. He had signed the book. Just as she was turning away, she swiftly slipped a shred of paper into his hand. Then she was gone and the next reader was already flourishing his book. He hadn't had the time to read the paper till twenty minutes later, when his German publisher, Ursula, managed to pluck him away from the winding line of readers for a short break. The only thing written on the paper was a series of numbers he immediately recognized—a BlackBerry PIN number, BBM, for instant messaging.

Later that night, after a never-ending event at the Institut français on Kurfürstendamm with a fastidious journalist who asked only the most obvious questions, the ones he could no longer face answering but knew he had to ("How much of the book is taken from your own life?" "Did you ever find a letter like that for real?" "Is Margaux Dansor modeled after your mother?" "How did your family react when it was published?" "Did Toby Bramfield buy the rights the week the book came out?" "Is it true you have a cameo in the movie?" "What is your second book about?"), he got back at last, very late, to the refined privacy of his junior suite at the Ritz-Carlton on Potsdamer Platz. He kicked off his shoes, turned on the TV, zapped through the late-night news and porn channels, delved into the minibar for champagne, and sprawled out on the sofa, shoving aside boxes of chocolates, welcome cards, baskets of goodies, books to sign for the sales reps. It was too late to call Malvina. He'd do that in the morning. He took the scrap of paper from his pocket and stared at it for a while. On the TV screen, a frenzied threesome was going at it with gusto. He turned the sound down, had a gulp of champagne, watched them for a while. Then he typed the BBM PIN code into his phone.

He should not be doing this, he knew. That catlike green-eyed woman spelled trouble.

JOURNALISTS APPEARED TO BE fascinated, almost morbidly so, by his father's death in 1993, as if that episode represented the core of his inner self, his essence. They craved each detail of the day his father died, or, rather, the awfulness of the precise moment when his father disappeared, when it was understood that he was not coming back, and how, as an eleven-year-old boy, Nicolas had undergone such trauma. Before Hurricane Margaux, Nicolas had not talked about Théodore Duhamel's death to anyone, not even to his ex, Delphine. It had been difficult choosing the right words, strange feeling them roll around his mouth for the first time like a foreign dish his palate balked at. But then he discovered, with a sort of secret pleasure, that the more interviews he gave, the more Théodore Duhamel took on a new, virtual existence, an unexpected renaissance. His words resuscitated his father, fleshed him out, dusting away the forlorn mantle of stiffness that had settled with the passing of time, brandishing the triumphant and true image of what Théodore Duhamel used to be. "My father was my Gatsby," he once confided in an early interview, and Lord knows how many times that line had been quoted, copied, Tweeted. When asked to describe Théodore Duhamel, Nicolas was discouraged. How? Listing his height, the blaze of his blue eyes, his square chin, his long, gangly arms and legs wasn't enough. Even photographs of Théodore Duhamel posing with Nicolas, age six, in front of the battered but elegant silver Jaguar E-Type, a cigar emerging from the white of his smile, or standing astride his black Hobie Cat at the Miramar beach in Biarritz, did not suffice. How to describe the way women would look at his father, all women, young and mature, staring at him? Nicolas suspected the journalists would never grasp the complexity of Théodore Duhamel's seemingly sunny personality, simply because no one had, not even his wife or his son. Théodore Duhamel was a scintillating comet that seared through the fragile canvas of his son's boyhood, an alpha and an omega of interrogation and perplexity, an alluring realm of uncertainty, a no-man's-land of chiaroscuro where legend and reality intertwined. "Is it true your father has no grave?" was one of the favorite questions. And Nicolas invariably replied, "Well, his name is on my grandparents' tombstone at Père-Lachaise, but as his body was never found, technically, yes, my father has no burial place."

The earliest memory Nicolas had of his father was his voice. A nasal voice, loud, sometimes irritating, that rang in one's ear like the rich toll of a bell. And the laugh! High-pitched, sensual, at times reduced to a short howl or a snort. It took people by surprise. Théodore Duhamel used it like a weapon. He wielded it artfully, Nicolas discovered, in delicate situations—with uptight teachers, ungracious shop assistants, frosty bankers. Most of the time, it worked. But that ploy infuriated his mother, his grandmother. They saw through it. When Théodore Duhamel winked at his son over the dinner table, flaunting a down-turned mouth as if to convey, *Those women!* Nicolas shivered with pride; yes, he was part of the team, just the two of them, the secret team he formed with his father, like Paul Newman and Robert Redford in *Butch Cassidy and the*

Sundance Kid, his father's favorite movie. He was Sundance; his dad was Cassidy.

What did his father do? From early on, Nicolas slowly grasped to what extent his job was shrouded in mystery. His father did not leave every morning wearing a suit and a tie, carrying a briefcase, like François's father, kissing his wife good-bye on the doorstep. It was his mother, Emma, who took off when it was still dark, a chunk of croissant crumbling from her fingers, rushing in order not to be late for her students. Théodore Duhamel did not make an appearance till ten, and the puffy-eyed look he harbored in the mornings was another of Nicolas's earliest memories. "What does Papa do?" he asked his mother when he was eight or nine, as he never knew what to write in the school forms that asked for his father's profession. "Hmm," reflected his mother, "why don't you ask Papa?" (Nicolas could have been imagining things, but wasn't there a smile hovering on her lips?) So Nicolas obediently asked his father outright while Théodore was watching the news, a glass of whiskey in hand, and his father had replied, eyes glued to the screen, "I can't describe what I do. It doesn't boil down to one word." Nicolas felt a lump in his throat. What was he going to tell his school? Couldn't he leave that entry out? Only write Mother's profession: Teacher. Did they really have to know what his father did for a living? Théodore Duhamel finally glanced over at his son, took note of his distress, and gulped his whiskey down with relish. "Just write 'entrepreneur,' Sundance. That will do the trick." Nicolas nodded. "How do you spell it?" His father spelled it out slowly. Nicolas had no idea what it meant. He asked tentatively, "What is an entrepreneur?" His father poured out another whiskey and ignored that question. Then after a moment of silence, he added, "If anyone asks you, just say you can't give any details because it's too dangerous." He'd lowered his voice to a whisper. Nicolas felt the thrill run up and down his spine, and he nodded. Later, he looked up the word *entrepreneur* in the dictionary. "A person who organizes and manages a commercial undertaking, especially one including a commercial risk," he read. The definition made Nicolas feel even more puzzled. His father had no office. The dining room was his lair; he would sit in there for ages, staring at the television even if it was turned off, puffing away at a cigar.

The bitter smell invariably brought his father back in a flash. Théodore Duhamel was fussy about cigars. He refused to buy them anywhere but at the Davidoff shop on the avenue Victor Hugo, where he spent hours choosing between a Monte Cristo N°2 (obus), an Upmann Sir Winston, and a Hoyo de Monterrey Excalibur Legend Crusader. Théodore Duhamel did not like being interrupted when he chose them, except by the vendor or a pretty woman. Nicolas noticed that pretty women often came to the shop. They waited, bored and beautiful, as the usually short, bald, and ugly men they accompanied also took their time. Nicolas had often watched his father chat up the ladies. Most ingenuously, he would hand a Havana to the lady, and sometimes the lady would stroke it in a slow and strange manner. Often, he would slip his card to the smiling lady behind the fat, bald man's back. His father's card was dashing. In bold red lettering, it said *Théodore Duhamel, International Entrepreneur*. Nicolas often heard him on the phone while Emma was out, using a suave, low voice, and expressions like "my beauty," "my lovely," and he had seen how his father looked at women in the streets, his eyes raking over them, that smile on his lips. Did his mother know about this? Did she mind?

Théodore Duhamel had a business acolyte, a guy Nicolas had seen around the house since childhood. His name was Albert Brisabois, but his father only ever called him Brisabois. He was a short, sturdy fellow with a fleecy ginger beard and a paunch. When Nicolas got home from school, Brisabois and his father were usually locked up in the dining room. Smoke wafted from under the closed door. His father's loud snort was heard from time to time above the low murmur of voices. When his mother arrived, she would glance at the closed door, raise her eyebrows, and say, "Hmm . . . your father is working. Don't make any noise." (Nicolas could have been imagining things yet again, but wasn't that another discreet smile?) He would share a quiet dinner with his mother in the kitchen, just the two of them, which he rather liked, while Théodore Duhamel and Brisabois pursued their conversation. "What are they talking about?" he once asked his mother as his father's shout of a laugh echoed down the corridor. "Business," she replied matter-of-factly over the leek and potato soup. And Nicolas was left to muse about what "business" really meant.

One Saturday, Nicolas and his father were walking down the Champs-Elysées on their way to lunch at the Pizza Pino. Théodore Duhamel suddenly gasped, turning a horrid shade of white. He pushed his son to one side and ducked. "Sundance, I've spotted an enemy. We need to go undercover." At first, Nicolas thought his father was joking, but his face was ghastly, so pale that Nicolas felt frightened. He was shoved into the nearest shop. His father pretended to examine an array of silk scarves with marked interest. He did the same. His father waved off an obsequious saleslady. "Whatever you do, don't turn around." His father's voice was normal, a trifle subdued, but the livid hue of his face was terrifying. Nicolas stared at the scarves (years later, he can still remember their design: pink and purple, rather hideous, nothing his mother would ever wear), and it seemed to him that they stood there for ages, petrified. Finally, after an eternity, his father muttered, "All clear. Let's get the hell out of here." They fled the shop, hand in hand, faces down, the collar of his father's coat raised around his neck like a shield. Théodore Duhamel's complexion had gone back to normal, and Nicolas felt relieved. His father dashed into Fouquet's, dragged Nicolas down a flight of stairs, and plonked his son onto a chair. "Wait for me here. Won't be long." His father disappeared into a phone booth. Nicolas could hear his voice quite clearly. "Brisabois. It's me. I saw him on the Champs-Elysées." A long silence. "What the fuck are you going to do about it? Have you thought about the consequences? Have you really? Do you have any idea—" Another long silence. "I pray to God that you are right." Then his father replaced the receiver as loudly as possible, as if to convey the enormity of his irritation to Brisabois at the other end of the line. After their ritual Regina pizza, on their way home in the metro (Théodore Duhamel rarely drove the battered but elegant E-Type in town, only out of it), Nicolas timidly asked his father who it was he had seen. His father grinned down at him and said, "All is under control. No worries." But Nicolas did worry. When he got home, he did not breathe a word of what had happened to his mother, although he longed to.

Another mystery was his father's relationship with his mother. After her husband's death, Emma Duhamel had stated (and Nicolas had heard her say it) that Théodore Duhamel was the love of her life. But during the eleven years that Nicolas had shared of his father's existence, there were few memories of a loving and passionate marriage. He eventually understood that his father had had affairs and that his mother had ignored them. Had she suffered? Had she had affairs, as well, more discreetly? When they met, in 1980, Emma was twenty-one, a brilliant philosophy student, and Théo was twenty, working in the photo department at *Paris Match* magazine. They met in a nightclub, Castel, on the rue Princesse and fell promptly in love (even though Emma was going out with a Belgian guy she'd met at the Lycée-le-Grand, and even though Théo was dating a Norwegian model named Janicke, who had graced the cover of *Elle*). They married because he, Nicolas, was on the way. It seemed to Nicolas that his mother put up with his father, that she treated him like a child prone to tantrums. Emma was only thirty-four when her husband disappeared. There were other men, but no one important enough for Emma ever to consider another marriage.

What Nicolas missed about his father was his boyish audacity, his endearing craziness. "Your father was as mad as a hatter," Emma admitted more than once. "Thank God you are the serious type, like me." His father could not resist a practical joke. Some were downright foolish. Others commanded the utmost respect. Like pouring gallons of bubble bath in the place Victor Hugo fountain just as an "enemy" was walking out of the church with his new bride. The entire place was soon invaded with mountains of foam, like in the Peter Sellers movie *The Party*. Like letting fifty white mice out of their cages at a famous socialite's cocktail party (to which he had not been invited). But what Nicolas was the most nostalgic about were the bedtime stories. Nicolas said in a TV interview, "I believe that my father's fertile imagination, the outlandish stories he used to whisper to me before I turned the light off, somehow shaped the writer I later became." Nicolas liked to think back to those moments with his father in his bedroom at rue Rollin, the room he grew up in, lined with his Tintin, Astérix, and Picsou books and his posters of Harrison Ford as Indiana Jones and Han Solo. His mother rarely put him to bed. She left that job to his father, who took it seriously. Nicolas lay tucked up under the sheets, his head propped on his father's chest, taking in whiffs of Eau Sauvage and the scent of cigar smoke that seemed to drape itself around Théodore Duhamel's person, even if the Monte Cristo had been extinguished hours ago.

Nicolas's favorite story was the one about Lord McRashley. (Where did Théodore Duhamel get that name? No doubt from an old Louis de Funès movie called *Fantômas contre Scotland Yard*, which Nicolas had watched time and time again with his father.) It was morbid and frightening, like a tale by Edgar Allan Poe. Lord McRashley lived alone in a freezing castle, far away, where the north wind would blow, sounding like the howl of ghouls in the deep of the night. Lord McRashley had dinner served by his faithful butler, Jarvis, every evening. Holding a flickering candle in a heavy silver candlestick, followed by an army of black bats, Lord McRashley would then totter up to his rooms, situated at the top of the highest tower of his castle. Up and up the twisting stone steps he went, very slowly, bent over with the weight of years, heaving and wheezing, and every night it took a little longer, as he wasn't getting any younger. The stern portrait of the late Lady McRashley—all angles and bones—glared down at him as he made his way up. There was a narrow landing with a chair between two flights of stairs, and he always paused to rest there for a moment. There he sat, gasping for air, until he felt strong enough to resume his ascent. The long and narrow landing, as ill-lit as the rest of the stairs, was lined with ancient spotted mirrors, and Lord McRashley could see himself from the back, reflected dozens of times, getting smaller and smaller and smaller. One evening, he happened to notice a black speck at the back of the last reflection. He dismissed it as a blotch on the mirror. But evening after evening, to his growing dismay, the dark blemish seemed to become steadily larger, drawing closer with each mirrored layer, creeping up on him, and he became afraid to go up the stairs, dreading to see the black form looming bigger and bigger each night. Consumed with anguish, he asked Jarvis to come up with him one night, and he nearly fainted when Jarvis vouched he saw nothing, nothing at all, and all the while the hideous silhouette (or whatever it was, and how Nicolas shivered at those very words) had glided even closer. There were no other stairs that led to his bedroom at the top tower, and it was with fear in his heart that Lord McRashley tremulously climbed them, until one fateful evening he saw that the loathsome horror was only one reflection away. He could see it all too clearly now, a vision of abomination, a skulking nonentity, a grimacing and sinister mummy like form, draped in a black cloak. Was it a man? A woman? At that point, his mother usually barged into the room, scoffing. "Théo, is this a proper bedtime story for a six-year-old?" Théodore Duhamel waited till she closed the door again, flashing his downturned mouth (Those women!) and rolling his eyes at his son, saying, "Well, Nicolas, do you want the end of the story?" Nicolas would clutch his plush rabbit, Thumper (from *Bambi*), jump up and down on the bed, and yell, "Well, of course. What do you think!" Even if Nicolas knew the story by heart, even if he had heard it dozens of times, he still begged for it. And so Lord McRashley crept up the stairs ever so slowly, candle wax dripping onto his shaking wrist, and even the silent army of black bats did not dare go up with him this time, as if they knew. When Lord McRashley got to the landing, he found he did not have the courage to look up at the mirror. His old knees quaked and nearly gave way, his old heart fluttered painfully, and drops of sweat trickled down his weathered forehead. He finally mustered the strength to raise his face toward the mirror, whimpering like a child, and he hardly had time to utter a strangled moan, because—*whoosh!*—a black shadow pounced out of the mirror and gobbled the old chap up in one go (while his father's lean hand grabbed Nicolas by the collar of his pajama top). And that was the end of Lord McRashley.

"Your father is a hero to you. Is that why you made Margaux Dansor's father, Lucca Zeccherio, a hero, as well?" Nicolas was often asked. His father was no hero, he told the media over and over. Born in 1960, Théodore Duhamel had fought in no wars, taken no stands, resisted no danger, defended no territory. He had not battled against cancer or some other illness; he had not written a world-changing thesis; he had not invented a revolutionary mathematical formula. He was no artist, no writer, no painter, no musician, no film director, no singer, no athlete. "That scene in *The Envelope* when Margaux is in a plane with her dad and the plane is hit by lightning, did that really happen to you and your father?" the journalists invariably asked. Yes, it was true, at age ten he'd been in a plane with his father and the plane was struck by lightning, but he'd turned it into a different scene, wrote it in another manner. That was Margaux's story, not his. He had become accustomed to journalists desperately contriving to find similarities, however minor, between the book and his life, searching for a pattern that he could not decipher and which held no interest for him. "Why did you write *The Envelope*?" To that very frequent question, he gave one answer: "Because I had that story to tell."

Nicolas has dreamed of the thunderstorm episode time and time again since his father died. He also thinks about it whenever he boards a plane. He still sees his father's long back, ensconced in a green loden coat, the glossy curls of chestnut hair tumbling over his collar. His father told him to go sit by the porthole. "You'll have a better view, and I need to stretch my legs in the aisle seat." Those long legs, how vividly Nicolas recalls them, swathed in beige corduroy or jeans, and the leather moccasins (from Florence) casing the thin, narrow feet. This was not the first time Nicolas had flown alone with his father. His mother had remained in Paris, stuck with her students, and Nicolas had been whisked off to Basel with his father, who had to meet a client—a client who never turned up. They ended up buying Swiss chocolates and having an enormous meal at the Trois Rois Hotel. ("No need to tell your mother about the client not showing up." Nicolas had nodded at his dad mannishly. But he wondered why his mother should not know.)

The flight was a bumpy one, the bumpiest Nicolas had ever experienced, and he began to feel queasy. The thought of the *Rösti* and strudel churning in his stomach was not pleasant. The plane bounced up and down dizzyingly, like a frenzied bumper car. Nicolas did not dare take his father's hand, although he longed to. Now he felt both ill and scared. He glanced up at his dad's face. Théodore Duhamel appeared to be fast asleep. Nicolas stared at the rich, full mouth, the square chin, the lush eyebrows. Another half hour before they reached Paris. How could his father sleep through such turbulence? All the other passengers were quivering. He wished his mother was there. He would have hung on to her for dear life. He longed for her touch, her perfume, her soothing voice. As Nicolas peered out of the porthole at the billowing black clouds, whispering for his mother, a terrifyingly loud clap was heard, like a hundred lightbulbs exploding at once, and a blue haze bolted smack into Nicolas's face. The plane lurched to one side. Passengers screamed in terror. Nicolas sat there, wide-eyed, speechless, certain that his last day had come, that they were all going to die right there and then, that the plane was going to drop down to earth with a crash and they would all perish. All around him, he could hear the worried babble of voices, the scuffle of flight attendants scurrying down the aisle, a baby wailing, and he glimpsed a sea of faces turning back toward him, to where the blue light had blazed with such strength. "Is he all right?" asked the man sitting across from them. "Poor little fellow," cooed a plump lady in front. "How brave he is!" At last, his father's tanned, lean hand found its way into his. "This is extraordinary!" gasped Théodore Duhamel, shaking Nicolas's limp hand with gusto. "Nicolas, *you* are extraordinary." Nicolas gaped. What was his father talking about? Had he not realized how frightened his son was? The captain's grave tone was heard above the din. Everyone went quiet. "Ladies and gentlemen, please remain calm. A rare event has occurred. Our plane was hit by lightning. There is no damage to the aircraft and I'm told of a very brave young gentleman in row fifteen. We shall be landing in Paris shortly, so please return to your seats." Nicolas blinked. Hit by lightning? He could hardly believe his ears. His heart pumped away like a little drum. "And do you realize," his father said breathlessly, "that the lightning struck your window, Nicolas? The lightning chose you. Out of all the passengers sitting in the plane, the lightning chose you." Nicolas glanced up at his father. "What does that mean?" Théodore Duhamel beamed down at him. "It means you are exceptional. Now, I want you to do so something for me, Nicolas. Listen to me very carefully. I want you to write this down right now. I want you to describe exactly how you felt when the blue light exploded in your face. Do you understand? You need to capture this moment before it goes away forever, like taking a photo, but with words. Get it?" Théodore Duhamel pressed on the buzzer and summoned the flight attendant. She seemed flustered and agitated by the event. "Oh, you are the brave boy the captain was talking about! I'm glad you are all right." Nicolas basked in the unexpected attention. "We need a sheet of paper, please. My son has something important to write," said Théodore Duhamel in his bossy voice. He handed Nicolas his pen as the flight attendant rushed off to get paper. Nicolas remembers the feel of the pen in his youthful fingers, still warm from his father's breast pocket, where he usually kept it, next to a cigar case. Théodore Duhamel's pen was a vintage Montblanc, engraved with the initials T.D. It seemed oddly heavy in Nicolas's hand, its black coat silky and shiny, and when he unscrewed the top, he saw that the golden nib was dotted with blue ink.

What was he supposed to write? His heart sank. He did not enjoy writing, the act of it. It was a scholarly, fastidious enterprise, summoning the creased forehead of Monsieur Roqueton, his principal, always ready to pounce should he misspell a word. Why was his father asking him to do this? His father had never bothered with homework. That was his mother's role; she was a teacher, after all. But he did not want to disappoint his father. Had Théodore Duhamel not said that Nicolas was extraordinary? No, he could not let his father down.

As the plane circled toward Orly airport in a grove of dark, rainy clouds, but on a smoother glide this time, Nicolas wrote. Unaccustomed to his childish loops, the fountain pen spluttered, but he mastered it, tongue clenched beneath his teeth, and the words came, beaded together, flowing out of him and onto the paper, joyful little creatures set free, giving him the most unexpected pleasure. He wrote a full page, which he anxiously handed to his father as the plane landed. His father's eyes darted from word to word; then he shouted, "Yes!" making his son jump. "That is it! That is absolutely it! How clever of you to compare the blue haze to Rascar Capac's crystal globe!" Nicolas had been afraid that linking the incident to Tintin's adventures with a frightening mummy (one of his favorite reads) might trigger his father's scorn. On the contrary, Théodore Duhamel raved all the more. He thumped Nicolas on the back so hard, the boy nearly choked. "How brilliant! I knew you could do it!" When they got home, his father read the page to his mother, who listened quietly and nodded her head. She liked it, but she seemed less enthusiastic than his father.

It was not until a full fourteen years later, when Nicolas sat down to write the first pages of *The Envelope* with the same sputtering Montblanc, that he experienced the joyful, uplifting pleasure once again. The exact one, the one he had felt in the plane as a boy, the one that swept him into a secret world of which he was the only sovereign. A pleasure so keen, so pure, that he had grinned to himself, remembering Rascar Capac and the blue haze.

I'M GOING BACK UP to the room," mutters Malvina. Her face looks ashen, peaky.

"Do you want me to go with you?" Nicolas says feebly, making no move to get up, incapable of relinquishing the sun's golden touch on his skin.

"No," she says, struggling to her feet. "I'll send you a text message if I feel worse."

"You don't want any lunch?" he asks. He's been looking forward to their meal up by the pool.

She grimaces and takes off. Nicolas watches her walk laboriously to the elevator. He'll check on her later. As soon as she is out of sight, his hand reaches for the BlackBerry, like a greedy kid aims for the cookie jar once his mother has turned her back. He now has an unexpected time niche to indulge in one of his favorite activities. He reads his personal e-mails, keeping Sabina for last. Dita wants a reply for her three queries (none of which he is thrilled about, and he wonders at this—how and when did he become reluctant about meeting students in a high school, answering a journalist's questions by e-mail, or posing for another glossy magazine).

Alice Dor wonders where he is and why he hasn't been responding to her e-mails. Nicolas knows she is worried he might take off and give his next book to another publisher. So concerned that she offered Nicolas the most expensive contract she ever proposed to a writer. (Pure folly, thought Nicolas when he signed his name at the bottom of the page, next to hers. How could she pay him that much money for a book he hadn't even written, that wasn't even in his head? He hadn't had the heart to tell her then and there that, no, he had not started to write yet, because he found it much more exciting to travel the world and meet all these people who admired him.) Alice was terrified—yes, that was the word, *terrified*—Nicolas might be snared and pulled in by all those other publishers out there, swimming around him like hungry sharks, especially since the Oscar. She knew that they had already begun to court Nicolas, sending their lieutenants to invite him to lunch at La Méditerranée, on the place de l'Odéon, at the Closerie des Lilas, or for drinks at the Lutetia bar at six. They would soon finally move in themselves, calling him directly. Nicolas has turned them down politely. For the moment. Alice trusts Nicolas, but how far will these publishers go? She is aware they will up the ante, that the figures can become obscene, and how could Nicolas possibly resist? Nicolas thinks of Alice's intelligent golden eyes, her deep voice, her surprisingly delicate hands. The woman who changed his life. The woman who sold his debut novel to forty-five countries and to Hollywood. The woman who wrought Hurricane Margaux.

Alice was a friend of Delphine's, the same age as she was, nine years older than Nicolas. Delphine's daughter, Gaïa, and Alice's daughter, Fleur, attended the same primary school on the rue de l'Ouest. It was Delphine who suggested he show the manuscript of *The Envelope* to Alice in 2007. She had started up an independent publishing company a couple of years back, one that was doing rather well. She had left a much larger company, taking all "her" authors with her. In that batch was the best-selling Basque writer Marixu Hirigoyen and Sarodj Ramgoolan, a young Mauritian literary sensation, the talk of the last Frankfurt Book Fair.

"I'm fine," Nicolas writes to Alice, thumbs flying over the Black-Berry, "just taking some time off. Back on Sunday." Dutifully, he calls his mother. No answer at the rue Rollin apartment. He tries her mobile, gets her voice mail immediately. He mumbles, "Hi, it's me, just checking in. I'm in Italy, with Malvina for the long weekend. Hope you're okay. Big kiss." Where could his mother be on a Friday morning in July? Perhaps he should have brought her here to the Gallo Nero, instead of Malvina. Maybe he should start thinking about his mother for once. The last time he saw her, she seemed tired, fed up with her students, with Renaud and his shilly-shallying, and thankful the school year was coming to its end. She had mentioned going to Brussels in July, staying with her sister, Roxane. Perhaps she was there now, in the tall house on the rue Van Eyck, full of Roxane's lanky teenagers, and then they would all go have lunch at Tervuren, where their mother, the cozy and endearing Béatrice—his maternal grandmother—lived. Nicolas convinces himself that his mother is with her family and not alone in Paris. He finds it morally more comfortable, yet he despises himself for it all the more.

Next on the guilt list, François. Nicolas sends a text message, choosing the cowardly way out, instead of calling him directly. "Hi, dude! How are ya? Miss u! In a secret place writing my new book, which I've nearly finished! Give me some news? Khûbe." He knew, with a sinking heart, that François would not answer his text message. Even though he signed it "Khûbe," his old khâgne nickname, it would not soften François. The silence would go on. It would go on until Nicolas actually called François and set a date for lunch, a drink. But would François come? François's silence stemmed from anger, jealousy, bitterness. He had seen the articles in the magazines (how could he not?), the shoots with Robin Wright, the four-page spread of the new duplex on the rue du Laos, the ads for the watches and the cologne; he had also seen the more serious articles in the *Figaro Littéraire,* in the *Monde des Livres,* in *The New York Review of Books,* analyzing the meteoric success of a young, unknown Frenchman who had touched so many hearts. François could not step into a bookstore, in France, in Europe, in the United States, without being confronted with posters of Nicolas and display stands of *The Envelope* in every language. "Of course François is jealous of you," scoffed Lara during a recent lunch. She is Nicolas's best female friend (meaning girlfriend in the true sense of the word, not a girl he's slept with, but a girl he's been friends with since their khâgne years.) "How can he not be jealous of you? Everyone envies you; even I sometimes do." She cackled at his outraged expression and took another bite of her quiche Lorraine. "Oh come on, Nicolas. For years you are a charming, hopeless, good-for-nothing nincompoop, flunking exams, living off your mother, then an older woman, and all of a sudden you lose your passport, and wham! You write this novel that is read all around the world—by twelve-year-old kids who don't like to read, by grannies, by housewives and businessmen, by First Ladies and actors. We still love you, but we are jealous. And poor François just can't say it to your face."

Nicolas starts to send a BBM to Sabina. A soft feminine voice is heard above him. He looks up, squinting against the sun, annoyed at the interruption.

"Excuse me, you are Nicolas Kolt, are you not?"

The accent is pure Italian. She is in her late thirties, wearing a floppy hat, dark glasses.

He nods once.

"I just want to thank you for your book. . . . You must have so many people telling you that, but . . . I just wanted to tell you. . . . It's a lovely book . . . . It helped me during a black moment of my life. . . . I have a family secret, too, and reading Margaux's story was . . . very helpful. . . ."

He nods again. "Thank you."

"Alessandra," she simpers.

"Thank you, Alessandra."

He smiles, but it is a tight smile, the one he uses when he wants to be left alone, when he does not want to answer any more questions (especially this one: What are you working on now?) but, all the while, is refraining from hurting the other person's feelings. She goes away and he sighs with relief. In the beginning, it was a thrill being recognized. When he took the metro, people's eyes lingered on him longer than necessary, and he could see them whispering to one another, "Isn't that the writer?" It had happened all at once, after the big photo shoots came out in *Paris Match,* after the prime-time TV shows, after the posters in bookstores. All of a sudden, his face had gone public—his gray eyes, his long sideburns, his square chin, his boyish grin. And then it started happening outside France. The only way to remain incognito was to cover his head with a baseball cap. Had he been unnecessarily callous to that fan? There might come a day in the near future, especially if there was no new book, when he would no longer be recognized. To remove the unpleasantness of that thought from his mind, Nicolas sends a BBM to Sabina. "Tell me what you are doing now. Tell me exactly." He is aware of the danger, of his foolishness, but he does it all the same. He has not seen Sabina since the first time he laid eyes on her, last April in Berlin, but he has been exchanging countless BBMs with her since then. At first, the tone was friendly, laid-back. And then one evening in May, when he was in Alsace for a book festival, the messages slipped into something else. Cordial still, but decidedly sexual. Since then, Nicolas has become wary about his exchanges with Sabina when Malvina is around. Sabina answers him immediately, always, as if she is waiting just for that, for him to contact her. When he reads "Sabina is writing a message" on the screen, his pulse quickens and he feels an erection stirring underneath his bathing suit.

"Nicolas Kolt has a 'thing' for older women," French *Elle* wrote last year in a long feature. He had not denied it to the journalist, a peach-skinned creature in her twenties. Yes, he had always fancied the mature woman; yes, he had had a long love affair with a woman who was nine years older than he was; yes, Margaux Dansor was his idea of perfection at forty-eight; yes, Robin Wright embodied her brilliantly. He did not tell the young journalist about Granville, but he knew well enough that what had happened on the beach with Véronique and Nathalie when he was seventeen had no doubt sharpened his inclination.

Sabina's BBM comes through. "I will tell you exactly. I want to take you in my mouth." His heart pumps crazily.

Nicolas decides to go for another swim fast, before his erection becomes embarrassing. The satiny touch of the water on his loins is delicious. He is alone in the sea, and he revels in this privilege. The heat is fierce now, shimmering and hazy. Most of the guests have gone up to the pool restaurant. He swims until his shoulders and legs ache, until he is out of breath. He sits for a while on the edge of the concrete slab, feeling the sun sizzle the salty water off his body. He thinks about Sabina's BBM and cannot help grinning. Well, he's not doing any harm, is he? Neither is she, right? Nobody is getting hurt.

Speedboats are bringing clients in for lunch at the Gallo Nero. They roar up to the impressive yachts and sailboats anchored in the bay, collect passengers, and come back. Nicolas watches as they arrive. A patrician family steps ashore. Probably wealthy Romans or Florentines. Regal grandparents, elegant mother and father, a tribe of well-groomed children, girls in flowery smock dresses, ribbons in their hair, boys with crisp shirts and Bermuda shorts. They look like they are posing for *Vanity Fair*. Later, another boat brings in two sisters, breathtakingly beautiful, one clutching a bag that is the distinctive blue of a famous New Yorker jeweler, and the other the leash to a clumsy, joyful Labrador who nearly tumbles into the sea (this makes Nicolas chuckle). Both sisters wear huge sunglasses, and their hair is tied back in artfully disarrayed chignons. Their small square faces remind him of Natalie Portman. They leap ashore, nimble and graceful, laughing at the dog's antics.

Nicolas tears himself away from the dreamy contemplation of the lovely sisters and makes his way back to the room. It is coming up on two o'clock. In the cool penumbra, Malvina is stretched out on the bed, fast asleep. He puts a careful hand on her forehead. It feels clammy but not hot. There is nothing left for him to do but to go have lunch.

He is ushered to the same table he had at breakfast, and notices that the French are once again on his left. The husband is eating with marked appetite, wolfing down pasta. He has been playing tennis and has not changed. His face is red and sweaty, his white polo damp under the armpits. Madame, head wrapped in an ungainly turban, makes deft, deadly swipes with her fork at her prosciutto, her jaw working. They do not exchange one word. On Nicolas's right, the brunette with the gorgeous bosom eats her bruschetta alone. The Belgian family, gregarious and jolly, order more chilled white wine. The Swiss couple peck at their salads and nod at him when he looks their way. He nods back. From where he is sitting, he has a perfect view of the entire terrace, yet he is partially hidden behind a parasol. Alessandra, his fan, lunching with an older version of herself, certainly her mother, cannot see him, and he is thankful. The *Vanity Fair* family, at least ten of them, appears overly affectionate with one another. They eat, drink, and kiss one another with loud smacks during the entire meal. He watches, eating his *granceola* club sandwich. But when the Natalie Portman sisters arrive, he has to put the sandwich down, they are so riveting. They must be twins; they are identical, down to their Cape Cod Hermès watches. The Labrador sits at their feet, panting. A server brings it some water, which it laps up noisily. Nicolas strains his ears to catch what language the sisters are conversing in.

"If you lean any farther, you'll fall off your chair, pal," says a nasal masculine voice.

Startled, Nicolas turns around. A hunched man in his late for-ties is standing there, wearing a crumpled T-shirt and faded jeans, holding a glass of rosé. He looks decidedly familiar, and with a shock, Nicolas realizes it is Nelson Novézan, the Franco-British novelist and Goncourt Prize winner. They have met several times—on TV shows, at literary events. Nicolas is surprised Nové-zan actually acknowledged him. His surliness is notorious.

"How you doing, pal?" Novézan drawls, staggering to the empty seat in front of Nicolas and dropping himself into it. He seems drunk. He lights a cigarette and holds it between his middle and ring fingers, a trademark gesture of his.

"Fine," says Nicolas, amused. From close-up, Novézan's skin is blotchy and unhealthy-looking. His hair shines with grease, as if he has not washed it for weeks.

"On holiday, are you, pal?"

"No, I'm here writing my book," says Nicolas.

"Really? Me, too." Novézan yawns, revealing unappetizing yellowed teeth. "Writing in the lap of luxury. I'm so happy with my work. Coming along fine. This is by far my best novel. It will be out next year. You'll see, it will be huge. My publisher is thrilled. So am I." He clicks his fingers at a passing waiter and motions for some more rosé. "Been here before, pal?"

"Nope, first time."

A flash of the yellow teeth. "Thought so. Marvelous place. Otto is a friend of mine. The director, you know. I get the same room year after year. The one with the best view. Splendid. That's the fucking brilliant part of being a best-selling author. Right?"

Nicolas nods, giving him the same tight smile he gave Alessan-dra.

The rosé comes.

"They're always turning up their noses at me because I'm not ordering some fancy Italian wine." Novézan pours himself a glass with an unsteady hand.

"How old are you, pal?"

"Twenty-nine," answers Nicolas.

A short grunt. "What the hell do you know about life, at twenty-nine?"

"How old are you?" retorts Nicolas, point-blank, longing to kick those stained teeth in.

A shrug. "Old enough to know better."

He smokes in silence while Nicolas scrutinizes him. Over the past ten years, this man has published four books. The last two were big best-sellers in Europe and in America. Nicolas has read them all. During his struggling khâgne years, Novézan fascinated him. The man was now an arrogant literary legend. The more famous he became, the ruder he was to journalists and readers. His novels were misogynistic, crude, and beautifully written. People either loved his work or hated it. No one was indifferent to it. Recently, Nicolas saw Novézan at a book fair in Switzerland, where, in the foulest mood, he publicly insulted his assistant because the taxi she had ordered for him was late. Nicolas recalls how the woman remained calm, and yet she was quivering from head to toe while Novézan ranted and raged, spewing four-letter words in her direction for all to hear.

"Clever move, that little book of yours," Novézan mutters, slurping down the rosé.

"What do you mean?"

Another yawn. "Well, drawing on that passport episode. I mean, the idea was out there, hanging in front of our noses. Look at me, French father born abroad, English mum, me born in Paris. . . . It could have happened to me." Nicolas says nothing, revolted by what the man is insinuating. "I mean, the seed was there, pal, for all French citizens faced with having to prove their nationality because of that absurd new law. You went out there and you wrote it. Clever move. Did it sell well in the end, your little book?"

"Reasonably well," says Nicolas in an even voice, realizing that at last he has the upper hand, and inwardly writhing at "your little book."

"Like what?" drawls Novézan, carelessly rising to the bait.

Nicolas pauses before the coup de grâce. His eyes linger over the lovely sisters, then travel up to the ocher house where Malvina sleeps.

"Thirty million worldwide," he says quietly.

That shuts Novézan up for a couple of minutes. Nicolas feels the spurt of triumph within him wither away. How despicable of him to flaunt his sale figures. Who is he trying to impress? The aging, fatigued, vain author sitting in front of him?

"Are you here alone?" he asks Novézan politely.

"Can't get any writing done if there's a woman in my room. So I text, and she comes running." Novézan makes an explicit, vulgar gesture with his mouth and hands.

Nicolas cannot help smiling. He stands, putting his cap back on his head. "I'm off for a swim. Want to come?"

Novézan waves him off. "No thanks. Going back to work, pal. Lots more to write. Such an inspiring place! My juices are flowing. How about yours?"

Nicolas ignores that last question. Novézan rises as well, reeling on shaky, skinny legs. They part, clapping each other on the back like old buddies. Before Nicolas gets into the elevator, he checks his BlackBerry. To his surprise, and annoyance, there is a photo of him posted on his Facebook page. A photo taken this very morning from up near the pool. The fan's name is Alex Brunel. The profile picture is a Granny Smith apple, which gives him no inkling of what he or she looks like. Alex Brunel's page is a private one, no access. Luckily, there is no mention of where this photo was taken. Four hundred and forty-five people have already "liked" it. This has happened to him before. Fans see him in the bus, in the metro—which he has never stopped taking, despite his new-found fame—discreetly click away with their phones, and then publish the photo on his wall, as a tribute. It's never bothered him till today. He looks at the photo closely. A telltale black-and-white parasol is in view. A person who really wanted to find out where he was could put two and two together. There is nothing he can do.

He can almost hear Delphine's voice: *This is the price you have to pay, Nicolas; and this is what you wanted, isn't it?* He scrolls down to read the comments. "Mmh, sexy." "Gorgeous." "Hey, Nicolas, take me with you!" "Italy or Greece?" "Way to go!" No one mentions the Gallo Nero, thankfully. He could delete the photo, but Alex Brunel, whoever he or she may be, might be offended. He or she might even post other photos of him. He has learned to be careful with his fans. Angry fans are bad news. He checks his Twitter feed. No mention of his Italian escapade by his followers. He looks up his own name, just to be on the safe side. Nothing. He does not do that often, nor does he Google his name much anymore. He used to, in the beginning. It was secretly thrilling to discover all those blogs and Web sites mentioning his work, then the movie. But for every dozen positive remarks, there were the few negative ones. The ones that hurt. On Twitter once, some influential Web journalist had Tweeted, "Stop telling us to read that awful Nicolas Kolt shit. Why does this guy sell so many books?" That had been Retweeted hundreds of times.

When he gets down to the beach, he sees Malvina waiting for him. Her cheeks seem pinker. He asks how she is. She says she threw up, felt terrible for a while, but is fine now. Probably a stomach bug. He lies down next to her and holds her hand. He tells her about Nelson Novézan and their conversation. He mimes Novézan's famous sneer, his cocked eyebrow, the way he holds his cigarette.

"You should have posted that on Twitter," she says, grinning. "With a photo of him."

"I'm taking a Twitter break," says Nicolas. And then he adds cruelly, "He looks like an old dog."

Malvina asks if he saw the new picture on his Facebook page. She checked it out on her iPhone. Nicolas frowns and admits he is not happy about it. He is craving privacy. He wants time for himself, time for them, three days of peace. Three days of sun.

"I wonder who posted that photo," whispers Malvina.

Nicolas whispers back, "I don't care," and kisses her glossy hair.

It is less hot now; the long shadows of the afternoon creep slowly along the concrete beach. They are served tea, *cantucci,* and slices of melon. An Asian couple in their fifties are installed nearby. The man is bald, Buddha-like, with a flashy orange bathing suit and an ostentatious Cartier Pasha. The woman is pale, her hair a perfect black helmet. She wears a long blue kimono. They nod and smile to the staff, who bow and smile back. Nicolas catches them murmuring "Mr. Wong" at the end of each sentence. Mr. Wong must be very important; he is certainly getting a lot of attention. Mrs. Wong cannot stand a single ray of sunshine on her skin, so two parasols are joined above her by the complying attendants, who give her just as much "Mrs. Wong" until a grinning, head-shaking Mr. Wong says, "No no! Not Mrs. Wong! No no! Miss Ming!" Mr. Wong and Miss Ming then smile and nod to everyone next to them, including Nicolas and Malvina, who smile back.

Nicolas notices more newcomers. Two young men of his age, although one could be a little older, already in his thirties. One is long and thin, geeky-looking, short blond hair, John Lennon glasses, plunged into his iPad. The other is tanned, smooth-skinned, and hairless. They both wear the same watch. Gay? American? Canadian? They, too, nod and smile at Mr. Wong and Miss Ming, then look at each other and giggle. Malvina finds them cute. A little farther off, the Swiss play chess. The Belgians are back. Father and son go for a swim, mother reads on, and daughter steadfastly tans, eyes closed.

Nicolas can see the Belgian mother has gotten to the end of his book, probably the part when Margaux decides to go to San Rocco di Camogli to find out who her father's family was. She knew nothing about them, down to their name, Zeccherio. Nicolas is reminded of the shock he felt when he saw his father's real name for the first time in 2006. He had been to the town hall of the fifth arrondissement with his *livret de famille* and his birth certificate because his passport had expired. Renewing it was usually a quick deal for any French citizen. A couple of weeks at the most. An unpleasant surprise awaited him. The woman behind the counter said to him, "I'm afraid we cannot renew your passport, Monsieur Duhamel. Your mother was born in Belgium, and your father in Russia."

Nicolas had stared at her blankly. "So?"

"According to the new governmental laws, French citizens with parents born in other countries now have to prove they are French."

Nicolas gaped.

"I've never heard of this law! I was born in France, madame, right here, at the Saint-Vincent de Paul hospital. I am French, and have been French all my life."

"I'm afraid that being born in France is no longer a reason for being automatically French, monsieur." The woman handed him a square of paper. "In the past couple of years, jurisdiction has been tightened on cases like yours. Those with parents born abroad. You are not the only one in this situation. You need to go to this address, the Pôle de la nationalité française, in the thirteenth arrondissement. They will study your dossier, and if they decide you can be French, they will deliver a certificate. This is called a 'certificate of French nationality.' It is the only way for you to obtain your passport. This may take several months."

Nicolas felt his jaw drop. "How on earth do I prove I am French ?"

"Call the Pôle and bring in the data they need."

"And if I'm not French, than what am I?"

"Stateless, monsieur. *Apatride*."

Nicolas left the town hall in a daze, went home to Delphine's apartment. He searched the Internet for governmental laws concerning French citizens with French parents born abroad. He discovered, to his consternation, that these laws had been recently toughened. Thousands of people all over the country were enduring the same trauma. How had he not heard of this? Fascinated, appalled, he read several interviews with famous writers, singers, and actors who were having to go through the Kafkaesque and humiliating procedure of proving they were indeed French. Many had denounced the entire process and had severely criticized the government.

Nicolas finally summoned up enough courage to call the dreaded Pôle de la nationalité française, where he was put on hold, listening to "Spring" from Vivaldi's *Four Seasons* over and over again, till he felt nauseous. At last, a female voice was heard, indifferent, unsympathetic. He was told to go to the Pôle in three weeks' time, on Tuesday morning at eleven, with his parents' birth certificates.

"But both my parents are French, even if they were born abroad!" said Nicolas plaintively.

The woman clicked her tongue. "There is a doubt concerning your nationality, monsieur. You must now prove that you're French." (Nicolas later told François and Lara, over a glass of wine, that this whole affair felt like a tasteless joke, as if France had reverted to her Vichy years. He told them about what he had learned online, relating the numerous articles, and the negative image this was giving France around the world. François had asked why his father had been born in Russia; Nicolas believed it was because his grandfather had taken his grandmother on a trip there when she was pregnant and she had unexpectedly given birth to his dad in Saint Petersburg.)

How was he supposed to get a hold of his parents' birth certificates, given they had not been born in France? Nicolas was informed by the charmless lady at the Pôle that French citizens in that precise situation obtained their birth certificates through the central service of the Registry Office in Nantes. Thankfully, this could be done online. Nicolas filled in the forms, specified he was the son of the late Théodore Duhamel and Emma Duhamel, née Van der Vleuten, explaining that he needed these papers to renew his passport.

The certificates took four days to arrive by post at the rue Pernety. They got there on a rainy day. A day Nicolas would never forget.

The first certificate read "Emma Van der Vleuten, born March 18,

1959, Edith Cavell Clinic, Uccle, Belgium. Father: Roland Van der Vleuten, born Charleroi, 1937. Mother: Béatrice Tweelinckx, born Liège, 1938."

Then he read "Fiodor Koltchine, born Улица Писарева, Leningrad, USSR, June 12, 1960. Mother: Zinaïda Koltchine, born Leningrad, USSR, 1945. Father: unknown. Died: August 7, 1993, Guéthary, France." There was a fine handwritten sentence at the bottom of the certificate and an official stamp: "Adopted by Lionel Duhamel in 1961; from now on known as Théodore Duhamel."

A pit opened up somewhere in his stomach. Nicolas sat there, incredulous, frozen, staring down at the piece of paper. He did not pick up the telephone. Instead, he marched straight to his mother's apartment on the rue Rollin. He got there out of breath, wet, and anxious.

"You need to explain," he said, shoving the birth certificate under her nose. Sitting in the large armchair by the fireplace, a startled Emma Duhamel had stared down at the paper, then back to her son with those fog-filled eyes.

"Oh!" she gasped.

"Well?" he grunted, still breathless.

Silence.

"Nicolas, its a long story," she said at last, nervously fingering her bead necklace. "Please sit down."

According to Théodore Duhamel, the Atlantic Ocean was the king of all seas. Little did he know that it would one day claim his life. He had never enjoyed holidays on the Riviera, where his parents owned a villa overlooking Cannes. For him, the Mediterranean Sea was a cesspool full of impotent septuagenarians flaunting tans, face-lifts, and diamonds. He despised the smooth, glassy water and the lack of tides. In the late sixties, a classmate invited him to the Basque country one summer, where he was smitten by the rolling, frothy waves, the green mountains, the humid wind, the unpredictable weather forecast. He did not seem, at first glance, the rugged outdoor type, but he was more of an athlete than he appeared. He learned to surf as a boy in Biarritz with a bunch of young local surfers, of whom he was the youngest and probably the most enthusiastic. Nicolas remembers that as a young boy he would sit on the beach with his mother—pale and stoic, her nose buried in a book—while Théodore Duhamel rode the waves with his surfer friends. He stayed in the water for hours on end, wearing a black wet suit, which gave him the slinky appearance of a seal, and by the end of the summer, his chestnut locks had turned gold, bleached by the sun and the sea. "Surfer widow," Emma's friends dubbed her, mocking her for her endless waits on the sand with her son, and there was no way they could ever have suspected that their affectionate nickname would, one summer, ring horribly true.

For the first ten summers of Nicolas's life, his parents rented a poky apartment overlooking the Côte des Basques. It had a grandiose view over the ocean, facing south, and one could glimpse Spain creeping out along the coast like an outstretched arm. Every morning, Théodore Duhamel rose early and stared out to sea like the Ancient Mariner. Nicolas liked to watch him stride down the long and winding path to the beach, surfboard tucked under his arm. With binoculars, Nicolas could then observe his father on the sand, waxing his board with sure, precise movements (he can still remember the smell of that wax, and its name: Sex Wax, although it had nothing to do with sex, as he one day discovered.)

Nicolas made Margaux Dansor's father into a skier. But the two sports were linked in his mind. They were both action sports that involved gliding on a natural surface; they were both risky, the participants in search of the highest wave, the steepest slope. In the summer of 1990, when Nicolas was eight years old, Théodore Duhamel bought a catamaran, a black Hobie 16 that could ride the crest of the waves like a surfboard. Théodore Duhamel sailed his Hobie Cat audaciously, to such an extent that even his phlegmatic wife gasped with fright when the sleek boat was nearly overturned by a powerful shore break.

Whenever Nicolas endeavored to describe his father to journalists, it was the memory of him sailing his Hobie Cat that he wished to convey, his wet suit, his cigar clamped between his teeth, his hair streaming behind him, waving to his son and wife as he drifted by. "There goes your man," he heard his mother's friends say. "Oh, look at him, Emma. What a prince!" And Nicolas would wave back, breathless with pride. The boat darted close to the shore, riding in on the wave like a surfer, then carelessly and effortlessly turned back at the very last moment, swooping high over the foam, black sail swinging over and swelling up again.

The Hobie Cat washed up with the tide near Hendaye two days after the disappearance, its mast smashed and its sail torn. But his father's body was never found. It had been a muggy, humid August day in 1993. The waves were no bigger than usual. Théodore Duhamel told his wife he was sailing down to Guéthary to see his surfer friends. If the wind was strong, as it was that day, it usually took him under one hour from the Port des Pêcheurs, where he kept his boat. Nicolas did not see his father leave (that morning, he was at his tennis lesson), but when he got back at lunch, he did glimpse the small pointed sail as it appeared behind the Gothic peak of the Villa Belza. He knew his father could not possibly see him at such a distance, but he waved to him all the same. He had wanted to go to Guéthary with his father, but Emma refused, because of the tennis lesson. She became flustered when she had to pay for lessons that her son did not attend. If Nicolas had gone sailing with his father, would he have prevented his death? Would they both have died? Those questions still haunted Nicolas, eighteen years later.

Nicolas remembers the harrowed look on his mother's face when she finally called the surfer friends in Guéthary as the sun was setting. Théodore had "been and gone," chirped his laid-back pal from California, Murphy. "I'm worried," she admitted. Nicolas was only eleven, but he felt a gnawing in his gut. Then she said softly, "I'm going to have to call the police." He could not bear hearing what his mother had to say to the police, so he left the room and went to stand on the balcony, where his father had stood that very morning. He put his feet where his father had put his, and placed his hands on the railing, exactly where his father had placed his hands. He watched the darkness of the night sweep up into the sky and the slow, steady beam from the lighthouse shine through the black, and he was afraid, more afraid than he had ever been in his life, ten times more afraid than when the plane was hit by lightning. His mother came out and cradled him in her arms. He dared not look at her face. He stared out at the immensity of the sea and thought of his father somewhere out there, and he started to cry.

The minutes slipped by, endless and dreadful. The night came, and people started to turn up. He was given something to drink, and someone made a meal. The apartment was soon packed with friends, and he was cuddled, kissed, cajoled, but it did not make him feel any better, and he watched his mother's face become paler as the night inched along. He finally fell asleep, exhausted, on the corner of the sofa while people continued to talk, drink, and smoke, and when he awoke, bleary-eyed, at dawn, his mother was crying in the bathroom, and he knew his father had still not been found.

"When there is no corpse," he told the journalists, "no coffin, no undertaker, no grave, no Mass, no obituary, it is hard to accept that someone is dead. When the Hobie Cat was found, we all longed for the body to be, as well. But it never was. To this day," Nicolas said over and over again in his interviews, "I still hope against hope that my father might walk through that door. He would be fifty-one today. I know it is impossible, because I know my father most probably fell off his boat and drowned, but there is still that inkling, that possibility, that he might still be alive, somewhere, somehow. Margaux Dansor, unlike me, does find out the truth about what happened to her father. But her story is not my story. Let's say I invented her story in order to try to answer my unanswerable questions about my own father." The journalists asked again and again, "And what about your name? Did you change your name when you wrote the book? How did Nicolas Duhamel become Nicolas Kolt?" Nicolas tried to answer them with the same patience each time. "Kolt is a abbreviation of Koltchine, my father's real name. When I was told the book was going to be published, all of a sudden, Duhamel made no sense."

Théodore Duhamel would never read *The Envelope*. But the book was dedicated to him.

To my father, Fiodor Koltchine (Saint Petersburg, June 12, 1960–Guéthary, August 7, 1993).

THE SUN IS SLOWLY sinking behind a high, rocky hill. It is not going to set in the sea, in front of them. Nicolas is disappointed. He was expecting a glorious pink sunset. Most people have turned their chairs away from the horizon, worshiping the final golden rays being swallowed up by the looming hill. He is secretly proud of the fact that for the last hour or so he has resisted the temptation of glancing at his BlackBerry. Mr. Wong and Miss Ming are playing mah-jongg. The gay couple are listening to the same iPod and swinging their heads in the same movement. The Belgian family is having a last dip. The Swiss are dutifully reading the papers. Alessandra and her mother seem to be fast asleep. The hairy man is puffing away on a cigarette, phone clamped to his ear, oblivious to the fact that his buxom girlfriend is chatting up the French guy (whose wife is no doubt at the spa). A puce-faced, tipsy Nelson Novézan makes a quick appearance, a pitiful sight in faded swim shorts that sag around his equally sagging buttocks. He plunges a toe into the water, yelps, and scuttles back to the elevator.

Boats are coming in again from the yachts, bringing more

exclusive clients to the Gallo Nero for drinks and dinner, and perhaps to spend the night. Once again, Nicolas thinks of the book he has been lying about to his entourage. One day soon, he will have to sit down, be responsible, and write that novel. No more procrastination. No more sloth. But how? If only energy for the book could come flowing in like those elegant guests smoothly riding in on the black Rivas. He remembered that when he started *The Envelope,* it was as if Margaux Dansor took him by the hand and led him onward. He could feel her hand, the texture of it, smooth, a little dry; he could feel the tug, the pull. He saw Margaux Dansor perfectly, as clearly as if she had been standing in front of him. It had been effortless creating her. She looked nothing like Emma Duhamel, his mother. Nor did she have Delphine's auburn hair, white skin, green eyes. Margaux had a long Modigliani-like face, hazel eyes, thick silver hair. She was a piano teacher. She lived in the rue Daguerre with her husband, Arnaud Dansor (a doctor), and their two girls, Rose and Angèle. One day, she had to get her passport renewed. Margaux soon discovered this was an impossible feat, according to recent laws, even though she had been born in the chic suburb of Neuilly-sur-Seine, near Paris. All this because her mother (Claire Nadelhoffer) had been born in Landquart, Switzerland, and her father (Luc Zech, who died in an avalanche when she was a child) in San Rocco di Camogli, Italy. At the Pôle de la nationalité française, Margaux was told to bring in every single document she could get ahold of concerning her father's family—birth, death, and marriage certificates going back to her great-grandfather, military service carnets, tax forms, Social Security cards—in order to prove her French nationality. And it was by perusing all these papers, by delving into the past, that Margaux Dansor stumbled upon the unthinkable.

At the mention of the name Koltchine, Emma Duhamel had cleared her throat on that wet October day in 2006, nearly five years ago, when her son confronted her with her late husband's birth certificate. It had taken her a while to decide how she was going to explain this to him as fluidly as possible, and Nicolas could see how complicated this appeared to be for her. She paced up and down the room, her hands going from her bead necklace to her hair, which she smoothed back in a calm gesture, but Nicolas could see those hands were trembling.

"I suppose you could say it all began with your grandmother," Emma finally said, using the philosophy teacher's voice, the one he disliked, higher-pitched and louder than her usual tone.

"Dad's mother?" he said.

"Yes."

"Nina?"

"Her real name was Zinaïda Koltchine."

"Is that Russian?"

"Yes."

"So she was Russian?"

"She was."

"Not French?"

"She became French when she married Lionel Duhamel."

Nicolas stared at his mother. "What are you trying to say?"

Emma Duhamel took a deep breath. "Your grandmother left the USSR in the early sixties. With her baby boy, Fiodor Koltchine."

"So she was married to a guy called Koltchine?"

"No. Koltchine was her maiden name."

Nicolas looked down at the birth certificate. Born in Leningrad on June 12, 1960.

"How old was Nina when she had Dad?"

"Very young, I think."

"So Lionel Duhamel is not my grandfather?"

"No, he's not, technically. But he adopted your father, gave him his name, and raised him as his son."

"So who is my grandfather?"

"No one knows."

Nicolas digested this in silence.

"Why did you wait all these years to tell me this?"

Emma took a while to speak. She seemed out of breath, distraught.

"When I married your father, we had to get paperwork ready for our wedding. That's when I saw his birth certificate and his real name."

She paused again.

"Did you ask him about it?"

"I did. But your father refused to answer me. I sensed that I could not talk to him about it. We never mentioned it again. The only person who brought up the Russian connection after your grandmother's death was your aunt Elvire. And that was only once. I didn't tell you because I was waiting for the moment when you would find out by yourself and be old enough to handle it. I believe that moment has come."

At the Pôle de la nationalité française, on another rainy day, Nicolas waited for over an hour in a crowded, narrow room. An old man next to him dabbed at his tearful, reddened eyes. He could not understand what he was doing here, he told Nicolas in a dignified, trembling voice. His passport and *carte d'identité* had been stolen, so he had gone to the town hall to get new ones. He was told that because his long-dead parents had been born abroad, he now had to prove he was French, at ninety-two, due to the new law. He was a retired doctor, a pediatrician, born in Paris; he had received the Légion d'honneur, he had fought for France during World War II, and now what was his country doing to him? Nicolas did not know how to comfort him. He could only shake his head and pat the old man's hand.

Time crept by. The rain pattered against the windows. Children and babies whimpered. Bored teenagers played with their mobile phones. Others read. Some people slept. Nicolas looked down at the papers in the folder on his knees. The Russian connection. Zinaïda Koltchine had been born in Leningrad in 1945. Her son, Fiodor, in 1960. Nicolas stared down at the dates. She was fifteen years old when she became a mother. Nicolas was baffled. He had never realized how young his grandmother was when she was still alive. Lionel Duhamel, her husband, now in a geriatric hospital, was fifteen years older than she. Nicolas had never noticed that age difference, either. He now realized Nina Duhamel had been only forty-eight when her son died. How extraordinary that he had not realized this earlier. But then, there was an age, a very young age, he recalled, when everyone over thirty seemed to be a crumbing wreck. There was nothing exotic about Madame Duhamel. Nothing Russian, not even remotely Slavic. No accent. No high cheekbones. She was merely a distinguished, chain-smoking, sophisticated bourgeoise who ran her household with an iron fist and who enjoyed glamorous summers on the Riviera. He had not been close to his paternal grandmother, preferring the motherly warmth of his Belgian granny. Nina Duhamel liked to be called "Mamita" by her offspring. She died in 2000 of lung cancer, at fifty-five years old, seven years after her son's disappearance. Nicolas's eyes wandered back to the folder. Fiodor Koltchine, his father. Born of a stranger. Fiodor Koltchine. Even the name made him shiver, as ominous and as unfamiliar as Keyser Söze, the enigmatic gangster in his favorite movie, *The Usual Suspects*.

A question mark had popped up in Nicolas Duhamel's conventional family tree. He obtained his *certificat de nationalité française* easily enough, as his grandmother became French when she married Lionel Duhamel in 1961, and Nicolas had the necessary papers to prove that official act. But the question mark remained, hovering in his mind, looming larger and larger, buzzing about like an annoying mosquito, even as his new passport was issued. Who had fathered Zinaïda's baby? And what had his own father, Théodore, known about his origins?

He had questioned his aunt Elvire Duhamel, Lionel and Nina's forty-three-year-old daughter. She was a wiry woman, divorced, who lived in Montmartre with two cats. Her teenaged children, Alina and Carlos, Nicolas's cousins, lived in Barcelona with her ex-husband, an alcoholic Spaniard. Their phone conversation was a fleeting, unsatisfactory one. "On her deathbed, Mother told me my brother had another name, a Russian one, and that he wasn't Lionel's son. What? Why did she tell me? She had just been diagnosed with lung cancer, Nicolas! She thought she was going to pop off any minute. Guess she wanted a clear conscience. She ended up living another six months, mind you. She never mentioned it again. And don't you dare go talking about this to my father. He's dotty enough as it is." Lionel Duhamel, approaching seventy-six, suffered from Alzheimer's and was in a geriatric hospital. Nicolas was confronted with the disagreeable reality of dementia and old age whenever he went to visit his grandfather (who, in fact, was not his grandfather, as he now liked to remind himself, with a touch of angst). With Emma's help, Nicolas found the family tree he'd drawn in class with such care as a boy at the elementary school on the rue Rollin. The Belgian branch on one side, the French on the other: Duhamel and Van der Vleuten. There was nothing French about him, he realized during that long wait at the Pôle de la nationalité française. The irony of it nearly made him chuckle out loud, but the sobbing old man next to him girdled his mirth. He was no Duhamel. He was Russian and Belgian. He was a Koltchine– Van der Vleuten mix. And he would probably never find out who his paternal grandfather was. That mere thought opened up an abyss under his feet. Nicolas Duhamel's placid, tranquil existence was no more. That gray day, as he waited over two hours at the Pôle, staring down at the papers on his lap, he felt a subtle shift in the world around him, as if unknown hands were tampering with his fate.

That was the day Nicolas Kolt was born, but he did not know that yet. And that was also the day Margaux Dansor first wove her way into his existence.

It took Nicolas under a year to write *The Envelope*, and it irks him to recall the smoothness of that routine, now that he is faced with the growing bulk of his procrastination. As he sips his fruit cocktail, he thinks of how he used to rise at dawn with ease and enthusiasm, before Delphine took her daughter, Gaïa, to school; he'd make tea and sit at the kitchen table. He wrote the novel by hand, in black notebooks like the empty one on his lap now, and then he typed the text into his MacBook, and it all flowed miraculously. Perhaps Delphine's kitchen is the only place he can write? He misses Delphine. He misses his life with her. The simplicity of it, the rhythm of it. Before Hurricane Margaux, Delphine was the busy bee of the two of them. She worked in a real estate agency and spent her days showing apartments to clients. Delphine was the one who found the rue du Laos duplex for them—or rather, for him. She never ended up living there with Nicolas, as their breakup took place the week he moved. She and Gaïa stayed in the modern building on the rue Pernety, just above the post office, and Nicolas went to live in the huge duplex by himself.

Before he embarked on the adventure of the novel, Nicolas rose late, puttered around, gave his philosophy lessons, went to pick up Gaïa at school when she was too small to go home alone. He did the shopping along the rue Raymond Losserand—he was a favorite with the long-haired fishmonger, the Algerian fruit vendor, the beaming dry-cleaning lady from Haiti, Claudia—he did the washing, the cooking, the laundry. He did not mind being a kept man. It gave him a thrill to hear Delphine's key in the lock, her face lighting up when she set eyes on him, her pleasure at the meal he had prepared, the wine he had chosen. Gaïa was put to bed and told a story, and then they had the evening to themselves.

When Delphine and Nicolas met for the first time in 2004, he was twenty-two. There had been nothing thrilling in his life since his trip to Italy with François in the summer of 2003, after the debacle of his studies. He still felt the brunt of his mother's discontent, although Emma never voiced it. Their cohabitation in the rue Rollin apartment was a strained one. Emma wanted him to move out, yet she could not bear the idea of being alone. Nicolas longed for freedom, but his tutorials did not bring him enough money to pay rent on his own.

One fall evening, Lara (who had not passed the khâgne exam either, but who did not care, as she had just landed a job at a prestigious magazine) took him to L'Entrepôt, a trendy restaurant in the fourteenth arrondissement. After Lara left, a woman asked him how he was feeling. He was drunk, sprawled over the bar, wrapped in a dreamy, nauseous stupor, but lucid enough to notice she was attractive, with creamy white skin and auburn hair. Delphine took him back to her place, five minutes away, but it took over half an hour to get there, as he could barely stand up. He blacked out as soon as he collapsed on her sofa, and opened bewildered eyes the next morning, confused as to his whereabouts. She was reading, sipping a cup of coffee, wearing glasses and a man's shirt, with nothing much underneath. He fell in love with her then and there.

After the breakup in 2009, it was in the splendor of the rue du Laos apartment that Nicolas realized he no longer had the energy to write. He put his lethargy down to Delphine's departure. "I don't like who you have become, Nicolas," Delphine had said bitingly on the phone during that final and awful conversation. "I don't like the full-of-himself, arrogant little bastard you like to pretend you are and that maybe you really have become." He tried to interrupt her, feebly, although he knew it was useless. Delphine, once she was started, was like a freight train; nothing stopped her. And so out it all came. Nicolas stood on the top terrace of the duplex, looking out to the Champ de Mars and the Eiffel Tower, braced himself, and listened. "Of course, we all know that being exposed to such an overwhelming success is risky. I'm not saying you've been un-faithful to me. I know—I hope?—you haven't, and I'm not even talking about that. I'm talking about how you used to care for people. You used to care, Nicolas. You used to listen. You were there. That's gone. Now you're a hot It Boy everyone hungers for. And the worst thing is, you've grown to like it. . . . No, don't inter-rupt me. You never used to be vain. Now you look at yourself in shop windows, for Christ's sake. Whenever you go anywhere, even into a supermarket, you check to see if someone has recognized you. You Google yourself all day long. You spend hours reading posts on your Facebook page. You seem to think that tracking down the Nicolas Kolt hashtag on Twitter is more important than talking to me, or my daughter, or your poor mother. Where is the Nicolas Du-hamel who used to wash dishes and crack jokes when I got home? Now you're either on a book tour or getting drunk at some cocktail party. This is not the kind of life I want with you. I'm thrilled, re-ally, that the book has changed your life and that the world is at your feet. . . . No, don't interrupt me. But that book opened our bedroom door to thousands of people. I can't stand that anymore. I could, if you were being more mature about it. But you are not. You are like a spoiled little boy who got too many presents for his birthday. Listen to me, Nicolas. Gaïa and I are not coming to live with you. You are going to live on rue du Laos all by yourself. Maybe you'll finally wake up and see what you're doing to your life. Life isn't one big book tour, Nicolas. Life isn't about being recognized in the street by adoring readers. Life isn't about how many people follow you on Twitter and how many friends you have on Facebook. Please tell Nicolas Kolt that I'm not impressed by him. Good-bye." She hung up. Since then (this was two years ago), Nicolas has swallowed his pride and Delphine has stopped being so resentful. They have not gotten back together, but they remain friends.

The rue du Laos duplex felt like a gigantic white box for the first two weeks. Nicolas kept waking up in the middle of the night, disoriented, wondering where he was and why Delphine was not in bed with him. Why did this space feel so huge, and he so puny? His mother, when she came to visit, said tentatively, "Hmmm . . . It's big, isn't it?" At first, he threw wild, loud parties where people danced, screamed, tossed bottles from windows till dawn, and the police were called. He was informed by the building management that if this went on, he'd be thrown out.

Six months after the breakup, Nicolas felt the need to get back to the book. The one that obsessed him, although he had not written a line of it. Why had his stamina fizzled out? What had happened to Rascar Capac and the blue haze? Where was the key to the secret world he used to disappear into?

Nicolas had Gaïa's pink room (the one she never moved into) repainted a subtle and soothing blue, he bought a long and narrow black table from Vitra, a new chair, a new lamp, and he sat down to write. All he could see was Delphine's face on the screen of his MacBook. After twenty minutes of nothing (nothing meaning a few sentences typed out at a snail's pace and promptly erased), he pushed the laptop aside and tried pen and paper. Where was his father's Montblanc? He searched high and low for it. He had not seen it since the move. He decided that he could not write his new book without it. He did not dare call Delphine; she was probably busy showing apartments to clients and would not appreciate being disturbed, especially by him. So he texted her. "Hi. Sorry. Do you know where my father's Montblanc is, by any chance?" And she texted back. "No idea. Good luck." He finally found it in a jacket he hadn't worn for a while.

Armed with the Montblanc, Nicolas sat down once more, pen poised above the paper. His new cleaning lady shuffled about quietly, anxious not to disturb his concentration, and he felt so embarrassed that he actually pretended to write. He wrote a love letter to Delphine that he knew he would never send.

It soon became clear to Nicolas that he would get no writing done in the duplex. Its grandiosity somehow warped his creativity and accentuated his indolence. He tried to write in a nearby café on the avenue de la Motte-Picquet, but he became distracted by watching passersby come and go.

At his wit's end, Nicolas decided to rent a seventy-five-square-foot room at the top of a nearby building on the avenue de Lowendal, five minutes away. It had the aspect of a monk's cell, with a cracked, jaundiced washbasin in one corner and a scaly radiator in the other. It gave onto an identical bourgeois building on the other side of the courtyard and seemed perfectly peaceful. Nicolas was delighted. This was just what he needed to get the writing process back into swing and to put his sloth at bay. He bought an old school desk at the flea market, a plain wooden chair from Ikea. The only luxury was a tall, slim Costanza lamp. This is great, he thought, striding with energy and purpose to his new cubbyhole of an office with his Montblanc and his Moleskine. Humming, he took the derelict, antiquated elevator, which made alarming noises all the way up, and installed himself at the desk. Nicolas stretched his arms, unclenched his fingers, and started to write. Again, he wrote to Delphine. He wrote her a long, beautiful (he was convinced it was beautiful) love letter. This was an excellent beginning;

it would turn out to be a moving, tender love story. He imagined Alice Dor's enthusiasm—he could even see the cover of the book—and he already pictured himself talking about it to journalists, "After the breakup, I was so distraught . . ." As he gazed outside, he caught a flitting motion in the apartment directly in front of him. There were three little windows lined with green-and-blue curtains. The movement happened again, and Nicolas, astonished, saw a young nude woman running from one room to the other—or rather, prancing—arms outstretched, head held high with the grace of a ballerina. Her pert breasts bounced up and down enticingly; her dark hair rippled down her back. Nicolas could see her perfectly, her pale, smooth skin, her round buttocks, tight and muscular, her flat belly and the delta of trimmed pubic hair. Intrigued, aroused, he put his pen down and continued to look. Impervious, she continued her flouncing, and he wondered how it was possible that she had no idea she was being watched. Perhaps she did know, and she liked it. It was difficult to tear his eyes away from the naked ballerina and return to the sentences on the paper. Even more so when she effortlessly lifted her leg, an ankle in her palm, offering him a remarkable view of her pudenda. Nicolas felt his throat become uncomfortably dry. He was never going to get any writing done at this rate. Or he would have to paste paper in his window.

The next day, he (reluctantly but bravely) turned his desk away from the window so that the tantalizing ballerina was out of view. He managed to regain some sort of concentration. Just as he was happily scribbling away, describing Delphine's hips under the shower, he heard a grunt, so loud and so near, he thought it came from just behind him. There it was again, masculine, low and rumbling, and definitely sexual. It came from the room on his left. His heart sank. He sat there, helpless, as the grunts gained in intensity and rhythm. How was he ever going to get any writing done at all with a nude ballerina and an audio version of the *Kama Sutra* behind paper-thin walls? The grunts became groans, and a foreign language could be heard. A loud thump made Nicolas jump, then a bang, followed by screeches that curdled his blood. He crept up to open the door a crack. More crashes, cries, and thumps. A silhouette stepped out from the next room and startled him. He made out a hugely tall person of undetermined gender and of pyramidal form, meaty latex-swathed thighs and stilettos. Another burly figure appeared, equally monstrous, wearing a Louis XIV–style wig of cascading platinum curls, knee-high black leather boots, fishnet tights, and a plastic minidress. Nicolas gaped as the two creatures lumbered toward the elevator, making the floorboards shudder, chatting in Portuguese. Hookers? Transvestites from Brazil? Whatever they were, he would only be able to write when they were not around.

Then, when things seemed to have calmed down, a young man whom Nicolas never saw rented the room on the right. He spent his life there, mournfully strumming away from morning till night on a badly tuned guitar and bleating out the same James Blunt song in an unbearable falsetto. Nicolas wanted to murder the young man. One afternoon, a female voice was heard along with the mewl. The young woman's voice was perhaps even worse than the young man's because it was so tragically off-key. Nicolas understood, with a sinking heart, that his neighbor had invested in a karaoke machine. The couple slaughtered "Imagine" and butchered "Let It Be." Next came "Summer Nights," "All by Myself," and "My Way." It was so excruciating to listen to that Nicolas began to laugh. He laughed so hard that tears came. He even taped some of the karaoke with his mobile so he could play it for his friends. The following day, the young couple went through endless successions of rapid, brutal sex. Nicolas endured it all—the bedsprings creaking wildly, the labored breathing. It did not turn him on in the least. It was perhaps worse than the karaoke. The young man squealed like a pig being slaughtered and the young woman remained stoically mute except for a final terrifying croak that did not sound human. Nicolas found he could not bring himself to bang on the wall to complain. What if one of them was a fan, the clinging kind? The kind that would come knocking every ten minutes? He could not risk that. So he bought earplugs at the pharmacy on the avenue de Lowendal. He shoved them as far as he could into his ears, so that the squeals and croaks became faint. Now he picked up the regular thump of his own heart. It was a strange and disconcerting sound, but infinitely better than the dreadful duo.

As Nicolas sat at his desk day after day, getting up from time to time to look out of the window (always hoping for a glimpse of the ballerina), he found his concentration to be disastrously fickle. Anything distracted him. Even the old lady on the seventh floor, a bent-over, century-old, white-haired granny, was interesting to watch. She spent the day reading, resting, then going out to her terrace and cooing at her plants, the birds, the blue of the sky. Once, she fell asleep in her deck chair, her head tilted to one side, her skirt askew, revealing frail, knobby knees, and she slept for so long, he feared she might have died. Luckily, she stirred, woke up, and hobbled off again. Nicolas felt like James Stewart in *Rear Window,* reveling in the permanent show his neighbors had to offer. On the fourth floor, a young mother played with her small children with patience and pleasure, and he enjoyed watching her. On the fifth floor, a woman who looked astonishingly like a Pedro Almodóvar movie actress (It had to be her! How could it not be her?) paced up and down, perpetually on the phone, a cigarette hanging from her lips. When she sat at her desk and opened her computer, if he strained his eyes, he could just make out what she was looking at.

A final fatal drawback came with a team of workers turning up one morning on his floor. A room was being redone. Through gritted teeth, Nicolas endured pounding, hammering, grating, drilling. The noise was horrendous, even with his earplugs. The workers gibbered away from dawn to dusk, portable radios turned on full blast, saluting him cheerily as he walked past, offering him sandwiches or a drink. He asked one of them how long the refurbishing was going to last and learned, to his dismay, that four rooms were being renovated, and then a scaffolding was to be installed, and the entire building restored, as well. The embellishments would take at least six months.

Nicolas gradually understood that no writing would go on in his monk's cell. And after that, an even more bitter realization emerged. There would be no writing at all. There would be no book.

How PEACEFUL IT IS to be here, tucked away from the turmoil of the world, the worrying news of a global crisis, bloody bombings, the sexual scandal involving a New York hotel maid and a French politician.

Nicolas's hand is itching for his BlackBerry, but he knows he cannot look at it with Malvina sitting next to him. Especially with a new BBM from Sabina. Sometimes he marvels at this woman he has seen only once, sending him such intimate messages. What is he sure of? Very little. In the beginning, when their messaging was still trivial, she mentioned she was married, that she had two daughters, not much older than he. She lived in Berlin, in Prenz-lauer Berg, with her husband. Nicolas likes to think back to the short moment she stood in front of him when he signed the book for her. He can bring it all back: her trench coat, the way the belt was drawn tightly around her slender waist, her sleek ash-blond bob, and the way she looked at him. Younger women never had that expression. They were too coquettish—they tittered; they minced—or they were drunk and swaggered vulgarly like men.

She stared down at him with a tiny smile, and those catlike eyes—translucent, like little pools of water—never blinked. When she handed him the piece of paper with the BBM PIN code on it, their fingers had touched, but that was the only time their skin made contact. To take his mind off the unread BBM and its enticement, Nicolas reaches for his father's Hamilton Khaki, tucked away next to his phone in his bathrobe pocket. He looks at it quietly and feels a kind of peace flow through him. He thinks of his father going to buy the watch for his son's tenth birthday. Did his father already know what he was going to purchase, or was he advised by a salesperson? He thinks of the Hamilton Khaki lying in his father's palm, the blue eyes gleaming down at it, examining it, and then, later, the memory of the long fingers fixing the strap on to Nicolas's wrist. He can still feel those fatherly fingers against his own skin.

One last boat roars in. At first, Nicolas thinks it has to do with a trick of the setting sun, some sharp gleam of the light on the sea, an odd reflection. That face on the boat. He puts the watch away, takes off his sunglasses, places his hand visorlike above his nose, has another look. His pulse quickens. The face comes steadily closer with the approaching boat. He puts his sunglasses back on, a little too fast, fingers fumbling, and looks again. His notebook and the Montblanc fall to the ground with a thump. The boat is near now, bobbing up and down as it begins its approach, weaving its way through the other Rivas lined up along the pier, the purr of its motor subsiding. He leans forward, gropes around under his deck chair for his cap, screws it tight to his head.

"What is it?" asks Malvina, intrigued. Nicolas does not answer.

Mesmerized, he watches the woman clumsily get out of the boat, helped by a hotel attendant in black. There are two people with her, but he barely notices them. She is the last to set foot on the concrete beach. Her bulky figure is swathed in a white djellaba. He makes out the telltale snow-white ponytail à la Karl Lagerfeld beneath the panama, the curve of the nose, the tight red stretch of the lips. He has never met her in real life, never seen her in the flesh, but he has seen enough television appearances and read enough articles to know it is unmistakably her. She lumbers up the stone steps toward the hotel elevator, holding on to the attendant's arm. She moves slowly, and Nicolas sees what a big, sturdy woman she is, much larger than she appears to be in photographs, massive, even. Her skin is alabaster white, speckled with a swarm of freckles. There is no grace about her, yet he cannot help thinking she has a dramatic majesty, like a medieval queen assessing her kingdom. She never glances down. Her square chin is raised high, giving her a fierce arrogance heightened by the ironic set of her mouth. She disappears into the elevator.

Nicolas lies back on his chair. Malvina pinches his arm, startling him.

"Nicolas! Who is that woman?"

He takes a deep breath. "Dagmar Hunoldt."

The name means nothing to Malvina. Her only solace lies in the fact that Dagmar is over sixty, overweight, and about as attractive as a beached whale. But she cannot understand why Nicolas has gone silent, scratching the top of his head, which he does when he is confused or upset.

Malvina waits for a while before she speaks again. She watches the other clients gather their things and go. Mr. Wong and Miss Ming are the last to leave, walking slowly up the steps. The sun has disappeared behind the hill.

"Who is she?" Malvina asks at last, unable to hold her curiosity back any longer.

Nicolas lets out a sigh. Malvina cannot tell whether it is a sigh of excitement or fear.

"Dagmar Hunoldt is the most powerful publisher in the world."

Malvina waits, biting her thumbnail. Nicolas goes on, whispering, so that she has to lean forward to hear him.

"And she is here at the Gallo Nero. Out of the blue."

Malvina asks, "Is that good news or bad?"

Again, Nicolas does not answer. His mind is racing. Did she know he was on the island? That Facebook picture! One of her lieutenants or scouts must have spotted it on his wall. Maybe she was not far off, perhaps on a friend's boat, and she just dropped by for a couple of days. But maybe she came for him. Maybe she came just for him.

Nicolas recalls the first time he ever heard of Dagmar Hunoldt and tells Malvina about it. It was two years ago. He was having lunch with Alice Dor and her (now ex-) boyfriend, Gustave, at Orient Extrême, near the rue de Rennes, and he had noticed how Alice's face had suddenly changed. She seemed to be no longer listening to what Gustave was saying. Nicolas turned his head to check where her gaze was lingering, near the entrance of the restaurant. A group of people was standing there, nobody he recognized. But then, what did he know about the publishing world at that point? It was a hazy, nebulous matter, a complex network of names, places, and logos that he could not decipher. It would take him a while to apprehend it.

"Oh!" exclaimed Alice.

Gustave looked across at Nicolas and shrugged.

"What?" Gustave asked finally as Alice kept staring. "Or who?"

"Dagmar."

That was the first time Nicolas heard her first name. Dagmar. He had found it old-fashioned yet powerful, exotic. The name evoked Vikings, tall, buxom, flaxen-haired creatures, wearing winged headgear and iron brassieres. Was Dagmar a Scandinavian writer? A muse? A literary agent? A bookseller? Whoever she was, the startling slant in Alice's eyes did not suggest a mellow relationship. The group of people walked by and Nicolas did not pick out anyone who looked vaguely like a Dagmar—or rather, what he wished a Dagmar would look like. Alice remained silent for a while, until Gustave nudged her and mouthed, *So?*

She waved her hands around, which is what she did when she was at a loss for words.

"Who is Dagmar?" insisted Gustave. (He was a banker, not familiar with the publishing crowd.) "From the look on your face, we gather she's not your best buddy."

Alice scowled. "She certainly is not."

Nicolas and Gustave exchanged glances over their maki.

"The suspense is unbearable," said Gustave.

Alice turned her face once more toward the group of people sitting at the back of the restaurant. She then said, leaning toward Gustave and Nicolas, "Dagmar is the most feared, the most respected, the most famous of all publishers. She holds the publishing world in the palm of her hand."

When Nicolas repeats this exact sentence to Malvina, she says, "Wow!" in an awed voice. Then, plucking at lint on her towel and lowering her voice all the more, even if they are now alone, she asks, "Is she here because of you?"

The vain part of Nicolas would like to say, Yes, yes, of course she is here for me, Malve. What are you thinking? She has already sent three people indirectly to try to lure me away from Alice Dor. Suzanne Cruz, pert, pretty agent from L.A. with a shrewd smile. Guillaume Bévernage, French publisher, known for his audacious alliances with Dagmar Hunoldt. And finally, Ebba Jakobson, powerful New York agent, also known for her close working relationship with Dagmar. Three lunches in the most exclusive restaurants of Paris, New York, and Santa Monica, and three polite nos to the juicy contracts, the unbelievably high advances. Nicolas now remembers reading about Dagmar Hunoldt recently in *Newsweek* magazine, and he recalls a couple of lines that had both amused and impressed him: "Hunoldt has the sharpest instinct about a book, about an author. Her entourage considers her utterly ruthless, extraordinarily intelligent, and totally perverse."

The lucid part of Nicolas mutters, "I'm not sure. She could be here on holiday. There is no way to find out."

"Does she publish Novézan?" asks Malvina.

Nicolas laughs curtly.

"No! Novézan's not that big in the United States. I'm bigger than he is."

"Does Novézan know who she is?"

Nicolas stares at Malvina, noting again, distractedly, how pale she is.

"Malve, Dagmar Hunoldt is like the Madonna of publishing."

"Well, not physically."

"Of course not physically," snorts Nicolas, exasperated. "I mean that she has that power. She is that powerful. Get it?"

Malvina nods meekly. Nicolas feels a twinge of guilt and squeezes her hand. It is getting cooler. The staff members fold up chairs, towels, and tables and take down the parasols. It is time to go back upstairs and get ready for the evening.

As they go up in the James Bond elevator, Nicolas cannot stop thinking about Dagmar Hunoldt and her presence at the Gallo Nero. He forgets Sabina's BBM, unread on his BlackBerry. He forgets to phone his mother, who has still not returned his calls. He forgets about contacting François. He has even stopped thinking about Delphine taking showers with other men. He marches into the room, accompanied by the silent and pale Malvina. He does not glance at the new array of flowers, fruits, the turned-back bed, the chocolates thoughtfully placed on the pillows with the weather forecast for tomorrow (sun, thirty-two degrees centigrade). He hardly looks at the card from Dr. Otto Gheza, the hotel director, propped up on the desk, asking them to attend a cocktail party tonight. Instead, he goes out on the terrace, looks out to the sea, and he thinks.

How will he say no? Can one say no to Dagmar Hunoldt?

An even worse thought comes and makes him cringe. How can he ever tell Dagmar Hunoldt, if she has indeed turned up at the Gallo Nero for him, that there is no book, that he has been lying to his publisher, to himself, to the world? Will he have to lie to her, as well?

JOURNALISTS WERE PERSISTENT IN trying to find out why Nicolas had decided to remain with Alice Dor despite his impressive success. It was public knowledge he was coveted by every single
publisher and agent on the planet. So why did he stick with a
small independent company? Nicolas indefatigably gave the same
answer. Alice Dor changed his life when she said yes to *The Envelope* on that dark winter day in 2007. She read *The Envelope*
because Delphine, her friend from the school where they took
their little girls each morning, and with whom she shared a coffee
from time to time, had urged her to read it. She had guessed Delphine was having an affair with a younger man, because she had
seen him drop off Gaïa as she was dropping off Fleur, and she had
put two and two together. Now she knew why Delphine had those
stars in her eyes and that spring to her step. The young man, whose
name was Nicolas, was rather charming, thought Alice, who preferred older men herself. He was tall and well built, she noticed
one spring morning, glancing at the ripple of muscles under his
black T-shirt. He had short, dark hair, with long sideburns and

fog-colored eyes. And his mouth, of course, was terribly noticeable, full lips and a large white grin. Not only was he pleasant to look at; he was also friendly, as Alice soon discovered. Polite, gentle, well-behaved. And it was fair to say that when Delphine handed her the manuscript over coffee one morning, Alice felt a spark of curiosity.

She had fifteen manuscripts to read that week, all of them piling up on her desk. Alice brewed a cup of coffee, put on her glasses, and started *The Envelope,* determined to write a nice note to Delphine, and to the young man, about how promising it was for a first effort. The first thing that struck her was the tone. What did she know about Nicolas Duhamel? Only what she could see (the sideburns, the friendly grin, the muscles under the T-shirt) and what Delphine had told her: a khâgneux who gave philosophy lessons and who had lived with his mother (a teacher) until he met Delphine. Delphine had said only this: "Just read it, Alice. Please." The tone of the book had nothing to do with a young man. It floored Alice to such an extent, she even wondered if Nicolas Duhamel was really the author. Here was Margaux Dansor talking. Margaux, salt-and-pepper hair, forty-eight years old. Not Nicolas Duhamel, twenty-five. The novel was filled with Margaux's intimate feelings, her fears, her bravery, her fragility, her discoveries. Margaux, finding out that her long-dead father was not who she had been led to believe. Margaux, finding out the truth, scribbled on a sheet of paper in a white envelope, hidden away in an old family home in Camogli, a small Ligurian village. A truth that nearly destroyed her. A truth that ended up shaping her, giving her new wings. The other characters were credible, appealing, and complex. Arnaud Dansor, Margaux's husband, trying to keep up with his wife's quest, to understand it. Their daughters, teenagers Rose and Angèle, perturbed by the voyage of discovery their mother had embarked on. Sébastien Zech, Margaux's brother, furious with what his sister was "digging up," smearing their family name. Alice admired the powerful depiction of Margaux's absent father, the compelling Luc Zech, alias Lucca Zeccherio.

What Alice liked best about the book was Margaux Dansor herself. Her sense of humor, her wit, her audacity. A piano teacher who taught Bach and Mozart but who listened to disco music on her iPod. In fact, her husband, Arnaud, called her "Silver Disco Queen," to the embarrassment of their daughters. Margaux danced by herself, in her room, in her kitchen, to "Stayin' Alive," with the smooth moves of a female Travolta. There was a boundary between the serious piano teacher and the relentless, inquisitive woman hot on the trail of a perturbing family secret. Alice thrived on the amusing details that Nicolas Duhamel painted of his heroine: her fear of driving (a bad accident at the age of eighteen, which left a long crooked scar on her calf); her dire cooking (her husband, Arnaud, was the good cook); her infatuation with the color blue (which explained why Margaux compulsively bought anything that was that color, be it a hot-water bottle, a rolling pin, an ashtray, although she didn't smoke); her inability to sit in a window seat in a train or a plane (a weak bladder was the real answer, which made Alice laugh); her hopeless command of mathematics (a true handicap when the euro made its appearance in 1999); and her prowess for imitating Céline Dion to perfection.

Three hours later, Alice finished the novel in tears. She was not expecting such a dramatic ending, the opposite of a sugarcoated Hollywood finale. Alice had to take off her glasses, wipe them, blow her nose, make another coffee, and breathe deeply. She was bewitched by the story, by Margaux. How had this young man pulled it off? Where had he planted his roots to shape such an unforgettable heroine?

Alice decided to call him. No need to wait. No need to call Delphine first. She checked her watch. Five o'clock in the afternoon, on a cold December day. His mobile number was written on the front page of the manuscript. And so Alice Dor made the phone call that was to change both their lives.

"Is that Nicolas Duhamel? . . . Hello! This is Alice Dor. Am I disturbing you? . . . No? Good. I'm going to publish your book."

She was used to the sharp intake of breath she often heard on the other end of the line. She enjoyed calling authors to tell them she was going to publish their work, and she liked doing it with her usual abruptness.

But Nicolas Duhamel had remained strangely silent.

"Are you there?" she asked tentatively.

"Yes," he said. "Yes. Thank you."

"Can you come and see me? We need to discuss a couple of things."

And he had arrived that very evening at her office on the rue de Rennes, on the corner of the boulevard Raspail, and she still remembers the way he walked in, striding in, his hand outstretched, the warmth of it. He was taller and thinner than she remembered. There was an earnestness about him she immediately liked. Yes, she could see Margaux Dansor in there somewhere, behind that engaging smile, in the way he sat down, calmly, crossing his legs, leaning toward her with a well-bred expectancy she enjoyed.

"I liked your book," she said quietly, with that deep, gruff voice he was just discovering. He soon learned that when Alice Dor said "liked," she meant "loved." She was the discreet type, never going for the superlative.

He sat there, dumbfounded, devouring her with those mist-colored eyes, perhaps taking her in properly for the first time. He remembered her, of course, as Delphine's morning coffee friend, Fleur's mother, a brisk brunette in her mid-thirties, who always seemed in a hurry. And now this woman wanted to publish his novel. He glanced around at her office, stacked perilously high with books, manuscripts, pens, papers, a computer, the customary paraphernalia of a publisher. There were photographs on Alice Dor's cluttered desk of her daughter and of her most famous authors, cheek by jowl with invitations to book launches and award ceremonies, contracts, files, notes, cards, and delicate purple orchids rising regally out of the mess.

"I don't know what to say," he finally mumbled.

"Did you call Delphine?" Alice asked, smiling.

"No. I was waiting to see you, waiting to see if this was really true."

"So call her! Call her now."

"You call her!" he said, smiling as well.

Alice telephoned Delphine, who screeched with joy. They all went out to dinner at a noisy restaurant near Saint-Sulpice, where Alice's boyfriend, Gustave, the jovial banker, came to join them. They drank champagne, laughed, celebrated, and clicked their glasses to Margaux Dansor.

None of them had any idea that the book would touch so many hearts, become an Oscar-winning movie. None of them suspected that Nicolas Duhamel would gradually shed layers of his sympathetic aura to become Nicolas Kolt, a trifle more blasé, a touch less openhearted. But somehow Nicolas guessed that the golden-eyed woman sitting in front of him had given him the kiss of life. She believed in him. "Why should I leave Alice Dor?" Nicolas replied to the journalists. "She sold the rights to my book around the world, and to Hollywood. Why would I want to be anywhere else?"

"But don't you want more money, more glamour, more everything?" his friend Lara had insisted recently. "You're not even thirty. Why not go for those much bigger publishing companies? Alice gave you your chance, sure, but why stay with her?"

"Because I owe her that," replied Nicolas. "Because I owe her everything."

"You sound like a boring, faithful husband," sneered Lara.

"Fuck off."

Lara tickled him under the chin, taunting him.

"Oh, what a bad temper . . . Wonder why. Have you really started that new novel yet, by the way? Or have you been too busy answering your fans on Facebook?"

Nicolas's palm itched to slap her jeering face. Everyone seemed unnecessarily keen to know about his upcoming book. Alice appeared reasonable when she prodded him gently about it. She put no apparent pressure on him, but he picked up her anxiety like a lightning conductor. He could feel her anguish growing like the ominous black speck in Lord McRashley's mirror, looming larger by the day.

How could Nicolas possibly confess to Alice Dor, now that she had bought the book for such an exorbitant advance because she was terrified he'd succumb to the lure of bigger publishing houses, that there was no book at all? How could he confess to Alice Dor that in the past six months, since they'd signed the new contract with panache, he'd been merely resting on his laurels, lounging in the delectable veneration of his fans, flying business class, sipping champagne, accepting gifts, posing for photos, signing autographs?

Alice Dor had bought nothing.

I N THE QUIET LUXURIOUSNESS of the pink marble bathroom,
Nicolas takes a shower. Through the splash of running water,
he hears Malvina's voice from the next room. She is on the phone
with her mother in Warsaw. Nicolas listens to the complex reso-
nances of a language he understands nothing of. He has never met
Malvina's mother, but he has seen photographs. The emotionally
intense divorced forty-something woman has the same green-blue
eyes as her daughter. Conversations with her mother always last
awhile, so Nicolas knows he has time to check his BlackBerry.
The device is hidden under the towel on the floor.

As Nicolas gets out of the shower, he glimpses his reflection in
the full-length mirror and notices the beginning of a promising
tan. He turns to admire it, the white of his firm buttocks contrasting with the bronzed hue of his long, muscular back. He leans to
pick up the BlackBerry with a humid hand. Sabina's BBM is still
unread. He clicks on it, bracing himself. The words leap out. "I
want you to come in my mouth." An electrifying shiver etches its
fiery path up and down his thighs. It's as if Sabina is here, right

now, on her knees on that marble floor, glistening lips half-open, eyes raised to his, defiant, wanton. He gives in to the erection coming on. Do I have time? he wonders hurriedly. Yes, he does, only a matter of minutes. He can feel the velvet of her mouth close around him, the pull of her cheeks and tongue. He can see the ash-blond hair falling back from her face as she works on him. He can see her long, elegant hands, her manicured nails, her golden wedding band. He can make out the moist noises her mouth and tongue make as she moves faster, still staring up at him. He sees both his hands on each side of her head, his fingers curling in to grab fistfuls of silky hair, making her head move even quicker. The orgasm builds up, powerful, and he teeters on its edge before he surrenders to it.

"Are we going to that cocktail party?" Malvina asks, dangerously near, just outside the bathroom door. Nicolas's eyes jolt open. He gasps at the reflection in the mirror. Him, slack-jawed, naked, triumphant erection in hand. He chokes. He hadn't heard Malvina end the conversation with her mother.

"We could!" he gulps hoarsely, shoving the BlackBerry behind a box of Kleenex and hiding his tumescence with the towel in one frantic move.

A tap of high-heeled sandals. Malvina steps into the bathroom. She is wearing a turquoise dress he has never seen. It is close-fitting, low-cut, and reveals every inch of her figure, but there is nothing vulgar or cheap about it. Her long, dark hair is combed back and tied with a black velvet bow.

Malvina looks suspiciously around the bathroom. Nicolas continues to dab himself with the towel, trying to look careless, normal, feeling his cheeks blaze red with guilt. Malvina continues her inspection. The BlackBerry is nowhere to be seen. His erection is dwindling by the second. Close call, he thinks. He beams at her.

"You are beautiful," he says earnestly, and means it.

"Why are you so red, Nicolas?"

"Sunburn." He grins sheepishly, caressing the velvet bow with his fingertips.

"Will Dagmar thingy be at the cocktail party?"

"No idea."

"What will you do if she is?"

"Say hello, I guess."

Nicolas rushes into the room to dress, heart athump the sultry heaviness lingering in his loins.

Later, at dusk, they walk down to the terrace together, hand in hand. Nicolas is wearing black jeans, a white shirt, and a new dark green jacket. He is aware of what a striking couple they make, his towering height contrasting with her sylphlike grace. He never used to have those thoughts when he walked in the street clasping Delphine around the shoulders. He didn't care, back then, what he looked like. But since Hurricane Margaux, Nicolas cannot go anywhere without trying to decipher how he comes across to others.

Nicolas realizes he has left Dr. Gheza's invitation in the bedroom, but it appears they do not need it, as they are ushered into a private area near the pool by a smiling waiter wearing the customary black suit. "Welcome, signorina. *Benvenuto,* Signor Kolt."

Gentle music is playing, not too loud. A cool breeze blows, but the heat of the day remains in the air, lingering like a steamy caress. Candles flicker lazily. The sea is splendid and inky blue. Guests laugh, drink, and chatter. Waiters glide by with trays of beautifully presented tidbits. Nicolas and Malvina sip chilled champagne, gazing out to the darkening sea. Nicolas relishes the Ruinart, but also the sensation of being safe in a peaceful bubble of sumptuousness. Moments earlier, the news was on television, and he had watched placidly, a Coca-Cola in hand, even though what he saw on the screen was disturbing, with its customary quota of bloodshed, financial crashes, political conflicts, and sex scandals. He turned the television off, and the dramas of the day vanished. He knew that in the next room, and for all those around him now, it had been the same. Wasn't the Gallo Nero a hideaway rich people went to so they could forget the turmoil of the outside world?

Nicolas is beginning to discover, with intertwined awe and guilt, how time slows down here, inching along at snail's pace, as if coated with molasses. More important than anything else is what wine to choose at table, which earrings to wear, which cigar to savor. Nicolas sees that the guests tonight have perfectly pressed blazers or dinner jackets and ties. Most women (except the creature holding on to Nelson Novézan's arm) are exquisitely turned out. Nicolas takes in their attire. Not an easy move, as Malvina is monitoring every flicker of his eyelashes. The Belgian wife is wearing a flowing apricot jersey dress with a flattering crossover neckline. The Swiss lady swimmer, long and lean, is spectacular in an off-the-shoulder floor-length emerald green number. The voluptuous short-legged brunette oozes sex appeal in a plunging scoop-back gown embroidered with glittering sequins. The blond French wife carries off a glamorous wrap dress with Parisian panache.

Nicolas looks around the terrace for Dagmar Hunoldt, wondering nervously what he should say to her, how he should introduce himself. But she is nowhere to be seen. Mr. Wong and Miss Ming, in matching black-and-red silk kimonos, bow their heads regally. The gay couple, cooly elegant in white-and-beige suits, are conversing with Alessandra, the cloying fan, and her mother, both in bejeweled djellabas.

Nelson Novézan, already tipsy, leans on the overripe blonde squeezed into a leather pantsuit on his arm. This must be his sex queen. Nicolas grins, holding his glass up to them. Novézan leers back, ogling at Malvina in her turquoise dress, taking her in from head to toe with a lecherous smile. Malvina turns her back to him, disgusted.

The Natalie Portman twins arrive with their Labrador, and they are such a sight that everyone swivels to admire them. Nicolas does it discreetly while Malvina turns to ask for a glass of water. He notes their vaporous pale pink chiffon frocks, their slim golden thighs, their vertiginously high red-soled pumps, and the strands of hair tumbling from artfully disheveled chignons. Just before

Malvina's gaze comes swinging back to him like an accusing boomerang, Nicolas glances down to the Labrador with a benign smile.

A balding man with tortoiseshell glasses and a navy blue blazer introduces himself as Dr. Otto Gheza, the hotel director. The man standing next to him is an actor. Tall, blond, American, in his fifties. Nicolas cannot remember his name. It is on the tip of his tongue. He smiles and nods, feeling foolish. For God's sake, he has seen enough movies with this guy. How could he forget his name?

"When can we expect your new book, Signor Kolt?" says Dr. Gheza brightly.

Nicolas smiles back, the thin, tight smile. He has an answer ready for that question. He fires it. "As soon as I've finished it."

"My wife loved *The Envelope,* by the way," drawls the American actor, puffing on a cigarette. "Bawled her eyes out for days. I only saw the movie, didn't get around to reading the novel. Robin was amazing as Margaux, wasn't she? Bet you loved the movie."

Nicolas nods. As the American rambles on, he realizes that most of the people on the terrace seem to have taken in who the actor is, and they appear to be sending nods and smiles the actor's way. He also notices they have recognized him, as well. The Belgian wife, her champagne level high, makes a clumsy beeline for him, ignoring Malvina, Dr. Gheza, and the American actor. Her name is Isabelle and there is nothing Nicolas can do or say to make her shut up.

"Oh, oh, oh," she says breathlessly, batting her eyes and clutching her pearls as if they are about to slip from her pulsing jugular. The heat has made her makeup clammy, and it's weaving its way into the wrinkles of her face. "I cannot believe that you are here, on this island, tucked away on the Tuscan coast, away from the madding crowds, while I'm reading that book of yours! Wait till I tell my sister and my mother. They read you before I did, you see, and they kept telling me, 'Isabelle, you have to read Nicolas Kolt.

You are going to love that book.' I couldn't read the book before now, you see, I've been so busy. I have a shop on the avenue Louise in Brussels. Do you know Brussels? Of course you must; I read somewhere that your mother is Belgian. This is unbelievable. You are going to have dinner with us, aren't you, with my husband, my son, and my daughter? How divine. What do you think? Oh, let me just take a picture of you so I can send it to my sister. She is going to be green with envy. Now wait a minute. I can never figure out how these phones work. Where do I need to press—"

The pear-shaped daughter utters only one word, loudly, but it brings her mother back to reality. "Mother."

"Oh, dear, I'm so sorry. I got carried away. I only wanted to—"

Nicolas, embarrassed, looks out to sea as the daughter firmly steers the mother away.

"I guess you get that a lot, don't you?" The American actor grins. "Hell, I used to, in my heyday."

"Now now," scoffs Dr. Gheza "I'm sure ladies still fling themselves at you today, Chris."

Chris. Nicolas racks his brain. A blond American actor in his fifties named Chris. The guy's face is so familiar. But nothing is surfacing. Once again, he scrutinizes the terrace. No sign of Dagmar Hunoldt's imposing silhouette. Was it really her? How can he find out? He can ask the receptionist. On his way down to the pool tomorrow morning, he can do that offhandedly: "Oh, by the way, has Dagmar arrived?"

Malvina is talking to the gay young men. She seems less shy, less self-conscious. Nicolas is relieved. She is a true loner. Her idea of a perfect evening is curling up on the sofa in front of the TV, her feet tucked in his lap. He looks on. How pretty, how young she is. When he was with Delphine, she looked after him. Now he is the one mothering Malvina. It is a pleasant feeling, but at times it overwhelms him. Her personality is tricky to handle. Confronted with her long silences, Nicolas never knows which attitude to choose. Sometimes his impatience takes over. She reminds him of

Delphine's daughter, Gaïa, the champion of the pout and tantrum. Nicolas carefully avoids eye contact with the Belgian lady (now drunk, lipstick smeared over her teeth) as well as with Alessandra and her mother, who are slowly but surely creeping up toward him in a maneuver to hem him in. He nods to Mr. Wong and Miss Ming, then makes a dash for the bar.

Nicolas has already had three glasses of champagne. Perhaps a fourth one would be a mistake. He asks the barman for some sparkling water. It is surprisingly hot, even though it's evening now. As he drinks, Nicolas thinks of Sabina. He cannot suppress a smile. What the hell is he doing, frankly? Leading on a housewife from Berlin with sizzling texts? Sexting, instead of texting. A part of him feels slightly ashamed. Does he really have to engage in this? Wouldn't it hurt Malvina terribly if she ever found out? Nicolas brushes the guilt away. He's doing nothing wrong, after all. It's a virtual business, no flesh to flesh, no exchange of body fluids, no contact. It's not as if he's having an affair. Of course, it would be difficult to explain to Malvina, if she ever stumbled on a message from Sabina. But that's not going to happen. His BlackBerry never leaves his sight, and even if she finally were to get her hands on it, she'd have to get by that password.

"Anything else, signor?" asks the barman. He is a burly man in his late thirties, with a warm smile. The name tag on his black lapel reads *Giancarlo*.

"No, I'm fine, thanks," says Nicolas.

"I hope you are enjoying your stay at the Gallo Nero?"

"Yes, I am. Thank you, Giancarlo."

"Nice weather, isn't it? If you like the heat, of course."

"I do," says Nicolas. "I came here for three days of sun."

"It's nice to see people your age. Most clients here are older."

Giancarlo mixes a cocktail with an energy that Nicolas finds interesting to watch.

"Some summers, it's depressing," the barman adds with a grimace, lowering his voice. His Italian accent is enchanting. "I shouldn't be saying this with Dr. Gheza nearby, but believe me, it can be like a retirement home sometimes." He winks.

"Come on, man." Nicolas chuckles.

"No, it's true, signor! I enjoy seeing young blood here. Not always the case, you know. Tomorrow, however, will be a great day for young blood."

"Why?" asks Nicolas, intrigued.

"Photo shoot for a famous fashion magazine. They're flying in the hottest models." Giancarlo cocks an eyebrow. "Is your girlfriend the jealous type, signor?"

Nicolas stares at him, deadpan.

"Malvina is beyond jealous."

"She can't be more jealous than my wife."

"Try me," says Nicolas.

The barman gets going on another cocktail with the same ardor.

"Well now," Giancarlo muses, shaking away, "Monica cannot stand that I even glance toward another woman. I did not say 'at'; I said 'toward.'"

"Ditto," says Nicolas.

"I see. There's more. Monica has a crazy obsession with my ex-girlfriends. She is convinced I am still in love with them."

"Ditto."

"And this: Monica goes crazy if I check my phone too often. She thinks I'm having an affair or something."

Nicolas laughs and says, "Sounds like Monica could be Malvina's sister."

The barman laughs, too.

"Your girlfriend won't enjoy tomorrow, signor. Too many dazzling young ladies frolicking around. Perhaps you will need to stay in your room all day. I'm joking, of course. You're a writer, I believe?"

"Yep."

"Sorry, I don't read."

Nicolas has heard that sentence so often, he wonders how it is possible he has sold so many copies.

"I mean, I don't read books," Giancarlo adds hastily. "Of course I know how to read."

"Of course," says Nicolas.

He realizes he is hot, thirsty, and dying for a drink—and not water.

"I'd like some champagne, please, Giancarlo."

"Of course, signor. Coming right up."

The glass is handed to him. Nicolas gulps half of it down. Then he turns around and checks out the terrace. No fans edging up on him. Malvina still talking to the gay couple. No Dagmar Hunoldt.

"All clear?" whispers the barman.

"All clear." Nicolas smiles.

"How do you get your inspiration, signor?"

Nicolas wonders if Giancarlo has any idea how often he is asked that question and how thin his patience is wearing, a fatigued battery about to render its last dying spark. He downs the last of the champagne and makes a wide sweeping gesture toward the terrace, the sea, the yachts.

"This is my inspiration," he says with exaggerated panache.

"You mean we are all going to end up in your new book?"

"You could." Then Nicolas states, ironically, "If my new book only existed."

Nicolas expects Giancarlo to pounce upon this precious unexpected bit of information, to move in relentlessly, to demand explanations—What do you mean, signor? There is no next book?—and he squares his shoulders, closing his eyes, preparing for the onslaught, but oddly, the man does not react. Nicolas opens his eyes, almost disappointed.

"You see that lady?" whispers the barman. "The one over there, talking to Dr. Gheza?"

Nicolas turns, to see a tall, slim, red-haired woman with a stupefying black dress of leather and lace, slit up the sides. Her fine spike-heeled shoes are buckled leather contraptions that suggest bondage and other delicacies.

"Who is she?" asks Nicolas. The woman's heart-shaped face is vaguely familiar.

"Cassia Carper. She is the editor in chief of that famous fashion magazine I was telling you about. She will be orchestrating the photo shoot tomorrow."

The woman is middle-aged, but her figure is that of a young girl. Nicolas takes in her legs, slim and shapely.

"Ah, yes, Signora Carper, she is something. Every year, she comes here with her daughter and her husband. She does a photo shoot each summer. You'll see. It's a sight. You'll probably want to put it in your novel. . . . Ah, good evening, signorina. Would you care for some champagne? I was telling Signor Kolt about the cruise ships."

Malvina, as usual, has crept up, unheard and catlike, and is now standing by Nicolas's side. She says cooly, "No, I'd like some water, please. With ice. What about the cruise ships?"

Smooth move, Giancarlo, marvels Nicolas as they all turn toward the sea, the very direction he was facing moments ago when he was checking out Cassia Carper's legs. A giant vessel is hovering nearby, blazing lights glittering like jewels on the dark blue sea.

"You see, signorina, they sail by and salute the Gallo Nero."

"Salute?" repeats Malvina.

"Yes, in Italian, we call it the "inchino"; it means the ship comes as close as possible to us and blows its siren. Usually, they sail at least four or five miles away from us, but in the summer, they come in only a mile away. Here is your water, signorina."

They observe the gigantic white cruise liner as it makes its steady approach, bedecked with lights like a floating, top-heavy, gaudy wedding cake.

"That's the *Sagamor*," says Giancarlo. "One of the biggest ones. On its way to Civitavecchia, the last stop of a luxury seven-day cruise."

The guests around them hold up their glasses to the *Sagamor,* so Nicolas and Malvina do the same. Looking at the boat's ungainly multilayered decks, Nicolas imagines clusters of people grouped along the railings, tiny black ants waving back at them, and he makes out the muffled roar of music, of laughter, of singing, of merrymaking as the enormous mass slowly surges past. He thinks fleetingly of all the stories that could be told about those passengers, who they are, where they've come from, and what lies in store for them. All this is his inspiration, as he has just jestingly declared; all this could get him started on the new novel. So why can't he get off Facebook, kick himself in the ass, forge a path into the raw material at his disposal, tap into a vein, thrive on it? He has literary possibilities right here, at his fingertips. But he knows, deep inside, how much he lacks the drive to write. It is so much easier to pretend to be writing, to take himself seriously, to play the part. When is he going to stop the lies, though? Oh well, he will think about that at the end of his stay here. For the moment, there are still two more languid blue-and-golden days ahead. Two more days for doing nothing. *Far niente,* that's what they call it here.

The deep boom of a siren blasts through the night three times.

"The inchino," says Giancarlo.

The *Sagamor* leaves a trail of froth on the black water in its wake. Nicolas decides to go up to dinner. As he turns to leave, Malvina on his arm, he murmurs good-bye and winks discreetly at Giancarlo with the eye that Malvina cannot see. Giancarlo nods, polite and poker-faced, but Nicolas knows he has acknowledged the wink.

Up on the higher level of the terrace, Nicolas and Malvina are shown to a table that is not the best one with the best view. Nicolas frowns. He angrily demands to be put at that table. The headwaiter answers that is not possible; it is reserved for another guest.

"Do you know who I am?" Nicolas coldly asks the man.

"Of course. You are Signor Kolt," stammers the waiter.

"I want that table."

Dr. Gheza is summoned. There is a bright smile on his face.

"Signor Kolt! That table is yours. It should have been given to you in the first place. Please excuse us."

The headwaiter is told off and banished. They sit down.

"Why did you have to do that again?" says Malvina.

Nicolas ignores her as he discards the pinch of guilt that takes over, only for a couple of seconds. He notices that most of the guests are looking his way and smiling. Yes, they have recognized him. Oh, look! It's the writer! Is it him? Yes, it's really him. The members of the *Vanity Fair* family, a vision of Italian elegance, raise their glasses to Nicolas. He smiles and does the same to them in return.

Cassia Carper is at the next table, sitting with a dapper white-haired man and a teenage girl. Nicolas has another peek at her legs and shoes while Malvina peruses the menu. He scans the restaurant. Dagmar Hunoldt is nowhere to be seen.

"Why are you frowning?" asks Malvina.

"I'm just hot."

He takes his jacket off, hangs it on the back of the chair. He is not hot, but there is no other way to explain the frown. Nicolas is longing to check the BlackBerry in his trouser pocket, but he cannot face Malvina's ire if he dares. Still no news of his mother. And François never called or texted back. And Sabina . . . That last BBM . . . He can hardly wait for the next one. And did Alex Brunel post a new photo on his Facebook wall?

Nicolas wonders, giving in to another twinge of remorse as he nibbles on some grissini, if he will ever be able to disconnect himself from his phone, from his e-mails, from Facebook, from Twitter. Will he ever be cured of this addiction? Maybe he should go someplace where there is no mobile reception, no Internet access. What about those writing residences, monasterylike places where recalcitrant authors are sent, locked up, and forced to write? He visualizes himself hunched over sheets of paper, Montblanc in hand, scribbling away in a bare, high-ceilinged room overlooking a magnificent landscape. Twice a day, a scrawny, grim woman in black, reminiscent of Daphne du Maurier's Mrs. Danvers, would wordlessly bring him a tray with tea, bread, and soup.

The waiter's voice pulls him back to the refinement of the Gallo Nero. Malvina has ordered a sea bass fillet with broccoli cream. Nicolas chooses oyster risotto and tuna tartare. When the food is brought to them, they eat in companionable silence. The meal is excellent, and so is the Orvieto. The chef comes to visit the tables and tells Nicolas how much he loved *The Envelope.* His family is from Camogli, and he knows exactly where Bob and Nancy's white house is. Nicolas thanks the chef. Then comes the dreaded question: "And what is your next book about, Signor Kolt?" Nicolas blandly delivers the habitual answer he has in store—"You'll just have to wait and see!"—with the faux beam of a smile that goes with it.

At the end of the meal, Malvina says she is not hungry for desert, so they go back down to the swimming pool and order drinks. The air is balmy and sweet. The sea murmurs from afar. They sit on deck chairs and look out at the silvery water.

"Happy birthday," says Nicolas quietly, handing her the small square box. Malvina opens it. The Rolex gleams in the moonlight. She stares down at the watch in her palm.

"Do you like it?" Nicolas asks tentatively. "It took me a while to find that one. I thought it was perfect for you."

"A Rolex . . . ," Malvina murmurs. "Well, yes, I like it, but . . ."

Nicolas stops smiling. "But what?"

"A Rolex, Nicolas. That's the kind of present you give your mother." He sighs. "Jesus, Malvie. Can't you just say thank you?"

"Thank you," she mumbles quickly. "It's lovely. It really is. Thank you."

He fumbles to fasten it on her wrist. The Rolex hangs there chunkily. He is terribly disappointed. The moment is ruined, not only by her remark, which stung, although he can't quite explain why, but also by how wrong the watch looks on her. He recalls the joy he felt when he bought it, the certainty that she would wear it with such grace.

"I'm tired," Malvina whispers. The nape of her neck is delicate and fragile, her skin paler than ever. She seems to droop like a wilted flower.

"You want to go back to the room?" asks Nicolas, but she is already on her feet, and he has no choice but to follow. It is only eleven o'clock. He does not feel sleepy, and the idea of going to bed now is unappealing. He hears the temptation of music and laughter from the bar behind them. Malvina strides on ahead in her high heels, surprisingly fast.

The room has been prepared for the evening while they were out. It is cool, calm, and inviting. The bedcover has been turned down, a white rose and a box of chocolates delicately placed on the pillows. The curtains are drawn and the night-lights are on. The air conditioner purrs, set at a perfect temperature. Fresh towels await them in the bathroom.

"Kiss me," says Malvina.

Nicolas kisses her. But in his mind, he thinks of Sabina, whom he has never kissed, and when he touches Malvina's high white breasts, he thinks of Sabina's mature skin, which he has never even seen. It is Sabina's mouth he feels, Sabina's mouth he craves.

※

Saturday,
July 16, 2011

You're so vain, you probably think this song is about you.

—CARLY SIMON

WHENEVER NICOLAS CHECKED INTO a new hotel during his frequent book tours, he had to submit to a necessary personal routine that enabled him to get through the night smoothly. In his previous life, as Delphine's lover and as a private tutor to irredeemable students, he had not traveled much. The only trips he undertook were those to Brussels, to visit his mother's family, and the Italian spree with François. His new fame propelled him worldwide. Nicolas discovered, at twenty-six, what the words *jet lag* truly meant. Between 2008 and 2011, he traveled to nineteen countries. At first, he thirstily lapped up novelty and thrill, delighted to be discovering new cities, new people, new challenges. Two years later, the intensity of the traveling began to take its toll, and he found that when he arrived at his hotel for the night, sleep eluded him, in spite of his exhaustion. Although he was always put in the best hotels, some rooms, even if they were stylish and elegant, had the word *sleepless* stamped all over them. Feng shui, his friend Lara insisted, an ancient Chinese discipline that had to do with whether your bed was facing north or south and if any mirrors were reflecting bad vibrations. Nicolas had scoffed at her. He now knew, as soon as he crossed the threshold, whether he was going to sleep well or not. It was like the first impression of a person's face. When Nicolas was standing in a room, looking around, taking possession of it, he sensed what was wrong. Perhaps it did have something to do with feng shui; however, he never admitted this to Lara. The bed wasn't in the right position, or the table took up too much space, or the chair was wrongly placed, a picture on the wall irked him, a coverlet was turned down in a crooked line according to his eye, a curtain was drawn in a manner that bothered him. His routine meant that he shoved the furniture around until he felt comfortable. At times, the color of the walls disturbed him. Or the smell, especially if the premises were overperfumed. Frequently, he went back to the reception desk to ask if he could be put elsewhere.

There were two memorable stays. One was in Venice, where he found himself in an entirely mirrored room that had no windows. He had not noticed that detail when he checked in, as he had been impressed by the lobby, a dizzying universe of silver icicles and black marble floor that seemed liquid, and by his room, a shimmering pink suite where his image was reflected back at him dozens of times, like in Lord McRashley's sepulchral staircase. Even the telephone, a glittering mother-of-pearl spiral, was a work of art, and so was the shower, a scintillating contraption of knobs and tubes he hardly dared touch.

After his book signing at the Libreria Toletta, in the Dorsoduro, Nicolas returned with the beginnings of a headache. He ignored the complicated shower, swallowed an aspirin, and went straight to bed. In the middle of the night, an icy hand had girdled his heart. He awoke with a start, fumbled with the light switch, hoping to turn the bedside lamp on, but he turned all the lights on instead, causing a glaring, blinding blaze that made him blink. He could no longer breathe. A monstrous weight flattened his chest, pinning him to the mattress. The mirrors placidly sent his panicked reflection back to him as he lay there, frozen, gasping like a goldfish plucked out of its bowl. He felt as if he were being buried alive. He managed to drag himself out of bed, legs weighing a ton, and struggled to his feet, meaning to open a window for a salvaging gush of fresh air, but there was no window to be found in the vast pink suite. Only the hum of the air conditioner and the expanse of mirror after mirror. Nicolas checked the bathroom, only to discover there was no window there, either. Was he having a nightmare? He pinched himself hard. What time was it? He didn't care. If he didn't get out of this room, he was going to die right now. He was going to topple flat on his back, full length on the pink carpet, and pass away. He could already imagine the headlines of the *Corriere della Sera*: BEST-SELLING AUTHOR FOUND DEAD IN VENETIAN HOTEL. Nicolas flung the door open and staggered downstairs. In the silver-and-black lobby, the receptionist behind the desk stared at him as he careened past. She wondered if he was on drugs. It wasn't until the cold nipped at his flesh that Nicolas realized he was standing outside in the middle of the night, wearing next to nothing. But he was breathing. He was alive. He was going to be all right. As long as he never went back to that windowless room again.

The other sleepless stay was in Madrid. The hotel was luxurious, with a jade green pool and a cluster of palm trees on a tranquil patio. He had gone to bed early by Spanish standards, after a successful event at the Casa del Libro. His Spanish publicist, Marta, had informed him with an apologetic smile that he'd have to be up "not too late" for a crucial breakfast interview with a top journalist from *El País*. Nicolas fell asleep after his routine of pushing things around until he felt at ease. The bedchamber was spacious, the pale yellow walls were soothing and pleasing, and there was no noise, as the room did not give onto the lively street, but the patio.

In the dead of night, diabolical cackles jolted him awake. Who was in his room? It sounded like an entire group of people. How had they gotten in? What on earth were they doing? Nicolas turned on the light and got up. There was no one, no one at all. Then he made an unpleasant discovery. The locked door by his bed was a connecting one that opened into another suite. Nicolas understood that behind the door, a merry bachelorette party was in full swing. The ladies began to dance to the "Macarena," howling with glee, sounding like a herd of hysterical elephants on a rampage through the bush. Nicolas could not bring himself to share their mirth. It was four o'clock in the morning and his wake-up call was in two hours. Should he join the ladies, get drunk and dance? He ended up wearily asking the receptionist for earplugs and then missed his call. He also missed the crucial interview with the important journalist.

As Nicolas walks down to the breakfast area, wrapped in his fluffy white bathrobe, holding his Montblanc and his Moleskine, he realizes that the two nights he has spent at the Gallo Nero did not require a feng shui routine. He felt spontaneously comfortable. But wasn't that to do with the luxury of the resort? Everything here seems designed for the comfort of guests, down to the tiniest detail: the delicate way soaps are laid out near the basin, the fresh sheets and their honey and lemon fragrance, the bowls of fresh fruit, the warm welcome of the staff, the kindness of the housekeepers. There is a simplicity about the Gallo Nero that makes it like no other fashionable hotel. It is, as Nicolas realized upon arrival, like being invited to a friend's home. The beauty of the Gallo Nero, the sea and its blue lure, the lush garden, the gentleness of the breeze, add to its charm all the more. He imagines that the glamorous Roman heiress and the dashing American pilot he read about on the Web site, who had built this villa forty years ago because they were in love, somehow live on. At least, their spirit does. Might they not make an appearance, hand in hand? She, tall and tanned, a barefoot brunette with a patrician nose and a Pucci tunic, and he, the rugged Steve McQueen type, wearing a pair of faded Levi's and a white T-shirt.

Nicolas is shown to the same table he had yesterday. It is not even eight o'clock, and he is not tired, although he's had little sleep. How was it he was able to get up so early and with such buoyancy? He thinks of last night, of the unexpected events that took place, and he smiles, thanking his father for those sturdy Koltchine genes, the ones that can deal with the morning after. The sun shines with Italian splendor, glorious and powerful. Nicolas orders tea and looks around him. Only the Swiss couple are already having their breakfast, and they greet him. He salutes them back. No Dagmar Hunoldt. Does she have all her meals in her room? Is she still here? Nicolas prefers to think about last night. There is one precise image that will not leave his mind. He smiles again, a slow, sensual smile. The waitress who pours his Earl Grey notices what an appealing young man he is. Nicolas glances up, and she grins back.

"*Grazie*," he says.

"*Prego*," she replies.

Malvina is upstairs, still asleep. She has no inkling of the events that unfurled after she snuggled into the large white bed. Once her breathing became regular, Nicolas retreated to the safety of the toilet, where he felt sheltered enough behind the locked door to check his BlackBerry. He first looked at his Facebook page. The elusive Alex Brunel had posted another photo. There was Nicolas, unmistakably Nicolas, sitting at the bar, facing Giancarlo. He had been photographed from behind, from the higher terrace, but he was recognizable; one long black sideburn could be glimpsed, and the square shoulders in the dark green jacket. Two hundred and ninety-six friends had already "liked" it. Nicolas did not read the comments. The photo filled him with dread. He hated being stalked. Last year, a disturbed young person had e-mailed him numerous photographs of herself naked, her body covered with dozens of his books in different editions. When he had not responded, she managed to secure his home address, and he had found her lurking around rue du Laos. There had been nothing amiable about the way she glared at him from afar. Recently, a middle-aged man wrote to him several times to politely declare he was going to throw acid in Nicolas's face at the next book signing. These isolated episodes had been dealt with by Alice Dor and the police, but they had made Nicolas nervous. Nicolas nearly deleted the photo from his timeline. He toyed with the idea of blocking Alex Brunel, so that he or she could no longer post on his wall. But for the moment, there had been no threats from Alex Brunel. Nicolas had tiptoed back to the bedroom. All was quiet. He looked out to the balcony. A beautiful night. Maybe he should order limoncello? The room-service waiter would awaken Malvina. Earlier on, she hadn't wanted to go on making love. She explained she was still feeling queasy, that she needed sleep. What about a dash to the bar? He left the room, closed the door in silence, and ran to the bar like a bat out of hell. Giancarlo welcomed him with a broad smile and handed him an icy shot of limoncello. Nicolas swallowed it in one go. It felt marvelous. He had another. It felt even better. The bar was empty, apart from a group of people farther off, near the pool. They were smoking, laughing, and dancing. Nicolas glanced up at the restaurant terrace to see if the mysterious Alex Brunel was waiting stealthily in the shadows, brandishing a smartphone to take another picture, but there was no one to be seen. Nicolas decided to call François, who had never gotten back to him. It was midnight, and François had a family now, a wife and kids (Nicolas could never remember their names), but he could not put it off any longer. After a couple of rings, François's taped voice was heard, that serious and earnest voice Nicolas missed. "You've reached François Morin. Please leave a message and I'll get back to you. Thank you." Nicolas left a long-winded, clumsy monologue. He tried to be witty, like in the old days, and failed. He hung up, feeling miserable. After a third limoncello, a desperate recklessness filtering through him, Nicolas called his mother's mobile for the fifth time that day. Answering machine. No one at the rue Rollin, either. Why was she not at home at nearly one in the morning? Why was her mobile turned off? This was unlike his mother. What if something had happened? When he at last looked away from his phone, the blond American actor was standing next to him, swaying slightly on unsteady feet.

"Howdy," the actor drawled, clapping him on the shoulder. "What about a refill, dude?"

Before Nicolas had time to draw breath, the actor was already ordering Caïpiroskas from Giancarlo. There was nothing else to do but drink. Nicolas could not face the idea of the silent bedroom and the sleeping Malvina. The evening had been a disappointment. The Rolex incident had left a bad taste in his mouth. No harm in a couple of drinks. He still had two days to enjoy at the Gallo Nero. Why not drink a part of the night away? No one was there to tell him not to. What was the actor whining about? His marital problems? His waning career? Whatever it was, it sounded as if it was coming from far away, muffled, distorted, like from the end of an endless tunnel. Nicolas nodded and drank. The American did all the talking and just as much drinking. The night deepened. Under the bittersweet coating of sugar and lemon, Nicolas felt the vodka permeating through him, heating his limbs, softening edges, drawing a fuzzy cobweb over his vision. He watched the group of people dance and sing while the American rambled on. It seemed that the same music played repeatedly: "Hotel California," by the Eagles. Nicolas heard a warning signal in his head when he nearly tumbled off his stool. Delphine's voice echoed in his mind. *Nicolas. You're drunk. Again.* He ignored both the signal and Delphine's voice and drank on. The rest of the bar episode was a blur, until Cassia Carper turned up in her electrifying dress and shoes. She had a phone glued to her ear. Who could she be talking to at this time of night, using that voice, so low, so throaty? She ordered champagne, and sipped it alone, standing up at the bar, next to him, still talking, but Nicolas noticed she was watching him out of the corner of her eye, her glance trailing back to him again and again. Every time he looked at her shoes, it gave him a thrill. Then, somehow, there had been Cassia Carper's hand on his leg as she leaned over to sign her bill, her white hand and its red nails, splayed out on his knee, deliberately, like a possessive starfish, and he had felt the warmth of her palm and fingers seep through his jeans. The chain of events had become confusing. The American actor vanished. Nicolas found himself with a glass of champagne in his hand and Cassia Carper's tongue in his mouth. How long that situation lasted, he could not tell. By the time Nicolas got back to his room, it was three in the morning. He could not walk straight. His magnetic card was not working or he was too inebriated to use it properly. He fumbled about in the dark for a long moment. Just as he was about to give up and fall asleep on the threshold, the door clicked open, and he went straight to the bathroom, as quietly as possible, but every noise he made resonated thunderously, at least in his head. He stripped with difficulty, stepped into the shower, and turned the cold water on full blast. He felt better. He dried himself off and drank thirstily from the tap. Then he looked at his BlackBerry. There was a little blue spotted signal on the screen. A BBM. From Sabina. He locked the bathroom door. There was hardly a chance Malvina would wake up now, but he wanted to play it safe.

There were no words in Sabina's message, just a photo. The photo was so unreal that Nicolas had to peer at it several times in disbelief. Was he imagining things? Was he that intoxicated? He stared as hard as he could. No, he wasn't imagining anything. There were Sabina's thighs, opened wide to the mesmerizing triangle, a tangle of honey tendrils, and two fingers dipped in the sweet pink wetness.

"Would you like some more tea, Signor Kolt?"

The waitress smiles at him again. Nicolas nods and watches the hot liquid filling his cup. He knew he could not keep that photo. It was too dangerous. So he had looked at it for a long time, crouching on the marble floor of the bathroom. If only he'd still had his iPhone, he could have zoomed in for a savory close-up, which the

BlackBerry did not manage so well. The flashing red light had announced a new BBM from Sabina. "Your turn."

Nicolas discovered, dismayed, that the act of photographing one's genitals and obtaining a satisfactory result was not an easy deed. The Caïpiroskas and champagne had not helped, either. At first, Nicolas was able to capture only his hip bone or his belly button, but finally he got the angle right. His penis resembled an unappetizing undercooked hot dog. His scrotum had the wrinkled aspect of purple-hued cabbage. There was no way he could send those pictures to Sabina. After what seemed hours, he managed a shot of his waning erection and sent it off, convinced Sabina had no doubt fallen asleep. But her answer appeared immediately. "Make yourself come. I will do the same." It did not take him long, and he did think of her, and of the pink intimacy on his BlackBerry, although the memory of Cassia Carper's slippery tongue sped things up.

Nicolas finishes his breakfast and goes down to the sea. He has the bathing area to himself, and the staff is delighted to welcome the first customer. The ballet of the chair, the parasol, the towel, the newspaper, and the fruit juice ensues. He gives in to it. He is then left alone, except for a nearby waiter hovering at his beck and call.

Nicolas observes the loveliness of the scene around him, the clarity of the water, the silvery fish, the boats zooming along the horizon, far away. He strides to the water edge, takes off his bathrobe, and dives straight in. For a short while, he swims fiercely, kicking into the cool sea. Not a trace of a hangover. His mind is crystal clear and his limbs tingle with energy. What a pity those two assets cannot be used for writing the book. He turns around, treading water, observing the ocher villa perched on the rocky hill, the gray cliff, the quiet beach area. He has never been afraid of the sea, although his father most probably drowned in the Atlantic Ocean. Nicolas has not been back to Biarritz since his father died, and of that, of going back there, he is afraid. He has turned down several invitations to book signings in Biarritz and in the area because he cannot face laying eyes on the Côte des Basques and the Villa Belza, the very spot where he saw his father's black sail for the last time.

Nicolas flips over to his back, returning to the shore. He flings his arms backward, slicing the water vigorously, legs pumping. His hand encounters a mound of flesh and the top of his skull jolts against something soft. A gurgle is heard. He turns around, faced with a goggled white sea lion wearing a flowery plastic cap. The sea lion quivers with indignation.

Dagmar Hunoldt.

His heart nearly stops.

"I'm so sorry . . . ," Nicolas mumbles. He feels his cheeks burn through the wetness.

Dagmar Hunoldt coughs, splutters, and chokes for a few endless moments. Nicolas reaches out to grab her forearm, as the sea is deep, and they both have to swim in order to keep to the surface. Her alabaster flesh feels surprisingly firm under his fingers.

"Are you all right?" he asks.

"Fine, thank you," she wheezes in that deep voice he recalls from TV and radio interviews.

"Would you like to rest, out of the water?"

"No, no," she tuts, "I'm fine. Just watch where you swim, young man."

She has a faint accent, which is impossible to trace.

"I'm sorry," he mutters again. "I thought I was alone."

She seems to have regained her composure and glances at him through her steamed-up goggles.

"Well, you are not alone."

"I'm very sorry."

Nicolas has said he's sorry three times. Dagmar Hunoldt says nothing in return. Perhaps he should exclaim right now, joyfully, Oh, hello! How nice to see you! But she glares at him in such a manner, he does not dare. She has not recognized him. But maybe with his hair wet, he looks different?

A waiter calls to them from the beach area. He wants to know if the signora is all right.

"*Va bene, grazie,*" Dagmar Hunoldt shouts back, flashing her terrifying white smile. Nicolas remembers reading somewhere that she speaks seven languages. Her origins are mysterious. She has Danish or Norwegian blood, but also a zest of Hungarian heritage. Some Austrian or German ancestry, as well. She is now swimming away, an energetic breaststroke that propels her out in the distance. Should he follow her? Get out of the water? He decides to swim on as well, keeping her in his line of vision. Perhaps later, when she takes off her goggles, she'll laugh and say, Oh, it's you! Nicolas Kolt! He could suggest a coffee; they would have it together, up on the terrace. They could then talk, quietly, just the two of them. He doesn't dare think of Alice and how he would be betraying her just by listening to Dagmar Hunoldt. He concentrates only on the moment, on the astonishing coincidence (but is it truly a coincidence?) of being here with her, Dagmar Hunoldt, the most powerful woman in the publishing industry.

He is nervous; he has to admit it. She does have that effect on people, and the fact that she has not recognized him makes it worse. He has heard through the grapevine that she has, or had, a drinking problem, a fact that is usually hushed up, but he has listened to tales of her passing out at restaurants and then being carted back home by a faithful friend. He also remembers the scandal that took place at the Frankfurt Book Fair when she turned up at the Hessischer Hof bar late one night with a young girl on her arm. A girl young enough to be her granddaughter, he was told, as he was not there to witness the scene, but he had heard the story so often, it now felt like he had truly been there. A lissome beauty in a black velvet dress. Even at such a late hour, the bar was packed with important figures of the international literary circle.

For a while, Dagmar Hunoldt had cajoled the young girl, stroking her hair, her naked elbows, her hands in what had been mistaken at first for motherly attention, until she had tipped the girl's face to hers and had kissed her on the mouth in a hungry, unequivocal manner that had electrified the entire bar. Dagmar Hunoldt was notorious for her appetite concerning men, men of all ages, men of all milieus. It was murmured she had two husbands in two separate countries, that she had a son, now in his forties, and a daughter who was not much younger, and there were even grandchildren in a big European city, to whom she devoted much of her time. The Hessischer Hof bar episode had made it clear to the publishing intelligentsia that Dagmar Hunoldt also enjoyed women.

Nicolas reflects upon all this as he swims behind her, observing the roll of her massive white shoulders under the water. Should he be relaxed, jovial, casual? Or polite, discreet, reserved? His stomach hurts, as it does with the cramps he usually gets before stressful TV interviews, and that he fully experienced when he had to pronounce a few words live on CNN after Robin Wright got her Oscar, and there he was on the red carpet, a forest of microphones thrust at him, and behind that red-eyed camera, the entire world.

Dagmar Hunoldt swims for over forty-five minutes, a fast and sure swimmer. She is surprisingly fit, he notices. When she finally hauls herself out of the water, Nicolas is relieved, as he was starting to feel tired. A waiter hands her a towel and she wraps it around her thick midriff, plucking the plastic cap off her head and the goggles off her eyes. Her legs are slimmer than he would have thought, firm and muscular. He can see a skein of blue-and-purple veins running up her thighs. Her hair is pure platinum. She walks to her deck chair and sits. There appears to be no one with her. The Swiss couple have come down, about to embark on their daily swim.

Nicolas walks up to her. "Are you all right?" He does not know whether to say "Mrs. Hunoldt" or "Dagmar," and so, preferring neither, he decides to add nothing.

She peers up at him blankly.

"I bumped into you in the water . . . ," he stammers, pointing to the sea.

"Oh!" She smiles. "Yes, you did. I'm fine. Thank you."

She turns away.

Nicolas is baffled. She has not recognized him and she dismissed him as if he were a mere bellboy. How could she not know who he is? It's preposterous. It's surreal.

An idea slowly dawns on him. Maybe she is doing this on purpose. Treating him like a *vulgus pecum*. Perhaps this is part of her secret plan. Dagmar Hunoldt does nothing the usual way. She is not like any other publisher. She abides by her own rules.

"Would you like a drink?" Nicolas says suddenly.

She frowns. "What kind of drink?"

"Any kind of drink. Cappuccino, tea, champagne."

"Champagne? At this hour?"

"Yes," he replies, grinning. "At this hour."

She looks at him closely at last, taking him in, the muscular chest and arms, still glistening with seawater, the flat, tanned stomach, its lower part darkened by tiny swirls of body hair.

"Well, why not?" She shrugs.

"What would you like?"

"I'll have what you have."

"A Bellini?"

She nods appraisingly. Nicolas orders two Bellinis. He drags a nearby chair over, pulling it next to her, and sits. She has put her panama hat on. She bears a resemblance to Glenn Close, the actress. The pale skin, the hooked nose, the deep-set eyes. He wonders what she must have looked like when young. Too massive to ever be pretty. Yet he has to admit there is something darkly attractive about Dagmar Hunoldt.

The Bellinis are brought to them.

"Santé," says Nicolas, clicking his glass to hers.

He decides to wait for her to speak. There is no urgency, after all. If she has come here for him, then she must know how to go about her business. He feels curious, expectant, but he is not going to ask any questions. He must be patient.

Nicolas Kolt and Dagmar Hunoldt sip their Bellinis without a word. Around them, the beach area fills up. The Swiss couple have changed into new bathing suits. The Belgian family (with a low-profile and puffy-faced mother) orders coffee and fruit juice. Alessandra and her mother sunbathe. The gay couple peruse Kindle and iPad.

None of the guests have any idea of the importance of what may happen next, thinks Nicolas. Nicolas marvels at the originality of Dagmar Hunoldt's approach. She is like a huge white spider, spinning her web from a faraway corner, gently reeling him in, and yet she has not even breathed a word. He waits, tremulous, his Bellini almost finished. His glass is tarnished with specks of peach. The alcohol has gone to his head, but it is an enjoyable, giddying sensation. His legs tremble with excitement. He wants the moment to last. He enjoys the strong pressure of the sun on his back, the salty breeze, and Dagmar Hunoldt's overwhelming presence. Just by lowering his eyes, he can glimpse her wrist, thickset and sturdy, and one square, powerful hand. A fascinating hand. She wears a golden signet ring on her middle finger. The hand that has signed contracts for life-changing books. The hand that has plucked authors out of obscurity and transformed them into golden-haloed superstars. The hand that rules the literary world, that bends it to its will. What will her first words be? What if she gets straight to the point, going for the jugular? No, she is too subtle for that. She will not play it frontal. The more the minutes tick by, the more Nicolas is convinced of that. She will want it to be a lengthy matter; she will want to relish the conversation, like a gourmet meal.

He has not made up his mind about what his attitude should be. Surely she is aware he will put up a fight. He will not capitulate, at least not immediately. He wants to be seduced. He expects the usual song and dance, yet he hopes Dagmar Hunoldt will indulge in her best party piece just for him. He yearns for a dazzling literary courtship. As he stares covertly at the thick wrist, he is aware of being yet another asset, yet another gamble, yet another ploy. He knows she has done this many a time, turning writers into instruments, shaping them to her needs. He thinks fleetingly of *Les Liaisons dangereuses*. Will she play Merteuil to his Valmont? He has heard rumors about the inimitable parties in her apartment on Gramercy Park (although apparently last year, she moved to the Upper East Side), where she invited her authors, expertly mingling them with models, artists, heirs, geeks, opera singers, polo players, actors, or good-looking nobodies she met on the subway. He recalled other rumors about business meetings in her legendary white office on the top floor of the Flatiron Building, where she was photographed for *Vogue* and where, overlooking the breathtaking view on Broadway and Fifth, she would swoop in for the kill.

Their empty glasses are collected. Dagmar Hunoldt leans back in her chair, dabbing sunblock on her chiseled face, neck, and décolletage. From close-up, her white skin is flawless, almost wrinkle-free. Has she had a little nip and tuck? She does not talk to him, but he does not feel rejected. They are joined in a bubble of companionable silence. He prays that Malvina will not come down now and ruin this moment. Hopefully, Malvina, if she does appear, will remain her usual silent self.

Dagmar Hunoldt throws a couple of words to the horizon, to the boats, to the sea. Not to him.

"Mercury Retrograde."

Nicolas strains his ears. Did she say: Mercury Retrograde? (The hashtag #WTF, short for "What the fuck?" flashes in front of his eyes, but he is not on Twitter. This is real life, not Twitter.) If he says anything, whatever he says will sound stupid. So he says nothing. But perhaps nothing sounds just as stupid?

"Mercury Retrograde," repeats Dagmar Hunoldt, dreamily, staring out to the sky and the water, not bothered by the fact that he has not uttered a sound. "We have nothing to fear till August, but one must be wary."

Nicolas frantically pieces all this together in his mind. He feels like a dull-witted contestant on a TV show. The slow one who has not yet pressed the buzzer. How cruel she is to play with him thus, to inflict incomprehensible charades on him.

She turns to look at him. "Are you familiar with astrology?" she asks.

"No," he says truthfully.

"Three times a year, for about three weeks, the planet Mercury turns backward, meaning it's in retrograde. For those three weeks, everything comes to a standstill."

Nicolas nods, not quite knowing what is expected of him. Astrology is not his subject. It is his friend Lara's hobby. Lara would know exactly what Mercury Retrograde is all about. She was the kind of person who'd exclaim over lunch, "Oh no, he's a Scorpio. I knew it. Well, that's it, then. Forget it." Nicolas was amused at how much of Lara's life was regimented by Zodiac signs. He teased her mercilessly about it. "So, what do the stars have in store for you today?" he'd text. "Are you allowed to have a drink with an Aries at six?"

"What do you mean by standstill?" Nicolas asks carefully.

Dagmar Hunoldt spreads more sunblock on her nose.

"Well, that this is not the moment to clinch an important deal, to sign a contract, to buy a house, for example," she says. "You see, for those three weeks, delays occur. Problems arise. Mercury is the planet of communications. Letters are delivered, but late. E-mails are lost. Messages are not listened to. This year, 2011, Mercury Retrograde starts on August the second. I have important decisions to make at that point."

"I am more familiar with Hermes than Mercury," admits Nicolas, his old khâgne reflexes kicking in. He wonders what she means by contracts. Editorial ones, surely. Is this the first of a coded message of some sort?

"He of the winged ankles and upright index?" Dagmar Hunoldt smiles.

"The very one. The messenger of the gods. His Roman equivalent is Mercury."

"The thieving son of Zeus, I believe?"

"Precisely. His exact title is god of commerce, thieves, travelers, sports, and athletes. He also guided the souls of the dead down to the underworld."

"You seem to know him well."

Nicolas thinks of the tedious tutorials he gave to dissipated students who wanted more than anything to be as far away as possible from Latin, Greek, and philosophy. He remembers the long hours poring over books and exam copies, faced with bored teenagers pining for their smartphones or the quick puff of a cigarette.

"Hermes and I have crossed paths," he says.

He expects her to ask how, to ask why, and he is already wondering how to make his answer sound more alluring, but instead, Dagmar Hunoldt brushes his arm with a careless finger and whispers, "What about another swim, Hermes?"

She is up on her feet, already fastening cap and goggles. Before he can think of a sagacious response to her invitation, she dives swiftly into the water, swimming away with a neat crawl stroke.

Nicolas stands there, arms akimbo. He senses Malvina's sudden catlike presence at his side.

"What's the matter?" she asks.

He watches the flowery cap bob up and down, growing smaller by the second.

"Is that Dagmar?" she murmurs.

He nods.

"What did she say?" asks Malvina.

Nicolas sighs and scratches the top of his head. "She is pretending not to know who I am."

THERE WAS ONE QUESTION, it seemed to Nicolas, that journalists invariably asked whether they wrote for a prestigious magazine or an unknown blog, whether they had a TV program or a radio show, whatever their nationality. In the beginning, it amused him. At the present stage, it infuriated him. Had they not visited his Web site, where press clippings in different languages were posted for all to see? Had they not clicked on the FAQ section, where all the most obvious questions and answers were listed?

"How did you get the idea for this book?" There was no escaping this precise question. It was as inevitable as the passing of time, as the sun rising and setting each day. He had now mastered two answers: a long version and a short one, depending on the degree of connectivity he felt with the journalist. He more often found himself rattling out the short version with the assurance of a blasé actor reciting lines he knew backward. A long version, however, and a particularly long-winded one, had been proffered to a lucky journalist in Paris, although Nicolas had not planned it. It had just happened.

One afternoon, in the plush crimson bar of the Hôtel Lutetia, on boulevard Raspail, Nicolas was to be interviewed for a famous French radio station by a journalist named Bertrand Chalais. This was during the final upward climb of the book, the exhilarating months just after the Oscar, in 2010, where the entire world seemed to want to know who the young man behind *The Envelope* was. Nicolas was not yet weary of the attention, of the interviews. Bertrand Chalais had lean, bronzed features he instantly liked, young still, but with premature gray hair, like Nicolas's heroine, Margaux. He wore a Lip T18 watch, a Churchill Gold. They sat on an accommodating divan in a quiet area, as Chalais was to tape him. While Nicolas waited for the journalist, who was ten minutes late, he had observed the steady comings and goings of those who counted in the Parisian literary world: publicists with their authors, outlining book releases and launches, and publishers wooing yet more writers. It was an incestuous medley of familiar faces, one that Nicolas had become accustomed to. He was able to pinpoint most of the people sitting in the vast room, and he also knew, with a throb of pride, that he had been identified, too, and that there were murmurs and surreptitious glances sent his way.

Bertrand Chalais had explained that the recording would last over an hour and that he would edit it for his popular fifteen-minute talk show about books and writers. The rest was to be podcast for an exclusive online interview. Chalais installed the small, sophisticated taping device and the interview began. When the ineluctable question was asked, Nicolas launched into his well-oiled monologue about the Pôle de la nationalité française and his father's real name. There was something about Chalais's eyes, the way he looked back at Nicolas with chestnut-colored irises behind rimless glasses. The gaze that held his was good-hearted, benign, but also amused, slightly curious, as if the answer truly mattered to him and he really did want to know how Nicolas had gotten the idea to write *The Envelope,* as if he were not the umpteenth journalist to pop the question. Nicolas's answer slowly began to differ from the standard one. He found himself describing what had happened at the Père-Lachaise Cemetery, in 2003, and in 2006, just after the passport-renewal incident. As he spoke, he realized that he had never told a journalist, let alone a friend, or even a member of his family, about those episodes, either.

On August 7, 2003, exactly ten years after Théodore Duhamel had disappeared without a trace somewhere in the Atlantic Ocean, off the coast of Guéthary, an inscription was added to the Duhamel family tomb in Division 92 at Père-Lachaise by Théo's widow, Emma. There had been a gathering to celebrate this small but important affair, and Nicolas remembered the new gold letters of his father's name, THEODORE DUHAMEL, carved in the slab of granite, as well as the dates of his father's short life span, 1960–1993. He had not often been to that cemetery, apart from his grandmother Nina Duhamel's funeral in 2000, and a later visit to show Jim Morrison's tomb to an American exchange student.

Just after the family get-together with his grandfather Lionel, his mother, and his aunt Elvire, Nicolas had decided to stay on at the cemetery. It was a hot summer afternoon, and the vast, hilly graveyard seemed to be full of tourists. In a couple of days, Nicolas was to leave for Italy with François, after the recent failure of his khâgne. That afternoon, he wanted more than anything to spend time alone and no longer talk about it, or his future, which his mother kept harping about. What was he going to do now? she kept asking. He was only twenty-one. He could still enroll in another course; he had time. The more she went on, the more Nicolas closed up like a clam. How he missed his father in those moments. Théodore Duhamel would have encouraged his son to choose another path, whatever that path might be, and even if it wasn't a conservative one, he would have patted him on the back and taken him to lunch in a crowded brasserie where the staff knew him and revered him.

Nicolas was relieved to see the others walk away at last. For an hour, he ambled, stopping at the graves of Edith Piaf, Modigliani,

Jean de La Fontaine, and Colette. Oscar Wilde's tomb, covered with lipstick, amused him. He went back to the Duhamel family burial plot, which had one of those narrow, towering chapels built above it, like a Gothic phone booth. Nicolas sat inside, in the shade, resting his cheek on the cool stone. On the tomb next door, a couple of funereal wreaths were wilting in the heat. *For our papa* read one of the wreaths. *To my beloved son* read another. Nicolas stepped out of the chapel to decipher the name on the tombstone. FAMILLE TARANNE. There were quite a few of them buried under there. He turned back to look at the Duhamel grave. Quite a few there as well, going back to his great-great-grandfather Emile, whom he had, of course, never known. They were all there, except for his father.

There at his feet were the remains of his Duhamel ancestors, but not of the man who had sired him. Never had he felt so far away, so alienated from Théodore Duhamel than on that August day at Père-Lachaise. He missed his father, and with such intensity that he nearly cried, a strange sadness stirring deep within him. He wanted to pierce the mystery of his father's death, even if it proved hard to hear. As a teenager, he had asked his mother once, "What if Papa is still alive? What if he was hit on the head by his sail and fell into the sea, and then was saved by a stranger? And what if he lost his memory and can't remember who he is?" Emma Duhamel had murmured soothing words about the impossibility of such a story. His father had drowned. It had been a terrible accident, a tragedy. His body had not been found, but he was dead. How could she be so sure? Nicolas wondered. Was it more comfortable believing he was dead and gone?

Girlish whispers and laughs were heard from behind a burial vault. Curiosity got the better of him. Nicolas stood up, trod softly to the front of Division 92, and hid behind a mausoleum. Three young women were gathered around the life-size bronzed statue of a reclining man. They were pretty, with long flowery dresses and wavy hair. The statue was realistic, as if the man had just fallen moments ago, struck by a blow or a bullet, his coat flung back under him, his top hat knocked to the ground, marooned near his gloved hand. One of the young women was straddling the statue in a sexually suggestive manner while the others tittered and cheered her on. Nicolas watched, fascinated. The first was an energetic Amazon hungrily riding her prey. The second was gentle and smooth, swiveling her hips in an erotic figure eight, which made Nicolas catch his breath. The third cupped the statue's head in her hands, lying full length on it, offering her ample bosom to the bronze lips. The entire episode lasted several minutes, and Nicolas relished it. They ran off, still laughing.

Nicolas went to look at the statue. The man's uplifted face, his eyes half-closed, depicted death perfectly. No doubt a violent one. Victor Noir. Born in 1848 and killed in 1870. Not even twenty-two when he died. Practically Nicolas's age. Every detail was perfectly rendered, the lapels of the opened coat, the waistcoat, the shoes. While the entire statue was a coppery green, the area around the groin had been touched so many times, it was of a different color—a polished, glistening brown. There was a definite protuberance in Victor Noir's tight-fitting trousers, and the first button of his fly was undone. Nicolas leaned over and touched the copper bump, smiling as he did so. When he got home, he looked up Victor Noir on the Internet and learned he'd been a young journalist who was shot by a Bonaparte. But Victor Noir became even more famous because of the statue on his tomb; women came from all over the world to rub his pelvis, for good luck, fertility, or the chance of catching a husband that year.

"You had never heard of Victor Noir's grave?" asked Chalais, smiling. Nicolas said no, he hadn't, and that it had been a pleasurable and interesting discovery. It was not till 2006, three years later, he told Chalais, that he returned to the cemetery, a couple of days after he got his new passport. In his hand, he held his father's birth certificate. The weather was foul, a wretched, rainy October morning. Nicolas sat in the narrow chapel, shivering, his feet wet. Fiodor Koltchine. He kept having to pronounce it out loud. Koltchine. What now? What could he do in order to try to understand who his father was, where his father had come from?

The previous time Nicolas had been to Père-Lachaise, he told Chalais, he had wondered about how his father had died. But on that October day, it was his father's birth that obsessed him. He sat there, forlorn, and felt the immense longing for his father come over him again. The fact that there was no burial place and no body made it worse. He thought of Delphine's warm arms, of the comfort she would give him that night on the rue Pernety. He thought of his new passport, of the certificate proving he was now officially French. But who was Fiodor Koltchine? Who was his father's father? What had his father known about all this? What had his father's mother, Zinaïda Koltchine, told him?

When Nicolas left, he passed in front of Victor Noir's tomb. The place was empty that day. The bad weather had put off hopeful ladies coming to stroke his private parts. Nicolas could feel the wetness creep under his collar, seep through his coat. He stood there, his father's birth certificate sodden in his hand, gazing down at the statue. He felt completely alone. The sadness had gone, and in its place, another sensation was taking over. Rascar Capac's haze seemed to diffuse itself slowly in front of his vision, interlacing delicate blue filaments with the curtain of rain falling on the copper statue. Nicolas felt the urge to write, as he had in the plane fourteen years ago, and the yearning was powerful, enticing, and so unexpected that he no longer cared about the cold. Nicolas leaned over and touched the wet bump with feverish fingers. Then, in a daze, he took the long metro ride home. The first thing he did, he told Chalais, was to fetch the Hamilton Khaki watch. He always kept it by his bed. He then sat in the kitchen with a notebook and his father's Montblanc. He made some tea. He stared down at the watch, sometimes pressing its smooth glassy surface to his lips. Then, when he felt ready, he cracked the Moleskine open, placing it flat on the rickety kitchen table.

Chalais knew he was onto raw material. The interview had gone on for well over an hour, but he suspected the young man had more to tell. They ordered white wine. While they drank, Chalais entertained Nicolas with the piquant account of a recent skiing holiday with his wife and children. Nicolas listened, grinning. Another journalist was sitting not far off from them, a sparrowlike woman with long black hair. Nicolas had crossed paths with her several times at book fairs and literary prizes ceremonies. Laurence Taillefer. She was notorious for her causticity. Her portraits of writers in a weekend newspaper were both feared and respected. Nicolas wondered whom she was waiting for. She was reading her notes and biting the end of a pencil.

The bar was now full, a bevy of waiters attending to tables, and a pianist was playing "Georgia on My Mind." It was hard to believe that the lofty Art Deco hall, where the sophisticated literary circle of Paris drank champagne, had witnessed the horrors of World War II. During the occupation, Nicolas knew, the Lutetia had been requisitioned by the Nazis. When Paris was liberated in August 1944, the hotel was used as a meeting point for concentration camp survivors to find family members.

"Why is *The Envelope* told through Margaux's eyes and not yours?" Chalais asked. Nicolas was prepared for that question, as well. However, he did not mind answering it for Chalais. He described how Margaux built a protective distance between his own story and hers. Yes, he could have created a guy of his age, he said, anticipating the next question, which Chalais acknowledged with a smile. Instead, he'd chosen a more convoluted path—a middle-aged woman as narrator. "Why Camogli and not Saint Petersburg?" Chalais asked. From another journalist, this question would have annoyed Nicolas, because he had heard it so often. But Chalais's company was agreeable. Nicolas found himself enjoying the interview. That had not happened for a long time. Looking over his shoulder, Nicolas saw that Laurence Taillefer's guest had arrived: a young woman whose face meant nothing to him. No doubt some writer Taillefer would make mincemeat out of.

Nicolas leaned forward, so that Chalais's face was near his. He could see the spikes of the man's eyelashes behind his glasses. He nibbled at the peanuts the waiter served them. Why Camogli—why should he be willing to describe the precise details of that intimate chemistry, the intricate tinkering that occurred somewhere in the recesses of his mind? Did writers really have to explain? Why should they give away their secret recipe?

Bertrand Chalais chuckled, but in a good-humored manner, and Nicolas felt he was not being judged. When the taping was aired a few days later, it was pleasant to listen to, with piano chords and the low murmur of Lutetia guests in the background. Bertrand Chalais then published a long interview of him in a popular weekend magazine. Nicolas was photographed on Victor Noir's tomb, wearing a black suit and a tie. He gained more followers on Twitter, more friends on Facebook, and even more readers.

WHILE MALVINA TAKES THE elevator to the hotel terrace, Nicolas walks slowly up the stone steps, perplexed. He needs time to think. Why is Dagmar Hunoldt playing this game? At first, he was mystified. Now he is indignant.

When Nicolas gets to the terrace, still bemused, he sees the entire pool area has been requisitioned by a camera crew. Lighting material, drapes, reflectors, and clusters of large silver umbrellas are everywhere. A group of people is rushing backward and forward, yelling to one another and into their mobile phones. Others are busy typing on laptops and texting on smartphones. The peace and quiet of the Gallo Nero is shattered, but there is glamour hovering in the air. The women wear high heels; the men are suave, urbane. He remembers now: the photo shoot organized by Cassia Carper.

He decides to check his BlackBerry before Malvina sees him and pulls it out of his bathrobe pocket. One missed call. Someone whose number has a Belgian prefix has tried to reach him. No voice mail. When he calls back, he recognizes his aunt Roxane's voice. He explains that he left her a message earlier on, as he had not been able to get ahold of his mother.

Roxane is a younger version of Emma, with the same splendid complexion and misty eyes. She also has the same dry humor.

"You mean you have no idea where your mother is?" she says.

"Nope."

"Ha," she says, exhaling. "Well, then it's worse than I thought."

Nicolas does not understand what she is driving at. He does not find her amusing.

"What do you mean?" he asks.

Another sigh. Roxane says, "Look, I don't know how to say it, but this will come as a shock."

Nicolas feels a twinge of fear. Is this one of those life-twisting moments he will always remember? Is his mother ill? Cancer, or something equally horrible? Could it be that Emma hasn't dared tell him? And that he's forgotten to ask? That must be it. That must be why Roxane is acting strange. His legs feel weak.

"Just tell me, will you?" he barks down into phone.

"When is the last time you saw Emma?" Roxane asks.

"I can't remember," says Nicolas glumly. "Maybe last month. Or in May."

Silence. Finally, she says, "And all of a sudden you're worried?"

What is Roxane getting at? He asks, "Are you being critical because I haven't been in touch with her?"

"Absolutely."

Nicolas bites his lip.

"I know," he mumbles. "It's my fault. I've been busy. With this book to write, and . . . everything," he adds lamely.

"So busy writing that you can't check on your mother, see how she is, take her out to dinner, to lunch, on a trip?"

"Roxane. Please. Stop it."

"No, I won't stop it, Nicolas. I haven't seen you for a while. I mean in real life, because we all see you in magazines, on TV; we all hear you on the radio. . . ." Nicolas winces at the irony she unleashes upon him with apparent glee. "I wish I could say this to your face, but I'll do it just as well on the phone. I'm glad for your marvelous success, but I'm very sorry for you. I hope you will one day wake up and realize what a vain, stupid person you have become. Good-bye."

The line goes dead. Nicolas stands there, rooted to the spot, his phone still stuck to his ear. He can hear Roxane's voice ringing in his head. The sting of those words: *vain, stupid person.* How dare she speak to him like that! Who does she think she is? He should have said something; he should have interrupted her, put his foot down. Beneath the surface of annoyance and hurt pride lurks dread. He still does not know where his mother is, what's wrong with her. He should have dropped by to see her, invited her for a meal. Has it been over a month? Maybe even two? He now sees, as he looks out in despair at the blue of the water, how his mother has always been there for him. He has taken this for granted. He has never done anything for her apart from buying her a Rolex for her fiftieth birthday. What a letdown he has been. How selfish. Here he is, reveling in the self-satisfying spiral of his success, more obsessed with being recognized when he enters a restaurant than worried about his mother's health. He suddenly remembers a funeral he attended last year—for the mother of a friend of his. At the end of the Mass, his friend had read a heartbreaking letter to his dead mother in a low, broken voice. He explained how he had never bothered to know his mother better, that he now realized mothers were not immortal, that they were not there forever to care for their children. And he had never cared for her. Nicolas recalls the final sentences of the letter, when his friend, nearly sobbing, had described her death as the final misunderstanding of their non-relationship, and that he, breathless and lost, felt he was running after the train that was taking her away forever, and that it was too late. Nicolas grips the railing hard. He closes his eyes. He must speak to Emma as soon as possible. He must find out how she is.

"Hey you!" shrieks a childish voice, startling him. "What's wrong? Are you gonna be sick, or what?"

He glances down at a small boy, perhaps six or seven, although he isn't good with ages. The boy is dressed in black and has long golden hair. He could be mistaken for a girl, save for the square jaw and thick neck.

"Nothing's wrong," says Nicolas, looking around for the child's parents. Apart from the feverish photo assistants preparing the shoot, he sees no one who could resemble the boy's mother or father.

The kid has clear green irises with tiny pupils. He stares up at Nicolas fixedly.

"What are you doing?" the child says in the same whining voice. "Are you gonna throw up?"

Nicolas has little patience with children and little experience of them. Why do people persist in bringing their offspring to places like these, havens of serenity? Kids should be banned from luxury hotels.

"What's your name?"

"None of your business," the child whimpers. "You're rude."

"Where's your mother?" asks Nicolas, moving toward the terrace, where he sees Malvina waiting for him at a table.

"Stop asking questions!" shouts the kid, following him like an annoying gnat. Nicolas longs to shake him off, but he does not dare.

"Get lost," snarls Nicolas.

A frumpy woman appears from nowhere. Blond, with buckteeth and a sunburned nose, she is in her mid-forties.

"Is Damian being a pain? I'm frightfully sorry." She has a strong British accent.

Nicolas shrugs.

"I'm not too good with kids."

"I understand," she answers good-naturedly. "Damian can be rather daunting."

The boy has now rushed to the other side of the pool, both arms raised in a frightening salute. He hovers around the photo assistants, hopping up and down, red in the face, screaming. They stare down at him, appalled.

"Oh dear." The mother sighs. "I must go rescue those people."

"Good luck," says Nicolas. He guesses she is a single mother who had the child late in life and is bringing him up alone. She should have taken him to a place where he could play with kids his own age.

Malvina drinks tea, lost in her iPhone. He sits down next to her. He toys with telling her about Roxane and Dagmar, his two grievances of the moment, and decides against it. What could she do to help? Nothing. The terrace is full of guests watching the developments of the photo shoot. Dr. Gheza, having coffee at the bar, waves to them, a short, quick wave, which Nicolas returns. The Belgian family is enjoying a snack. Do they eat all day long? The gay couple are playing backgammon. Alessandra and her mother are writing postcards. Nicolas looks to see if Dagmar Hunoldt is sitting somewhere around the back, but she isn't. Mr. Wong and Miss Ming, resplendent in matching pink silk kimonos, nod to all. The Swiss couple are probably still in the water. The French couple, no doubt at tennis and the spa. The buxom brunette, perhaps still in bed. Has Nelson Novézan left? There are new faces Nicolas has not seen before: a group of Americans, some Italians, and an elegant German couple, who are sitting at the next table. Malvina has a disenchanted expression, accompanied by stony silence, which heralds trouble.

"Everything all right?" Nicolas asks.

She frowns. "No. But you're far too busy to care."

He does all he can to remain calm, biting down hard on his bottom teeth, clenching his jaws together. She deserves the same treatment as Damian. The boy, he sees, is being told off by his mother a little farther off. Before Malvina can summon words, which, Nicolas knows, can be just as unpleasant as Roxane's diatribe, whispers and murmurs are heard. Three models have appeared, wearing lingerie, perched on high heels, with a flock of hairdressers and makeup artists in attendance. Long-legged, long-haired, and, Nicolas notes with pleasure, not too gaunt. Two brunettes and one blonde. They laugh and joke with the assistants and makeup team, seemingly unaware that so many eyes are on them, feasting upon their youth, nudity, and beauty. Where do these girls come from? Nicolas wonders. From some sleepy small town in Oklahoma, or some remote Scandinavian island?

"At least close your mouth. You're drooling," snaps Malvina.

"What is wrong with you?" he asks.

She sighs. "I haven't felt well since we got here."

"Maybe you should see a doctor," he replies, trying with all his might not to stare at one of the brunettes, whose lacy thong barely covers her pelvis.

"Maybe," Malvina murmurs. "Oh, and by the way, there's another photo of you by Alex Brunel on your Facebook wall."

"What!" he exclaims.

Malvina hands him her iPhone. The photo was taken early this morning, while he was having breakfast alone. It has been "liked" hundreds of times.

"Shit," he hisses.

Who is Alex Brunel? Nicolas had only noticed the Swiss couple near him during breakfast. Could Alex Brunel be one of them? There was also the smiling, friendly waitress. Music blares, making them all jump. An old Sheryl Crow song, with a loud guitar. The models start to dance, gyrating their slim hips to the beat, throwing their silky hair back across their shoulders, arms held up to the blue sky, to the blaze of the sun. Nicolas notices a small young man in their midst, holding a camera. He had mistaken him for an assistant, or a hairstylist, but he sees now that this is the photographer. A photographer who is his age, not a day over thirty. He is wearing low-slung, worn-out jeans and a red sleeveless T-shirt. Nicolas can't see his face because of the camera, but he makes out a short mop of jet black hair. When the photographer puts the camera down, Nicolas discovers the skinny young man is a young woman. This makes him chuckle. A vintage Madonna hit is playing full blast. The three models dance as if they are in a nightclub. They sway together like fragile flowers in the wind, bending backward and forward, lips pouting, eyes half-closed, as if they are high. Even Damian, the little boy, watches in silence, transfixed. They are beautiful. The young photographer clicks away steadfastly, her legs bent, a comical smirk on her face as she works. Nicolas sees Cassia Carper standing behind one of the fashion stylists, surveying the scene with a studious expression, while one of her feet, enclosed in another heart-stopping sandal, twitches to the rhythm. Nicolas already knows how fabulous the photographs will look on the glossy paper of the magazine. Cassia Carper stares into the camera to check the shots with the young photographer. She has an eagle eye on every aspect of the session. Today, she is wearing a short white dress with no back. Her mouth is pink and shiny. She has not looked his way once. Did she really kiss him last night? Or was that part of an erotic dream? No, she did kiss him. He can still feel her tongue in his mouth, surprisingly clearly.

"Do you know that red-haired woman?" asks Malvina sharply.

Nicolas shrugs. "I think I met her at a cocktail party in Paris. Not sure."

He orders some tea before Malvina can embark on any other questions. He is beginning to wonder whether this holiday is a mistake. Despite the loveliness of the setting, the weight of the nonexistent book bears down upon him with all its might. Did he really think he was going to get a book started this way? Who was he fooling?

"I need to get ahold of my mother," Nicolas explains, so that Malvina won't get started when she sees him handling his Black-Berry. "I don't know where she is. I'm worried."

His publicist's number shows up on the screen. Why would

Dita Dallard be calling him on a Saturday, in the middle of his holiday? She knows it's best to e-mail him. She knows he doesn't like being disturbed. If she is calling, then it is because it's important. He enjoys working with Dita, a bright thirty-something girl with an impish smile, a curvaceous figure, and a fine sense of humor. When she started out with Nicolas, neither of them knew that *The Envelope* would be published all over the world, and that, as a result, the whole world would clamor for him. Dita began her career at Alice Dor Publications as an assistant four years ago, but when Hurricane Margaux started to blow, her initiative, ideas, and energy soon landed her the job as Nicolas Kolt's personal publicist.

As soon as he hears her voice, Nicolas knows it is not good news. Dita never stalls. He appreciates that. She only has to say "Laurence Taillefer."

"Tell me," he says.

"I don't think you should read her piece."

"Is it that awful?"

"Yes."

"It came out this morning?"

"Yes."

"Has Alice read it?"

"Yes. She wants you to call her."

Nicolas can see the page clearly, as if the article is spread out on the table in front of him. One full page, in a newspaper the whole of France reads on a weekend.

"Send it to me," he says.

"I don't think that's a good idea."

"I have to learn to face this, Dita," he replies.

She hesitates, then says, "Okay. Sending it now. Call me if you need me. Call Alice, or she'll get worried. And remember, Laurence Taillefer never liked you. This is not a surprise."

Nicolas mutters good-bye.

"What is it?" says Malvina.

He tries to smile. "A bad article."

He recalls that the last time he laid eyes on the redoubtable, raven-haired Laurence Taillefer was during his interview with Bertrand Chalais last year at the Hôtel Lutetia. She rarely interviewed authors, he learned. Her reviews decoded books, writers, publishing phenomena. She was capable of promoting an author to glory, or catapulting another to flames.

"Who cares about a bad article when you have millions of readers around the world?" says Malvina, reaching out to pat his hand.

She is right, of course. He should not even read it. Who cares, when so many people love his book, when it is still selling strong? But at this fragile, tricky moment of his life, he feels he has to know.

Dita sends the article by e-mail, and all he has to do is click on it.

"The 'Nicolas Kolt' Syndrome and Other Vanities," by Laurence Taillefer.

He looks down to his BlackBerry, shielding it against the sun with his hand. He can no longer hear the music; he no longer sees the models, the young photographer, Cassia Carper in her white dress, the guests sitting around him, as if they are all in a theater, watching a show. He has eyes only for the words that are about to leap out at him with venom, and against which he does not know how to protect himself. Perhaps not reading the article is the only protection, he thinks, glancing up once to the blue of the sea, then down again. It is too late. He has started.

At first, the words do not make sense; they are jumbled, incoherent, and he has to go back to the beginning and take it slowly.

Nicolas Duhamel lost his passport in 2006. Because both his parents were born abroad, according to new governmental laws, he had to prove his French nationality, even if he was born in France. This gave him the idea for *The Envelope,* as the world now knows. In those less glorious days before publication stardom, Nicolas Duhamel was a struggling private tutor. One can imagine him teaching Plato or Nietzsche to

young girls, the latter no doubt thunderstruck by his tene-
brous good looks. That is the problem with "Nicolas Kolt."
He is easy to look at, and easy to read. Too easy? *The Envelope* is on everybody's lips, in everyone's hands. Why? Isn't
this due more to the ingenious, bludgeonlike marketing by
his artful publishers around the world than to his talent?
"Nicolas Kolt" has become an inescapable, unavoidable brand
name. His rugged bad-boy features grace the covers of magazines, cologne bottles, ads for watches and sunglasses. "Nicolas Kolt" looks stunning on TV. He played a cameo part in
the movie of his book, and his innumerable fans adored it. (If
you don't believe me, check his Facebook page.) "Nicolas
Kolt" has become the cult writer of the famed Generation Y,
the breed who thrives on cut, copy, and paste, on channel
surfing, on social networking, on e-books and smartphones,
on "likes," "Retweets," and "pokes," on friends, fans, and followers, on vacuity and vanity. *The Envelope* is a less than
average novel, for a first-time novelist. It is neither terribly
good nor bad. It deals adequately enough with a dark family
secret. It strikes the right chords. It is an efficient sob story
your granny will love, and your young nephew might like,
too. Why are we still enduring its success, three years later?
Is this to do with Robin Wright's Oscar? What is it about *The
Envelope* that makes so many people read it? The answer is
because "Nicolas Kolt" is like an easy lay. "Nicolas Kolt" is a
success only because his publishers have decided he will be
a success, and, sheeplike, masses follow. "Nicolas Kolt," the
best-selling international author, read from Stockholm to
Seattle, adored by millions of followers around the world, is
no writer. He is a product.

At this point, Nicolas looks up again and gazes at to sea.
"Are you okay?" Malvina asks.
He does not answer. He thinks of Alice Dor, who is waiting for

his call. She would find the words to comfort him, one way or another, but he does not want to speak to her right now. He thinks of all the people he knows, reading the newspaper this morning over their breakfast tables; he thinks of those who will smile, or even laugh; he thinks of those who will be saddened; he thinks of his fans, of what will be written on his Facebook wall, on Twitter, in his e-mail; he thinks of those who won't care, and he longs to be like them. He cannot bear reading the rest. He decides to skip a large chunk, scrolling down on his BlackBerry until he gets to the end.

Nicolas Duhamel should distance himself from the frenzied social networking he's been indulging in. Perhaps he should stop Tweeting once and for all. The question is, will "Nicolas Kolt" ever write a novel again? Will he surf forever on the wave of *The Envelope*'s success, fueled by avid publishers raking in the profits, until those good looks wilt and another writer product takes over? There will be no new book from "Nicolas Kolt." He is too busy preening in the hundreds of mirrors held up to him.

Nicolas gets up, dizzy. He finds he cannot speak. There is a stark truth in the article that hits home, even if Laurence Taillefer laid it on thick. He feels weak. His mouth is dry. A pit punctures his stomach. He walks to the side of the terrace overlooking the sea, heedless of the music, the models, the chatter. Malvina follows him, her hand on his back. They stand there in silence for a while, staring out to the blueness. He thinks of Laurence Taillefer writing. He imagines her in her office, wherever that may be, hunched over her computer, choosing the cruelest words, the ones with the sharpest bite. Does she smile when she writes her articles? When she wrote this one? He should post something on Twitter, on Facebook, anticipating the reactions. The last thing he wants is his readers' pity. Nicolas feels hot in his bathrobe, and he yearns for the cool water. Another swim might revive his spirits. But what if he bumps into Dagmar Hunoldt again? He could not endure another repudiation, not in his present state.

"You said you wanted to call your mother," suggests Malvina gently.

She is right: That is what he should do. Get ahold of Emma. Keep calling until he hears her voice. He walks a little farther off, so that he can be alone. He still feels dazed, as if someone has hit him on the head. He calls his mother's mobile. He expects to get voice mail, and is startled when a man's voice is heard.

"Hullo?" says Nicolas.

"Yes?" replies the stranger.

"I must have made a mistake. . . . I'm looking for Emma Duhamel."

"This is her phone," the stranger replies politely.

Who is this guy? Nicolas wonders. Why is he answering my mother's mobile? His heart misses a beat. What if Emma is in the hospital and this man is a doctor? A doctor with bad news.

Stuttering, he says, "Is . . . is Emma Duhamel around?"

The stranger clears his throat.

"And you are?"

"I'm her son."

"Her son?"

"Yes, that's right."

There is a silence. Nicolas hears music, very faintly.

"Hullo?"

"I'm still here," says the stranger.

"Is my mother okay?"

"She's fine, yes, just fine."

Is Nicolas imagining things, or is the man on the other end smiling?

"Who are you?" he asks. "Her doctor?"

"What? No!"

"Well, who are you?"

Silence. Then he says, "I'm Ed."

Nicolas says nothing. Who the hell is Ed? A friend? A student?

"Your mother is still asleep."

His mother, still asleep at noon? She, who always stated that the early bird catches the worm?

"I see," he says aimlessly.

"I'll tell her you called."

"Thank you, Ed. Where are you, if I may ask?"

"Sure. In Saint-Tropez."

Nicolas nearly drops the phone.

"In Saint-Tropez?" he echoes.

"Yes. Staying with friends. On a boat."

"I see," says Nicolas again, bewildered. "On a boat?"

"Indeed," says Ed. "A very nice boat."

Ed has a young, friendly voice.

"And you are . . . a friend of my mother?" Nicolas asks tentatively.

Another silence. Music in the background, and the hum of other voices. Emma still asleep at noon. A disturbing image wafts his way: an unmade bed, rumpled sheets, bare skin, an intimacy he does not want to see.

Ed laughs, not an unpleasant laugh, but it grates in Nicolas's ear. Then he simply says, "Um . . . I'm her boyfriend."

T HE ENVELOPE WAS READ by people of all ages, of all nation-
alities, of all backgrounds, people who had nothing in com-
mon except his book. Nicolas began to meet and know his readers
when he traveled, but he also met them virtually through Facebook and Twitter. He found it quicker, more practical, to interact
with them by way of the social networks. However, that was also
time-consuming, he had to admit. He became engrossed in the
process. He seemed to be perpetually bent over his phone. He
even slept with it by his pillow. It irked his entourage. His mother
often asked him, with a weary sigh, if she had to follow him on
Twitter in order to get him to answer her. Alice Dor complained
that even during their lunches, he had to peek at his phone. Lara
teased him about the number of Tweets he posted every day. "No
wonder you still haven't finished your book," she taunted. He did
admit to her he was hooked, to such an extent that whenever he
tried to write, he disabled the Internet connection and left his
phone in another room. This never lasted. He inevitably went back
online, like an alcoholic reaches for another glass and hates himself

for it. He needed to cure his addiction. He knew programs existed to help people like him get over it. Everyone, these days, seemed to have an eye on their texts, their e-mails, on their Facebook pages, on their Twitter feeds. Couples dined in restaurants, eating in silence, face-to-face, each riveted to a phone. Even during funerals, weddings, movies, Nicolas noticed people glancing down at their phones. Those who deliberately did not have mobiles or computers were a mystery to him. Did they live in the Dark Ages? But now, as he was faced with the increasingly worrying chasm of his intellectual inertia, he began to wonder if maybe those people were right in removing themselves from the never-ending, hypnotizing enticement of being online. Was Internet overuse slowing brains down? Had his been addled? Nicolas had opened a Facebook page before he became famous, when he was still Nicolas Duhamel, but he had to close it down when Hurricane Margaux started to blow, simply because Nicolas Duhamel no longer existed. The new Nicolas Kolt fan page immediately attracted thousands of readers.

Online, his readers prepared surprises for him. He was entranced to discover one day that "Margaux Dansor" had befriended him on Facebook. Whoever had created that profile page knew his character as well as he did. There was Margaux, exactly as she was described in his novel. He never found out who had imagined the online Margaux, and it did not matter. He enjoyed interacting with his heroine. Many readers thought Margaux truly existed, and that Nicolas had put her in his book after he'd met her. He let some of them believe that. It amused him.

Nicolas used social networks because he liked to share, he told journalists. He liked to communicate, and he reveled in the feedback, not merely because it was often appraising but also because it was a challenge. His Tweets were never inane. He thought carefully about what he Tweeted, tailoring those 140 characters to perfection, using a wry humor his followers hungered for. He Retweeted breaking news, pleased to be the first one to do so, the first one who seized the information as it fleeted past, and passed it on. He answered his reader's questions as best as he could. Some of those dialogues became famous, and journalists brought them up during interviews.

The Assen episode was often mentioned. Nicolas's Dutch publisher, Marije Gert, had coerced him, despite his exhaustion, into accepting an event in a town named Assen, near Amsterdam. She had assured him that the drive would take under two hours, a good meal awaited them, the entire event would not last too long, his numerous fans were waiting for him with intense anticipation, and, most important, he would be back at the Ambassade Hotel before midnight, as he had an eight o'clock plane the next morning to Oslo for the rest of his book tour. Nicolas had accepted. But the supposedly swift drive out to Assen turned out differently. They got caught in rush-hour traffic jams and slowed down by construction, while monsoonlike rains poured down from the black sky. Marije, who was driving, hardly dared look across at her author, who was sprawled out in the front seat on her right, concentrating on his BlackBerry. They inched along the wet, jammed highway in silence. The drive took over four excruciating hours. What Marije never knew at the time was that Nicolas was Tweeting it all. He Tweeted about his fatigue, her cautious driving (chin to the wheel), the sluggish traffic, the rain, his painfully full bladder, his stomach rumbling with hunger, his growing reluctance to attend the event. He Tweeted descriptions of objects left in Marije's car by her children and husband (a skateboard, a tie, a map, a Barbie doll). He Tweeted about his exasperation, his impatience, his helplessness. One Tweet in particular created an incredible buzz: "This feels like when you know her orgasm is not going to happen for a very very long time. #drivetoassen." By the time they finally arrived, the event had been canceled. Everyone had gone home. Nicolas was too tired to be angry or disappointed. He slept all the way back to Amsterdam.

There was another event in Nicolas's new life as a best-selling author that had been a hit on Twitter. He was on his way back to

Paris from Los Angeles after the Oscar ceremony. Magazines and Web sites were full of photos of him posing with Robin Wright, she in a scarlet dress, he in a black tuxedo. Nicolas boarded the plane with a business ticket, but when it was known that he was on board, he was upgraded to first class, where he found himself entirely alone. He had never flown first-class, and he marveled at the attention and comfort. The plane was delayed, and as Nicolas sat in lonely luxury in the first-class cabin, he Tweeted. Every five minutes, it seemed, a flight attendant offered him drinks, food, a magazine to read, a chocolate, a perfumed towelette to wash his hands. He Tweeted away, posting photos of the delicacies coming his way. During the long wait for takeoff, he was given a pair of elegant gray pajamas, slippers, and a vanity case. He asked a flight attendant where the toilets were, and she ushered him to a door toward the front of the aircraft. Once inside the small square space, Nicolas could not find the toilet. There was a plastic cushioned bench, which he poked and prodded at in vain. He peered over and under the sink, tapped at a paneled mirror, hoping a secret device might make the toilet spring forward. Nothing happened. He pressed on all the buttons he could see. Meanwhile, he Tweeted about his misfortune, making thousands of followers around the world roar with laughter. "Stranded in first-class toilet in plane. But no toilet to be seen. #help." He hopped around the cabin, crimson-faced, wondering what to do. "Am I going to have to pee in the basin or what? #wtf. #firstclassnightmare." When he emerged, defeated, telling the flight attendant he had not been able to operate the toilet, it was her turn to laugh. That was the changing cabin, she explained, grinning; the toilet was just on the left. He had opened the wrong door.

And then, of course, there was the presidential lunch. Last year, just after the Oscar, Nicolas had been invited to the Elysée Palace by the First Lady. When Dita phoned him with news of the invitation, he had at first thought it was a joke. Dita insisted that, no, this was no joke. The First Lady's personal secretary had called her, and this was all real. So? Was he going to go, or not? Nicolas was wary of any political maneuver and the possible repercussions. He did not like to be branded, nor did he wish to reveal any political tendency. A political opinion was a private affair. He prudently asked Dita to find out who else had been invited. An hour later, she called back to announce that two other writers had been invited to an "informal literary lunch by the First Lady." She gave him the names—a man and a woman. He knew both of them, but not well. They had met at book fairs and on TV shows. He was the youngest of the lot. Curiosity got the better of him. Nicolas told Dita that he would go. He had never been to the Elysée Palace. Such an offer may not happen again. On the given day, he turned up, wearing his customary black jeans and black T-shirt. As he crossed the rue du Faubourg Saint-Honoré, two guards standing outside brandished stern palms and ordered that he remain on the other side of the street. He gave them his most winning Nicolas Kolt–like smile and wordlessly handed them a printed version of the e-mail confirmation he had received from the First Lady's assistant. They apologized and led him to the entrance. A man wearing an impressive uniform, white gloves, and an intricate gold necklace ceremoniously held out a silver tray. Nicolas understood he was to give the man his identity card. He placed it on the tray. The tray disappeared. His card was a recent one, with the notation "Nicolas Duhamel, also known as 'Nicolas Kolt'" on it. Another man appeared, this one wearing a gray suit. He handed the card back to Nicolas, beaming. "Monsieur Kolt, it is a pleasure to meet you. My wife loves your book. She cannot wait for the next one." Nicolas followed him into the large square courtyard where, on TV, his entire life, he had seen presidents come and go along those steps, greeting other presidents. His hand itched for his BlackBerry, but he knew he could not take photographs or Tweet, which would be seen as rude and inappropriate. He had not mentioned this lunch to anyone except Alice Dor, who had gasped and smiled.

The two writers were already in the dining room when he was ushered in. The woman, in her fifties, wrote popular crime fiction, which had been adapted for television. She was wearing a fuchsia silk dress and too much lipstick. Writer number two, in his forties, was a platinum-haired trendy troublemaker who wrote nihilistic books about sex, literature, drugs, and himself. He wore oversized Harry Potter–like reading glasses and a prune-colored velvet jacket, on which a coat of dandruff was steadily forming. They greeted him with false affection and contrived smiles. From the windows, Nicolas could see the green lawns of the famous private gardens. After a short wait, the First Lady appeared, all dimples and friendliness. Nicolas had never met her. She was shorter than he had imagined, in spite of very high heels. Her lustrous hair was perfectly set. The lunch was strangely silent. Waiters passed the dishes in a fluid ballet. The First Lady did all the talking. It was as if she were having a conversation with herself. Fuchsia and Dandruff nodded and smiled. But no one else spoke. Were they too impressed? He longed to take photos of the silver cutlery, the monogrammed crystal glasses, the beautiful Limoges porcelain plates, from which countless presidents and their illustrious guests had eaten. When the dessert was served, a delicate fruit salad with meringues and a dark red raspberry sauce—which Nicolas concentrated on in order not to spill it over the immaculate embroidered tablecloth or himself—he sensed movement and glanced up. Dandruff and Fuchsia were on their feet, faces flushed. Nicolas realized with a shock that the president had entered the room. He stood up swiftly as well, towering over the president, a stocky man. Before he could say anything, the president was shaking his hand and asking everyone to sit down again. It was a surreal moment. Nicolas had to stop himself from staring at the president, whom he had never seen in the flesh. His eyes took in the president's suit, his monogrammed, white shirt, his gold cuff links, his blue tie, his watch (a Scuderia Ventidue). Coffee was served, and all the while, the president talked. His wife acknowledged his every word with a nod of her head. The president's monologue was political, in view of the presidential elections the following year. Dandruff fired a couple of polished remarks, eager to shine. At the end of their exchange, the president began to talk about social networks, an expression of disdain on his face, which sparked Nicolas's interest. With a guffaw, the president revealed that he had recently met the CEO of Twitter and the CEO of Facebook. "Nice guys," he called them, with a scornful smile, his upper lip contorting, "nice young guys in jeans and T-shirts" (forgetting that one of his guests was wearing precisely that attire), "nice guys who think they are kings of the world, but honestly," the president went on, grimacing, "Twitter is Mickey Mouse saying hello to Donald Duck, and Facebook is Donald Duck saying hello back to Mickey Mouse, right?" Everyone roared with laughter. Nicolas laughed, too, because he felt he had to, because it was the thing to do in the present circumstances, but when the mirth died down, he regretted having joined in the fun. The Mickey and Donald sentence remained stuck in his head, and he could not stop thinking about it. As soon as he left the Elysée Palace, he Tweeted the phrase, quoting it with the president's very recognizable initials. It attracted attention immediately. The buzz on Twitter grew. Journalists wrote to him, called him, or called Dita, who found herself swamped. Everyone wanted to know more. Where had Nicolas heard that phrase? Under what circumstances? Had he met the president? Meanwhile, his quote was Retweeted hundreds of times, on both sides of the Atlantic. Alice feared someone from the palace press corps might call and demand an explanation. But the Elysée remained silent. "'Presidents should never invite writers to lunch,' said Mickey Mouse to Donald Duck" was Nicolas's final and popular Tweet about the matter.

Nicolas never Tweeted about the book he was pretending to write. But he was very loquacious about *The Envelope*. He had wanted to Tweet about the pride and incredulity of seeing his name on the printed page for the first time. He had corrected the galleys with the help of a sharp-eyed beauty named Rebecca, with whom, he learned, all authors from Alice Dor Publications were enamored, because she was quietly professional, dedicated to her work, and lovely to look at when she bent over the page, red pencil in hand, chestnut hair cascading down her back, sometimes revealing a white neck. Then he had been tempted to share the prospect of choosing the cover with Alice Dor and her talented artistic designer, Marie-Anne. Marie-Anne was worshiped by Alice Dor, Nicolas soon discovered. Marie-Anne had come up with the distinctive logo that symbolized the publishing company: two cherries with intertwined stems. There had been several cover possibilities, and he thought that perhaps he could show them to his followers. And, finally, he felt compelled to describe the unforgettable day he saw his debut novel for the first time in a bookstore, the pure joy of seeing it there, for all to read, offered, ready, full of promise. But he finally chose not to Tweet about any of it. That joy was his, and his alone. It was a past joy; no point going back to it. He remembered how he entered bookstores in a sort of trance, just to glimpse his book among all the others. If a person picked it up and read the back cover, he felt intense excitement. If they ended up buying it, he was overjoyed. At that point, when the press had not yet started writing about him, he could still stroll into bookstores without being recognized. He spent a long time in these establishments, pretending to be absorbed in some other work, spying on would-be readers. If his book was badly placed, he would surreptitiously put it back on the front piles so that it could be seen more easily. But as *The Envelope* slowly and surely gained readers and attention, Nicolas found that he no longer needed to replace the copies. They were already there, in towering stacks for all to see. He did not need to Tweet about those triumphant piles. His thousands of followers did that for him.

IT IS NOW LUNCHTIME at the Gallo Nero. Guests take their seats at the restaurant by the sparkling pool, protected from the greedy rays of the sun by soft beige parasols. Waiters serve food in the usual smooth routine. There are more new people, Nicolas notices. Two blond American women, anywhere between forty and sixty, with the bloated, tight features of recent plastic surgery and Botox overuse. They laugh with the harsh whinny of hyenas. "Oh my God," whines one over and over again. "You gotta be kidding!" shrieks the other. Behind them is an Italian family, the identical version of the *Vanity Fair* tribe of yesterday, same allure, same glamour. The photo shoot has stopped for the moment. Those in the fashion group are nibbling snacks by the bar before they start shooting again in the late afternoon, when the heat will be less oppressive. Nelson Novézan lunches with his girlfriend, hunched over his plate, and orders more wine. His face is particularly puffy today.

Nicolas sits at "his" table with Malvina. He looks around at the other guests and wonders why they are all here today. It seems that no event, however horrendous, scandalous, or heinous, could ever alter the Gallo Nero's supreme and insolent tranquility. Here, the sun rules, masterful, seconded by the sea and the sky in their ultimate blue glory.

Nicolas tells Malvina about the call to his mother, and how someone named Ed answered Emma's phone. He tries to describe the embarrassment of the situation, the relief on learning she was not ill, and, all the while, the realization he had not been in touch for so long that he knew nothing about his mother's life. He explains how Ed sounded disturbingly young, although, of course, he could be wrong; it was on the phone, and it is hard to judge a person's age just by his voice. Malvina smiles. Nicolas resents her smile. He was expecting empathy.

Next to them, Mr. Wong and Miss Ming seem keen to start a conversation in halting English. This is the last thing Nicolas wants. Why can't these people shut up and leave him alone? If they mention the new book, he will be tempted to throw them over the cliff. He is still stunned by the events of the morning: his surrealistic conversation with Dagmar Hunoldt; his aunt's discomfiting harshness; the startling knowledge that his mother has a young lover and that she is with him on a boat in Saint-Tropez; the abominable article by Laurence Taillefer, which now feels like the aftereffects of a punch in the stomach.

The American face-lifted ladies continue to howl with laughter. Nicolas yearns to throttle them.

"You live Paris, yes?" squeaks Miss Ming, her moonlike face wobbling as she nods her head up and down. It is impossible to guess Miss Ming's age. She looks like she is made out of porcelain.

"Yes, we do," says Malvina, understanding that Nicolas is too preoccupied or uninterested to answer.

"Ah, Paris," squeals Mr. Wong. "Very, very nice, Paris, yes!"

More nods and bobs of their shiny black heads.

"And you live in . . . ?" asks Malvina politely.

Miss Ming pronounces a few unintelligible words. Malvina

glances at Nicolas for help, but Nicolas is in that other world, where she knows she cannot enter. There is no point in speaking to him now. Unbeknownst to Malvina, Nicolas's head is full of women. The women of his day: Alice's expectations, Dagmar's snub, Roxane's causticity, Emma's secrets, Laurence and her contempt. The women of his night: Malvina's untroubled sleep, Sabina's BBM, Cassia's tongue. He wants to be anywhere on earth but here, now, trapped in this perfect blue luxuriousness with all the other rich, spoiled guests being pampered, waited on hand and foot. Perhaps the only comforting thought right now is of Sabina. Sabina, who set his loins on fire with text messages and photos. Sabina is the only solace he can take comfort in, at least mentally. The idea of her, or just thinking about the pink-and-golden triangle, brings him a sweet stab of secret pleasure.

The waiter comes for their order. Malvina chooses sautéed vegetables served with Gallo Nero's garden herbs and flowers and buffalo mozzarella; Nicolas has red mullet wrapped in zucchini blossoms, with black-rice cream and artichokes. Nicolas watches Novézan steadily drink rosé and wishes he could join him, so that they could drink together, wordlessly, with no explanation, just drink until they dropped. He notices the first stages of exhaustion settling upon him, no doubt last night's overindulgences finally taking their toll. There is a telltale dryness in his throat, and his eyelids prickle as if lined with sand. Malvina is doing her best to understand what Miss Ming is miming with pudgy hands. Mr. Wong tries to help by bouncing up and down in his seat and uttering another series of incomprehensible sounds.

"They want to know, I think, if you've ever been to China," whispers Malvina.

"Who cares?" Nicolas sighs. Malvina glares at him. Making an effort, he says that, yes, he has been to Shanghai, Beijing, and Hong Kong. He tries to describe his book promotion there, but he soon realizes that Miss Ming and Mr. Wong, despite their enthusiastic smiles and continuous nods, do not understand him. So he slows down, as if he is talking to an obtuse five-year-old, and this appears to work. Their meal is brought to them and they eat in silence until Miss Ming, her double chin quivering with anticipation, starts miming with her hands once again.

"I can't stand this," mutters Nicolas to Malvina.

"Just be nice," Malvina whispers.

They both concentrate on Miss Ming. She keeps pointing at Nicolas. They cannot make out what on earth she means. Mr. Wong huffs and puffs, sounding like a steam engine, offering to help in his own way, but this only makes matters worse. A piercing scream is heard. Everyone turns, to see the British woman stoically carry her yelping and kicking son away. Once the fuss is over, a now-pink Miss Ming resumes pointing at Nicolas and flapping her hands in the air like a plump, clucking hen.

The BlackBerry on the table flashes François's number on its screen. François, his savior! Nicolas grabs it with relief. "Have to take this, sorry." He scrambles to his feet, not looking at Malvina (he can already anticipate her whining: "You left me with those abysmally boring Chinese people to answer your phone . . ."), and rushes to the terrace. At last, François is calling him back. Good old François. He knew he could trust him. Always there when he needs him. François will never let him down. François will always be there, standing up for him. François is his only true friend. His one and only friend.

"Hey, dude!" he drawls, using the deep, exaggeratedly virile voice of their adolescence, expecting François to respond with "Hey, Khûbe!"

But there is an ominous silence on the other end of the line, like the blank moment after lightning, just before thunder strikes.

"Hullo?" says Nicolas. "You there?"

François's voice comes over loud and clear. "Who the fuck do you think you are?"

Nicolas finds he can no longer speak.

François's voice is cold as he goes on. "Calling me, last night, drunk, at one o'clock in the morning, leaving that pathetic message. You know I get up early to work, even on a Saturday. You know I have small children, a wife, whose names you never remember because all you're interested in is being Nicolas Kolt. How nice to hear you're writing your future best-seller on a paradisiacal island while the rest of us get on with our dreary, humdrum lives. I don't understand the person you now are. And I don't want to. Don't call me again. Don't bother."

"Wait!" whimpers Nicolas, at last finding his voice. "Don't hang up!"

"I haven't finished yet," says François icily. "I'll hang up when I have. I read that article by Laurence Taillefer, like most of France did this morning. She is right. You are a flash in the pan. You have become a product. I saw this coming. Delphine is the only one, apart from me, who saw it coming, too. The truth is, you can't even write a new book. You don't have what it takes to be a writer. To be a writer, you need to suffer; you know that. You need to have that hidden wound inside you. You need to bleed. You don't suffer. You don't bleed. You used to. You bled when you failed the exam. You suffered when you found out who your father really was, when you realized how he might have died. You wrote that book with your tears and your blood. You now thrive on your worldwide success. It's gone to your head. You've become blasé. You spend. You travel. You shine. You're in glossy magazines. You're the king of Twitter. The truth is, Nicolas, you'll never write anything ever again."

Silence. François is gone. Nicolas stares out to the azure beauty of the Mediterranean. How is it possible that what he is looking at appears calm, serene, when he is enduring inner hell? Boats sail, the sun shines, guests lunch and laugh, gulls soar. A perfect sight. It is not quite three o'clock. He is now convinced the rest of his day will be a series of disasters. What will be in store for him next? He dreads to think. He slowly walks back to the table, his legs unsteady.

His hands are trembling and he nearly drops his phone. He sees that his lunch is awaiting him. He is no longer hungry.

"I at last understand what Miss Ming is trying to explain." Malvina grins triumphantly, not noticing the expression on his face. "She wants to know what you do."

Nicolas feels more deflated than ever. He thought Miss Ming knew who he was. His book sold very well in China. Sitting down, in a sort of stupor, he halfheartedly mimes writing, then a book, flapping imaginary pages with his hands. Miss Ming watches with great attention, black eyes twinkling. She is thrilled when she finally comprehends Nicolas is a writer. So is Mr. Wong. They clap and bow. They have never met a writer. How exciting! How thrilling! They ask for his name and the title of the book. Wearily, Nicolas writes both on the paper napkin. They decipher it slowly. They nod and smile. Malvina smiles, too.

Then Mr. Wong taps him on the shoulder encouragingly. He says loudly and with a wide smile, "Maybe one day you will become very famous! Good luck, sir!"

IN AUGUST 1993, WHEN Théodore Duhamel disappeared off the coast of Guéthary, and after the black Hobie 16 was found near Hendaye two days later, his family waited. They waited to hear confirmation of his death. They waited for his body to be washed up. All through the rest of that bleak summer, Emma and Nicolas waited. They did not go to the beach. They did not go out. They stayed in the small apartment, and they waited. Nicolas wondered how the news was to be announced to them. A phone call? A letter? A policeman at the door? He could not bring himself to ask his mother. She seemed lost.

The same friends who came the night of his father's disappearance now came every day. They cooked meals for his mother and for him, they did the shopping, they cleaned the kitchen and the bathroom, and they made the beds. They hugged him, kissed him, called him "little fellow." Roxane, Emma's sister, arrived from Belgium with her husband. They stayed in a hotel around the corner. Nina, Lionel, and Elvire Duhamel came from the Riviera and stayed at the Hôtel du Palais. Nina kept saying, "Théo's had an accident.

He will be fine. He's in a hospital somewhere, recovering. We'll soon hear from him." How can she be so sure? Nicolas asked himself, watching his energetic grandmother pace up and down the living room, cigarette in hand, while Emma sat hunched by the phone with a dazed expression. When the phone rang, Emma jumped. She reached for the receiver, trembling, her face a white mask. Nicolas remembered her low voice murmuring over and over again, "No, no news. I'll call you. Bye. Thanks. Bye. . . ."

Every evening, Nicolas cried himself to sleep, clutching the Hamilton Khaki watch with all his might. Friends and family stayed late or all night. There were voices from the next room and the waft of cigarette smoke till dawn. Sometimes the door would creak open, and he'd feel his mother's tender hand on his forehead; then she'd slip away. The regular beam of the lighthouse flickered over the walls. The lighthouse had always fascinated him, ever since he was a young child. Its strong light helped boats come ashore to safety, even in the worst weather, even in the most treacherous currents. He had seen those crosses at the Rocher de la Vierge, near the Grande Plage, where hapless boats had been pounded to smithereens against the rocks by powerful waves. Why couldn't the lighthouse help his father come ashore? Was his father ever going to come back?

At the end of August, it was time to return to Paris. Emma had classes to start at the Collège Sévigné, and Nicolas had to go back to school. But Emma refused to leave Biarritz. Her husband's body had not been found. This meant that perhaps he was not dead. There was still hope. She repeated this to the police. They were kind to her; they tried to explain that Théodore Duhamel had most certainly drowned, but she would not hear of it. The Collège Sévigné gave her two extra weeks to stay on in Biarritz. But Nicolas had to go back to Paris with his grandparents to begin his school year. He stayed with them in their apartment on boulevard Saint-Germain, where the traffic was so loud, it could be heard through double-glazed windows. One late night, Nicolas could not sleep and overheard a strange conversation. Nina's voice was sharp.

"What are you talking about, Lionel?" she was saying. "Are you out of your mind? How dare you suggest such a thing?"

His grandfather sounded meek. "It was just a thought."

"A very stupid thought," she spat.

"I'm sorry, dearest. I know you hate it when I bring up Leningrad."

"Shut up, Lionel. For God's sake, shut up."

Nicolas had crept back to his room. What had they been quarreling about? What about Leningrad? What had his grandfather meant?

When Emma came back to Paris in mid-September, Nicolas returned to the rue Rollin to be with his mother. She seemed frailer and paler than ever. The apartment, without his father, had turned into a desolate remembrance land. It continued to exude his personality. Cigar smoke lingered in the dining room. Whiffs of Eau Sauvage could be caught in his bathroom, in his bedroom. His closet was bursting with his clothes, and his other things—his trousers, shorts, jeans, his cashmere sweaters, his ties, his shoes, his golf clubs, ski anoraks, gloves, canes, shirts. A bureau drawer held his cuff links, his black Montblanc fountain pen. But not his Doxa Sub watch, which had been on his wrist the day he disappeared.

Emma and Nicolas found themselves still waiting, like they had all summer long. They both went about their lives, schools, meals, but the only thing that mattered was the wait. It was exhausting and unbearable. Emma had been to see Nicolas's teachers to explain the situation. Everyone in class was nice to him. Other students stared at him and whispered behind his back, "His father drowned. But they still haven't found the body." The only person he felt he could trust was François. François's parents, Odile and Michel, and their other children, Victor, Constance, and Emmanuelle, became the only source of comfort in his eleven-year-old life. Every afternoon, after school, he went to their place on the avenue Duquesne, and he felt like he was part of a normal family. For a couple of hours, the dreadful thought that his father might never come back was held at bay. Whenever he got home with the new au pair his mother had hired and she turned the key in the lock, for a split second, Nicolas felt the flutter of a wild hope that his father had come home at last. Théodore Duhamel was wounded, or even maimed, or had lost an eye, but there he was, triumphant, safe. But there was no cigar smoke, no laughter, no father. Only silence.

Just before Christmas 1993, a red-eyed Brisabois came to visit them. He spent an hour crying into Emma's shoulder. How could such a wonderful man have disappeared? How could life be so cruel? Emma said nothing, patting his quivering round shoulders. Nicolas looked away, embarrassed. But the scene became even more embarrassing when Brisabois asked his mother for money, claiming that Théodore Duhamel owed him a rather large amount. Without a word, Emma got up to fetch her checkbook. This scene took place again the following year. Then, no one heard from Brisabois again.

Gradually, Nicolas learned to deal with other people's questions. He learned to say that, yes, his father had drowned, and that, no, his body had not been found. He pronounced the words with detachment. This did not mean he did not care. The distance he put between the words and himself was the only way to protect himself. Four years later, in 1997, after Princess Diana was killed in a car accident in Paris at the end of August, Nicolas watched the funeral on TV as her two sons walked behind their mother's coffin during the procession. Prince William was his age—fifteen. As the entire world sobbed for the dead princess, Nicolas felt the smoldering heat of resentment. Prince William knew his mother was dead. Perhaps he had seen her dead body. Prince William was perfectly aware his mother was in that coffin being carried through the streets of London, with white roses placed upon it, and a card where his brother, Harry, inconsolable, had written "Mummy" in a childish hand. William and Harry were going to be able to mourn her. Nicolas had not been able to mourn his father. Emma and he were still waiting for Théodore Duhamel to walk through the door at rue Rollin or for the phone to ring with news of a body found along the coast near Hendaye that could be his.

The years slipped by and the wait continued. The wait became their prison. Emma could not bring herself to empty her husband's cupboards. For five or six years, Théodore Duhamel's clothes remained in the apartment. From time to time, Nicolas would open the cupboard and look at them. They smelled of stale cigar smoke. And finally, they no longer smelled of anything except dust. What did his mother do with the clothes? He never knew and he did not ask. He was handed the Montblanc pen, which he cherished. But what he would have wanted above all was the orange Doxa Sub watch.

June 12 was his father's birthday. Each year, Nicolas knew his mother would be thinking of him, too, and how old he would be if he were still alive. And his grandmother would, as well, until her death. Each year on August 7, the day his father was last seen, Nicolas awoke with a feeling of dread. He saw himself as a frightened little boy, standing on the balcony, staring out to sea. The questions loomed as large as they had that fateful day: What had happened to his father? Why was he never found?

In 2001, a couple of years before the Italian trip and before he met Delphine, he had a short, intense love affair with a bossy, intelligent older girl, Aurélie. She was studying to become a doctor. The affair had not lasted because of her grueling workload; at least that was the reason she had given him when she decided to move on without him. One evening in early September, as they were at her place, near République, having dinner, she asked him about his father. Her queries were innocent enough at first, but they gradually became more pointed, and Nicolas guardedly asked her what she was driving at. She said she was surprised he and his mother had not asked more questions themselves. "Like what?" Nicolas had spluttered. (He often thought about that scene, recalling the beamed ceiling and picturesque view over Paris rooftops, and Au-rélie wearing a cherry-colored chemise that clung to her full breasts. The scene had later woven itself into *The Envelope,* but in a different form: Margaux having lunch with an ex-boyfriend, and the ex-boyfriend bringing up all the unmentionable questions about Luc Zech's disappearance and the avalanche.) Aurélie had poured them another glass of Chablis and said, "I mean, haven't you ever wondered why your father's body has never been found? Do you re-ally think he drowned? You tell me he was an entrepreneur. What if someone had wanted him dead? What if there was hush money involved?" And this: "Was your father truly happy? Was everything okay in his life? Do you think he could have committed suicide?"

Nicolas had sneered at all this sourly at first. He had never en-visaged those possibilities. But then he remembered Théodore Duhamel's shockingly white face that afternoon on the Champs-Elysées, and his strange telephone conversation with Brisabois at Fouquet's. "Brisabois. It's me. I saw him on the Champs-Elysée . . . What the fuck are you going to do about it? Have you thought about the consequences? Have you really?" his father had said. Later, Nicolas thought of those evenings when his father appeared worried, and so did Emma, when money was short, when there was only soup for dinner, and then all of a sudden a "contract" was signed, and money flowed—Brisabois turned up with Ruinart cham-pagne, and his father went to buy caviar at Petrossian to celebrate—until the next difficult "soup period."

That September night in 2001, Aurélie instilled the first doubt in his mind, the first inkling that perhaps his father's death had not been an accident.

"H EY," SAYS A YOUNG feminine voice.

Nicolas looks up from his notebook (in which he has written nothing, as usual) to one of the models for the photo shoot. She has her dark hair done up in a fancy twisted bun, but her face is free of makeup. She is extraordinarily pretty. Nineteen, or twenty. Malvina is asleep in the shade, a little farther off.

The heat is unbearable. It is the hottest moment of the afternoon, and the quietest.

"Hey," he replies, smiling.

"Got a cigarette?"

She has an American accent.

"Sorry, I don't smoke."

She shrugs. "Having fun?" she asks.

She is wearing a blue bikini. Her skin is tawny perfection.

"And you?"

She shrugs again. "Just another boring job. That Carper woman's a Nazi."

"Where are you from?"

"New York City, sir. You a police officer, or somethin'?"

He laughs. She looks at him sideways, impishly.

"You're the writer, aren't you?"

"That's me."

"The Envelope."

She lifts her eyebrows and smiles, baring small white teeth.

"What's your name?"

"Savannah." She rolls her eyes. "No comment." She jerks her chin toward the napping Malvina. "That your girlfriend?"

"Yes."

"She's always asleep."

"Have you been spying on us?"

Savannah looks away. "Kind of."

"How long are you here for?"

"Gone tomorrow, when this thing is over. We're flying to Paris for another shoot."

"How long have you been modeling?"

"Started when I was thirteen. Got spotted in Central Park by a scout. Boring story. Boring job."

"Why do you do it, if you find it so boring?"

"My dad died when I was a kid and my mother's alone, fighting cancer. What I bring in puts her in the best hospital, with the best care."

"Is she getting better?"

"Nope. She's forty and she's going to die. Don't stare at me like that, Mr. Writer. You going to put me in a novel, or what?"

Nicolas chuckles. She is rather irresistible.

"Are you writing a new book?"

He hesitates. Usually, he would have answered, with a serious expression, that, yes, indeed he was. Instead, he says, "I'm pretending to."

Savannah moves closer. She smells of sea salt and cinnamon.

"How come?"

Her voice is soft, friendly. She plays with a tendril of hair escaping from her chignon.

"Everyone thinks I'm writing a book, and I'm not. I'm procrastinating."

"You have writer's block? You're not inspired?"

"No. It's just that I'm lazy. I've become terribly lazy."

"So what are you going to do?"

"When I get back to Paris, I have to tell my publisher the truth. Tell her that this book is one big lie. She's going to be furious."

He thinks of Alice Dor, who has already left two messages. She wanted to know how he was bearing up after reading the Taillefer article. He still hasn't phoned her back. Alice Dor trusts him. She is waiting for the novel, patiently, kindly. For how long?

A waitress appears. Nicolas orders *aqua gassata* with lemon. Savannah is now dangerously close, her shoulder only inches from his own. The terrace is deserted, apart from the sleeping Malvina, hidden from view by a large, bright-cushioned sofa and parasols. Most of the guests have retired to their air-conditioned rooms for a nap, or ventured down to the sea for a swim. It is so hot that Nicolas feels beads of sweat forming on his upper lip. How easy it would be to lean forward and kiss that full mouth. She shares the same thought; he sees it flitting past in her green eyes: the promise of a kiss. Reluctantly, he draws away ever so slightly.

The water is brought to them. Nicolas pours out a glass for her, then one for himself. She says, "My favorite author, apart from you, is Salinger, you know."

"I'm honored."

She comes closer again.

"Salinger hated interviews, newspapers, radio, TV. He was a recluse. He lived in a remote house miles away from the city and grew his own vegetables and wrote for himself."

Nicolas smiles wryly. "Maybe I should try that. But I enjoy company. I'm no hermit. I like keeping a finger on the pulse of the world. I like meeting new people. If I lived in a cave, what would I write about? If I kept to myself, how would I discover what's going on around me?"

"Good point," she says.

Her finger, long and slim, traces the length of the glass. Nicolas tears his eyes away from it. He is fully aware that any minute now, Malvina might stir, open her eyes, and behold him with an astoundingly beautiful girl. He remembers the barman's warning.

He draws away again.

"Relax," she scoffs. "I know you have a jealous girlfriend. I've seen the way she looks at you."

"What about you? Do you have a boyfriend?"

"I have three," she replies seriously, studying her nails. "Anyway, you prefer 'mature' women. It's in every interview I've ever read about you. Older women and watches. Yawn." Another roll of the eyes.

A man calls her name from the upper terrace. "Coming!" she calls back, sighing. "Fun's up. Got to go have my face painted back on for Kapo Carper. Nice talking to you, Mr. Writer. Catch you later."

He watches her leave, admiring the nonchalant swing of her slim hips.

"Another one of your fans?" comes Malvina's weary voice from behind him.

He turns to look at her, bracing himself for the usual battle. She is so pale, he gasps.

"Malve, are you okay?"

"No," she whimpers. "I feel sick again."

He walks her slowly back to the room. She can barely stand. He places her carefully down on the bed, draws the curtain, gives her some bottled water.

"I'm going to call a doctor," he says firmly. "This can't go on. You've been unwell since we got here."

"Just something I ate," she murmurs. "Or the heat."

He calls the reception desk. He is told a doctor will come by in the late afternoon.

"Now you rest," he says, stroking her hair gently. Her forehead feels cool. "Just close your eyes, breathe slowly. The doctor will come and give you some medicine, and you'll be just fine."

"Stay with me," she begs. "Don't leave me. Please." He lies down next to her. She seems more fragile than ever, like a palpitating fledgeling with soft, tender wings. "Tell me you love me. Tell me you love only me."

"You're the only one," he says gently. He cannot bring himself to use the word *love*. The only woman he ever loved was Delphine.

"Tell me you'll never leave me."

He caresses her hair soothingly.

"I'm right here, Malve. Right here by your side."

"Promise me you'll never treat me like Justin did."

"I'll never do that; you know that, Malve."

Justin was Malvina's previous boyfriend, a stuck-up, arrogant guy who quoted Yeats and sounded like Hugh Grant. They had been together for three years. He unceremoniously dumped her after he found out she had started a simple friendship with a class-mate of his. He refused to speak to her ever again and e-mailed her photos of him burning her unopened letters. Then he plastered his own Facebook page with photos of him and a new girl-friend. He never bothered to find out how Malvina was after the breakup. It was as if Malvina had never existed. When Nicolas met Malvina, nine months ago, she was still getting over Justin.

"That girl, what did she want?"

He knows she means Savannah, but still, he asks, "Which girl?"

"The one you were talking to when I woke up."

"Just a girl who said hello."

"One of those models . . ."

"So?"

"Tell me I'm prettier than she is. Tell me."

He kisses her cheek.

"You are the loveliest. Now please rest."

She falls asleep within minutes. If it hadn't been for Malvina's feeling sick, he would have been outside, having a swim, working on his tan. He adores the splendid hour when the light evolves into a mellow gold and the heat recedes. Just his luck to be closed up in a room with his ailing girlfriend. And to think their last day is tomorrow. Malvina's breathing is regular, but he knows it is too risky to look at his BlackBerry. Earlier on, while she was resting by the pool, and before Savannah spoke to him, he had made the most of the quiet lull to catch up on e-mail and social networks.

There had not been a new BBM from Sabina, and he could not help feeling disappointed. Was the fun over? Had she grown tired of their digital exchanges? The Taillefer article had made his fans furious. How soothing it had been to discover the comforting messages posted on his Facebook wall. He scrolled through them, enraptured, feeling as if the stinging wound had been miraculously healed. But when he saw another photograph of himself by Alex Brunel, his wrath and exasperation were rekindled. There he was during the photo shoot, staring at the models with a rapacious smile. It had been taken from quite close, he noticed, so Alex Brunel must have been sitting near, and that thought made him even angrier. His fans loved the photo; it had been "liked" hundreds of times. He decided not to make any comment. On his Twitter feed, there were also references to Taillefer's article, but he skimmed through the Tweets, not wanting to read them in depth. Nor did he Tweet anything. In fact, he had not Tweeted since getting here. Many followers found that very surprising.

He glanced at his fan mail. There was an e-mail from an "S. Kurz" with an attached file. Subject: "VERY VERY PERSONAL." He clicked on it. It was from Sabina. "My BlackBerry is kaput," she wrote. "So I found your e-mail on your Web site and I'm writing to you this way, from my computer. And you know I can't stop writing to you, Nicolas. I need to know you are reading my words and that they excite you. Just thinking about you waiting for my words is erotic. So . . . Today I am wearing a dress that buttons up the front. I'm sending you a photo of the dress. It's pretty, don't you think? It can be opened very quickly by tearing the buttons open. Underneath, I am wearing nothing, as you will see in the second photo. Now tell me, Nicolas Kolt, what you will do to me once you have opened that dress. I want to know exactly."

The first photograph showed her standing in front of a full-length mirror, wearing a demure orange dress that was closed from her cleavage to her knees. Behind her, he could make out a double bed with a pale blue cover, and two black bedside lamps. He could not see her face, only the ash-blond shoulder-length hair and her neck. His heart started to beat faster. Perhaps it would be safer to go into the men's toilet. He checked Malvina and went, his breath short, his sweaty palm wrapped around the BlackBerry.

There was no one in the men's room. He clicked on the second photo. The orange dress was wide open, her hands firmly holding the lapels apart, baring her entire body. This time, he could see her face. She had the same expression—the one that aroused him so—as the day they'd met. The small smile. The intense gaze. The uplifted chin. The white breasts jutted out toward him, as if they craved his touch. She stood with her legs slightly apart, so that he could easily see her naked thighs, belly, and crotch. He e-mailed back from his personal e-mail account, not the fan one, typing as fast as he could: "What I would do to you, beautiful Sabina? I would kneel in front of you, and I would kiss your ankles and then your calves, very slowly, then your thighs, with a very hot, very wet mouth, working my way up to your—" He was interrupted by some-one coming into the men's room. His fingers froze. He waited for a couple of endless minutes. The person finally left. He went back to his e-mail, typing feverishly. "With my tongue, I will take my time to make you come. I want to do that very badly, Sabina. I can almost taste you in my mouth, I am writing this to you hidden in the men's bathroom of the Gallo Nero, and imagining my tongue in you is unbearably exciting." She e-mailed back within seconds: "Send

me a photo of you in the men's room; show me how hard you are."
This time, he was able to photograph his marmoreal erection with
no difficulty. He e-mailed it to her; then he swiftly made himself
come. It was a matter of seconds.

As he left the men's room, heart still thumping, he hastily read
her last e-mail: "Danke. So gorgeous, so appetizing. One day I want
to meet you again in real life, Nicolas Kolt, and I want to make you
come in such a way that you will never forget me. Maybe in Paris,
or if you come back to Berlin. Tomorrow, I will send you another
photo."

As he lies on the bed next to Malvina, Nicolas closes his eyes
and imagines meeting Sabina in Berlin. He imagines the hotel
room, her knock. He thinks of her smell and the feel of her skin.
Before he knows it, tiredness takes over, no doubt due to his short
night and lack of sleep.

A loud buzzer goes off and he takes some time to understand
someone is ringing with insistence at the door. His vision is blurred,
his mouth pasty. What time is it? Where is he? He had the strang-
est dream. His father and he were standing in the rain at the foot
of Victor Noir's tomb. His father's voice, unbelievably clear, was
still ringing in his ears. His father looked exactly as he had the last
time Nicolas had seen him, the day of his disappearance. He
could feel his father's hand on his shoulder, the weight of it.

Nicolas gets up with difficulty to open the door. A man is standing there, holding a briefcase.

"Yes?" says Nicolas, puzzled.

"Dottore Scaretti," says the man.

"Of course, come in."

The doctor silently examines Malvina, taking her blood pressure, listening to her heart, looking into her throat, her ears, prod-
ding her stomach with sure, careful fingers. He does not speak
any English or French. Nicolas is able to explain to the doctor that
Malvina has not been well since she arrived, that she vomited
several times. Perhaps food poisoning? Or some sort of intestinal

flu? The doctor says nothing. When he has finished his examination, he goes into the bathroom to wash his hands. He comes back, sits on the edge of the bed, and writes on a sheet of paper. He hands Nicolas his bill. Then he fishes in his briefcase and gives Nicolas a box. It is a pregnancy test. Nicolas stares at it, then back at the doctor. He points to the box, then to Malvina. The doctor says a couple of sentences in Italian, but he speaks too fast. Nicolas asks him to slow down. The doctor says *"Incinta"* several times and cups his hands in front of his stomach. His gesture is unequivocal.

The doctor leaves. Malvina gets up and takes the box from Nicolas. She is very silent. She locks herself in the bathroom. Nicolas waits, his head in his hands. He does not want to think. He lets his mind go blank. His eyes rove over the room, the cream walls, the large unmade bed, the uneaten fruit. Then, for some reason, he thinks of his dream: he and his father, in the rain, in front of Victor Noir's tomb.

Malvina comes out of the bathroom, and her smile is magnificent. In her hand, a plastic object with a blue cross on it.

"Oh Nicolas," she says breathlessly. "Oh, my love. I'm going to have your baby."

Sunday,
July 17, 2011

Vanitas vanitatum et omnia vanitas

I T WAS WIDELY KNOWN that Nicolas Kolt collected vintage
watches. This was no recent hobby. It was the first detail Nicolas noticed about people, after the color and shape of their eyes. In
the rue du Laos duplex, a small safe was fitted into the back of a
closet, where he kept his precious watches. There was one watch
he never talked about. One particular watch he did not own, one
watch that haunted him and that he thought about nearly every
day: his father's orange-faced Doxa Sub. Capitaine Cousteau's watch.
Robert Redford wore it in *Three Days of the Condor*. The Doxa
Sub was famous for its robustness. It could still function even in
the deepest parts of the ocean, where the pressure was at its highest. Théodore Duhamel had never removed his. He'd kept it on
even to sleep. When Nicolas was a little boy nestling in his father's
arms, he could hear two things: the beat of his father's heart and
the tick of his watch. If his father had drowned—the theory his
entourage seemed to agree upon—then Théodore Duhamel had
slid down to an aquatic void wearing that watch. Had it gone on
ticking even after his father had died, lungs full of salt water? Was

the watch still there today, a rusty relic embedded in sand or encrusted on a reef, while his father's body had disintegrated, nibbled away by sea creatures? Nicolas shared those morbid thoughts with no one. He'd harbored them since August 7, 1993. In the first year of his khâgne, when he read Shakespeare's *The Tempest,* the first lines of Ariel's Song were painfully evocative.

Full fathom five thy father lies;
Of his bones are coral made;
Those are pearls that were his eyes:
Nothing of him that doth fade . . .

During one of his watch quests, he came across an identical model. It happened in 1999, before Hurricane Margaux. The watch was on display in a place on rue de Béarn he liked to visit, if only to window-shop. It looked so uncannily like his father's that he felt compelled to go in and have a closer look. The watch was taken out of the vitrine and placed on a felt tray. He stared at it, dumbstruck, for minutes before he dared take it into his hands and fasten it. The same familiar orange face, the same tick, the same clasp. Should he buy it? It was expensive, but he could get his grandparents, mother, and aunts to participate. If he succeeded in passing his baccalaureat next year, which seemed likely, this would be an ideal present, as well as serve as his eighteenth-birthday gift. He pondered it for a while. Perhaps it would prove disconcerting and morally uncomfortable to be confronted with the orange face each time he glanced at his wrist. Perhaps it would make him think of his father all the more. He slipped it off and carefully put it back on the tray. He left the shop, fighting the overwhelming emptiness he always felt when he dwelled upon his father and his disappearance.

Those "waiting" years, between 1993 and 2003—until Théodore Duhamel was officially declared dead—when Nicolas aged from eleven to twenty-one, were difficult ones for the boy he was and the young man he became. He grew up in the perpetual shadow of his father, and yet his father was no longer there. When he met family friends, there was always an awkward pause and the inevitable exclamation: "Oh! He looks like his father, more and more. . . ." He was aware he had inherited his father's height, his long arms and legs, the shape of his face, his mouth, his nose. Only his mist-colored eyes were Emma's, not his father's blue ones.

His mother had kept the press clippings from the summer of 1993, when *Sud-Ouest,* the local newspaper, published a couple of articles about Théodore Duhamel's disappearance. She stored them in a navy blue cardboard box in her desk, and Nicolas knew exactly where that box was. The articles had become yellow and faded, and he wondered why she had decided not to throw the clippings out. Who was she keeping all this for? He asked her. "One day," she replied, "you will want to know more about your father. This may happen when you become a father yourself, or even before. So I've kept everything. His letters, his photos, his bits and pieces. You can look at this whenever you want."

But Nicolas never did. For more than ten years, he shied away from the box, as if just glancing at it could hurt him and bring up the dull ache, the empty pain. In September 2001, when Aurélie, his girlfriend of the moment, had raised the first questions and doubts concerning the causes of his father's death, he had been tempted to rummage around in the box. But he did not feel ready.

Nicolas was drawn back to the box five years later, when he discovered his father's real name was Fiodor Koltchine. At that time, he no longer lived on rue Rollin with his mother, but on rue Pernety with Delphine, where he'd been since 2004. Emma and he had both been relieved that at the age of twenty-two, he was leaving the family nest. When he had packed up all his belongings, his mother waving at the front door, it had been with a mixture of elation and nostalgia. He had, with his mother's approval, kept his keys to the apartment on the rue Rollin. Whenever he came back to his childhood home, he prudently rang the doorbell, aware that his mother had a life of her own, and not willing to be confronted with it in a manner that might prove to be unpleasant for anyone. His mother was discreet about her lovers. She sometimes named them, but her son rarely saw them. After a while, he forgot to ask. He later became entangled in the giddying ascension of his fame, and his mother's love life did not interest him enough for him to inquire about it.

In October 2006, that same rainy week after the conversation with his mother about his father's real name, he returned to the rue Rollin at lunchtime and rang the bell. He needed to look through the navy blue box. His mother was not there. No doubt she was with her students at the Collège Sévigné. He let himself in and took off his wet shoes in the entrance. The box was in its usual place in Emma's desk. He took it into the kitchen, made himself some tea, and sat down. He was still inwardly reeling from the shock of seeing the name Fiodor Koltchine on the birth certificate and trying to work out the pieces of the puzzle of his father's life. He was not sure why he was doing this, or what for, but he did know that he had to go through the box, that he would not rest or feel at ease until he had found some answers.

Earlier on, he had shared a coffee with Lara on avenue du Maine, near the magazine where she worked, and he had shown her the birth certificate. She had been stupefied. She had fired off questions. Why had his mother kept this from him? Emma could have told him in 1993, when her husband disappeared. Nicolas answered that his mother thought he was too young at eleven to know. Then she had waited until he found out by himself, which was what had happened. His father had never wanted to talk about it with her. Why was the whole matter such a secret? insisted Lara. Who was trying to hide what? From whom? "There is an element of shame, of guilt here," Lara went on, flushed with excitement as the rain continued to patter on the windowpanes of the café. "This is a typical family secret," she whispered, "that everyone tries to hush up for years, and that comes swinging back like a boomerang." Nicolas had placed a cautious palm on her arm. What was she talking about? Wasn't she getting carried away? This was just the banal story of a young girl getting pregnant and quickly marrying another man to give her fatherless child a name. Lara stared at him over her croissant. "Fatherless?" she had hissed. "No child is ever fatherless, Nicolas. Except the Virgin Mary's, of course. But we're not talking about that. We're talking about who slept with your fifteen-year-old grandmother in Leningrad, in 1960. It wasn't a cozy time for teenagers. You couldn't waltz down to the nearest bar and pick up a boyfriend." Nicolas was taken aback. He had never thought of that. He had conveniently forgotten about the Cold War and communism. Later, at rue Rollin, he opened the navy blue box with apprehension. There was nothing in there that his mother had not told him about, he reminded himself. But he soon understood that what he feared the most was the intensity of his feelings. He was afraid of the power of the emotions that would take over once he delved into his father's past. For thirteen years, he had learned to bury everything that concerned his father, to steer away from it, to try to keep the emptiness and longing for him at bay. He had learned to live without his father. As he looked down at the box, he measured now how much he missed Théodore Duhamel. Fiodor Koltchine. He had missed his father for most of his existence. His father, the beautiful stranger.

His mother had filed all the elements in the box. They were labeled "Articles," "Photos," "Important Papers," "Letters," "Notes." He started with the articles, the yellowed *Sud-Ouest* ones.

Parisian entrepreneur Théodore Duhamel, age 33, set out two days ago from the Port des Pêcheurs, Biarritz, to Guéthary on his catamaran, a Hobie 16. He arrived in Guéthary at approximately 10:00 A.M. on August 7, and spent an hour with friends of his, the Australian surf champion Murphy Nash, who resides in Guéthary, and his wife. Théodore Duhamel sailed back to Biarritz but did not come home. His wife, Emma Duhamel, and his son, Nicolas, age 11, have been waiting anxiously for him since. The police and gendarmes have searched the coast from Anglet to Hendaye, with no results.

There was no photograph accompanying this article, but the following one was illustrated with a grainy black-and-white picture of his father, taken in Paris at a dinner party. He was wearing a suit and tie and holding a champagne flute.

CATAMARAN FOUND ON HENDAYE BEACH

The black Hobie 16 belonging to the Parisian entrepreneur Théodore Duhamel (33), missing since August 7, was found yesterday, partially wrecked, on the beach of Hendaye. It was formally identified by Emma Duhamel (34), his wife. The gendarmerie has stated that a body has not yet been found. Théodore Duhamel, according to other boat proprietors, was an experienced sailor and surfer, well accustomed to the area's danger zones. The weather conditions were good and the current on August 7 was not powerful. The Parisian entrepreneur and his family came to Biarritz every summer and rented an apartment overlooking the Côte des Basques. They were popular with the locals, especially the surfing community. According to their surfer friends, the Duhamel couple, parents to 11-year-old Nicolas, had a happy marriage. His wife stated that there was no reason for her husband to take his own life.

Nicolas read the obituary notice in *Le Figaro,* published in the "Carnet du Jour" of August 7, 2003.

Ten years ago, on August 7, 1993, Théodore Duhamel disappeared at sea, off the coast of Guéthary. His name will be added today to the family grave in Division 92 of Père-Lachaise Cemetery.

Mr. and Mme. Lionel Duhamel, his parents

Mme. Théodore Duhamel, his wife

Nicolas Duhamel, his son

Mme. Elvire Duhamel, his sister

Nicolas turned to the notes and letters. The sight of his father's slanted black scrawl was like a slap in the face. Nicolas had not seen it for years and there it was, as if his father had written those sentences moments ago with his Montblanc. Nicolas marveled at the intimate power of handwriting, how personal it was, how enduring. How was it that the handwriting was still there on the paper in front of him, while his father had disappeared without a trace?

He discovered incomprehensible lists of names, places, dates. Entire paragraphs that had been crossed out and rewritten. Nicolas pored over them, hoping for one detail, one clue. But nothing came. His mother had tied a red ribbon around a dozen letters that had her maiden name and an address in the sixth arrondissement on them. He guessed they were the first love letters from his father to her. He did not want to read them. He felt as if he were lifting a curtain on their past intimacy. In the next pile were bills, sums, and invoices. Some of them involved surprisingly large amounts. The tax documents also displayed figures that startled Nicolas. He had no idea his father had earned so much money. He also discovered his father had often paid his income tax too late. He read several long-winded letters to the officials at the tax department, in which his father explained in great detail the complicated reasons why he had not been able to pay what he owed on time. The letters were flawlessly written, with perfect grammar and spelling, which had not been his father's forte. Nicolas understood his mother had probably written them as her husband dictated.

He went on to the photo file. The first one he pulled out was of his parents, dated on the back 1980, taken by a certain Maxime Villanova. A large black-and-white glossy portrait of them, standing up against a white background, no doubt shot at the *Paris Match* studios, where his father had worked when he met Emma. Nicolas had never seen the photo before. Théodore Duhamel, at twenty years old, younger than Nicolas was now, and Emma were magnificent. They wore black leather pants, boots, and black shirts opened to their navels. They had the same long, tousled hair, and pale, perfect faces. They looked like rock stars, an eighties version of Patti Smith and Robert Mapplethorpe.

The following photograph was from a series Nicolas had often seen. He and his father posing in front of the Jaguar, his father smoking his cigar, a proprietary hand on his little boy's shoulder. Then came another unknown one. Nicolas was five or six. They had attended a summer wedding at Arcangues, and they had arrived late. Nicolas smiled as he remembered all those faces turning back to look at them as they walked into the church, his father holding himself tall, like a crowned king, wearing a salmon pink jacket and trousers, with no shirt. His naked tanned chest drew gasps from the other guests, especially the women. Nicolas was dressed in a white-and-blue sailor suit. Emma was not in the photograph. Perhaps she was the one who took it. There were more photographs, which he glanced over, conscious of the quick beat of his heart: the ill-fated Hobie 16 in front of the Hôtel du Palais, on the Grande Plage in Biarritz; Emma and her sister, Roxane, at a fancy dress party; his aunt Elvire the day of her wedding with Pablo, in Sevilla; Nicolas as a baby in a pram at the Jardin des Plantes.

And then there was an old black-and-white one of a plump, dark-haired young girl cradling a toddler in her arms. He had no idea who it could be. The girl did not look like anyone he knew. Nicolas turned it around. He recognized his grandfather's handwriting. "Théodore. Paris, 1961." The round-faced teenager was Zinaïda

Koltchine with her illegitimate child. She was gazing down at the baby with evident pride, but also, thought Nicolas, with an expression of curiosity mingled with wariness. She was very different from what she would later become—a slim, sophisticated bourgeoise. How could she have transformed herself to such an extent? wondered Nicolas. She could only have gone that far because she desperately wanted to. It seemed that when she left the USSR forever in 1961 to become Nina Duhamel in Paris, she also left her former life behind her. Nicolas put the photograph in his wallet.

Looking through the "Important Papers" file, Nicolas stumbled upon a copy of Zinaïda's birth certificate. Nicolas read that her parents, his great-grandparents, were named Natacha Levkin (born Petrograd, 1925) and Vladimir Koltchine (born Petrograd, 1921). He wondered about them. Were they still alive? Did they know who the father of the baby was? How had Zinaïda met Lionel Duhamel, a wealthy young businessman fifteen years her senior? What had Lionel known about his teenage wife's past?

Nicolas took the birth certificate and put it in his pocket. As he sat there in his mother's kitchen, he remembered, for the first time in thirteen years, the conversation he'd overheard in his grandparent's apartment on the boulevard Saint-Germain just after his father disappeared. Lionel's apologetic tone: "I know you hate it when I bring up Leningrad." Had Théodore Duhamel ever questioned his mother, and what had she told him? There were no answers. But those queries became the starting point, unbeknownst to him, of the novel that Nicolas was going to write. They were the foundations he was slowly laying down, without even realizing it, of Margaux Dansor's story.

As he placed the box in his mother' desk and put his damp shoes back on, Nicolas slowly began to see what he had to do in order to understand who his father was, and where Fiodor Koltchine had come from.

NICOLAS LEAVES THE ROOM quietly at dawn, when the sun starts to diffuse its golden rays through the curtains. He has not slept, even for a few minutes. His entire body aches and his head throbs painfully. The thought of Malvina's pregnancy disturbs him to such an extent, it feels like a hangover, which is not the case, even if he did spend most of the night in the bar. He had been too appalled to get drunk. How had he let himself get into this situation? Nicolas wants to bang his head against a wall. He was convinced Malvina was on the Pill. He had even seen her take it before she went to bed. He had asked her once, in the beginning of their relationship, last year, whether she was taking it, because he hated using condoms, and she had replied, yes, she was. He had never doubted her word. Had she forgotten to take it? Had she wanted to do this, to become pregnant with his child? Had she done this to trap him? He remembers how her eyes shone with that strange gleam when she had said, rapturously, the pregnancy test in her hand, that she was going to have his child. *His child.*

He walks down to the beach area. There is no one in sight. It is far too early. There are no deck chairs, no parasols. He sits on the edge of the concrete slab, his feet dangling in the water, and watches the sea. She cannot have this child. It would ruin both their lives. It would ruin the child's life.

His head in his hands, he goes over the events of last night. After the doctor left, Malvina cried with joy, hugging him with all her might. He was too stunned to utter a word. She had called her mother, and he went to stand by the window, shaking. The conversation went on and on. She cooed and giggled ecstatically. He stood there, a rigid statue, horrified. She finally hung up.

"My darling love," she whispered beseechingly, "come to me."

He said firmly, "Malvina, we need to talk."

She frowned. "Don't ruin this lovely moment."

"We need to talk, now," he insisted, trembling, hearing the anger distort his voice. "This can't wait."

She got up from the bed and wound her arms around his neck.

"We'll talk in the morning, okay? We don't need to talk now, do we?"

He sighed with exasperation. "We need to talk right now, Malvina. This can't go on. I'm not going to sit here and not talk about it."

He tried to pry her clinging arms off his neck. She backed away and stared at him, narrowing her eyes.

"Why are you so furious? This is such good news!"

"Good news?" he nearly screamed. "What the fuck?"

"This baby is the best thing that's happened to you, Nicolas Kolt."

And with that, she disappeared into the bathroom. He heard the water running.

"Malvina!" he shouted, rattling the door. She had locked it.

The anger erupted. He could not spend another minute with her in this room. He grabbed his BlackBerry, some cash, and, for some unexplainable reason, the Hamilton Khaki watch, then left, slamming the door. He was so incensed that he did not nod back to the gay couple and the Swiss couple, who were on their way to the bar for predinner drinks. He did not see them. He saw nothing, except how he had been duped. He went to stand on the terrace near the pool. Luckily, there were only a few people there. He sat down on a chair and felt his thighs tremble. What was it? Fear? Rage? Perhaps both. A waiter came to ask him if he wanted something to drink, and he shook his head wordlessly. There was only one person he wanted to talk to right now. There was only one person who could understand him and listen to him. Delphine. He pressed the speed-dial key linked to her name. He imagined her, looking down at her phone, seeing his name flash on her screen. She did not pick up. He got her voice mail, and the sound of her voice still made his heart flutter. He left no message.

Nicolas sat there, shivering with despair. Then the screen lit up and her name appeared. She was calling him back. He fumbled to take the call.

"Sorry about that, Nicolas. Phone was at the bottom of my bag, as usual!"

He was so overjoyed to hear her, he nearly choked.

"Delphine . . ."

"I read that Taillefer article this morning. Ouch."

"Yeah. I read parts of it. Not the whole thing."

"Don't read the whole thing. Where are you?"

"In Italy. And you?"

"In Normandy. With a friend. How's the book coming along?"

He paused, then said, "It's not."

She waited for him to speak. She knew how to do that. How he missed her sense of timing.

"Malvina is pregnant."

She said carefully, "Was this planned?"

"No!" shouted Nicolas. "No, of course not!"

"What are you going to do?"

"I don't know!" he almost wept. "She's overjoyed. She wanted this. I was conned. I'm such an idiot."

"You need to talk to her."

"She won't listen! She thinks this is the best thing that's happened to her! She's fucking overjoyed!"

Delphine kept her calm. "You must be feeling miserable. But let me ask you this. You're not going to like it, but I must ask you all the same."

"Go ahead," said Nicolas.

"Are you sure this is your child?"

He was shocked.

"Well, there is no way of knowing, of course, but I do think so. She is faithful; at least I think she is."

"You may want to think about a paternity test."

Nicolas laughed grimly.

"Delphine, you don't get it. I do not want her to have that child. I'm not going to wait till the child is born to check if it's mine."

"So you don't want this baby at all?"

"No!" he shrieked, beside himself with anger. "I do not want this baby. At all!"

He became aware that the people behind him were staring. He turned away from them.

"Why?" she asked in her calm, quiet tone.

"Why?" he echoed, lowering his voice. How could he tell her? Would she find him even more pathetic? Of course she was going to find him pathetic. He was totally pathetic. Is there a man standing next to her? he wondered. Some guy who's eavesdropping on all this? At the end of the conversation, the guy would question her. She would sigh and say, "That was my ex, the writer." Normandy, she had said. He imagined one of those old-fashioned, charming hotels in Trouville, or Cabourg, an antiquated room with a balcony and a view of the gray-blue sea. At this hour, they were getting ready for drinks downstairs, and Delphine was wearing that green dress he loved, the one that set off her auburn hair and white skin. . . .

As he was still not answering, Delphine went on gently: "Do you love Malvina, Nicolas?"

"No," he said, immediately. "No, I don't love her." He yearned to say, I love you. You. You. I have never stopped loving you. Delphine. You. I have not stopped thinking of you. I miss you so much, it is killing me. He did not say those words, but it seemed to him they had been uttered all the same, and that somehow she heard them as they lingered, unspoken and omnipresent, hanging in the silence between them.

"Then you must tell her," said Delphine. "You must tell her that there is no future with her and this baby. You must tell her now."

Now, as he looks out to sea, Nicolas thinks of Delphine's words, her advice about telling Malvina. It is now Sunday morning, and they are to leave tonight at six o'clock. A car is picking them up to take them to the airport. He has all day, their last day, to talk to her. After his conversation last night with Delphine, Nicolas paced up and down the terrace, his hands clenched. Going back to the room was out of the question. Having dinner with Malvina was, as well. But where could he go? He was locked up in a golden-caged prison of luxury with the elegant guests who were now arriving at the bar in yet another procession of designer dresses and jewels. He did not want to say hello to any of them, so he looked away, to the sea, to freedom. He did not care if Dagmar Hunoldt was there, somewhere behind him; tonight, he had nothing to say to her. Tonight, he had no patience. Dr. Gheza, in a resplendent white blazer, asked him if everything was all right and if Signorina Voss was better. Nicolas replied, unsmiling, that yes, thank you, she was better. Dr. Gheza announced, with a Chesire cat–like grin, that tonight was Samba Night, an exclusive concert for the happy few, with a Brazilian band coming to play just for them. He was very much hoping that Signor Kolt and Signorina Voss would join in the fun. Before Dr. Gheza could add another word, Nicolas cleared his throat, muttered, "Excuse me," and promptly walked away from the bar, to the dismay of Alessandra and her mother. He wandered into the lobby, trying to give a purpose to his step, and sat down despondently on one of the sofas, picking up a magazine and leafing through it without seeing it. What was he going to do with himself this evening? The last person he wanted to see or to speak to was Malvina. Yet how could he get away from her for a couple of hours? They were on an island. He was stuck. He did not even want to check his BlackBerry, which lay in his pocket, ignored. The woman behind the reception desk smiled at him. Her name tag read *Serafina*. An idea came to him. He leaped to his feet. He asked Serafina if there was any chance he could dine somewhere else than at the Gallo Nero. She replied, still smiling, that of course that was possible. A boat could take him anywhere he wished along the island's coast. There were some charming restaurants on the other side, only thirty minutes away. Should she make reservations for him? No, no, he said, delighted to hear this. No reservations. When was the driver free? Serafina said that Davide was at his disposal and ready when he was. Nicolas was overjoyed. Where should he meet Davide? At the pontoon, she told him, thinking that Signor Kolt really did have the most magnificent smile. He thanked her and then went straight to the James Bond elevator. He could hear the Brazilian band starting up with "Mas Que Nada." Who cared? He was escaping. He chuckled with glee. Down at the pier, a tall young man his age, wearing a black jacket, awaited.

"*Buona sera,* Signor Kolt," said the young man, giving a polite little bow. "*Sono* Davide."

Nicolas smiled back, thrilled, and stepped into the glossy black Riva, feeling his spirits soar. The boat headed out to sea, motor growling in a throaty crescendo. Nicolas stood next to Davide, shoulder to shoulder. The wind whipped his hair and seawater sprayed over his face. He glanced back at the Gallo Nero, at the glittering lights of the terrace shining out to them, and he felt like a bird set free, breathing heady whiffs of sea air. Davide asked him where he wanted to go, shouting to be heard, and Nicolas shouted back, he had no idea, Davide should choose for him, a simple place to eat and drink. "Somewhere uncomplicated," he yelled. "Somewhere not like back there." He gestured toward the receding Gallo Nero. Davide nodded, and Nicolas felt the camaraderie between them; he felt that somehow Davide understood that he needed to get away, even if Davide had no idea what Nicolas was running away from—a pregnant girlfriend and an overdose of luxury. He was glad that he had not had time to change for dinner, that he was still wearing his bathing suit under his shorts, his black Gap T-shirt, and his Converse sneakers. He looked like any other twenty-nine-year-old guy on a summer evening.

Davide drove on swiftly, the boat rising and falling, sometimes landing with a jerky bump, which made Nicolas careen into him, and he had to steady himself, which made them both smile, sharing that unspoken boyish complicity that warmed his heart, and then Davide let Nicolas put his hands on the wheel, and he felt the exhilarating vibrations of the motor filter up through his palms. Around them, the shadows grew as the sun backed down behind the hill, the water deepened into a blackish blue, and the hot air was suddenly laced with cooler strands. Davide slowed down, approaching a small town with a high circle of faded pink and blue houses. Nicolas made out a large, quaint villa with a crumbling facade, a leafy garden, and an arbor with tables and chairs beneath it. Davide pointed to the villa. "Villa Stella," he said. "Very nice. You will like it." Then he handed him a card with a number on it. Nicolas was to call him when he wished to return to the hotel. Nicolas thanked him. Before he got to the wrought-iron gates, he sent a text message to Malvina. "We really need to talk. Gone somewhere else to think things over. Back later." Then he pocketed the phone and Davide's card.

He was seated under the arbor at a large table with other customers. It was a noisy, joyful crowd, with young children, but that did not bother him tonight. The families were Italian. There were no tourists. A teenaged girl, who spoke little French or English, smiled at him shyly as she offered him a glass of white wine. She explained there was a set menu. Gnocchi to begin with, and then fish. She couldn't say what the fish was, but she assured him it was very good. Nicolas was delighted. He sat back, sipped the wine, which was chilled and dry, the way he liked it, and looked around him. A large fig tree sent its enticing perfume his way. Through its green luxuriance, he could glimpse a silvery moon. He watched the Italian families laugh and be merry. He watched the young girl serve the dishes with careful yet awkward gestures, which made her all the more touching. The meal he ate at the Villa Stella was one of the best he'd ever had in his life. It was simple, rustic food, lovingly prepared by some buxom mamma in the kitchen, a faded apron tied round her ample hips, dyed black hair drawn back in a bun. It brought back his Ligurean summer with François. He loved the fact that the table surface felt a little greasy, that there were still crumbs from the previous customer's meal, that the noise level was deafening. This was the Italy he preferred, the real Italy, nothing to do with the antiseptic perfection of the Gallo Nero. He did not feel lonely as he sat there, drawing a sensual pleasure from each slow mouthful. He did not think of Malvina, of the baby. He did not think of Laurence Taillefer's article, of his mother and Ed, of Dagmar Hunoldt. He did not think of Delphine, of Alice Dor. He did not think about the nonexistent novel he had been lying about for so long.

He laid the Hamilton Khaki on the table in front of him and thought of his father, Fiodor Koltchine, and how he would have done anything in his power, how he would have invoked any god, succumbed to any voodoo, risked any occult pact in order to summon his father to his table at the Villa Stella tonight.

As he spent his days hunched in front of his computer, not writing, surfing relentlessly, feeling woolly-brained and lethargic, Nicolas became obsessed with the writing processes of other authors—living authors, dead authors, best-selling ones, lesser-known ones, French, British, Indian, Spanish, Italian, Canadian, Turkish, American authors, any authors. He scoured the Internet for details on how they wrote. Many, it seemed, were inspired by events, conversations, or other books. And once the idea took form, how did they actually write their novels? Nicolas thirsted for each and every element of information. How long did it take? Did they write notes? Did they research? Did they plan an outline? Was it detailed? Or did they simply sit down and write, like he had written *The Envelope*? Nicolas learned that Russell Banks did not enjoy writing fiction on his computer, as it cramped his flow. He wrote his first drafts by hand, with a rough outline to map his way. Nelson Novézan admitted that writing was such an agonizing business that he needed alcohol, drugs, and sex to get on with it and locked himself up in five-star hotel rooms. Margaret

Atwood, who Tweeted as much as Nicolas did, printed out her chapters and stacked them on the floor, changing their order when she needed to. When she got an idea for a novel, she had to write it down on the first scrap of paper she could find, even if it was a paper napkin. He discovered that Orhan Pamuk also wrote by hand, following a structured plot he doggedly stuck to. Michael Ondaatje literally clipped and pasted entire paper paragraphs into multilayered notebooks. Kazuo Ishiguro edited ruthlessly, cutting out parts that were over a hundred pages long. Jean d'Ormesson did the same, salvaging a mere three pages out of three hundred one summer. Katherine Pancol wore a pen around her neck to jot down ideas, ate chocolate and sipped tea while she worked. William Faulkner drank whiskey. F. Scott Fitzgerald drank too much. W. H. Auden swallowed Benzedrine. Charles Baudelaire had to wrap his aching head in strips of cloth dipped in sedative water. Emile Zola wrote best at Médan, his country home by the Seine. Daphne du Maurier found her inspiration at Menabilly, her Cornwall estate, where she wrote in a gardener's hut under the trees in order to get away from her children. Ernest Hemingway delivered five hundred words a day, every day. Ian McEwan, one thousand words. Tom Wolfe, eighteen hundred. Stephen King, two thousand. James Joyce needed one full day just to produce a couple of sentences. Georges Simenon wrote a novel every four months and found the names of his heroes in the phone book. Vladimir Nabokov wrote on index cards. Virginia Woolf, Victor Hugo, and Philip Roth wrote standing up. Truman Capote had to lie down with a coffee and a cigarette. Roald Dahl slid into a sleeping bag before sitting on his chair. Salman Rushdie wrote first thing in the morning, wearing his pajamas at the desk. Marcel Proust wrote in bed late at night. So did Mark Twain. Haruki Murakami started to write at 4:00 A.M. So did Amélie Nothomb, using a blue ballpoint pen. Anthony Trollope from 5:30 A.M. to 8:30 A.M. Amos Oz took a forty-five minute walk at 6:00 A.M and then got to work. Joyce Carol Oates preferred to write before breakfast. Toni Morrison wrote at dawn, in order to watch the sun come up. John Steinbeck puffed away at a pipe. Guillaume Musso listened to jazz. Dorothy Parker typed with two fingers. Serge Joncour wore earplugs and lifted dumbbells. Simone de Beauvoir wrote eight hours a day, pausing for lunch. Paul Auster, six hours. Emily Dickinson wrote on a tiny desk. Joanne Harris, in a stone shed built by her husband. Marc Levy, on a table made from an old door placed on trestles. The Brontë sisters, in their dining room. Nathalie Sarraute and Ismail Kadare, in cafés. P. D. James, in her kitchen. Jane Austen, in a room that had a squeaky door, which warned her of anyone's arrival. Gustave Flaubert rewrote his sentences over and over again. Gabriel García Márquez could work only in familiar surroundings and never in hotels or on a borrowed typewriter. Annie Proulx started her stories by writing the ending first. Delphine de Vigan needed a long breather between two novels. Maupassant needed women; Cocteau, opium. Nicolas stopped researching. All the information he gleaned ended up depressing him. His feelings of inadequacy increased tenfold.

As he sat enjoying his meal at the Villa Stella, Nicolas tried to analyze the reasons why he couldn't summon the energy to write. Was it only because he had been lured into the gluey and inextricable trap of the Internet and social networks? Hadn't he been eviscerated by three years of a nonstop book tour? Perhaps his fame had in truth transformed him into the vain and uninteresting person Roxane and François were now convinced he was. Or was it because he was no writer, just a product, as the Taillefer article had so harshly pointed out? The taste of limoncello was sweet and lemony on his tongue. He wished this starry night under the fig tree could last forever. One of the Italian families was celebrating a birthday, and he watched it all, the cake, the candles, the faces gathered around their loved one, the singing, the cheering, the kisses, the embraces, the opening of presents. He could describe this so easily, the grandparents, regal and benign, the storm of boisterous children, the salt-and-pepper father, the mother beaming with pride, the young boy who was fifteen today, not yet a man, but full to the brim with the promise of swagger and style. He watched the father reach over and ruffle his son's hair, and once again he felt the ache for his own father. He thought of everything he owed to Fiodor Koltchine. If he had never seen his father's real name on the birth certificate, he would never have written *The Envelope*. He took a while to think this over. If he had never written that book, would he still be living with Delphine and Gaïa over the post office, on the rue Pernety? Would he still be a private tutor? It seemed impossible to go back to that old life, however charming some elements of it had been. Hurricane Margaux had spoiled him. He was now used to luxury, to flying in business class, to the best hotels. He'd had no idea about the strange and unexpected path he was about to take when the book was published, about how a book could change a life.

He really was extraordinarily shiftless, he thought, uncomfortably, as he watched the Italian family leave the restaurant. This could not go on. He must force himself, exert discipline, stop being so idle. It was all there, at his fingertips. If only he had the stamina to do it! He could write about a luxury seaside hotel and its elegant guests; he could write about a famous publisher and her unexpected appearance and what would ensue; he could write about an uninspired author; he could write about his ex, her hips in the shower, her perfect timing, and how he still loved her; he could write about an absolute cretin being trapped by a pregnant girl-friend; he could write about a sultry housewife from Berlin; he could write about his mother's mysterious love life. He could write about anything; he could write about everything. He had done it once. He could do it again, if he got his act together. Instead of thinking about it, he had to do it—physically do it. Write it. Rascar Capac's blue haze was out there somewhere. He had only to track it down and get to work.

When Nicolas called Davide to go back to the Gallo Nero, it

was late. They sailed through the darkness, gliding over the black sea. This time, Nicolas sat in the back and observed the cloudless sky, the stars. When they arrived, he thanked Davide, clapping him on the back. He had nothing to tip him with, as he had left a large tip for the young blushing waitress, but Davide did not seem to mind. He said that if ever Nicolas wanted another ride, he should just call him. Nicolas walked up to the bar. The Brazilian party was over, but the bar was still full. He noticed new faces he had not seen before. Sophisticated Spaniards, one woman, pretty, and three men. Her husband, brother, and father, he guessed. A French family, the image of refined elegance; the mother small, lithe, and tanned, with black hair touched with silver, the balding but dashing father wearing a pink shirt and beige trousers, and two sleek children in their early twenties. The beautiful Natalie Portman sisters were back, each with an eager suitor on her arm. Saturday night was a busy night at the Gallo Nero. Or was it Sunday now? Nicolas checked his watch. It was. He had no intention of going back to the room and confronting Malvina. He ordered sparkling water from Giancarlo, who intuitively understood his mood was awry tonight. The blond American ladies were sitting not far off, heavily made up, their necks cluttered with jewelry, martinis in hand. He could not help listening to their conversation. Their voices were so loud that everyone was listening to them, or was forced to. Were they really talking about a beauty parlor where they'd had their pubic hair dyed? He had to make sure. They were. When they saw him turn around, they shrieked with laughter and sent air kisses to him. The next thing he knew, Giancarlo was handing him a martini.

"This is from the American ladies," Giancarlo murmured. "I think they like you."

Nicolas turned around again and smiled at the ladies. Then he took his drink and went to join them. They welcomed him warmly. Their names were Sherry and Mimi. Sherry was from Palm Springs, and Mimi was from Houston. They were friends and widows. They punctuated each sentence with a giggle and a double flounce of their hair, like headbangers from a hard-rock band. Nicolas was confused by this at first. Then he understood that they did it in order to convey emotion, as their skin was so tightly stretched over their cheekbones and their eyelids practically stitched open, like Alex DeLarge in *A Clockwork Orange,* giving them the glassy, fixed expressions of dried-out mummies.

"Of course we know who you are," gushed Sherry, baring her impeccable white teeth, "and we love, love, love and totally adore you, but we are not going to bother you with that."

"You already have far too many fans here," Mimi went on, waving her crimson-nailed fingers, "all those people who have read your book."

"And all those people who saw your movie!" gushed Sherry.

"It's not my movie," corrected Nicolas, as he always did; "it's Toby Bramfield's movie. He's the director."

"Oh my God, you were so cute in that movie," rhapsodized Mimi, clutching her ringed hands to her inflated bosom. "In that scene where Robin Wright sees her father's real name for the first time, you're right behind her, aren't you?"

Nicolas nodded, patiently. How many times had he heard that sentence? Impossible to count.

"Mimi, honey, give the poor sweetie a break, okay?" hissed Sherry, poking her friend's shoulder. "He's here on vacation, remember? Time to relax!"

"Relax?" echoed Nicolas ironically. "I wish."

They both did a bit of heavy head bashing so he could understand they were upset.

"Why?" they asked in lugubrious sisterly chorus. "What happened?"

"Forget it," he said, taking a gulp of the martini. "I want to hear about you. When did you arrive? Do you like it here?"

It was like pressing a button. He sat back and listened. They loved it here. How could they not love it here? They loved the spa, the bar, the rooms, the view, the food, the service; they loved the whole thing. As they babbled on, Nicolas was reminded of his first book tour to the United States, in 2009, when *The Envelope* hit the *New York Times* list. He had never been to America. The first stop was New York City, then Washington, Atlanta, Miami, L.A., and San Francisco. Alice Dor had gone with him, accompanying him during the full two weeks of the tour. He had just broken up with Delphine, or rather, she had just left him, and he boarded the plane in a red-eyed stupor. He had an affair in every city, discreetly, of course, as Alice was never far and he didn't want her to think he was a heartless womanizer. Alice, being close to Delphine, knew about the separation and was aware it had been Delphine's decision. Nicolas's favorite U.S. affair was with Norma, in New York. They met at a party given by his American publisher, Carla Marsh, on the rooftop terrace of the brand-new Standard Hotel, in the Meatpacking District. He met his translator for the first time and the team who had designed the cover, as well as the entire marketing staff. Norma was a photographer, covering the event for a magazine. A couple of years older than he, she was a willowy brunette with a purposeful stride. She had taken pictures of him all evening, until he had begged for mercy. They spent the rest of the evening walking downtown, wandering through the Village, stopping in bars for a drink, getting steadily tipsier, and when they at last reached her place in Brooklyn Heights, very late, by taxi, he was too jet-lagged and too drunk to manage to kiss her or even to take her in his arms, although he very much wanted to. When he woke up the next morning, he was confronted with the most stupendous view of New York City he could ever have imagined. Norma's family had lived here for forty years. But none of them— her grandparents, her parents, her brother and sister—could ever have expected what they would witness on September 11, 2001. "It was like being a helpless spectator sitting in the best seat at the most horrifying, fascinating, and evil performance in the world," Norma said as Nicolas sat up in the bed, rubbing his eyes, wordlessly staring at the city glistening in its silver splendor. "I felt at first I could not photograph what I was seeing. It was horrendous. We saw it all, from the first plane striking at eight-forty-six A.M. to the second tower crashing down. We stood here, all of us, thunderstruck, then screaming like crazy. I can still smell what the wind was sending our way—burning ashes, smoke, huge clouds of gray dust. Then my hand reached out for my camera. I took the photos. I had to. I cried as I took them, but I had to. My mother yelled at me, appalled. She said, 'How can you do this, Norma? People are dying.' And my father said, 'Let her take them. That's what she knows how to do; that's what she does: She takes photos. Let her do that.'" Norma showed the photographs to him. They were in a large black album. They were beautiful, and horrible. Looking at them made her cry softly. Nicolas took her hand and stroked it as she cried. After a while, Norma said, smiling through her tears, "You're so cute, you Frenchie." She kissed him on the mouth, lingeringly. "Now please do what you've come here to do." America loved him. The Frenchie. The tall, dark Parisian with the delightful accent. They loved him, his book, his looks, him. His six-city tour was a roaring success. Readers stood in line for hours to get their book signed, handed him letters, pictures, cards, flowers. But from that first triumphant voyage to America, what he remembered most vividly, what he enjoyed thinking about the most, was Norma, the long-legged photographer from Brooklyn Heights. Her tears, her sensitivity. But above all, the combined grandiose vision of the great city and Norma's sinuous back, her rounded hips as he took her from behind in front of the view.

Mimi and Sherry were indefatigable. They ordered more martinis, which he did not touch, and chattered the night away. He listened, or appeared to listen, but his mind wandered to the room where Malvina slept. Pregnant Malvina. A loathsome sensation of dread invaded him. The bar slowly emptied; the American ladies left at last, kissing him affectionately and patting him on the cheek, as if he were their grandson. Only the Spaniards remained, smoking into the night. The Spanish woman was very beautiful—glistening hair, perfect tanned features, glowing eyes. Nicolas gazed at her through the smoke, incapable of going back to the room. She finally left with her three men. Giancarlo closed up the bar and came to say good night.

Nicolas wandered aimlessly around the terrace. It was getting on toward three o'clock. Everyone at the Gallo Nero was asleep. There were no boats out at sea tonight. Too late. He went to stand by the stone steps that led to the beach area. A cool, perfumed breeze blew at his hair. The water called out to him, beckoning. Hastily, he removed his shoes, T-shirt, shorts, and, on an impulse, his bathing suit—there was no one around, after all—and left them in a little bundle. The water on his naked body was a satiny delight. When was the last time he'd done that? Midnight dips in the nude? He couldn't even remember. Probably with Delphine. He swam for a while, then hauled himself out of the water and dried himself with his T-shirt. He shivered. He welcomed the cool sensation. He pulled on his bathing suit and shorts. When his hands were completely dry, he checked his BlackBerry. A text message from his mother: "Hello! Give me a call. Love." He thought of her and Ed. He imagined the boat, the sea, the port, the throng, the drinks in the evening, his mother in those long linen dresses she wore in the summer. He wondered how old Ed was. Why did this bother him so much, when he himself preferred older women? Would he feel less uncomfortable if his mother was dating a man of her own age, or older? An e-mail from Alice Dor: "Nicolas, you haven't been returning my calls. Please let me know that everything is all right. I am worried. That Taillefer woman is notorious for that kind of article. It must not get to you or discourage you in any way. Please call so we can discuss it. Are you enjoying the Gallo Nero? How is the book doing? I'd love now for us to talk about it. I do feel I've given you enough time to find your way into it. Please get back to me. All best, Alice." He sighed as he read this. He was expecting this reaction, but the fact that he had seen it coming did not make the situation any easier. Nicolas knew he could not put off his conversation with Alice any longer. This was the first time she'd mentioned the book directly. There could be no more stalling. He had to come out with it. He had to tell her the truth. The idea of it made him want to curl up and wither away. What was Alice Dor going to make of his lying? He loathed disappointing her. He could not face letting her down. But he had been doing just that, letting her down, behind her back. Letting her think there was a book. Letting her pay him that enormous sum for nothing. He toyed with idea of replying to her e-mail. No, he'd do it tomorrow. So many things to do tomorrow. Confront Malvina. Confront Alice Dor. Bloody Sunday, he thought, grimacing in the dark.

A recent e-mail from Lara: "Hey, man, how are you? Just saw on Facebook that you're living it up in some gorgeous hideaway. How's the book? When are you back? I'm stuck in Paris and going crazy. All people talk about in this shitty magazine is what DSK did to that maid in the hotel. I mean, so what! Call me or text me. Miss you. L." Alarmed by the Facebook reference, Nicolas went straight to his Facebook page. He was horrified to see that two new photos had been posted by Alex Brunel. One was of him and Davide roaring off in the motorboat. It had already reaped hundreds of "likes." The other, posted not even an hour ago, was of him at the bar just after Mimi and Sherry had left, staring wistfully toward the beautiful Spanish woman. Why hadn't he been able to spot Alex Brunel? He mentally went over the events of the night. But the bar had been full, and he hadn't taken everyone in, and why should he have, after all? He had only noticed the new people. The French family. The Spaniards. Who else had been there? He thought hard. Maybe the German couple. Maybe Alessandra and her mother. He couldn't remember. There were more reactions on Twitter to the Taillefer article, which he did not have the courage or the curiosity to read. Then the little red light flashed, indicating he had a new e-mail. His personal account. It was from Sabina. Before he opened it, he made absolutely sure he was alone. He walked up and down the beach area quickly, using the BlackBerry to guide his way like a torch. It was pitch-black. Nobody was there. Alex Brunel was not spying on him. He was completely alone. He was safe.

Nicolas went to sit on the far edge of the concrete slab, close to the cliff. From there, he could not be seen, even from above. He smiled in the dark. The BlackBerry glowed in his hand like a strange jewel. He opened Sabina's e-mail tremulously. It was a photograph of her on a large double bed—the same bed as in the previous photograph of her in the orange dress. Sabina was naked, her hair tousled, her back arched, on all fours on the bed. He did not know who had taken the photo (her husband? a lover?), if it was an old one, a new one. He did not care. The effect of the photo was instantaneous. He wrote back, pleadingly, "More. Please. Now." Another e-mail came flying in. The same bed, the same pale blue cover. But this time, Sabina was on her back. There was nothing left to the imagination. It was all there, exposed in its luscious rosy glory. And these words: "Now tell me, Nicolas Kolt, exactly what you would do to me right now if you were really here. And please, no romance." What would he do to her? As he began to touch himself, staring down at the photo glowing in the dark, he knew exactly what he would do to her. He would ravage her. It would be as simple as that. There would be no tender caresses, no foreplay. No making sure she was on the same level, no being worried she was paces behind. No being careful about going too fast, about hurting her, no wearing a condom. He could do exactly what he wanted in his own personal dream world. The orgasm was so fast, so powerful, he nearly dropped the phone. It took his breath away for a few seconds. He had to go back into the water to clean himself up. Then he wrote to her, his breath still short, describing with fast, furious sentences what that photograph had inspired in him. He did not tone it down. He wrote it as it came. He did not care about the typos. Even if they were obscene words, he did not steer away

from them. No romance, she had stated. He did not fear her reaction. Never in his life had Nicolas Kolt written anything so pornographic, so steamy, to a woman. At the end of the e-mail, he
wrote, "Can you call me? Soon? I want to hear your voice. I want
to hear you come. Call me." And he added his number.

When he got back to the room, very late or very early, there was
a note for him on the pillow. Malvina was fast asleep. He took the
note into the bathroom to read it. "I am so happy. Our baby. Our
baby! I love you. Malvie."

"HELLO, HERMES," COMES THE low rumble of an unmistakable voice.

Nicolas, startled, looks up. Dagmar Hunoldt, wearing a white bathing suit, goggles, and a bathing cap, is smiling down at him, a mountainous pale form against the blue sky.

"What about a swim?" she says.

Without waiting to find out whether Nicolas is coming or not, she climbs down the ladder and flings herself into the water. She moves away with an energetic backstroke. Nicolas discards his bathrobe and plunges in, following her. The beach area is still deserted. They are the only ones in the sea. The water is cool this morning, vivifying and choppier than usual. Nicolas finds that keeping up with Dagmar Hunoldt is difficult. She seems to have a secret inner strength that keeps pushing her forward. He acknowledges his lack of sleep but is irked by the fact he has to swim as hard as he can to keep abreast. The woman is past sixty. How does she do it? She is heading for the large reef, at least half a mile away. Nicolas grits his teeth with the effort. It would be too humiliating for words if he had to return to the shore. They are now far from the Gallo Nero. How foolish, how proud can he get? This is ridiculous. All this to keep up with the great, the unique, the one and only Dagmar Hunoldt. All this to impress her. How much longer can he hold out? And, dreadful thought, each stroke outward means another stroke inward. He is already thinking about the way back. He feels drained. He looks up and sees with relief that the reef is straight ahead, coming nearer and nearer. Dagmar Hunoldt is pulling herself onto it, clambering up with the clumsy power of a polar bear. Nicolas's fingers at last grasp the rough surface of the large rocky reef, and he nearly cries out with joy.

"Come on up, Hermes," she calls, taking off her bathing cap and smoothing back her white hair.

Nicolas tries to quiet his ragged breath and crawls up the reef, all the way up, to where she is sitting. He crouches next to her, and wishes he could stop his lips and hands from trembling.

"Did you enjoy that?" she asks after a while.

"I did," he replies, still breathless. "But you're quite a swimmer. It's not easy keeping up with you."

A slow, sensual laugh.

"I was born a swimmer. My mother always said I knew how to swim before I could walk or talk."

They both look back at the Gallo Nero, an ocher spot on the gray cliff. Nicolas wonders how he is ever going to manage the swim back. He might as well make the most of the rest they are having now. But what if she suddenly wants to get going? He will have to stall her. Ask her questions. Prevent her from getting up and swimming away.

"Where did you learn how to swim?" he asks.

"Up north. Where I was born."

"Isn't the water very cold there?"

"It is. But you get used to it. What about you? Where did you learn to swim?"

If Dagmar Hunoldt knew anything about him, she would have known this. She would have known, as the entire world knew, that Nicolas Kolt spent his childhood summers in Biarritz, that he learned how to swim at the Port Vieux with his father. She would have known, like millions of readers, that his father drowned in the summer of 1993. She was obviously sticking to her little game. Pretending not to know him. Well, he could play that game, too. He could also pretend he had no idea who she was. Why hadn't he thought of that before? He nearly laughs out loud with triumph.

"I learned to swim with my father," he replies. "I was six or seven years old. South of France."

"Are you French?" she asks, still gazing out to the Gallo Nero.

"Yes," he says.

Of course she knows he is French. She knows he had to prove he was French in 2006, because his father was born in Russia and his mother in Belgium. That's how he got the idea for the book. She knows that, crafty, cunning woman.

"And you live in Paris?" she goes on.

"Yes. What about you?"

A seagull circles above their heads and they look up to it as it flies near, then swoops away.

"Oh, here and there," she says evasively. She lies back on a flat part of the reef, closes her eyes, and sunbathes. He wants to do the same, but there are no more flat bits for him to recline on. So he remains where he is, sitting next to her. He looks down at her massive body. Even from very close, there is nothing flabby about Dagmar Hunoldt. Her skin shines with sunblock, giving it a milky, translucent hue. He is curious about her love life. Is she with a man or a woman right now? When was the last time she made love? Who was the last person to glide between those parted, heavy thighs? What is she like in bed? What does she do best? His stomach rumbles loudly and he remembers he hasn't had breakfast. His thoughts stray to Malvina, to the unpleasantness of the scene that will take place later on. How do you tell a woman you don't love her and you don't want her child? He can already see Malvina's heart-shaped face crumpling up in agony.

"Is this your first time at the Gallo Nero?" asks Dagmar Hunoldt.

Thinking about Malvina is banished for the moment. He is thankful.

"Yes," he replies. "And you?"

"I came here long ago, with a friend. It hasn't changed. It has a timeless perfection to it. The ideal place for an epicurean like me."

"I don't think poor old Epicure would have enjoyed it at all."

She sits up and turns around to glance at him, moving the straps of her bathing suit down across her shoulders. He looks at the pure white skin.

"Really? Why?" she asks.

"The Gallo Nero is far too luxurious for Epicure," says Nicolas. "He was into frugality. He much rather preferred a cool glass of water to quench his thirst than a celestial Château d'Yquem."

"You're saying that we have deviated from the original meaning of what epicurism really is?"

"We have indeed," replies Nicolas, fingering the raspy surface of the reef. "Nowadays, an epicurean is a fat guy with a cigar snoring in a hammock after a six-course meal washed down with gallons of wine."

Another laugh. She goes on. "Well, I did mean what I said. I am a complete epicurean when I come here. In the noble sense of the word, not the fat guy in the hammock. I'm not referring to the food, however good, or the service, however remarkable. I mean that when I am here, I am away from the turbulences of the outside world, from the tragedy and chaos that rage on in our cities. When I am here, I treasure rare moments of precious serenity."

Dagmar Hunoldt pauses and turns her gray-blue eyes to his. He stares back at her. How can he confide he feels precisely the same? It would be like sucking up to her, like groveling. Her words strike a chord deep within him. He longs to tell her. But perhaps that's what she is striving for. Perhaps that is her way of seducing him. Of winning him over. Of making him leave Alice Dor for her. How can he make sure? He has no way of knowing. He can only sit here on that reef and listen. Her voice is gentle and dreamy. He feels he could listen to it for hours.

"When I swim here, when I am in the water, I feel a sort of communion with nature. Even if I swim fast, even if I push myself, I am at one with the sea. I love to swim; I swim every day, wherever I am, even in swimming pools that reek of chlorine and sweaty armpits. Here, swimming is like going back to my childhood. The pleasure I feel when I come out of the sea, when I sit down to rest, when all my limbs are crying out for mercy, is overwhelming. I bask in the sun, like I am doing now, and there is nothing more exquisite. If I were to describe it to you, Hermes, I would say this. The pleasure I feel at the Gallo Nero is a delicious, dreamy summer afternoon after wild, violent lovemaking."

She gets up, and Nicolas knows she is about to take off. He reaches up to touch her hand.

"No, wait," he says. Her fingers linger in his for just a moment. "I want to hear more. About you and Epicure."

This is only a partial lie. Although he dreads the long swim back, he wants her to go on talking. He wants this moment on the reef with her to last longer, even if it is only for a few more minutes. Is he falling under her spell? Isn't this what Dagmar Hunoldt does to writers? She acts like no other publisher. She is one of a kind. What was that sentence he read in a magazine? "Her entourage considers her utterly ruthless, extraordinarily intelligent, and totally perverse."

He stands up next to her. The breeze blows at them, salty and cool. She looks almost beautiful in the pale morning light. Her clear-cut profile and its chiseled features have a regal purity. Being near Dagmar Hunoldt feels like being sucked into another planet's orbit. A frightening and alluring pull. He is standing so close to her now that the white skin of her arm is grazing his chest. He does not feel the tickle of the familiar sexual thrill, but something else, a strange osmosis, an unexpected communion that unsettles him.

"Forget the fat guy in the hammock," whispers Dagmar Hunoldt, and Nicolas leans in closer still to catch every word. "What does he know of Epicure? Nothing. He is like those rich Romans who vomited their meals in order to wolf down some more. What Epicure relished, and you know that, Hermes, was not the pleasure of eating, but the satisfying sensation of having eaten just enough." She pauses. Then she puts her cap back on, and her goggles, and Nicolas follows her, mustering his strength. But she now swims at a slower pace, and Nicolas thankfully discovers he can keep up. He asks if he can borrow her goggles. She complies. He glides into the turquoise underwater world, admiring a fleet of round blue-striped fish, jagged rocks dappled with the sun and studded with black sea urchins. When they arrive at the beach area, the chairs and parasols have been installed. They are offered towels by a smiling waiter. Nicolas looks around for the bathrobe he left on the concrete slab before the swim. The waiter runs to get it. His BlackBerry and the room key are still in his pocket, along with the Moleskine and the Montblanc.

"Breakfast, Hermes?" asks Dagmar Hunoldt. Before he can reply, she tells the waiter that they'll have it down here, not up at the buffet. "Do you prefer coffee? Tea?" she asks him briskly.

He says tea, wondering if she ever lets anyone make up his own mind about anything. She is used to giving orders, he can tell. Their table is installed in the blink of an eye and they sit down. The Swiss give them a little wave as they set off for their swim. The gay couple nod jovially. Another day at the Gallo Nero. His last day. Except that he is having breakfast with Dagmar Hunoldt, tête-à-tête. Nicolas begins to feel nervous again. What is he to do if she goes on pretending she has no idea who he is? What if he were to lean over, bang his hand flat on the table, making her jump, and say, Okay, Dagmar, enough with Epicure, Hermes, and Mercury Retrograde. You know perfectly well who I am. Cut the crap. Maybe she likes that kind of attitude from men, action *à la hussarde,* no small talk, no fussing around, even a spot of virile vulgarity. Maybe that is what she expects from him, to be ballsy, to cut to the quick, to be efficient, concrete, to the point. As their coffee and tea is brought to them, along with the morning papers, in French, Italian, German, and English, Nicolas feels his courage fizzling away like a deflated balloon. His anguish rises when he notes that the choice of newspapers includes the French one with the disastrous Taillefer interview. How awful if she starts to read that one under his nose. The photograph is large and very recognizable. He cringes as her fingers hover over the pile. She picks the *Times.* He exhales with relief.

Dagmar Hunoldt leafs through the newspaper nonchalantly. She reads a long article about the French politician and the hotel maid. She sips her coffee and munches a croissant. From time to time, she looks up at him and smiles, a clone of Glenn Close. Her white hair shines platinum in the rising sun. She has not even asked him what his name is. And she has not even told him hers. Such supremacy. Such arrogance. He both admires her and resents her for it. Making him feel like a little Mr. Nobody. Yet she smiles at little Mr. Nobody; she makes him feel he is her friend, that she enjoys his company, enjoys swimming with him, having breakfast with him, and that this is a privilege. How can she do that so masterfully, wonders Nicolas, ignoring his identity on one hand, and making him feel special, chosen, on the other? Has she read the Taillefer article? Probably. Everyone in publishing has read it. What is she like with her authors? he asks himself as she stirs her coffee. Does she act motherly? Is she authoritarian? Patient? Does she ever sleep with them? He is aware that she is not going to pronounce a single word during the entire meal. She is not going to speak to him. But every five minutes, she looks up at him and smiles. Her eyes twinkle. He feels the companionable bubble close around them, like yesterday morning, when they shared the Bellini after their swim. No need for words. Being together is somehow enough. Sharing an indefinable moment. Dagmar Hunoldt does that very well. She is a master at it.

The beach area is now full. Mr. Wong and Miss Ming bow and smile. The Spanish woman appears in a bright pink bikini. Her body is appetizing, delicately plump and tender. Mimi and Sherry, oozing with makeup and perfume, send air kisses.

Nicolas knows it is time for him to go back to the room with leaden footsteps, to confront Malvina.

"I have to go," he murmurs.

Dagmar Hunoldt looks up from the newspaper.

"Thank you for spending your morning with me, Hermes," she says, and there is a gentleness in her voice that warms him, even if he longs to say, My name is Nicolas Kolt; you know that.

She asks for a pen and some paper. He wonders why. He watches her scribbling. Her number? Her e-mail? His stomach churns again, making him wince. Oh! Here it is, then. Here is her offer. On a piece of paper. Not orally. But written. Written words, written numbers. He grasps the edge of the table to steady himself. He certainly has not seen that coming. The hand that has signed so many contracts. The hand that has changed the face of publishing. Dagmar Hunoldt is making him an offer. She is not doing it the usual way, because she is no ordinary person. And all these people down here with them, applying sun lotion, dipping toes into the water, listening to music, reading a book, are miles away from imagining that the most famous publisher and the most talked-about author of the moment are entering negotiations over breakfast, wearing bathrobes after a swim at a luxury resort on the Tuscan coast.

Dagmar Hunoldt hands the paper to Nicolas and smiles briefly. He knows this is a dismissal. He mutters good-bye and leaves. When he gets into the James Bond elevator, heart pumping hard, fingers shaking, he looks down at the paper.

No name. No e-mail. No number. No sum.
Only three sentences:

The smell of freshly cut grass after an exhausting hour mowing the lawn.

Opening the shutters to a golden morning after a wondrous night of sex and slumber.

To the storm of an orgasm, Epicure far preferred the quiet sweetness of its aftermath.

I N 2008, WHEN NICOLAS met Toby Bramfield, the African-
American director who adapted *The Envelope* for the screen,
they hit it off right away. Toby was perhaps eight years older than
Nicolas, a tall, angular fellow with dreadlocks and a dash of Jimi
Hendrix. He wanted to stay close to the book, he told Nicolas and
Alice, over drinks at L'Hôtel on rue des Beaux-Arts (where Oscar
Wilde had died in 1900, a fact that Nicolas found morbidly fascinating). He had already spoken about the role to Robin Wright's
agent, and he had high hopes she would say yes. This was right up
her alley, he told Alice and Nicolas; this was just the kind of part
she could not say no to. Nicolas listened, enthralled. In 2008, the
book had only just started its worldwide career, and he had no
idea, nor did Alice, just how far and fast that career would go. The
fact that a director had bought the rights so swiftly after publication, that his novel was going to become a movie, had been a wonderful and unexpected surprise. Toby Bramfield was not a famous
director, but neither Nicolas nor Alice minded. He had made a
couple of good films with relatively well-known actors that had

attracted moderate attention. All of them were adapted from novels. Toby Bramfield himself had no idea how Hurricane Margaux was also going to transform his own life, forever. He wrote the script himself, always keeping Nicolas in the loop, making sure Nicolas knew and approved of what he was doing. Nicolas felt thankful for this. He had heard of numerous painful cases where the author was shut out of the filming process, where the author was not part of the new adventure in any way. Often, the author ended up not liking the movie at all. Toby Bramfield seemed to thrive on Nicolas's feedback, as if it drove him on, as if he gained energy from it.

The first time Nicolas read the screenplay, he was put off. It dawned on him that he had to read while envisioning the scenes and the acting in his head. Once he got over that first unsettling sensation, he understood what Toby Bramfield was doing, how he had made a movie out of his book. But the real shock came later, when Nicolas went to the set for the first time in Paris, during the rue Daguerre scenes, shot in a studio and in the street itself. He was warmly welcomed; everyone had read the novel and had loved it. He sat behind the director, awed by the intricacy of the electrical rigging, the lighting installations, the complexity of the sound engineering, the minute details of decor, costumes, makeup, the fact that each and every person on the set had his or her precise and important part to play in making the movie possible. When Nicolas saw Robin Wright emerge from the changing rooms, her hair dyed silver, exactly like Margaux Dansor's, wearing blue tennis shoes, a blue shirt, and white jeans, his jaw dropped. Here was his heroine, his Margaux, the disco-loving piano teacher come to life. He was so moved, he could hardly speak, and only managed to shake her hand. Toby Bramfield let him play a cameo part in the Pôle de la nationalité scene, also shot in a studio. There had been over fifty extras, a mix of people who looked like all those he had crossed paths with that day in October 2006, during his long wait. He was placed next to Robin Wright as she sat staring at her father's birth certificate, hypnotized by a name she had never seen, Lucca Zeccherio, instead of Luc Zech. He had been bowled over at how actors could take another person's inner turmoil and transform it into their own. They were like sponges, sucking in emotions. When he said this to Robin Wright between two takes, she laughed. "If we actors are sponges, then what are you writers? Even bigger sponges. Don't forget we are all here today because of you, Nicolas Kolt. Because of what you wrote." He had treasured those words. He still did.

Nicolas saw the movie for the first time in 2010, just before it was released, in a private screening room in New York. Alice was with him, as well as his American publisher, Carla Marsh. Toby Bramfield was to join them at the end of the viewing. For the first few moments, Nicolas could not respond to the film, as if a door had been slammed in his face. Had he been foolish to trust Toby Bramfield? Then the movie began to spin its magic, and Nicolas forgot about his book. He saw only Toby's vision of *The Envelope*, and he saw it was one he could relate to. He loved the score, composed by a young Austrian musician who had managed to create a haunting theme that perfectly evoked Margaux and her contrasts, with piano solos that wrung his heart. He laughed during the witty dialogues with Margaux's teenage daughters, Rose and Angèle, played by two young excellent actresses. He gripped the edge of his seat during the ugly confrontations between Margaux and Sébastian, her younger brother. He was moved by the perfection of the performances of Robin Wright and the actor who played her husband, Arnaud. What he loved above all was watching Robin Wright dance to disco music, alone in her kitchen, then in the nightclub scene in Genova, with Silvio, her Italian ally. The film rang true; it flowed. There was nothing contrived or fake about it. Nicolas felt tears well up during the flashbacks to Lucca Zeccherio's past, his charisma, his flamboyance, his tragic death, the body that was never found, carried away forever by an avalanche in the Swiss Alps. From the parts filmed at Camogli till the very end, when Margaux discovers her father's secret and wonders how to tame it so it will not destroy her own life, Nicolas cried gently, embarrassed to be doing so while seated between Carla and Alice, until he realized they were weeping as well, blowing their noses, wiping away tears. When the lights came up, they hugged one another, red-eyed and wordless, and that was how Toby Bramfield discovered them when he walked in. He flung his bony hands skyward and shouted, "Hallelujah! They're crying! They're crying!" Later, after the movie was released, Nicolas saw an interview with Toby Bramfield on TV. He was saying, "The book and the movie have the same DNA; I like to think of them as sisters." Nicolas also cherished that sentence. And he began to think about the intimate DNA of the book, of how he had fathered it. And how he had decided to put aside a pivotal scene about what he had experienced in October 2006, just after he had rummaged through the navy blue box in his mother's desk. That scene, which happened in the geriatric hospital with Lionel Duhamel, had been a turning point not only in his life but also in his imagination. He now saw, with the distance offered to him with the passing of time, that the scene had been part of the writing process, that it had been at the core of the novel, and he knew now how much he owed that scene, however horrific it had been to endure. The shock of it had forced a dark new path into the recesses of his mind. A bright light was shining down that path, heading where, he did not know, but he knew he had to take that path, had to write about that path, but not about the light that had revealed the path to him. He would never talk about that scene to a journalist, to another writer, not even to anyone close to him. He was to keep it to himself. He felt that, like a photographer framing a picture, instinctively understanding what to include in that picture and what to keep out, he was aware, as a writer, of what he wanted to show in his book, and what was to be kept hidden forever.

Lionel Duhamel passed away in 2007, at seventy-seven years old. He did not witness his grandson triumphantly metamorphosing from Nicolas Duhamel to Nicolas Kolt. He had been hospital-ized in 2004, when it became evident to his daughter, Elvire, that he could not longer reside in the boulevard Saint-Germain apart-ment, where he had been living alone since his wife Nina's death in 2000. His mind was slipping. He left the gas on, could not re-member his name, and could not find his way home. He became aggressive with his family, his neighbors, with the young nurses who came to care for him daily. The doctors diagnosed Alzheim-er's. He had not wanted to leave his apartment, but he had not been given a choice. The hospital was situated near the rue de Vau-girard, not very far from the rue Pernety. Nicolas had not been to visit his grandfather for a long while. This had become an ordeal. Most of the times, Lionel was medicated, sedated, and bland, and the visit went well. But the atmosphere of the hospital, its stench, the vision of the demented elderly patients who were confined there, was always unbearable.

On that October evening in 2006, which was to alter many as-pects of his life, Nicolas bought a bunch of flowers near the metro station on the rue Raymond Losserand and walked to the hospi-tal. It was growing dark and the air was heavy with a bitter humidity. It was rush hour and cars slowly drove along the streets, sending noxious fumes into the air. The hospital was glaringly lit up and overheated. Nicolas took off his coat as he came through the door. Lionel Duhamel lived on the last floor, the closed one, the one for the crazy old people. Most of the patients wore magnetic bracelets on their wrists. If they wandered beyond the entrance, a blaring alarm would go off. Nicolas always kept his eyes down when he entered the ward. He could not get used to what he was con-fronted with each time he came: the rows of wheelchairs, the wizened, wrinkled faces, the distorted smiles, the lolling of tired heads. Some patients sat there half-asleep, drool running from dry, cracked lips. Some stood up, resting on canes or walkers, staring into nothingness, twitching, scratching. Others shuffled by with zombielike gaits, nursing an arm, one shoulder higher than the other, one foot dragging behind, cackling, moaning, or singing. He sometimes heard screeches and howls from a far-off room and the calming, pacifying tones of a doctor or a nurse. The most terrifying patients were the ones who looked normal, sitting in front of a game of chess or solitaire, groomed and presentable, no stains on their clothes, no trembling hands, no sign of dementia. They spoke well; their speech was not slurred. They resembled any well-to-do grandparents, happy to be visited. They ogled him as he walked by, and he had learned not to look back at them, because if he did, their madness lashed out at him through their glittery eyes, blazing after him like a trail of fire. He had learned to keep away from them. Once, a respectable-looking granny had grabbed him by the crotch, silently and savagely, with a salacious smirk, flaunting a yellowed-tip tongue at him.

The nurses attended to them all with a patience he found heroic. They were insulted, ignored, jeered at, hit, all day long. How could they do this job? Looking after old people was not much fun, he imagined, but demented old people surely made it even worse. When Nicolas arrived that evening, the dinner had been served and was being cleared away. The air was stuffy and fetid, a lifeless mixture of dreary hospital food, probably cabbage, and the ammonia-tinted whiff of detergent, no fresh air, just the reek of old age and neglect, of forlorn old skins that had the aspect of dried-up parchments stitched with stringy white hair. The wheelchairs had been placed in front of the strident TV. Half of the patients in front of it were asleep. Why was dinner served so early in hospitals? Didn't it make the night even longer, even more unbearable? Did these people know that when they left this place, it would be in a coffin?

Lionel Duhamel, wearing a bathrobe, was sitting in an armchair near his bed, staring down at his feet. He did not move when Nicolas entered. Nicolas had already seen him in this state. He sat down on the edge of the narrow bed and waited for the old man to acknowledge his presence. Lionel Duhamel had never liked mingling with the "old fools," as he called them. He had his meals in his room, and he watched his own television. The room isn't too bad, thought Nicolas. But it still seemed bare, despite his grandfather's having lived here for the past couple of years. Pale lime walls, a pack of cards, a comb, and some magazines. And to think his grandfather had lived in a large apartment full of books, paintings, ornate furniture, a grand piano, majestic tapestries, exotic carpets. What had happened to all those things, wondered Nicolas as Lionel at last looked his way with watery oyster-colored eyes that blinked at him a few times.

"Théodore," said Lionel Duhamel. "How nice to see you."

Nicolas was used to this, as well. But the first time had been a shock.

"Hello," he replied, smiling back. "Some flowers for you."

Lionel Duhamel gazed at the flowers blankly as if he had no idea what they were. Nicolas unwrapped them, threw the paper in the wastebasket, and went to fetch a tall plastic vase he knew was in the bathroom, as this was not the first time he'd brought flowers. Elvire had suggested laying off chocolate, as the old man had a tendency to wolf them down in one go, and spend the next day suffering from diarrhea. Nicolas arranged the flowers and took them back to the room, where the old man was still sitting, motionless.

"They look nice, don't they?" Nicolas asked.

"Yes, they do," said Lionel Duhamel. "Thank you, Théodore. Very kind of you. How are you doing at school?"

"Very well," said Nicolas.

"I'm glad to hear it. Your mother will be pleased. And what about that geography lesson?"

"I know it by heart."

"Excellent. Well, I must be getting ready. The baron is coming for dinner."

"Wonderful news," said Nicolas. He found these conversations surrealistic, no matter how many times he'd had them.

"But it is so much work when the baron comes." Lionel Du-hamel sighed. "I have to polish all the silver and get the crystal glasses out, and the tablecloth with his crest on it. The baron wants salmon and crab. So much to be done."

"Is that what he usually has?" asked Nicolas.

"No! Of course not! I already told you! Before the elevator got stuck! Remember?"

"Yes, of course," said Nicolas. "I'm sorry, I forgot."

The old man was agitated now, his eyebrows meeting in a vee over his nose. He started to complain in a high-pitched whine that grated on Nicolas's ears.

"They came this morning, Théodore, again. No one saw them, only me. People are so stupid here. They steal things. As if I can't see them. They have no idea. Goons! Complete idiots! Fools! They don't know that the enemies spread a poisonous paste all over the windowpanes, so that if you touch it, you die. I tried to wash it off, and the stupid nurse got angry. Moronic fat cow!"

Nicolas thought of the birth certificate in his pocket. He looked across at the grumbling old man, observed his shiny bald head, his plump, flabby pink face. For twenty-four years, he had considered this man his grandfather. His blood, his flesh. "Papi," as he called him. Weekends with Papi, going to the theater and the Louvre with Papi, visiting Montmartre with Papi, and Versailles, as well. Learning about the Sun King with Papi. Papi knew so much. He knew all the right dates and where all the important battles had been fought and who had won them, and if a king had been a Ca-pet or a Bourbon. It turned out that Papi was not his grandfather. Papi was not his flesh, not his blood. Papi had raised a fatherless boy and had given him his name, Duhamel. Papi knew all about Fiodor Koltchine. He was the only person in the world who could tell Nicolas anything about Fiodor Koltchine.

Nicolas had not come unprepared. He reached for his wallet, took out the photo of Zinaïda and Fiodor dated 1961, the one from the navy blue box in his mother's desk, and handed it to the old man.

The doctors had never said not to talk about the past. They had never warned him or Elvire that it could be a bad idea. He wasn't doing anything wrong. He was only hoping for an answer, hoping that somewhere in that tired, old, confused brain, a light might switch on, a spark might fly.

The minutes ticked by, and the old man said nothing, staring down at the photograph. A faint shout was heard from down the corridor, along with the metallic voices from the TV. The rubber wheels of a chair squealed past. A door slammed.

Nicolas wondered whether he should speak. The old man seemed stricken. The photograph in his fingers trembled.

"She never wanted you to know," said Lionel Duhamel at last, very clearly. "She didn't want anybody to know."

His voice sounded like his voice from "before," his normal voice. His Papi voice, of the old days. Gone was the whining of a moment ago.

Nicolas nodded, hardly daring to breathe. He was afraid of ruining the moment. So he remained silent, biting his lips. The shouting took up again down the corridor. He prayed it would not distract Lionel Duhamel.

The old man said, with the same calm, dull voice, "That letter came, that summer. At the end of July. You read it, didn't you, Théodore?"

"Whose letter?" whispered Nicolas.

"Alexeï," said Lionel Duhamel tonelessly. "The letter Alexeï sent."

A long pause.

"Who is Alexeï?" asked Nicolas gently.

The photograph slipped to the floor and the old man started to bawl silently, mouth gaping open, tears splattering down his plump cheeks. His frame was racked with sobs. He began to moan loudly, holding his head between his hands, rocking back and forth. Nicolas sprang to his side, grasping his arms, trying to calm him.

"Stop it!" spat the old man, furiously pushing him away. "Get away from me! Get away!"

The gnarled hands clutched at his throat, and Nicolas was shocked at the vibrant strength left in those old bones. For a brief and horrible instant, he thought he was going to black out. His vision grew wobbly; he could hardly breathe. At last, he was able to shove himself away and dislodge the viselike grip around his neck. Lionel Duhamel wheezed and spluttered. His eyes were enormous, bloodshot, filled with hatred.

"Papi, it's okay, relax," Nicolas whispered soothingly, terrified that a doctor or a nurse might turn up because of the racket and tell him off, or, worse still, order him to leave. He found the photograph under the chair and slid it back into his wallet. He rushed into the bathroom, took some Kleenex, and dabbed the old pink face. "Calm down, Papi. Please calm down. Everything is fine, I promise, just relax."

Lionel Duhamel blew his nose, still quaking, but the tears had stopped. He asked for some water. Nicolas filled a paper cup. He watched the old man gulp it down.

"Are you all right, Papi?" he asked, patting a sagging shoulder.

The flabby pink face seemed to swell with fury.

"Who are you? I've never seen you before!" hissed Lionel Duhamel, his eyes still huge, injected with red. "Get the fuck out of my room, or I'll call the police. Get the fuck out!" Nicolas left as fast as he could, racing through the long, brightly lit corridors, past the wheelchairs and the TV, down three flights of stairs, out into the cold air, where he gasped with relief. He ran all the way to the rue Pernety. He got there breathless, dizzy, still reeling from the violence of the scene. His throat hurt and he had difficulty swallowing. Delphine was not home yet, and Gaïa was with her father for the evening. He fished around in his pockets for the keys. No keys. On his key ring, he had the rue Pernety key as well as the rue Rollin one, and also a spare set to his mother's car, which she lent him from time to time. He must have dropped them on the way home or, worse still, left them in Lionel Duhamel's room at the hospital. He tried calling the hospital, asked for the third-floor ward, but it was busy. He ran all the way back, cursing. There were no keys on the glistening sidewalk. When he got to the third floor, he was not allowed back in by a snappy nurse, who said visiting hours were over. She grabbed his arm, but he ignored her, pushing past, yelling that he had left his keys in his grandfather's room.

His grandfather had been put to bed and was fast asleep when he slid the door open and slithered into the room. He turned the bed light on, frightened that this might wake the old man up (how could he face those dreadful eyes one more time?), but Papi did not budge, snoring peacefully away, as if nothing had happened, as if he had not tried to strangle his grandson. There were no keys. Nicolas searched every inch of the room and bathroom, in vain. He looked into the wastebasket. It had been emptied. He saw himself unwrapping the flowers. His keys had been in his hand, for some reason, and he must have thrown them away with the paper. He left the room and went to find the snappy nurse. At first, she remained unhelpful. Then she began to be aware that Mr. Duhamel's grandson was more than agreeable to look at. He had the loveliest smile, beautiful lips and teeth, gorgeous eyes, such an interesting color, the color of a misty morning. He was so tall, so dark, what a change from those decrepit gnomes she dealt with all day long. Of course she would show him the shaft in the cellar where the rubbish was emptied every evening. She said she hoped he would find his keys in that awful mess. She told him her name was Colette.

Armed with gloves, Nicolas waded through a nightmarish man-size bin full of the waste produced by a geriatric hospital—stained cloths, used diapers, food-encrusted bibs, dirty napkins—his mouth and nose clenched against the horrific stench, fighting the urge to retch, until he found his keys miraculously stuck to the flowers' wrapping paper.

He thanked Colette, then walked home slowly in a daze, the stink of the bin on his clothes and hair. Delphine was still not there, but she had sent a text message saying she was on her way. He undressed and took a long, hot shower. When Delphine came back, he said nothing about his day and about what had happened with Lionel Duhamel. He couldn't sleep that night. He went into the kitchen with the black-and-white photograph of Zinaïda and Fiodor, and his father's birth certificate. He drank some water and sat down at the table. He sat there for a long time. The words came back to haunt him, like Lord McRashley's silent army of bats. *She never wanted you to know. She didn't want anybody to know. That letter came, that summer. At the end of July. You read it, didn't you, Théodore? . . . The letter Alexeï sent.*

Nicolas strides up to the room, the piece of paper Dagmar Hunoldt gave him still in his hand. What do those ridiculous sentences mean? He scrunches the scrap up into a tiny ball and shoves it into his pocket. How could she possibly not know who he is? And why had he been so meek? Sitting there sheeplike. He nearly kicks himself. The next time he sees her, he will just ignore her. It will be like looking through thin air. Yes, that's it. Dagmar Hunoldt does not exist. She'll have to come begging if she wants him to acknowledge her.

When he enters the room, frowning, Malvina is on the bed, a tray on her lap. She looks beautiful, although her beauty is the last thing to touch him at the moment. She smiles at him.

"There you are!" she says.

He sits down on one of the white armchairs facing the bed. He finds he has little patience left. It has been nibbled away by his lack of sleep, by Dagmar Hunoldt's incomprehensible behavior.

He is going to be blunt. For him, there is no other way.

"I don't want this baby, Malvina."

Her face hardly moves. He was expecting it to drop, to crumble. It remains perfectly smooth.

She takes a sip of tea. Then she says quietly, "We're going to get married, and you'll see, you'll be so happy. I know it."

He is too stunned to speak. When the words come out, they sound like a roar.

"Are you crazy, Malvina? Are you out of your mind? Marriage?"

She smiles serenely. "Yes, marriage, Nicolas. We're going to make this little person very happy. We're going to build a lovely home for him, or her."

He grabs her arm. The tray tilts sideways on her knees. Tea spills, staining the white sheets brown.

"Be careful!" she cries. "Look at the mess you're making."

He drags her out of bed. She is standing in front of him, wearing a short white T-shirt, appearing tiny, faced with his height. A frail slip of a woman. But there is no fear in the small face turned up to his.

"The mess!" he hisses. "Let's talk about the mess, Malvina. Let's talk about your mess. If you don't mind."

"What do you mean?" She is pouting like a little girl. Like Gaïa used to.

"I mean, how the hell did you get pregnant? I mean *that* mess. Your mess."

She shrugs and looks away. "I don't know. Maybe I forgot my Pill."

"I see. Maybe you forgot your Pill. Great. Wonderful. You forgot your Pill, you're pregnant, and now you want to get married. Right?"

"Yes!" she says, stamping her foot. "What's wrong with that? I love you. We love each other. We're having a baby. Don't you see the beauty of it?"

And now the tears come, as he had expected. He lets her cry; then he takes her elbow again, but more gently this time, and leads her back to the bed, sits her down. He has to tell her he does not love her. That he never did love her. That he still loves Delphine.

That he respects her, that he has enjoyed their time together, that she is a fine, emotional, intense, interesting person, but that there is no way he is ever going to marry her and bring up that child. Has she any idea what she is talking about? She is a child herself. How can a child have a child? He thinks of her and a baby, on the rue du Laos, and closes his eyes with horror. A baby! Bringing up a child. The responsibility of it. A child changes a life forever. She should know that. He should tell her. And him, a father? How can he be a father? He doesn't even know what a father really is. His own father died so long ago. Marriage! How can she even pronounce that word? She is like a little girl, dreaming of Prince Charming. He remembers her talking to her mother last night on the phone. She sounded elated, like this was the most wonderful thing that could possibly happen to her.

Malvina sobs into his shoulder and he holds her close. The words don't come. He thinks of her fragility, her loneliness. Malvina moved to Paris for him. She gave up her life in London, her studies, her friends, all for him. She never made any friends in Paris. She just sat at home and waited for him. He thinks of her ex, Justin, and how that guy destroyed her, broke her wings, posting scornful, odious messages on her Facebook wall for all to see, telling her over and over again how useless she was, how stupid, how lost and pathetic she was, that she had never made him happy, that he had obliterated every single memory of his relationship with her, that she was a nonentity, that she might as well jump out of a window or stick her face in an oven and turn on the gas.

The words stay buried within him. He feels trapped, as if a metal door has clanged shut right into his face. He closes his eyes with despair.

"Are you so very angry?" Malvina says softly.

"This is a shock," he admits as nicely as possible.

"I know. I can tell."

She walks to the window. In that body, he thinks, that slim body, there is a minute bundle of cells that is growing and thriving with every passing second. Her cells, his cells, their baby. He cannot bring himself to believe it. Or accept it.

"I can give you more time," she says, looking out to the blueness. "For you to get used to the idea of being a father. I won't put any pressure on you. You need to finish your book."

"My book?" He laughs spitefully. "There is no book."

"What do you mean?" she says, turning back to him, alarmed.

He says, robotlike, "There. Is. No. Book."

Silence, and then she says, "I don't understand. What have you been writing for the past year?"

"Nothing. I've been pretending to write. I've been lying to all of you."

Her eyes are round with shock. "So what have you been doing all this time?"

"Nothing!" he yelps. "Nothing!"

"But everybody thinks . . . ," she begins.

"Yes, everybody thinks!" he echoes, waving his hands.

"Why?" she asks simply.

He snorts. "Because. Because!" he yells.

"What are you going to do?"

"I have to tell Alice." The mere thought of that makes him want to howl.

"I'm sorry," says Malvina.

"About the baby?" he retorts, a little too fast.

She scowls. "No! About the book."

"Malvina, we still need to talk about this. About how I feel. Do you understand?"

She nods. "We can take it slowly," she says. "We don't have to get married right away. We can wait till the baby is born. And once the baby is here, I'll take care of everything, I promise. I know you will love this baby. I love it already! Have you thought about names yet? I'm so excited. Oh, my darling Nicolas. I'm the happiest girl on earth. Please don't look at me like that."

Later, at lunch, Nicolas notices how Malvina is glowing. Gone is the sullen, glum creature spying on his every move, checking the way he looks at other women. Even when Savannah undulates by, wearing a bikini the size of a stamp, when the Spanish lady removes her top and exposes charming, pert breasts, and when the Natalie Portman sisters prance in and out of the pool in an adorable aquatic ballet, she remains impervious, gazing at him with idolatry, a proprietary hand on his arm. She has not looked at her iPhone once, a miracle, as she usually monitors every single item posted about him on the social networks. She is like a queen. Her radiance says to all, Yes, I am having Nicolas Kolt's child. Yes, I am the chosen one. I am that woman. I am the one. He wants to crawl under the table and weep.

This was meant to be a restful, inspiring escape. Yesterday afternoon, after François's devastating phone call, Nicolas begun to understand that this was not the case. He somehow knows, with dread, that it is not over. There is more to come. What, he cannot tell. But all his guards are up. His armor is on. It is as if the lovely scenery, the sun, the guests, the staff are all part of a play. It is a sham. They are all onstage. Behind the coat of luxury, tragedy lurks. Only this time, Nicolas gears himself up for it. He is ready.

"Mind if I join you, pal?"

Nelson Novézan, wearing a stained blue T-shirt and grimy jeans, slides into an empty chair at their table, plucks a grissino from the bread basket, and grins at them.

"That Taillefer article was something," says Novézan, his mouth full. "She's such a bitch. She hates my guts, too."

"Really?" asks Nicolas.

He is secretly relieved that Novézan has sat down, uninvited. His presence, however offensive, creates an unexpected and welcome barrier between him and Malvina. Novézan appears to be in a friendly mood. His usually sullen face is beaming. He pats Nicolas confraternally on the arm.

"She wrote a worse article about me last year. Don't you remember? Said I was a misogynistic, racist bastard who loved and respected only one living creature on earth: his cat. When you get ripped to shreds by Taillefer, it means you've made it. Welcome to the party, pal." He slaps Nicolas's shoulder. "This calls for celebratory drinks. Hey, Salvatore, Giuseppe, or whatever your godforsaken name is, get over here! I'm packing up and about to go. Leaving after lunch. So sad to leave this gorgeous place. What about you guys?"

"Leaving tonight," replies Nicolas.

He watches as Novézan grabs the wine from the waiter and serves them each a large glass. Malvina puts her hand over hers.

"Being a good girl, are you?" slurs Novézan.

Malvina radiates with pride. She places a protective palm on her flat stomach and nods. Luckily, Novézan does not notice the gesture.

"How's the writing going, pal?" He does not pause to hear Nicolas's answer. Nicolas sighs with relief. "I'm happy with mine. This is going to be enormous. Should be out next August. Hope your book isn't coming out then, because mine is going to blow everyone's away."

Nicolas makes the most of the pause Novézan takes to down his entire glass of Chianti in one gulp. "Did you notice Dagmar Hunoldt is here?" Nicolas says.

Novézan splurts wine on the tablecloth. He looks around. "What, here? Now? At the Gallo Nero?"

Nicolas nods. "Not right now, but definitely here."

"Did you talk to her?"

"I've been swimming an hour with her every morning."

"And . . ."

Nicolas shrugs.

"Did she make you an offer, pal? Come on, you can tell me."

Nicolas feels tempted to pronounce the three sentences on the paper, which he remembers by heart. But Dagmar Hunoldt did not recognize him. Novézan would weep with laughter over that. So he says nothing.

"Dagmar," says Novézan, whimsically. "I know a writer who slept with her. Atomic bomb, he told me. I never fuck women her age, but I'm tempted. How interesting that she's here. What a pity I'm leaving. I wonder if she'll come after this new book of mine."

"What's it about?"

"As if I'd tell you!" taunts Novézan, wagging a scornful finger under Nicolas's nose. "You wouldn't tell me about yours, would you?"

"Oh, mine? It's about the vanity of writers," quips Nicolas.

Malvina flashes a surprised glance at him, and Nicolas shrugs at her, as if to say, Hell, why not?

Novézan lights a cigarette, puffing at it. He says, "You think writers are vain?"

"Some of them."

"Well," says Novézan, studiously picking his nose, "why shouldn't they be? Writers hold the keys to the world, don't they? They re-create the world. So they should be vain. Literature is a kingdom where writers rule, like kings, like emperors. A kingdom where emotions do not exist, where truth does not exist, where history means nothing. The only truth is the words on the page and how they come to life. That's why writers are vain. Because they are the only ones who know how to bring those words to life."

Novézan lets out a large belch and squeals with laughter at Malvina's cool stare. Alessandra and her mother send disapproving glances from the next table. All through the meal, Nicolas and Malvina endure Novézan's monologue. His problems with his mother, who resented his books and who voiced her disapproval in a recent interview. His problems with his teenage son, who is in re-hab. His problems with his ex-wife, who always wants more money. His problems with an ex-girlfriend who has been posting intimate details about their past relationship on a spiteful blog, where he is not named but where everyone can recognize him. His problems with his landlord, his neighbor, his assistant, his publicist, his den-tist, his aging cat, his hair loss. Novézan does not mention the sex scandal involving the French politician and the New York hotel maid, which is on everyone's lips. He does not talk about anything except himself. He is wrapped up in his own universe. Nothing else seems to interest him. Is it with that scorn, that egocentrism, that he writes such powerful books, thinks Nicolas. Are his novels spawned from the utter disdain he feels for others, for women, for society, for political leaders, for the intelligentsia? At the end of lunch, when the bill comes, Nicolas expects Novézan to make a gesture toward his pocket, to say something about splitting the bill. But Novézan remains silent and lights yet another cigarette. Nicolas remembers hearing from a journalist that Novézan is unbelievably stingy. The journalist told Nicolas that Novézan, one of France's most famous novelists, who owns an apartment in Paris and one in Brussels, a house in Dublin, and a villa on the Costa del Sol, never lends anyone money, never pays for anyone's drinks, anyone's meal, never gives a tip to a taxi driver, a deliveryman, an usherette, and always counts his change.

Nicolas charges the three meals to his room. Novézan stands up, plants a slobbery kiss on Nicolas's cheek, tries to do the same to Malvina, who shrinks away; then he leaves, waving. Nicolas watches him disappear into the building with a mixture of admiration and revulsion—exactly what he feels when he reads Novézan's books.

"Is your new book really going to be about the vanity of writers?" Malvina asks.

Nicolas smiles. "Why not? I'm tempted."

"Nicolas," says Malvina. "Your BlackBerry."

He glances at the phone on the table. ALICE is flashing on the screen.

"Are you going to pick up?" Malvina whispers.

He had not been able to tell Malvina the truth about their relationship earlier on. He had to be brave now and tell Alice what he had promised to reveal. No more beating around the bush. He notices that the Belgian family and Alessandra and her mother are too near. This is going to be one of those private conversations.

He rises, takes the phone, and moves away, where he can stand alone and not be heard.

He braces himself and answers. "Alice," he says.

There is silence, an ominous one, like the one before François spoke, and he feels a sort of dread spill through him.

"Alice, are you there?"

He picks up an odd sound. Could it be a sob? Another one comes. It definitely is a sob. Alice Dor is crying. He can no longer speak.

"Nicolas! How can you do this to me?" Her voice, usually low and poised, is a croaky moan. "I trusted you. I've trusted you since the beginning. I thought we were a team and we worked together hand in hand. I made a mistake. I guess Delphine was right after all."

"Alice, please . . . ," he says, filled with consternation. "You mean the book? I have started it. It's just not as advanced as you may think it is, but I have started it. I promise you. You must believe me. Of course you can trust me."

"Be quiet!" she yells. He has never heard Alice Dor yell. He is stunned. "Stop it, Nicolas! Have the decency to tell me the truth. I always knew you might leave me. But I never thought you'd do it this way."

Malvina comes to his side. She must have seen his face. She holds on to him. He feels her warmth, her love. Somehow, it helps.

"Alice . . . ," he says again.

"No, let me finish." Her voice is calmer now. The sobbing has stopped. But the pain is still there. He can hear it. "You know very well what difficult times we in the publishing industry are going through. People read less, buy fewer books. We publishers have so much to work out, with the advent of e-books, the slow death of printed books. Booksellers are worried; bookstores are closing down. Publishing deals mean so much more than they used to in a world where everything is changing—for writers, for publishers, for readers. And you chose this particular moment, when you know how fragile all this is, to do this to me. You know I run a small company. You are my star author. You are the reason I can publish other authors. We all live off you. But you used to say, with such grace, such elegance, 'Alice Dor changed my life.' And I used to answer, with earnestness and truth, 'Nicolas Kolt has changed mine.' I'm not talking about money, Nicolas. I'm not talking about your very generous contract and your ample royalties. No, I'm talking about trust. I wonder if you know what that word means anymore. I'm saying to you now, and I want you to answer me now, how can you do this to me?"

Nicolas is so bewildered, he cannot speak. Malvina strokes his hand gently. He can hear the thrumming of his heart, the voices coming from the restaurant behind them, Alice Dor's ragged breath.

"What do you mean?" he stammers helplessly, knowing this will unleash her fury.

She yells again, and he can hear the outrage, hear the suffering.

"It's all over Facebook! It's all over Twitter!"

He finds it difficult to breathe.

"Alice, can you hold on, please?"

He mutes the BlackBerry with a trembling finger.

"Malvina, give me your iPhone."

Malvina hands it to him. His heart pounds. On his Facebook page, there are two photos posted by Alex Brunel fifteen minutes ago. They were taken during his breakfast this morning with Dagmar Hunoldt. Appalled, Nicolas sees the photos through Alice's eyes. He sees what she saw. In the first one, Dagmar and he are rubbing shoulders, wearing the same bathrobes, seated at the same table. Like old friends. Like accomplices. As if they had shared something special. A swim? A conversation? More? Much more. In the second photo, Nicolas is standing up, and Dagmar's right hand is in his. The precise moment when she handed him the piece of paper. He is gazing down at her, and she is smiling.

"Alice, for God's sake, it's not what you think! I can . . ."

But Alice Dor is no longer there. Alice Dor has hung up on him.

He tries to call her back. He calls five, ten, fifteen times. She has turned her phone off. He leaves message after message, sends three pleading e-mails, six texts. He is distraught. Malvina leads him back to the room. She strokes his hair gently. They have a late checkout, she reminds him, but they need to start packing; the chauffeur is picking them up at six to drive them to the airport. That is in a couple of hours. He should pack now, and then what about a final swim? "Isn't that a good idea," she says, smiling, "a final swim?" He nods, his mind miles away. Nothing else matters. Only Alice. How is he going to explain this to her? Will she ever believe him?

As Malvina begins to fold her clothes, Nicolas remains frozen, standing in the middle of the room. How can ever he win Alice's trust back? How could he have been so stupid, so vain? Yes, it was a question of vanity. It was all vanity. He had felt flattered, tempted, enthralled by Dagmar Hunoldt's presence, infuriated by the fact that she pretended not to recognize him. Look where that has landed him. How could he not have foreseen that Alex Brunel (whoever Alex Brunel is) would post other photos? He should have blocked that account. He should have done that from the start.

The phone vibrates in his pocket, startling him. That must be Alice, calling him back. She will be angry at first, but he will explain it all, and he even has that piece of paper in his pocket with those crazy sentences about Epicure to prove it. She will come around. He will make sure she does. He will do everything in his power for her to forgive him.

The number is a private one, not showing up on the screen. He hesitates. Perhaps Alice is not at home; perhaps her battery has run out, and she is calling from another phone, another place. It can only be Alice.

But the voice he hears when he takes the call is not Alice's voice. It is that of an unknown man.

"Nicolas Kolt?" The voice is clipped, polished, with a Germanic ring to it.

"Who is this?" he asks uneasily.

"Hans Kurz."

The name rings a faint bell. Enough to make Nicolas feel uncomfortable.

A pause.

"Yes?" says Nicolas carefully. "What do you want?"

"What do I want?" A dry laugh rings in Nicolas's ear. "Now, you listen very carefully. You were stupid enough, Herr Kolt, to send e-mails to my wife, in which you left your phone number and in which you also mentioned where you were staying. So it was easy for me to contact you."

"I don't know what you are talking about," Nicolas says firmly. "You've dialed the wrong number."

His tone must sound contrived, because Malvina stops packing and turns all her attention to him. Hans Kurz continues, his voice louder now.

"Oh, I see, you are not alone. Your unsuspecting girlfriend, I imagine. Poor thing. I've seen her Facebook page. In a relationship with Nicolas Kolt. Malvina Voss. Very pretty. Very young. Poor little Malvina. She adores you, doesn't she?" Another ironic chuckle. "How uncomfortable this must be for you, Herr Kolt. What a pity Sabina's BlackBerry is kaput. BBMs are so practical, aren't they? Nobody can intercept them. But it's a different story with e-mails, isn't it? So easy to read someone else's e-mails. And to pass them on, too. To forward them. To send them on to unsuspecting people. And that last e-mail of yours was so very graphic, wasn't it? The one with your phone number in it. Where you describe to my wife exactly how you are going to fuck her. In great detail. Oh, you wrote that beautifully, Herr Kolt! You had a hard-on, didn't you? Probably more exciting to write that kind of crap."

Malvina is now standing close to him. She can probably hear Hans Kurz's guttural tone.

"Who is it?" she whispers.

"I can't hear you," shouts Nicolas into the phone, turning away from her. "This is a bad connection."

"Pathetic excuse. You leave my wife alone, Herr Kolt, or I will come in person to the luxury hotel you are staying in, the Gallo Nero, and I will kick your arrogant face to a pulp, until your beloved fans no longer recognize you."

Nicolas turns the phone off. His hands are shaking, but he manages, somehow, to keep a normal expression on his face.

"What did that person want?" Malvina asks, frowning.

"No idea," says Nicolas. "Some creep. Wrong number."

He goes out to the balcony. He finds he cannot think properly. Every thought is sluggish. He feels numb. How long will it take? Not long now, he guesses. As soon as she finishes her packing, or even before, Malvina will check her iPhone. There is nothing else to do but wait.

He feels like those people frantically protecting their home against an oncoming tornado. Boarding up windows, piling sandbags in front of doors, stocking up on water, sugar, pasta, batteries, and flashlights. He waits. Down below, he sees the flow of the unhurried pace of the Gallo Nero's rhythm, disconnected from reality. An iridescent butterfly wings by. Valets come and go. A gardener tends to the plantation. Guests stroll past with tennis rackets. Others head to the spa in their bathrobes. The Swiss can be spotted in the sea, on their way back from their afternoon swim. The American ladies are having tea in the shade. He can hear the "Oh, my God's" from where he stands. The terrible Damian runs by, followed by his exhausted mother. Dr. Gheza and an elegant man are talking near the cypress trees. The gay couple play badminton on the lawn, dressed in white, like a scene out of *Brideshead Revisited*.

Five o'clock on a sunny Sunday afternoon in July. One of those perfect, golden afternoons. A bomb is about to explode. He waits.

As usual, he does not hear Malvina walk out to the balcony. He picks up the crackling electrical rage emanating from her and spins around.

Her face is a tight white mask, her eyes two glittering blue marbles. Voicelessly, she hands him her iPhone in a smooth, fluid gesture that would look perfect in a video clip or an ad, he thinks absurdly. He glances at the phone, but there is no need to read the whole thing. He knows it is a copy of his explicit e-mail to Sabina, forwarded by Hans Kurz to Malvina via her Facebook page. He wonders how old Hans Kurz is. Probably in his fifties, he guesses. What does he look like? The balding type, with a beer belly, or one of those tanned, fit, spruce guys who watch their weight and work out?

"Nothing happened," he mutters, giving the phone back to Malvina. He steps back into the room.

She follows him. Her voice rises to a screech. "What? Is that all you have to say? 'Nothing happened'?"

Nicolas feels disconnected from the scene. It is as if he is sitting on the sofa, arms crossed, watching both of them. He is calm, stony-faced, almost placid. She is like a crazed moth, flitting around a flame, frying its wings.

"Nothing happened?" she shrieks. "Did you read this? Were you drunk when you wrote it? And the photo? Can you explain the photo?"

"What photo?"

The iPhone is once again held up to his face with the same slinky gesture, and he is confronted with the image of his erection photographed in the men's bathroom of the Gallo Nero. The one he sent Sabina via his personal e-mail.

"Look Malvina," he says with a sigh, "I know this is unpleasant, and a shock to you, but nothing happened with that woman."

He is reminded, as he pronounces those words, of President Clinton, and what he had nebulously grasped of the Lewinsky case when he was a teenager, joking about it with François and Victor, aroused by the cigar element and the stain on the dress, and he now remembers Clinton's reddish face on TV when the president stalwartly stated, "I did not have sexual relations with that woman." Hadn't the public prosecutor then said snidely, "Define sex, Mr. President." Sabina made him come five or six times, albeit virtually. But those orgasms were not virtual. They were due to Sabina, even if Sabina happened to be in another country. "Define sex, Mr. President." Nicolas closes his eyes. He should have thought of the possible complications when he sent that e-mail from his private account. He should never have answered her first e-mail.

Malvina nearly spits at him with rage. Her tiny fist pummels his arm. "You keep saying that. 'Nothing happened.' How dare you!"

"But it's true," he insists. "I only met her once, at a book signing in Berlin in April."

"Who is she?"

"She's from Berlin. That's all I know."

"How old is she?"

"I don't know."

Malvina snorts. "Oh, yeah, sure, you don't know. A cougar. The kind you can't resist. One of those desperate housewife types who has the hots for you. And she came on to you, right?"

"She gave me her number," admitted Nicolas. "We exchanged a couple of text messages, and, well, you know, it came to this."

"To this!" howled Malvina, brandishing the iPhone, her face twisted in utter disgust, "It came to this," she says, reading his message: "'I'm going to grab your hips, Sabina, and I'm going to fuck you so hard, you will hear the sound of—'"

"But I never touched her!" shouts Nicolas, interrupting her, "I never kissed her. I never slept with her. I have never seen her since then. Nothing happened!"

"That is the most pathetic excuse I have ever heard. Nothing happened? You send this woman a two-page e-mail where you describe all the things you want to do to her, the most pornographic stuff I have ever read in my life, stuff you've never even done to me, your own girlfriend, and you dare tell me nothing happened?

And meanwhile, you buy me a Rolex for my birthday and you act like Prince Charming. Shut up with your 'Nothing happened.' You sound like Valmont in that book and movie you love, repeating 'It's beyond my control' over and over again. 'Nothing happened.' Shut up! Luckily, her husband seems to agree with me. He so kindly sent this to me, along with that gross photo. That's what you are, Nicolas. Disgusting. Gross. You are revolting."

"Oh, come on Malvina." He sighs. "I know it wasn't very elegant of me, but I wasn't having an affair with this woman. I wasn't being unfaithful."

She pounces on the word *affair* like a wildcat with all its claws out.

"Yes you were! That's exactly it. You were having an online affair. You were having an affair. It's the same thing. You were cheating on me. You betrayed me. What would you have done if you had found that out about me? If you read dirty e-mails I sent some guy?"

He nearly says, I don't think I would have minded quite so much, because I am not in love with you. He cannot bring himself to pronounce those words. But then he thinks of Delphine, and what he might have felt if she had been having an online affair, a virtual affair, with some man. The thought sobers him. He begins to feel guilty. Poor Malvina. It must have been a dreadful shock, reading that e-mail, seeing that photo. She is, after all, deeply in love with him.

"I'm sorry, Malvina," he says softly. "I'm sorry I hurt you. The truth is, I don't care about that woman. I care about you. I'm so sorry."

Her back is turned to him, and he tentatively puts his hand on her fragile shoulder. He expects her to turn around, break into tears, and sob into his chest. Then they will kiss, probably make love, and he will be forgiven. Malvina shrugs off his hand and resumes her packing without another word. She goes into the bathroom, gets her things there, fits them into her suitcase, and zips it up. Her gestures are precise. She does not look at him once.

When she at last turns around to glance up at him, there is no softness, no forgiveness. Her face is still the stony mask. There is such hatred in her eyes that he takes one step back.

"It's too late for being sorry," she hisses, wheeling her suitcase toward the door. She takes her bag, places her iPhone in it, and slides a jacket over her dress. "I'm leaving now. I'll take an earlier car and an earlier plane back to Paris."

"What?" he says, bewildered. "Wait—"

"You heard me," she snaps, her hand on the door handle. "I'm leaving. But remember this. I am carrying your child. I'm entitled to many compensations. I'm not talking about Rolexes. I mean as the mother of your child. Long term. Things will work out my way. We will have this baby and we will get married. You will be my husband. I will be Mrs. Nicolas Kolt. Whether you like it or not."

She opens the door and walks briskly out of the room. The door swings shut.

Nicolas kept seeing lionel Duhamel's red eyes. He kept feeling the pressure around his throat. He went about his day, not mentioning the scene with his grandfather to anyone. He gave his tutorials, did the shopping, went to pick up Gaïa at school at four-thirty. While she was playing in her room, and before Delphine got home, as he prepared dinner, he called his mother and his aunt Elvire with the same questions. Did they know who Alexeï was? Had they ever heard of a letter he sent Nina? Emma was mystified. She could not understand what her son was getting at. She did not remember that name, or a letter. "Why?" she asked. He said it was a conversation he remembered from long ago, nothing important. He was blunter with Elvire. He told her that her father had mentioned this to him the night before. She was furious. The hospital had called her that morning. Lionel was not at all well; he had slept badly and was aggressive with the staff, to such an extent, they'd had to increase his medication. "What the hell do you think you're doing?" she said, her voice booming over the phone, and he could visualize her wide-jawed pink face, which looked very much like her father's. "No, that name and a letter mean nothing to me, but let me be clear about this, Nicolas. Do not go back there again without warning me, and when you do visit, do not talk about those things, because that is obviously what upset him. I don't care who that Alexeï was and what that letter said. My father is an old, confused man and he deserves a peaceful end. Do you understand?"

The last person he called was Brisabois. It took a while tracking him down. He hadn't seen him since he had come asking for money a year after his father's death, in 1994. The phone number in Théodore Duhamel's address book was no longer in use. There were other Brisaboises listed, but not the one he wanted. He finally found a Brisabois on Facebook who happened to be Albert's daughter. Nicolas had no memory of Brisabois's having a child, but luckily, she remembered that her father had worked with a certain Théodore Duhamel in the late eighties and early nineties. She gave him her father's number.

Brisabois agreed to meet Nicolas in a café on the place des Ternes. It was pouring, and it seemed to Nicolas that it had not stopped raining since he discovered his father's real name. Brisabois's ginger beard had gone white with the passing of time. But otherwise, he remained the same jovial fellow Nicolas remembered. They ordered tea and coffee, and Nicolas got straight to the point. He showed Brisabois the birth certificate.

"Did you know my father was called Fiodor Koltchine?"

Brisabois nodded.

"I saw it on some official paper when we were young. I asked him, but Théodore didn't like talking about it. I knew he was born in Saint Petersburg. He used to show off with that. It made him exotic. Different from us. But tell me more."

"My father came to France as a baby with his mother, in 1961. He was adopted by Lionel Duhamel, who had just married Zinaïda Koltchine, my grandmother. She was fifteen years old. Lionel was thirty. I found all this out when I had to renew my passport because of those recent governmental laws."

"And so now you want to know more about your father. Right?"

"Yes. This is going to sound awkward, but what did my father do? His job, I mean."

Brisabois stroked his beard. He smiled. "I knew you'd ask that question one day," he said.

Nicolas pointed to the birth certificate. "I know nothing about his real family or how he died. It's not unhealthy curiosity, Albert. It's just me, his son, his only son, trying to work out who he was. And you were close friends. Weren't you?"

"We were. Since our school days. Lycée Montaigne. Théodore was not a good student. He left school when he was seventeen. I found it amusing that he married a brilliant khâgne student, who then became a teacher."

"So tell me about his job."

Brisabois looked out to the place des Ternes, where cars waited, gridlocked under the rain. People scurried by in forest of glistening umbrellas. Up ahead, the Arc de Triomphe loomed, draped in humidity.

"Let's just say your father had a gift. He was gifted at bringing people together."

"A business angel?"

"No, it was more underground."

Nicolas stared at Brisabois. The minutes ticked by.

"You don't mean drugs? Or governmental secrets?"

"Not drugs."

A pause.

"My father was a spy?"

"I don't like that word," said Brisabois, drumming his fingers on the table. "Neither did Théodore."

"A secret agent?"

Brisabois chuckled. "Oh, come on, Nicolas. Do I look like a secret agent to you?"

"You're not going to tell me, are you?"

Brisabois only grinned.

Nicolas felt the mystery shrouding his father become even more opaque. Brisabois was giving nothing else away. Nicolas discreetly peered around the café. Nobody seemed to be observing them. Was Brisabois afraid? He looked so normal, so quiet. A middle-aged man with a paunch. You'd think he was a professor or a historian. No one you would ever notice. Nicolas leaned forward. His voice was a whisper.

"Albert, do you think my father was in some sort of danger when he died? Do you think someone . . ." He floundered, not daring to voice his thoughts.

"Do I believe he was killed, you mean?" said Brisabois briskly. "No, I don't. But your father always took risks, even if he had parents, a family, a young child, a wife. He couldn't help it. That was the way he was."

"Did my father ever mention the name Alexeï to you?"

Brisabois frowned. "I don't recall him mentioning that name."

"And do you remember my father ever talking about a letter from Russia?"

Another pause.

"A letter?"

"Yes, a letter."

Brisabois played with his coffee cup. His fingers were short and square. There were stains on his jacket. He smelled rank. His glasses hung crookedly on his face. His hair was too long, curling over his collar. Where did Brisabois live? Nicolas imagined a dank apartment, ground floor, giving onto a sunless courtyard. Did he have photographs of Théodore Duhamel at home? Had he ever been jealous of his friend's charisma? It must have been difficult for Brisabois to walk down the street next to Théodore Duhamel. All those eyes, those hungry eyes, not on him. Emma used to make fun of Brisabois, in the old days, when Théodore Duhamel was still with them. She'd ask her husband, teasingly, if there was a

Madame Brisabois. Poor old Albert did look lonely at times, she said, and neglected, like a dog waiting for its master to come home, gazing yearningly at the door, pricking its ears at every footstep on the stairs.

"A letter . . . That's interesting. . . ."

"Is anything coming back to you?" asked Nicolas eagerly.

Brisabois nodded, slowly. He took off his glasses and wiped them with a corner of his shirt. He slipped them back on.

"That last summer, 1993 . . ." Brisabois hesitated.

"Yes?" said Nicolas. "That summer?"

"The last time I spoke to your father on the phone, the last time I ever heard his voice, he mentioned a letter."

Nicolas looked at the thick fingers on the cup, then up to Brisabois's face. "Can you remember what my father said, exactly?"

Brisabois exhaled sharply. "Nicolas, that was years ago."

"Thirteen years ago. Just try, please."

Brisabois ordered another coffee. He waited till it came. Nicolas waited, too, his legs quaking with impatience under the table.

Brisabois said in a low voice, "I remember. Théodore had just arrived in Biarritz. Must have been the beginning of August. Just before . . . He called me to discuss a professional matter. His voice sounded a little strange on the phone. Upset. Odd. I asked why. He just said this: 'I read a letter. A hell of a letter.' And that was it. That's all he said. I asked him whether it was to do with our business deals. He replied no, no, nothing to do with business. And that was it. Your father had affairs. You probably knew that, didn't you? I thought it was some woman, some woman in love writing a letter. There were always women in love, trailing after him. I dismissed it. I never thought about it again."

"Someone called Alexeï wrote it. In July. From Russia. I think he sent it to Nina, my grandmother, my father's mother."

"How do you know all this?"

"My nutty grandfather, Lionel Duhamel, spilled the beans."

"What do you think was in that letter, Nicolas?"

"Absolutely no idea. I don't even know who Alexeï is. But I'm going to find out. At least I'm going to try."

Brisabois's eyes twinkled.

"Right now, I see him, peeping out at me, in your face. You look so much like him. When you walked into the café, I had a shock. It was like Théo striding toward me. You are darker, and your eyes are not blue, but . . . When you were a kid, there was a vague resemblance, but now . . . Oh! It's both painful and wonderful to look at you."

"Do you miss him, Albert?"

"I miss him more than you can possibly imagine. I miss his audacity, his bravery. Your father was like the hero of a novel. You don't often meet people like that in a lifetime. I still hear his voice, and I dream of him every once in a while."

"Do you think he's still alive, somewhere, somehow?" asked Nicolas.

"When you never find a person's body, you can imagine anything. Did your father long for a new start? Did he stage his own death? Is he living another life on the other side of the globe? Does he have a new family, a new wife, new kids, a new name?"

"Was it an accident?" continued Nicolas. "Was he unhappy? Did he want to end it all? Was he upset because of that letter? The letter Alexeï sent."

They looked at each other in silence.

"The worst part about your father's story is not knowing," sighed Brisabois. "Being left in the dark."

Nicolas thought of the past years. Growing up in the shadow of a father who had left no trace. He felt the old dull ache, the familiar pain.

"Being left in the dark," he echoed. "The story of my life."

"You still miss him, too, don't you?"

Nicolas recalled those afternoons when he'd come home as a young boy, hoping against hope that his father had returned while he had been at school. "I have missed him every single day since

August seventh, 1993." Nicolas felt his eyes water up. He didn't care if Brisabois saw the tears. There was no shame. "I miss him even more since I've learned his real name."

Brisabois reached out and patted his shoulder comfortingly. Then he rubbed his hands. "So, what are you starting with, Nicolas? What's first on your list? How can I help?"

Nicolas smiled for the first time. "I'm starting with Saint Petersburg."

Once he obtained the visa, booked the airline tickets, the hotel, which all took a couple of weeks, he got an e-mail from Brisabois. The day of his arrival in Saint Petersburg, he was to take bus number thirteen from the airport. The bus went to Moskovskaïa metro station, on line two, which would bring him right up to the Nevski Prospekt station. Lisaveta Andréiévna Sapounova would be waiting there for him at four o'clock. She would then accompany him to his hotel.

"You won't notice Lisa at first," Brisabois had written.

"At first"—Nicolas wondered what he meant by that. Lisaveta was an "old friend," Brisabois wrote, a woman he'd met in the eighties, when Saint Petersburg was still Leningrad. She was a translator, he explained, and a quarter French. She knew her city backward and forward, and spoke fluent French. However, she had a complex personality; she wasn't the easy, outgoing type. "I call her my Russian princess," he added. "Oh, nothing happened between us. . . . Just friends . . . Alas . . ." Nicolas had smiled at this.

"Saint Petersburg?" his mother had asked, surprised, when he informed her of his departure. "With Delphine?"

"No," Nicolas had replied. "By myself. Just for a couple of days."

When he told his girlfriend, she had not pried. Delphine sensed something was on his mind and was taking up a lot of his time. Whatever it was made him silent, pensive. One morning, she found him sitting at the kitchen table with his father's old Montblanc in hand.

"What are you writing?" she asked.

"Nothing much. Just taking notes."

She had seen the birth certificate; he had shown it to her when it had arrived.

"Look, my father's name was Fiodor Koltchine."

"How do you feel about all this?" she had asked gently when he had been to see his mother on that rainy day.

"I don't know. Weird, I guess. Trying to understand. Trying to understand who he really was."

"I'd do the same thing," she said comfortingly, kissing his forehead.

Delphine lent him some money for the plane ticket. He had not wanted to ask his mother. He chose the cheapest hotel he could find, a central youth hostel. He took off in early November 2006, during the midterm school holidays. He would only miss a couple of tutorials.

How strange and lost he felt landing in a country where he could not read the signs. He had not thought of that when he had decided to come. As he took an endless escalator descending to the bowels of Moskovskaïa metro station, he prayed he was on the right train, heading to the right stop. He felt thankful that Brisabois had suggested a friend to help him out, as he did not even know how and where to begin. He hoped Lisaveta Sapounova might be helpful. He had no one else to turn to.

November was not a good month to visit Saint Petersburg, he had learned online. The crowds came for the famed white nights during the summer, when darkness fell for only two hours. He was to expect rain and cold. Well, he thought, Paris had not been very different in the past weeks, had it?

A fine drizzle greeted him as he emerged from the station. He stood on the Nevski Prospekt, his collar turned up, peering around for Lisaveta Sapounova. He supposed Brisabois had described him to her. Tall, young, dark, French-looking. He heard Russian being spoken around him, a rich, throaty language he understood nothing of, but that fascinated him, because it was part of him. He was, after all, half Russian. He found himself noticing his father's slanted blue eyes, turned-up nose, wide mouth in every person walking by. This was, somehow, his country, yet he knew nothing of Russia, except what his history classes had taught him. He knew enough to know that the Saint Petersburg he was looking at now, filled with the animated throng of people coming and going, carrying shopping bags, chatting into mobile phones, and wearing designer clothes, had little to do with Leningrad of 1960, the year his father was born to a fifteen-year-old girl during the Cold War. He thought of the poet Anna Akhmatova, returning to Leningrad in May 1944, and writing, "a terrible ghost that pretended to be my city." In his khâgne years, Nicolas had avidly read Blok, Bely, Gogol, Brodsky, all linked to Saint Petersburg, not yet knowing he himself had intimate ties to the city through his father.

"Nikolaï Duhamel?" came a feminine voice. She pronounced his name the Russian way. It enchanted him.

He looked down at a small, slender woman with a scarf tied around her head. Forty-five, or a little less. She held out a cold hand. Her face was stern.

"I am Lisaveta Andréiévna Sapounova."

She held her chin up high, as if she was proud of her name, or herself. He noticed two beauty spots, one near her left eye, the other by the corner of her mouth. Brisabois's Russian princess.

He followed her, head down. It was pouring now. She led him up the broad, brightly lit avenue, crossing a couple of streets, and finally stopping in front of an old building on the corner of another large, noisy avenue. They stepped into the lobby to take shelter.

"This is the youth hostel," she said. "I hope you will be comfortable."

He nodded. She was intimidating. But not unpleasant to look at. She handed him a folded sheet of paper.

"This my address. I drew you a little map," she explained. "Not far from here. So you can get there easily. I have time after tomorrow to show you. Sightseeing. The museums, the churches, the canals."

He looked down at the paper: elegant feminine handwriting, a neat drawing of which streets to take to reach her place.

"Did Brisabois explain anything?" he asked.

She seemed puzzled. "Explain? He just asked me to show you around."

Nicolas cleared his throat. "I am not here for sightseeing. Although it's very kind of you."

She frowned. "Well, what have you come for, then?"

He smiled. "To visit ghosts."

He could tell she did not understand, so he hurriedly added, "I've come to find out more about my father and his family. He was born here. He died when I was a boy."

A group of wet and merry young people stepping into the lobby jostled into them. They moved aside to let them past.

Lisaveta Sapounova took off her scarf. She had thick, lustrous dark hair, coal black eyes, smooth white skin.

"To find out what?" she asked.

"Who my father was. Where he came from."

She looked up at him in silence for a few seconds, then smiled for the first time. It made her seem years younger.

"*Da*. I will help you," she said, nodding. "Come day after tomorrow, for breakfast."

"*Horosho*," he said. It was one of the only Russian words he knew.

She smiled again, repeated the word, with the right accent, and asked, "Good. Do you prefer coffee or tea?"

"Tea, thank you."

"Nine o'clock. Day after tomorrow. *Do svidania*. Till we meet again."

She slipped away. Nicolas went up to the fourth floor. The place was clean, well kept. Some friendly Swedes shared his room. It was also their first night in the city. Their names were Anders and Erik. "What about a drink, a bite to eat?" they suggested. They'd met some girls earlier on, locals, who mentioned a fun bar not far off, with a band playing. Why didn't he tag along? Nicolas did not want to spend the evening alone, so he accompanied the Swedes to the café, up another large street, through more persistent rain. The basement café was packed. The local girls were loquacious and entertaining. They spoke good English and ordered pickles, bouillon, blinis, vodka. One of the girls, Svetlana, got rapidly tipsy and excessively affectionate. Nicolas had a hard time keeping her off his lap. She kept climbing back on. Even after a couple of vodkas, she did not attract him; in fact, it was the opposite. As a loud band began to play and the small place became even more crowded and smoky, Nicolas lost them. He missed Delphine and wished she was here to share this with him. He felt tired and decided to leave.

On his way back, he got lost. In places, the wet streets smelled sour, as if the water was bringing up the odor from the sewers. A large golden church glowed through the darkness, a beautiful neoclassical structure, and he stared at it in awe before hurrying along. After more roaming, he found himself looking up from a canal at such spectacular onion-shaped domes, they made him forget the rain. A kind soul took pity on him and showed him the way back to the youth hostel. When Anders and Erik returned, more than drunk, he was asleep. They stumbled about the room, laughing inanely. Nicolas didn't mind. He turned the light back on and watched them trip around the place, laughing along with them. The people in the next room came knocking, annoyed with the noise. It was late. The Swedes finally dozed off. One of them snored. Nicolas found that sleep eluded him. But it had nothing to do with the snoring. For the first time in his life, he was in the city where his father had been born forty-six years ago. That thought kept him awake for a long time.

Early in the morning, Nicolas used the communal bathroom as the others slept on. He planned to spend the day visiting the homes of his favorite Russian writers, those who had been born or who had died in his father's city. The rain had stopped overnight. The morning light was pearly, the air crisp and cold. Pushkin's house was by the Moïka canal. He found it easily. He had to bend over to get in through the low wooden door. A stern gray-haired lady barked at him in Russian, and when he blankly looked back at her, she gestured for him to slide protective plastic slippers over his shoes. He tiptoed through the silent blue-walled rooms and remained for a while in the poet's study, which was lined with books. There was his walking stick, his pipe, his favorite armchair. Alexander Pushkin had died here on January 29, 1837, aged thirty-seven, mortally wounded after a duel with a Frenchman who was courting his pretty wife. Nicolas found the same reverential, hushed atmosphere in Fyodor Dostoyevsky's apartment at Kuznechny Pereulok. Like Pushkin, Dostoyevsky had also passed away in his office, suffering from a lung hemorrhage, on February 9, 1881. Another grim babushka waved Nicolas away from the great writer's candlelit desk when he leaned in too far to admire its surface. This was where Dostoyevsky had written *The Brothers Karamazov,* where he'd prepared his famous speech for Pushkin's memorial celebration, where he'd drafted the last issue of his *Writer's Diary,* published posthumously.

Vladimir Nabokov's birthplace on Ulitsa Bolshaya Morskaya no longer looked like what it must have been when the writer was born there in 1899. It now housed the editorial offices of a daily newspaper. But on the ground floor, Nicolas happily wandered through high-ceilinged rooms, where he found the famous collection of butterflies caught by Nabokov himself, index cards with Nabokov's handwriting, his pince-nez and travel Scrabble set, photographs of him as a boy, and an old-fashioned typewriter. A sullen young man ushered him into a cubicle, where he was shown a video from 1963—in black-and-white, of appalling quality—on a squeaky TV that could only have been a relic of perestroika, but nevertheless, he could make out Nabokov's voice speaking English with a Russian accent, then his round face and his piercing dark eyes.

It was Anna Akhmatova's communal apartment near the Fontanka canal, where she lived for thirty years, that moved Nicolas the most, in a way he could not entirely explain or describe. The humble kitchen with its dingy sink bore the vestiges of troubled times, hardship, and suffering. It was from this tranquil spot that Akhmatova watched with dread as her city endured revolution, civil war, political terror, world war. He spent a while in her room, observing her low bed, her high wooden desk. When he left the premises, it was dark already. A large marmalade-colored cat mewed at him as he walked away.

The next morning, after a more restful night, he left the hotel early again with Lisaveta Sapounova's address in his pocket. He stepped out of the building, turned left, and took the second street on the left, following her map. He came to a large canal that he had already seen the day before, near Akhmatova's house. "Fontanka," Lisaveta Sapounova had written in her neat handwriting. He paused for a while, looking around him at the gray-blue expanse of water, the patrician buildings lining it, their subtle, mellow colors. He understood now that in the heart of this city, built on a marsh by a tsar who hated Moscow, everywhere he looked, his eyes would find something to feast on. But his father had hardly known his birthplace, he reminded himself. How old was he when he left? Six months? A year? Théodore Duhamel had remembered nothing. He'd never come back. Neither had his mother, Nina.

Lisaveta Sapounova lived in a weatherworn edifice that bore a dignified grandeur, its crumbling facade decorated with Greek-like pillars and high square windows. Nicolas went up a large antique staircase that seemed about to collapse; graffiti had been sprayed all over the peeling paint of the walls. "Door number three," she had written. He knocked. Nothing happened. He noticed a small doorbell, and pressed it. Somewhere in the recesses of the ancient house, a faraway tinkle was heard. Then the quick tap of footsteps. The old locks whirred and groaned. The door opened with a whine. Lisaveta Sapounova led him into a single enormous room with the highest ceiling he had ever seen. The view over the Fontanka was extraordinary. He went straight to one of the bay windows and cried out in delight. She watched him, nodding and smiling. He finally tore his eyes from the canal and looked at her. She was wearing a dark brown dress that had a 1940s look. Her hair was tied back. He could not help noticing her slim waist. She held herself straight, hands on a chair, standing in front of a round table, on which he saw a glistening samovar and a porcelain tea set.

The room was entirely lined with books—Russian, French, German, and English. In one corner stood an old-fashioned four-poster bed with faded gold-and-blue curtains. In front of the windows was a long desk, on which he saw a computer, notebooks, pens and papers, icons, and a miniature malachite pyramid. A sagging crimson velvet sofa and some Moroccan poufs were arranged facing a vast stone fireplace in which a modern kitchen unit had been built.

"This used to be a ballroom," Lisaveta Sapounova explained. "That's why it is so big. Years ago, everything was divided and split up. The Soviet era left its scars." She pointed to long marks and traces along the walls and ceilings. "Look, there. Another floor was built, to house even more people. It was knocked down, thankfully, in the nineties. I have only one room. One big room."

He wondered if she lived alone. There were no signs of a husband or children. He guessed there was a bathroom behind a folding screen.

"Please call me Lisa. Tell me about yourself," she said once they were seated. He watched her work the samovar. She had delicate white hands. No wedding ring. "Are you a student?"

He told her about his private lessons. Then he went straight on to how he had discovered his father's real name. He explained how his family had never talked about it. He showed her his father's and Nina's birth certificates. She looked at them and said, "Your grandmother was born in an ancient clinic near the Tauride Gardens, which is now a university."

"And my father?" asked Nicolas.

"Not in a hospital. Pisareva Street. I can take you to the address. It is not too far from here. We can walk."

She handed him some toast, butter, and jam.

"What else can I do to help you?"

"I don't know. I'm lost," he admitted sheepishly. "I don't know where and how to begin."

"Well," she said, "we could go to the registry office of the Admiralteysky District, which is the area your family lived in. Perhaps we can look up your great-grandparents."

"Thank you," he said. "This is very kind of you."

"In Russian, we say *spassiba*, Nikolaï." Again she pronounced his name in the Russian manner and flashed her rare smile at him. "And your father, Fiodor in Russian, Théodore in French. Did you know they were the same names?"

"No," said Nicolas.

"Did your father or grandmother ever speak in Russian?"

"No, never," he said.

They ate the rest of the meal in silence.

"Our city has a history of pain and glory, and we still bear that stigmata today," said Lisa Sapounova as, later, she led him along wide streets humming with traffic, sometimes pausing to point out a monument, a statue, a bridge, a church.

In the registry office, Nicolas sat waiting in a dismal, ungainly hall that throbbed with the legacy of beleaguered times and the oppressive stamp of *nomenklatura*. The people working there did not have smiling faces. Lisa Sapounova explained that this was the Russian manner, a sort of gruff protection. It did not mean they were all unfriendly.

A few moments later, she brandished a sheet of paper. "Look, Nikolaï," she said triumphantly. "That wasn't very difficult."

He glanced down at the sheet of paper. There wasn't a single word he could decipher.

"Oh!" she exclaimed, sitting down next to him. "I'm sorry. You don't read Russian. Let me translate. So. This, here, says that your great-grandmother Natacha Ivanovna Levkina died in 1982, and your great-grandfather Vladimir Nicolaevitch Koltchine in 1979. And, here, a list of their children."

"My grandmother Nina."

"Yes, Zinaïda, and the other child."

"The other child?" asked Nicolas, surprised.

He stared down at the paper.

"*Da*, look," said Lisa Sapounova. "This here means your grandmother Zinaïda Vladimirovna, born in 1945. She was born right after the siege, like many babies at that time. This, here, is another name, a brother born before her. You see?"

The cheerless hall fell silent. From down the corridor, Nicolas heard the patter of footsteps, some voices. Then silence descended, again.

"What is his name?" asked Nicolas warily, but he already knew.

"Alexeï Vladimirovitch. Born in 1940."

As he later followed Lisa Sapounova to this father's birthplace on nearby Pisareva Street, Nicolas was quiet. She seemed to understand, without having to be told, that he did not want to talk. He kept his head down, his eyes on the pavement. He did not look up once, except to admire the golden Baroque spires and domes of St. Nicholas Cathedral. He did not want to voice the questions that were whirling around in his head. Was Alexeï still alive? His great-grandparents' certificates bore no mention of his death. But their daughter's death in 2000 was not mentioned, either. Nicolas wondered whether he should try to find Alexeï. Was it worth going through all this trouble?

"It is here," said Lisa Sapounova, halting.

The tall ocher building in front of them was old, its facade a mesh of cracks and patchy spots. It had a large arched doorway, five floors, divided into numerous apartments. This area, Kolumna, had changed for the better and was still changing, explained Lisa Sapounova. It had been derelict and run-down for many years; some streets in the neighborhood were still insalubrious. It had a scruffy, poorer look to it. Nicolas looked up at the many windows, where he could glimpse potted plants, different colored curtains and blinds. Behind one of those windows, his father had drawn his first breath. Underneath that arched doorway, Zinaïda had left forever, holding Fiodor in her arms. He asked Lisa Sapounova if she had noticed his grandmother's age when Fiodor Koltchine, her son, was born. Lisa Sapounova said she had. Fifteen years old. His grandmother had probably hidden her pregnancy till the end, and the child had been born here, in the family home. It had no doubt been difficult for Nina's parents, for her. It was hard to imagine the lives of people living in this city forty-five years ago, she went on. So many aspects had changed drastically. Even she herself, born and bred in the city, who had witnessed the dissolution of the Soviet Union in 1991, found it arduous to describe the extent of the transformation. Nicolas asked if she had any idea how his grandmother could have met Lionel Duhamel, the young businessman who was to adopt her child, and to wed her, a year later, in France. No, she did not, and it would be hard to find out. But with a little imagination, one could think of options, she mused. If his grandmother had been a pretty girl, then it made things easier. Pretty girls got attention, even during the Cold War. Had Nicolas ever thought about the love factor? she asked, unsmilingly. The love factor did make things much simpler, didn't it? Maybe Lionel Duhamel had come to attend a conference at one of the universities, and perhaps Zinaïda had accompanied an older friend there. That was all it took. Love was all Lionel Duhamel would have needed to get Nina and her child out of the Soviet Union. Was Lionel Duhamel well-off? she asked. Did he have money? He did, Nicolas told her. Well, then, there was his answer, love and the right amount of rubles placed in the right hands. No need to look further, she said. Nicolas looked down at Lisa Sapounova, a trim figure in her dark raincoat. Perhaps she was right, he said, but to him, there was another element, something else. His grandmother had wanted to flee this country, to change her name, to never come back, to erase everything Russian about her. Why?

During long parts of the night, while Erik or Anders, along with a recently arrived Dutchman, snored, Nicolas lay on his back and thought of Alexeï. Was this the Alexeï who wrote that letter in 1993? Why had Nina never mentioned her family in Saint Petersburg, her parents, her brother? Why had she crossed them out of her life?

The following day, Lisa Sapounova met Nicolas at the youth hostel to inform him she had been able to locate where his grandparents were buried, thanks to a friend who worked at the archives office that held the records for all the Saint Petersburg cemeteries. The Volkovo Cemetery was situated at the south of the city. Metro line five took them straight there. Ivan Turgenev was also buried at Volkovo, she informed Nicolas on their way, as well as Lenin's mother. When they arrived, Nicolas was surprised. He had never seen a graveyard with so many trees. Although it was November, and most of them had lost their leaves, he imagined the greenness of spring and summer. The place was deserted and silent. The tombs bore Russian crosses, and on many were enameled photographs of the deceased. The more ancient tombs were slanted, mossy, their lettering faded. The alleys were long and humid, often muddy. Lisa Sapounova's small feet in their elegant high-heeled lace-up boots deftly avoided the puddles. The air was moist and earthy. Vladimir and Natacha. Nicolas knew nothing of them. How strange to be coming now to their grave. The great-grandson they never knew. It took a while for Lisa Sapounova to find the tomb. She kept looking down at her map. Suddenly, she stopped. She leaned over, put her hand on a railing surrounding a grave, and said in a low voice, "This is it. Here they are. Koltchine."

A Russian cross, made of stone. A black marble grave.

"Oh, wait!" Lisa Sapounova exclaimed. "Oh, look . . ."

Nicolas leaned closer. He could not read the names, but he saw the enameled photographs. A black-and-white image of a couple in their fifties: a man with a long, narrow face and a gentle smile, and a woman with rounded cheeks, a scarf around her head. Another photograph showed a younger man, with a face that was so shockingly like his father's that he gasped.

"Who . . . who is that?" Nicolas stammered, grasping the railing.

"The couple are your great-grandparents," said Lisa Sapounova. "The younger man is Alexeï, their son. Your father's uncle. He looks so very much like you, Nikolaï. It is astonishing." Stunned, Nicolas read the dates. Наташа 1925–1982. Владимир 1921–1979. Алексей 1940–1993.

He finally spoke, turning to look at her. "There is one more thing I need to know. The exact date of Alexeï Koltchine's death in 1993."

The answer came later, back in the gloomy registry office where they had been the day before.

Lisa Sapounova translated it for him. "Alexeï Vladimirovitch Koltchine never married. He had no children. He died in Saint Petersburg on July fifteenth, 1993."

Nicolas sits for a while in the room after Malvina's departure. Then he stands up and shakes himself like a drowsy animal coming out of hibernation. A new energy races through him. He dials the reception desk and reaches a woman who says she is Carla. Yes, he knows Signorina Voss has taken an earlier car and has asked to be put on an earlier flight, *grazie*. He asks Carla if it is possible for him to stay another night. And can his plane ticket be canceled and another one obtained for tomorrow afternoon? He is informed he will be called back in a couple of minutes. In the meantime, Nicolas sends an e-mail to Alice Dor. He writes to tell her she must not worry. He pleads with her to believe him. He is sorry for the misunderstanding, but there is no deal with Dagmar Hunoldt. None at all. When Alice wanted to sign the contract for the new book, she seemed in such a hurry, he hadn't dared admit he had not started to write. This is all his fault. He feels guilty; he feels terrible. He will return the advance. He will explain everything when he gets back tomorrow. They must talk. When can he meet her?

The receptionist calls him. Does he mind changing rooms? There are many new arrivals tonight, because of the party Dr. Gheza is throwing for some close friends to celebrate their wedding. He is most welcome to join the gathering, which starts at seven, on the terrace. The new room will be smaller, but with the same ocean view. Is that okay? Nicolas says of course, okay, no problem. He asks if someone can pick up his suitcase. He is told his suitcase can be packed for him by one of the housekeepers and that it will be moved to his new room on the next floor. He can go there as soon as he is ready. As for his transfer and flight the next day, everything has been taken care of and they are awaiting confirmation. Just before Carla hangs up, Nicolas says, "Can you tell me if Mrs. Dagmar Hunoldt is still here? Will she be attending the party tonight?"

He is asked to repeat the name.

"I'm sorry, I've checked, Signor Kolt, but we do not have a guest here under that name."

He is stymied. Is Dagmar Hunoldt registered under one of her husbands' names? He tries to describe her to Carla. A lady in her sixties. White hair, tied back, a panama hat. A heavier version of the actress Glenn Close.

"No," says Carla, "I'm afraid that does not ring a bell. I'll ask my colleague Lodovico. Hold on. . . . *Un momento* . . . Lodovico says maybe you mean Signora Jordaens? She was here with her husband, but she left this afternoon."

Nicolas asks Carla for the correct spelling of the name, thanks her, and hangs up. He picks up the BlackBerry, looks up Jordaens on Google. He sees photos of people who have nothing to do with Dagmar Hunoldt. He is mystified. Was it her? Or a woman who looked like her? Was she staying at the hotel? Or just coming in for an early swim and breakfast from a nearby yacht? He feels like he has been conned. Was he playing up to a total stranger?

MOM flashes on the screen.

"Hey!" he says, gasping with pleasure and relief.

Emma laughs. "You sound like you've missed me."

"I have!" he says. "You'll never know how much."

He wonders if she is still on the boat with her boyfriend in Saint-Tropez.

"How's Ed?" he asks cautiously.

"Fine. I suppose you're curious about him now that you've spoken to him?"

"Very curious. But happy for you."

"Are you having a lovely time in Italy, Nicolas? Are you working hard on your book?"

He looks around the beautiful room, noticing that Malvina has left the Rolex in the middle of the bed. It is lying there, useless and glittering, like a discarded toy. He picks it up and shoves it into his suitcase with a pang of anger.

"No," he mutters. "I'm having the worst time ever."

"What's wrong?" She sounds worried.

A knock on the door. He asks his mother to hold on. It is one of the housekeepers, coming for the packing. He is embarrassed to watch the woman handle his things while he is still in the room. He tells her he will help her; then it will be done faster. While she folds his clothes, he'll deal with the stuff in the bathroom.

Once he is in the bathroom, he resumes the call to his mother.

"Sorry about that. I'm in the middle of packing."

"What's wrong, Nicolas?"

"Malvina is pregnant. It wasn't planned. At least not by me. And she wants to keep the baby."

"I'm not surprised." His mother's voice is cold.

"What do you mean?"

"I never liked her. I never trusted her. Ever since the first time I saw her."

He sighs. "Why didn't you tell me?"

"What could I say? She was young, lovely. You thought she was soft and gentle, but I never saw that. I never saw that softness. I guess you were lonely, you were taken by her, and you were never over Delphine. That's how it happened. That's how these things happen."

"Yes," he says grimly, "and now I'm trapped. She left, earlier on, for reasons I don't want to go into right now, and all of a sudden, she was someone else. It was dreadful. Another woman. A stranger. She wants compensation. She wants us to get married. To get married!"

The last words ring out in the salmon pink bathroom.

His mother's tone is firm and strong, the teacher's voice. He had often made fun of that voice, but today, listening to it does him good; it reassures him.

"Nicolas, no one is going to force you to do what you don't want to do. Nothing, no one. You can get a lawyer onto this. You did not want this child. This is not your choice. You are not in love with this girl. Remember that."

"Mom, there's a baby on the way!"

"Perhaps. But you need to keep your calm; you have to stop panicking. She trapped you."

"Did you feel trapped by Dad when you got pregnant?" he asks.

"No! Of course not. We wanted you. You were everything we always wanted. We were so proud when we found out I was pregnant."

"But you were so young, both of you."

"Old enough to know we wanted to be parents. You were our decision. This is not what is happening to you today. She is turning that baby into a hostage. You are going to have to put up a fight."

He thinks of what lies ahead: the lawyers, the endless battle, the registered mail with recorded delivery, the mediators, and the child, the faceless child. He knows he will not shy away from being that father's child. He will legally recognize it as his own, if the DNA tests prove he is indeed the father. It is Malvina he will have to reckon with for the rest of his life, even if he now knows he will leave her. He will refuse to get married. But she will still be linked to him forever, as his child's mother. A fierce thought comes, and he does not fight it. What if she has a miscarriage? Those things happen; women lose babies in the early stages. Is it wrong for him to hope with all his heart that she might naturally miscarry?

"I miss you, Mom."

"I miss you, too, Nicolas."

"We have some catching up to do, don't we?"

"We do."

He says good-bye to his mother and returns to the bedroom. His suitcase is ready, and a bellboy is summoned. He thanks the housekeeper, tips her, and follows the bellboy to the new room. It is smaller, but just as comfortable. The sea view is perhaps even lovelier from here. He tips the bellboy and pulls the door shut. A strange, lonely peace comes over him. He lies on the bed and peruses his e-mails (no answer yet from Alice Dor), checks the social networks. He skims through. Nothing retains his attention. He puts the BlackBerry away. He might as well go down to the party for the newlywed friends of Dr. Gheza. But instead, he stays on the bed, hands crossed behind his neck. He thinks of Malvina taking off on a plane back to Paris. Her determination. The new assurance she now flaunts. The Rolex lying in the middle of the bed. He thinks of Delphine, and he wonders whether one day he will have the courage to tell her he still loves her. Would she laugh at him? Would she give him another chance? He thinks of Dagmar Hunoldt. Was it truly her? He would never know, unless he did meet her, one day. Mercury Retrograde . . . Epicure . . . And him, hanging on to every word. What a complete idiot! Roxane, François, and the sting of their words. Savannah, the luscious lips he nearly kissed. Cassia Carper, her legs, her shoes, and her tongue in his mouth. Sabina, her husband, and the e-mails, the photographs. He doesn't know why, but he smiles. He thinks of Laurence Taillefer writing her articles and stops smiling. Nelson Novézan. His leer. His tobacco-stained yellow fingers. His ego.

Alice Dor. Her tears. Her voice on the phone. Winning her trust back. Winning her esteem back. Writing at last. He is reminded of that unforgettable moment in her office when she said to him, four years ago, "Have you thought of publishing this book under another name? Or do you want to stick to Nicolas Duhamel?" He had replied immediately. "No," he said. "I want to sign it Nicolas Kolt." She had held out her hand to shake his and said, smiling, "Good. I hope to publish many other books by Nicolas Kolt."

It is only a shiver, a shudder, but he feels it: heady, intoxicating energy.

And he sees it: a tendril of blue haze unfurling in front of his eyes.

WHEN NICOLAS RETURNED FROM Saint Petersburg in November 2006 with a heavy cold, he sent an e-mail to Lisaveta Sapounova the morning after his arrival.

> *Dear Lisa,*
> *Thank you for your precious help. There is one final question I need you to answer for me. You are the only person who can help. It's going to sound strange, but here it is.*
> *I need to know how Alexeï Koltchine died. He was only fifty-three when he passed away, and I must know how. It's important for me. Is there any way you can find this out? I'm sorry for the trouble.*
> *I often think of you in your room overlooking the blue Fontanka.*
> *Maybe one day, I will come back. I would like that very much.*
> *Thank you again,*
> *Nicolas Duhamel*

Lisaveta Sapounova did not respond for a few days, but when she did, Nicolas had to print the e-mail and then read it on paper over and over again.

> *Dear Nicolaï,*
>
> *It was a pleasure to hear from you. And it is a pleasure to help you. I am presently sitting in my room, a trifle cold and damp today, drinking tea and translating. The Fontanka is still as blue and lovely, and we have had some snow already.*
>
> *I found the information you wanted rather quickly. Another friend of mine works for a newspaper and she has access to that sort of data, which I don't.*
>
> *However, I must warn you, Nicolaï, that what you are going to read is not happy news. I feel I must tell you. You are still very young. And now that I know you a little, I can guess you are a sensitive person.*
>
> *I have taken the liberty of translating the short article that was published in the local newspaper in late July 1993. Please find it herewith. I hope that reading it will not be too distressing for you.*
>
> *My thoughts and prayers are with you,*
> *LS*

The body of a drowned man was found floating yesterday morning at dawn in the Griboedov canal, just across from the Kazan Cathedral. The man has been identified as Alexeï Vladimirovitch Koltchine, fifty-three years old, an office clerk, unmarried, no children, living near Sennaya Square. His neighbors describe him as a gentle, timid man, with few friends, who led a quiet life. He had no problems at work, where he was employed for the past fifteen years. Forensic tests reveal a large quantity of liquor in the bloodstream. The body does not show signs of batter or foul play. There was a letter in Alexeï Vladimirovitch Koltchine's pocket, but the long moments spent in the water diluted the ink, and thus the writing was no longer readable. The police are pursuing their inquiries, but at this stage it has been impossible to determine whether Alexeï Vladimirovitch Koltchine stumbled and fell into the canal, or whether he decided to take his own life. He will be buried in his parents' grave at Volkovo.

ALEXEÏ. ZINAÏDA. FIODOR.
His Russian blood.

What had happened behind those walls in that old building on Pisareva Street where his father was born?

The brother. The sister. Five-year difference between them. The small, cramped apartment.

Had it been a hideous, forceful act? Had it been a secret, doomed, impossible love? What had Natacha and Vladimir known?

When Alexeï wrote to his sister in July 1993, some thirty years later, was he asking for her forgiveness? Or had Alexeï written to say he could not live without Zinaïda? That he was going to put an end to it all?

The letter retained all its mystery. Nicolas could see it perfectly, the envelope, dingy from its long trip from Saint Petersburg to Paris, made of plain white paper. The careful, curly handwriting. "Madame Lionel Duhamel. Boulevard Saint-Germain." Or had it been forwarded to the villa near Nice? Nicolas imagined the break-fast tray, toast, coffee, the pot of milk, jam, honey, the morning papers. She must have stared at that Russian stamp when the letter arrived. The leap of her heart when she understood her brother had written it.

How had the envelope found its way into Théodore's hands? Who had shown him that letter? Had Alexeï written a similar one to Théodore?

Suddenly, the novel was mapped out in front of Nicolas, like a runway lights up for a plane arriving by night: He had only to follow the lights, pinpricked in his head. The book formed around the mystery of a father. Mysterious in every way. The father's birth. The father's death. No one could tell. No one knew. People who did know were no longer alive to tell the truth, to reveal it in its entirety.

Nicolas never wished to be in his book. The choice was clear from the start. He needed to turn away from his own story to spin another tale. Yet what he invented had solid roots sprouting from deep within him. Roots seeped with his emotions. His turmoil. His questions. His searching. His quest.

Nicolas did not have all the answers. He had only possibilities. Choices. Exploring them the way he did in the novel both shielded him and offered him a form of protection, a manner of dealing with what the truth could be. Whatever that truth could be.

In his book, Margaux discovered the letter hidden behind a loose floorboard in the ancient Zeccherio household, near the small piazza. A letter lying there for years, waiting to be read. A letter from a brother to a sister. A farewell letter. A letter that said the unthinkable. Margaux had to sit down. Her knees gave way. She clutched the envelope to her heart and cried. Somehow, her father had read that letter, the one she was holding in her trembling hands, and her father knew what she now knew, that he had been born of the impossible love between a brother and a sister. The avalanche had been no accident. Her father had taken his own life.

"How dare you suggest something so hideous?" Elvire Duhamel

had screamed two years later, when she read *The Envelope* after it was published in 2008. "Have you lost your mind, Nicolas? You have no proof, no proof at all! All I can say is, thank God you are signing this book Nicolas Kolt and not Nicolas Duhamel. And thank God my poor father passed away last year, so he can never read this rubbish."

But Nicolas's mother, Emma, had been so moved by the novel that she had not been able to speak; she only held his hands and squeezed them. Later, she wrote him a note, which he kept.

> *Nico,*
> *I understand what you have tried to do. I see how you have filled in the blanks, your way. No one has the answers, but you have opened up doors, courageously; you have looked at truth in the face. You have done what none of us would have dared do. I am proud of what you have written. Bravo, Nicolas Kolt. My son.*

Lisaveta Sapounova sent him a handwritten card made of thick pale green paper. He also kept this one, preciously.

> *Dear Nikolaï,*
> *I read* The Envelope *with pleasure.*
> *You will be happy to know that the Russian translation of your novel, which I bought at the bookstore Dom Knigui, on the Nevsky Prospekt, is fluid, almost as good as what mine could have been.*
> *I was moved by your portrayal of Margaux Dansor and her family secret. You have written a powerful book, which I'm sure will become very successful.*
> *I do hope that one day, you will write a novel about your intimate connection to Russia, and to Saint Petersburg. Because, after all, you are half Russian. If ever you choose in the future to write about your own Russian heritage, in any*

way, please be assured that I would be willing to be your guide once again.

And perhaps this time, I will have the honor of translating the book myself, for you? Warm wishes from the Fontanka,
LS

At eight o'clock, nicolas changes into jeans and a white shirt and goes down to the terrace. A crowd is gathered around a buffet. It seems to him the guests are even more elegant than usual. Some men are wearing black tie, and he spots a couple of extravagant ball gowns. He is offered champagne and greeted warmly by Dr. Gheza.

"We are very glad you could stay with us for another night," says the hotel director. "Let me introduce you to the happy couple."

The newlyweds, in their late twenties, are named Cordelia and Giorgio. They seem glued together from hip to shoulder like conjoined twins. Cordelia wears an ivory satin dress and has pearls woven into her blond hair; Giorgio is in a perfectly cut white suit. Neither of them recognize Nicolas. I never get the balance right, he thinks despairingly as Cordelia glances superciliously at his jeans. Either people fall over backward when they realize he is Nicolas Kolt and become embarrassingly obsequious or they have no idea who he is and he feels snubbed.

A silver-haired crooner with smoldering eyes and a chocolatelike tan is installed behind the grand piano. His voice is deep and rich, with Sinatra-like undertones. He sings "La Vie en Rose" with such purpose, he could have written the song himself. Waiters bring a fancy pink wedding cake. People clap and cheer. The couple kisses. More clapping and cheering. Nicolas has another glass of champagne. As he drinks it, watching the night fall once again upon the Gallo Nero, he feels someone watching him. He whips around and is confronted with Alessandra, his fan, taking a snap of him with her phone. Her face goes beet red when she sees she has been caught.

All of sudden, it clicks. Alessandra . . . Alex . . .

"You're Alex Brunel." It isn't a question. It is a fact.

She nods, quaking.

"You need to take those photos off my wall," he barks. "If you don't do it, you'll be hearing from my lawyer. Do you understand?"

"But everyone posts photos on your wall!" she wails. "Why am I the one getting into trouble?"

He feels a vicious rage swirl up within him. He lets it explode. The wrath not only sparks from Alessandra's faux pas; it is rendered even more powerful by the unfortunate events of the past few days.

"I am here on a private holiday," he roars, not caring if guests are looking their way, surprised. "I did not want anyone to know where I was, nor who I was with, and now, thanks to you and your photos, everyone knows."

She cowers. He despises her flabby upper arms, her flowery perfume, her blue eye shadow.

"Of course," he goes on, fuming, "you have no idea of the damage those photos caused. You don't care, do you? What were you going to do tonight, huh? Post more photos? Well, now I've caught you, haven't I?"

Nicolas grabs his BlackBerry, shoves it into her face, and takes a photo, an unflattering one, where she is all quivering nostrils, double chin, and shiny, coarse skin. In an instant, it is posted on his Facebook wall, for his 250,000 "friends" to see. He writes, gloatingly, "A taste of your own medicine. Alessandra, alias Alex Brunel."

She turns and flees. Nicolas ignores the glances shot at him and finishes a third glass of champagne. He wanders over to the bar. The people here tonight appear to be as rich as they are boring. He listens to the mellifluous chatter. "Oh, darling, how marvelous." "Yes, Anastasia and Gaspard have just moved; the triplex has been redone by Fabien, and it is out of this world." "Did you see Paolo this summer? He has a new yacht." "I feel sorry for that revolting man's poor wife, after what he did to that maid." "We are here till tomorrow, then off to Rome, but Lorenzo is taking his plane—you know what he's like." "Wanda looks so thin. I wonder who her new doctor is?" "Hélène is leaving Rodophe, but she gets to keep the château."

He wishes Cassia Carper was here, with Savannah and the other models. He even wishes Novézan was still around. And Chris, the blond actor. The American ladies are not to be seen—perhaps not select enough to be invited to the party? The Swiss couple and the gay couple are not here, either. Have they left? Gone back to their pampered lives?

"Good evening, Signor Kolt." Giancarlo, the barman, smiles at him. "Signorina Voss is not with you?"

"She is in Paris, or on her way there."

"Are you enjoying the evening?"

Nicolas chuckles. "Not particularly. Those newlyweds look like a scene out of *Gossip Girl*."

"She is from the richest family in Italy," says Giancarlo, lowering his voice. "And he is part of the aristocracy. They were married yesterday in Rome; it was all over the papers."

"Thrilling," says Nicolas ironically. "I guess I'll have some more champagne."

The heiress and the prince are now dancing cheek to cheek as the silver-haired crooner launches into "La Mer," by Charles Trenet.

They are watched by doting parents, grannies, aunts, bosom buddies. Nicolas has rarely seen such a concentration of gems, plastic surgery, and luxury watches.

As he drinks the champagne, feeling giddy, he realizes he has Davide's card in his pocket. Maybe he should call Davide, get him to pick him up in the Riva, and go back to the Villa Stella for another delicious meal.

"That's strange," says Giancarlo, staring out to sea.

Nicolas follows his gaze. He spots one of the gigantic cruise ships on the darkening water.

"What is it?"

"The *Sagamor*. It is coming in so close. Look."

Nicolas notices the ship is much nearer than it was on Friday night. He can make out the enormous black letters of its name. A muffled rumor filters from the vast boat, the humming buzz of music, of hundreds of voices.

"You mean to do the *inchino*?" Nicolas asks.

Giancarlo nods. "Yes. But it hasn't blown its horn. And it never sails this far in."

Nicolas shrugs. "Maybe a new distraction on board?"

"Perhaps."

The huge boat does not seem to be moving. It has halted near the reef that Dagmar Hunoldt and he swam out to that very morning, blazing with hundreds of lights, sitting on the water like an oversized glittering building.

"What is it doing?" asks Giancarlo. "I see this boat twice a week, all through the season, and I've never seen it come so near and stop like that."

Waiters are now handing shrimp canapés to the guests. The crooner is deep into "Ti Amo." A group of people is slowly dancing. Cornelia and Giorgio exchange wet, amorous kisses. A scowling middle-aged man stops in front of Nicolas. He is wearing a tuxedo.

"You're the writer, aren't you?" he says bluntly, lighting a cigar.

He has a snarly, unpleasant voice.

The smoke wafts over to Nicolas, who welcomes the Pavlovian poke to his father.

"I am," he replies.

The man puffs away. "My wife absolutely adores you," he says tonelessly. Then he walks off, without adding anything else.

Nicolas sits at the bar, his glass in his hand. To think he is Nicolas Kolt, and he has no one to spend the evening with. He nearly laughs out loud. "Those women," as his father would say with a roll of his eyes and down-turned lips. Nicolas looks around him, his elbow resting on the bar, and he takes in each detail of the party as the moon rises and the night falls; the murmur of voices, the dazzling array of gowns, of jewels, the strum of music, the candles, the cigar smoke, the languor of the summer evening.

A young woman of his age, with long brown hair, stumbles up to him.

"You're that writer," she drawls.

She seems tipsy, or high, or both. She is wearing a silk and gauze taupe dress that is too short, revealing anorexic knees. A diamond the size of a grape sparkles on her finger.

She holds out an unsteady glass to Giancarlo. "Just fill it up," she says. "Vodka. Or whatever."

She hoots with laughter.

"Are you alone?" she asks Nicolas, focusing unnatural violet-colored eyes on him. She is not pretty—her nose is too large, her mouth crooked—but there is an appeal about her.

"Indeed," he replies.

She presses up to him. "Really? No girlfriend? A good-looking guy like you?"

He grins halfheartedly. "There was a girlfriend." He nearly adds, And now there's a baby, but he doesn't.

"I'm alone, too. I am so fucking bored." Another screech.

"Are you friends with Cornelia?" he asks.

"Cordelia," she says, correcting him. She is trying to sit on a high stool, and failing. He helps her up. "Yeah. I'm her older sister. The spinster."

"What's your name?"

"Liliana. But just call me Lily. Why are you here?"

"I was invited by Dr. Gheza."

"Fat old snob. Can't stand his guts."

"He's standing not too far away, Lily."

"So what? Who cares." She bats her eyelashes at Nicolas and wets her lips. "Are you going to put me in your new book?"

"Should I?"

"Seriously. Please do it. I'll pay you."

"Just tell me why I should."

"Why? Because I'm the pathetic older sister. The one no one has looked at since Cordelia was born. I'm the drug addict, the drunkard. I'm the one who gives blow jobs to my father's friends in their Maseratis and Ferraris. I give very good blow jobs, you know."

"I'm sure," he says, amused.

Giancarlo and he exchange glances.

"Do you want a blow job?" she asks, her voice slurred.

"Well, that's kind of you, Lily, but no, not right now. Please tell me more about why I should put you in my book."

She fumbles around in her purse, finds a pack of cigarettes, and lights one. She offers the pack to him. "You don't smoke, either?" she says when he shakes his head.

"No. But I drink—a lot. Go on. Tell me."

"You should put me in your book because I'm desperate. I live alone, in a magnificent apartment in Rome on the Piazza Navona. I have so much money, I don't know what to do with it. I haven't had a real boyfriend for years, but I've slept with over a hundred men since I was fourteen. I have a degree in law no one cares about. I'm much smarter than my sister, but, alas, I don't have her looks, so no one notices. Desperate characters are always more interesting, aren't they? You know that; you're a writer. Look at Anna Karenina. Or Madame Bovary. Although I wouldn't go so far

as killing myself. Afraid of the mess. Tonight, for instance, because I'm so desperate, I could do something foolish and ridiculous, just to ruin my sister's party. If you look over there, you will
see the way my parents are watching me. See, that spindly man
with the glasses, in black tie, and that pinched-faced woman in
green, drenched in diamonds. My parents. Look at them. They are
so worried that something might go wrong tonight in their perfect
world. And over there, look, my new brother-in-law's parents. Like
royalty, my dear. That posh lady in blue, wearing her ridiculous
tiara, and that bloated man with the white mustache. All these
people here tonight are the crème de la crème of Rome—bankers,
trophy wives, heirs, designers, politicians, masters of the universe
who fly in private jets and who get their monogrammed sheets
changed every day."

"Just how would you ruin the party, Lily?"

"I'm drunk enough already as it is, but I have a couple of ideas. I
could strip and jump naked into the pool. I could set some woman's
haute couture dress on fire. I could smash up the buffet. I could
call the Gallo Nero from my cell phone and tell them a bomb is
going to go off."

A loud explosion startles them, coming from the sea, from the
motionless *Sagamor*. Fireworks, popping upward like long-stemmed
white flowers.

"Looks like people on board know the famous newlyweds are
here tonight," says Giancarlo drily. "That boat has been there for
over an hour. Maybe they're hoping to join the party."

The guests clap and cheer again. More fireworks go off loudly,
shimmering into the black sky.

A woman's gushing voice is heard: "What a lovely idea! How
sweet of them!" Nicolas notices Dr. Gheza's looking out to sea with
a perplexed expression. A couple of smaller boats can be made out
in the dusk, speeding toward the *Sagamor*. Dr. Gheza walks
quickly to the bar and asks Giancarlo for the telephone. He speaks
staccatolike in rapid Italian that Nicolas does not catch. His hand

slices the air, moving up and down. His mouth is tight and thin. Then he hangs up and storms away. Lily translates.

"The old snob wants to know what those *cazzos* on board think they are doing. How the hell do they know about the wedding party? No one from the *Sagamor* is allowed to land at the Gallo Nero tonight. 'Get some men out there right now to stop boats coming in.' That's what he said."

Disco music is now being played. The silver crooner has gone. The golden honeymooners move with the smooth, sure steps of nightclubbers. "Dancing Queen," by Abba. Other couples join in; they twirl and strut, smiling and laughing.

"How I hate watching my parents dance," groans Lily. "It's almost as bad as imagining them having sex, which I'm sure they haven't for the past century."

"I think I must put you in my novel," says Nicolas. "You're just too funny."

"I knew I could corrupt you." She grins back. "Do you think writers are vampires? I mean do you use us? All the people you meet in your everyday life. Do you suck inspiring stuff out of us?"

"Yes, we do," he says grudgingly. "In a way. Only it's not that simple."

"I'd love to be a famous writer. I would write scandalous novels about my ex-boyfriends and get excommunicated by the Pope. I would have adoring fans lining the Piazza Navona just for a glimpse of me having a joint on my terrace. My parents would never speak to me again. It would be divine. Are you working on a new book? Or do you hate that question?"

"I hate that question." He laughs. "But I'll answer it. I'm supposed to be working on a new book."

"And you're not?"

"My publisher thought I had nearly finished it, when I hadn't even started it. Now, because of some stupid Facebook pictures, she thinks I've sold it to someone else. She's furious and hurt."

"So what are you going to do?"

"Write the book. Send it to her when it's finished."

"And what is the new book about? Or are you not telling?"

Nicolas smiles down at her. "You'll see."

They gaze out to the immobile *Sagamor.*

"That ginormous thing looks like a floating parking lot," drawls Lily. "It's ruining my view. Who would ever pay to spend time on such an ugly boat?"

"The cruises are popular with older people," says Giancarlo. "The seniors."

"I would rather die," groans Lily.

"My sister went," Giancarlo continues. "It is luxurious, signorina. The *Sagamor,* for instance, has four swimming pools, a theater, a movie center, a spa, six restaurants, a dozen bars, a discotheque. My sister loved it."

"A nightmare!" murmurs Lily. "Put me on one of those and I'll hang myself *subito presto.*"

Nicolas and Giancarlo cannot help laughing.

"At last! Look," Lily says, "it's turning. It's going away."

The angle of the brilliantly lit-up boat has changed and it seems to be heading in another direction.

"Wonder what took them so long," says Giancarlo. "A mechanical problem?"

The wedding party is dancing to "YMCA," by the Village People. The music is turned up louder. Everyone has blissful smiles. Dr. Gheza and Lily's mother are indulging in a sort of disco minuet.

"Ciao, *Sagamor,*" chants Lily in tune with the song. "Ciao, *Saga-mor!*"

"No, no, its not moving away," says Giancarlo, frowning. He screws his eyes up to see better. "This is . . . *O Dio. O Dio!*"

"What?" says Lily impatiently. "What do you mean?"

Giancarlo drops the lemon in his hands. He rushes to the part of the terrace that is closest to the seafront, leaving the party behind. He is followed by Lily, staggering on her high heels, and Nicolas.

The *Sagamor* can be seen clearly from where they now stand. It has not turned away. It is listing sharply to the right, against the reef. Flashing orange lights shine out from it like beacons, revealing panic-stricken movements of tiny figures scrambling along the decks. Several boats bob up and down on the water below, looking puny in comparison with the enormous slanting structure.

"*Madonna santa!*" says Giancarlo incredulously.

"*Ma che cazzo!*" screeches Lily, grasping Nicolas's arm.

The disco music is deafeningly loud, but the three of them can make out the blast of alarms and sirens coming from the boat, howling in the night.

"How did this happen?" asks Nicolas, hypnotized by the sight of the huge ship tilting to one side, an oversized, monstrous Humpty Dumpty.

"It came in too close," says Giancarlo. "The hull is damaged. The water is not deep enough inland for such a big vessel."

"What about those fireworks?" asks Lily. "Do you think they were for Cordelia and Giorgio?"

"I'm not sure if anyone on board knew the party was being held here, signorina. Dr. Gheza asked that it be kept secret."

"So you're saying that those fireworks were distress rockets?"

"Yes." Giancarlo nods. "Only we didn't realize there had been an accident. Everyone took too long to react. We were busy with the party."

"How many people do you think are on board?" asks Nicolas.

"Around four thousand," says Giancarlo.

"Why aren't they getting passengers off? What are they waiting for?"

A group of men appear on the lower terrace, just below them. They are armed, wearing blue-and-red uniforms.

"Oh! The police!" cries Lily with relish, clapping her hands. "*Mamma mia!* Looks like my prayers have been answered after all. Cordie's party is going to be so ruined."

DONNA SUMMER AND "LOVE to Love You Baby" resonate across the Gallo Nero. Cordelia and Giorgio, unfazed by the presence of their parents, eagerly show their entourage how unabashed their sex life is as they mime copulation to perfection, encouraged by clapping, whistling, and cheering.

With voyeuristic satisfaction, Nicolas watches the police savagely interrupt the dance and order the music to be stopped. Donna Summer lets out a final strangled whimper. The dancers stand in their finery, heaving and short of breath. Dr. Gheza's face is again as black as a thundercloud. Nicolas doesn't need Lily to translate. "What on earth do the carabinieri think they're doing?" he howls, pursing thumbs and fingers together in that most Italian gesture. "This is a private party, a wedding party, with very important guests. How dare they barge in this way?" The police wordlessly point to the sinking ship, visible from the other side of the terrace. The entire party rushes to where Nicolas, Giancarlo, and Lily are standing. Dozens of telephones are held up as pictures are taken. Everyone wants a photograph of the sinking *Sagamor*.

Dr. Gheza and a man in black, the one Nicolas remembers seeing on his first day here, seem to be arguing with the police. Dr. Gheza keeps repeating "No, no, no," staunchly shaking his head. Nicolas asks Lily what the fight is about.

"The police want to open the hotel to the people being rescued. Gheza is refusing, saying they are exaggerating, that the boat is only five hundred yards away and people can swim. It's a warm night, he says; the sea is not cold."

"What a loathsome bastard!"

"Didn't I tell you?" asks Lily self-contentedly.

The *Sagamor* is now completely slanted, tipping toward them, its starboard side almost covered in water. They can see inside the void of its single smoke stack. The sirens have stopped blowing and an eerie silence has fallen. How many people are still on board, wonders Nicolas. Have they been rescued from the port side? Where are they being taken to?

The argument goes on. Do the police have any idea of the importance of the guests here tonight? Gheza goes on, stamping his foot. Lily translates for Nicolas, whispering in his ear as the director continues, seething. Can they please acknowledge the prestige of his hotel, the luxury of it. The police only have to look. The wealthiest family in the country, a best-selling author, a well-known actor, a famed politician, respected businessmen—the Gallo Nero is the sanctuary of the rich and famous. He must protect them all. This haven cannot possibly be opened to strangers, and on top of it all, the flower beds and lawns will be ruined by helicopters landing. Have they lost their minds, or what? The *Sagamor* is not going to sink; it is lying on a reef. People are near enough to be rescued by boat and taken somewhere else, end of story.

Waiters continue to offer champagne to the guests, who chatter and point to the boat with awed whispers and excited giggles. Cordelia and her new husband pose for a photo, with the *Sagamor* in the background.

"Mamma is worried her jewels might be stolen if they open the hotel to the survivors, and Papa is convinced the paparazzi will gate-crash the party," says Lily. "Oh, and now the police are saying they've heard enough. The Gallo Nero is being opened to the Sagamor survivors. Look at my parents! Look at Cordelia!" She crows in delight.

It is like watching actors on a stage. A play a modern Oscar Wilde could have written. Dr. Gheza worried about helicopters ruining his flower beds, the bride's mother, fearing for her diamonds, while out there, maybe people are drowning, maybe already dead. Nicolas could sit back and merely watch. He could choose safe passivity. He could tape it all in that secret part of his mind and use it later for the book. He will use it, he knows. But not by choosing passivity. Not by standing here and looking on.

He takes Davide's card from his pocket and dials the number. Davide answers on the first ring.

"Hey, Davide! Remember me? Nicolas Kolt? You took me to the Villa Stella last night."

Of course Davide remembers. What can he do for Signor Kolt? Meet him at the pier, now? *Certo!*

"Where are you going?" hisses Lily as Nicolas turns to leave.

"Going out there."

She sneers. "Oh, I see. Playing Mr. Hero?"

He looks down at her with pity. "Why don't you come with me?"

"Me?" she says.

"Yes, you, the desperate alcoholic spinster."

"I'm not wearing the right shoes," she mutters, looking away.

"Good-bye, Lily."

He runs down the stone steps as fast as he can. Davide is standing by the boat, waiting. A group of people are huddled together, staring out to the agonizing *Sagamor*. He recognizes the Swiss couple among them.

"Can you take me to the ship, Davide?" he asks.

"Dr. Gheza says no." Davide falters. "He ordered us to stay here and to let no boat come in."

"I don't care about Dr. Gheza. He's busy arguing with the police right now. He's going to have to open the hotel to survivors; he has no choice. We need to go see if we can help in any way."

"Can we come?" ask the Swiss couple in unison. They are good swimmers, thinks Nicolas.

"Of course!" he replies.

A woman's piercing cry is heard.

"Wait! Wait for me!"

It is Lily, shoeless, waving as she rushes down the pier.

Davide helps her on board.

"This is the most exciting thing that's happened to me in years," Lily says rapturously. "And I'm not even high!"

As they approach the gigantic mass, a bitter smell comes wafting toward them, caught on the summer breeze—the stench of burned rubber and leaking fuel. The Riva bypasses the impressive bulk of the *Sagamor,* heading out to its port side. An apocalyptic scene greets them. Lily wails. Even the Swiss couple express shock. Davide is forced to stop the engine as panic-stricken people dot the water, screaming in anguish as they flounder. Little boats jam-packed with passengers bob crazily up and down by the huge white hull, where a long gash can be seen, like a gaping, bloodless wound. Patrol boats direct powerful spotlights up at the stranded ship, and they see that lifeboats can no longer be dropped down along the *Sagamor*'s flanks because it has listed too sharply. They hang there, crooked and useless. Up on the decks, highlighted by roving spotlights, more passengers wave and shout. The monstrous ship lets out creaks and groans, as if it's a living creature thrashing in pain, about to draw its last breath.

The Swiss couple stand up. She takes off her pumps, smoothing down her long black dress. He removes his dinner jacket and shoes. With the same harmony that Nicolas admired every day during their morning swim, they dive headfirst into black water littered with debris. They swim away, and rescue an elderly woman, cradling her head in their arms as they steadily bring her back.

Nicolas and Davide haul her on board. She looks frail, like a wet bird. The old lady cries, wordlessly, clinging to them, her back racked with sobs. She finally manages to say in French that she cannot find her husband. Where is he? They jumped together; he said he was right behind her, but she cannot find him. Please, can they help her find him? Nicolas asks her what happened. Lily takes the Swiss man's jacket and wraps it around the old lady. "We were in the middle of the gala dinner. There was a bang, deep down in the ship. The plates and glasses fell off the table. No one said what happened. We had no idea what to do. For an hour, we stayed there, in the dining room, and then they said to go back to our cabins and wait. The ship was tipping sideways, more and more, and then it rolled over, falling over to its side, and my husband said to get my life jacket quickly, that we must jump. We were not far from land; he could see lights. In the terrible panic, we jumped. Please find him! Please find my husband!" Lily tries to comfort her as the Swiss couple go back into the water.

Ahead, Nicolas notices a rope ladder dangling from the *Sagamor*'s lower deck. A man wearing a long black robe is clambering up it. Another man is watching him from a small boat, steadying the ladder with both his hands.

Nicolas kicks off his shoes.

"What are you doing?" pants Lily.

"Going up there."

"Are you crazy?"

Without listening to her, he jumps into the water. It is not that easy to swim in his clothes. The sea is greasy, dirty, speckled with floating rubbish. He swims slowly to the other boat. The man on board roughly asks him what he wants in Italian. Nicolas points to the rope ladder. High up above, the man in the black robe has nearly reached the deck. The other man laughs, shaking his head. "*Pazzo!* The boat is going to roll over even more and sink! That man going up, he's a priest. He's doing his job, saving souls. You should save your own!"

Before Nicolas can answer, a feminine voice behind him bursts out in vehement, crude Italian. The man shrugs, sighs, and seems to comply, holding out his hand to help Nicolas on board.

From the boat, Nicolas turns, to see Lily in the water.

"Shit," she says. "I forgot I had my contact lenses in. I just lost both of them in the sea."

"So you can't see a thing?" asks Nicolas.

"Oh, sure I can. They just make my eyes look like Elizabeth Taylor's. You know, violet?" She turns her attention to the man on the boat. "Hey, *stronzo!*"

Shrugging again, the man pulls her into the boat, then grabs the rope ladder.

"I don't know why I'm doing this," mutters Lily, seizing the ladder. She looks down at the sopping, ruined silk of her dress. "That was Prada, you know."

It is a taxing climb. Better not glance behind, thinks Nicolas as he grasps each rope rung with a wet hand. He sees Lily's bony feet above his head, her emaciated rump. Why is she here? he wonders. Redemption? Guilt? And what about him? He nearly laughs. Yes, what the hell is he doing? No time to think. Move on. Come on. One hand after the other. Slowly. Surely.

When they get to the deck, a disturbing silence greets them. From time to time, a muffled scream or shout is heard coming from far away. The acrid stink of burning rubber is stronger here. There is another smell: the reek of fear, of anguish, of death.

The *Sagamor,* by rolling onto its side, has a changed and disturbing topography. Walls have become floors. The hallways are now vertical shafts. Each surface is treacherously slippery, coated with a slick layer of water and oil. Chunks of broken glass hang like frosty icicles. They see clumps of elderly people clinging to railings in the cavernous orange-and-purple atrium, now horizontal. Some are being helped by the priest, who got there just before them. Other trembling white-haired septuagenarians are making their slow way to a higher deck.

"Why is there no one here to help?" asks Nicolas.

"I guess the younger, stronger people got off first," replies Lily. "They left the old folks behind."

They inch gingerly across the long hallway on bare feet, skirting shards of glass and long spills of oil. They come to a restaurant, now a vast swimming pool. Hundreds of tables, gilded chairs, and white napkins float merrily by, along with thick swirls of lobster, chicken wings, smoked salmon, lettuce leaves, and bread rolls.

The glaring lights overhead begin to wink and flicker with a buzzing sound.

"Is anyone here?" yells Nicolas.

"Remember Jack and Rose? Rose made it. Jack didn't."

"Shush, did you hear that?"

"What?"

A faint wail.

"Someone is here."

They strain their ears. They hear it again, distinctly. A final flicker and fizzle, and darkness falls. The general electrical system has failed. The only feeble light comes from luminous green squares over doors and emergency exits. It takes them ten minutes to find passengers trapped in a long hallway that has become a vertical, narrow well. The people have water up to their waists. The water is slowly rising with ominous gurgles. Nicolas peers down at terrified faces eerily lit up by the green signs. Not one of them is young. How many? Three, maybe four. They speak poor English.

Nicolas rushes back to the restaurant, fishes tablecloths out of the water. He wrings them out as best as he can, then ties them feverishly together, like sheets. They lower the tablecloths. Lily and he, heaving, breathless, their palms burning, chafing, and bleeding against the damp cloth, frantically fighting the slippery surfaces, bruising and grazing their elbows and knees, haul up three shaking, wet passengers one after the other. Two women and a man. All in their seventies or eighties.

Around them, the doomed *Sagamor* shudders and groans. Deafening cracks are heard.

"We need to get off the ship. Now. We have to go," Lily says.

"Wait," orders Nicolas. "There is still someone down there."

At the bottom of the shaft, a face is turned up to them. Nicolas sends the cloth back down. The person makes no effort to take it.

"Please!" he yells. "Please let me help you! Take this; I will pull you up."

No response.

"I'm taking them with me," says Lily. "Come now!"

"Do they know who this is? A friend of theirs?" asks Nicolas.

They shake their heads. No idea. They don't know who it is. Lily herds them along, protectively, leading them away.

"Are you coming?"

"I want to rescue this person!" he shouts back to her.

Nicolas is alone. He lies flat on his stomach, the twisted sheet in his bloodied hands. He hears the regular trickling of water surging, rising higher by the minute. If he goes down there, he will not be able to make his way back up.

"Can you hear me?" he says, his voice clear, ringing out in the hallway.

The face is upturned to him once more, and in the greenish light he sees it is a woman—an elderly woman with white hair. Her eyes are large and soft. He makes out the shimmer of earrings and a necklace. She has water up to her shoulders now and her face seems to float up to him, carried by the inky water.

"Please let me help you. Just catch this with both your hands, and I will pull you up. I will bring you up and take you off the boat."

Still no answer. Just the sweet, weary old face gazing up at him. He feels a strange sort of terror pluck at him. What if he cannot save her? What if she won't let him? He takes a deep breath. He must calm down. He must think carefully.

"You must be very tired, but after I pull you up, I will carry you; you won't have to walk."

Will he be able to carry her down the rope ladder, over his shoulder? He'll bother with those details later. The important thing is to get her out of the shaft.

"Do you speak English or French?"

The old lady shakes her head.

"What is your name?"

Silence. She will not answer him. The ship groans and cracks. Nicolas hears a scream from far away. Someone crying. He feels the fear grip him again. He must get off the boat. But he cannot leave the old lady behind. He cannot walk away and leave her there in that black well.

He jabs a finger to his chest. "Nicolas," he says. "Nicolas." He points down at her. "And you?"

"Natacha."

The accent is unmistakable. His heart leaps.

"You are Russian?"

"*Da.*" She nods.

"*Puzhalsta!*" he shouts. "Please! Natacha, let me pull you up. Let me!"

He desperately wishes he had learned Russian, his grandmother's language, the language his father never knew. How he wishes he could speak it now, to coax Natacha up, to win her trust. He is sure that if he were able to say a few sentences to her in Russian, she would listen to him, let him save her.

Natacha. His great-grandmother's name. In his mind, he sees the photograph on the grave at Volkovo, the scarf knotted around her face, the gentle smile.

He wants to pronounce her name in the most Russian way possible, as if it were written in Cyrillic, Наташа, as if the Russian blood running in his veins could somehow, miraculously, reach out and reason with this old woman.

"Natacha," he cries earnestly. "Natacha!"

She shakes her head.

"*Niet, Nikolaï.*"

She utters his name the Russian way, the enchanting way Lisaveta Sapounova used to.

The black water has reached her chin. She is not afraid. She smiles up at him bravely. He cannot bear watching her.

He knows he will remember that face, that smile, for the rest of his life.

He scrambles up, crying for help, screaming at the top of his lungs, tripping and stumbling along the slippery deck. If he finds someone, they can drag Natacha out. If he finds someone, she will be safe. But there is no one in sight. He shouts, his voice hoarse, his throat painful. The only noise he hears is the gushing of water making its inexorable progress. He remembers the BlackBerry in his pocket; he thinks maybe he can call for help. But the phone did not survive the swim. He hurls it furiously away.

Out on the deck, the moon, indifferent to the chaos, casts a silvery light over the disaster. Nicolas sees how much the ship has rolled, lying fully on its starboard side. Helicopters circle overhead, aiming spotlights at the *Sagamor*. He feels there is hope. If he can attract attention, if he can show those who have come to save them where Natacha is, then perhaps she can still be rescued. He stays on board, precariously perched on the railings, waving to the helicopters, tears streaming down his cheeks as the huge carcass continues to shake and crack beneath him. He can hear the yells of passengers below in the water, but he has only Natacha on his mind, saving Natacha, making sure Natacha is safe. How long he waits, he does not know. When the men with wet suits at last set foot on the ship, he leads them back to the restaurant, now filled with water, and he realizes with horror that the shaft is unreachable, completely flooded, and that there is no hope left at all.

A<small>T DAWN, THE FIRST</small> rosy rays of the sun reveal an unearthly vision, so startling, so shocking, so hypnotizing, Nicolas cannot take his eyes off it.

A gigantic white mass, sunk against the reef, half of it rising from the water, a beached monster revealing its vulnerable, wounded belly.

SAGAMOR.

The oversized black letters. SAGA, story. AMOR, love in Italian. MOR, mort, death in French. A story of love and death. Those words, too, fascinate him.

Nicolas stands on the cement slab. His face is bruised, his arms and legs ache, and there is a gash on his chin. His white shirt is torn, his jeans are in shreds, and his hands and feet are bloody.

Around him, a medical team bustles, handing hot drinks to survivors. How many? Hundreds and hundreds of them. They roam over the Gallo Nero, wrapped in blankets; they sit on the terrace, in the restaurant, on the lawn. They seem drained. Their eyes, like his, turn again and again to the capsized ship.

Helicopters come and go. Motorboats roar in and out by the pier. The place is swarming with people. Police officers are posted at every corner. Nicolas recognizes guests from the hotel. Some do their best to help and rush around; others are already taking off, venting about the heavy traffic jam blocking access to the main roads. Others, wearing bathrobes, placidly watch the scene from their windows. More still take photographs with their phones. Waiters try to do their jobs, serving guests, also offering to help. Dr. Gheza is nowhere to be seen. Nearby villagers have come, bringing food, beverages, clothes. The press has arrived. Numerous vans with satellite dishes pop up here and there; reporters lurk, cameras in hand.

"Aren't you Nicolas Kolt?" jabbers an excited woman with a press accreditation around her neck, thrusting a microphone at him.

"Who?" he asks.

"The writer."

He shakes his head. "Nope."

She turns away, disappointed.

Sorry, he feels like saying, Nicolas Kolt is indeed here, but he doesn't feel like talking. What could he tell you anyway? That there is an after and a before? That a page has been turned overnight? That Nicolas Kolt has never felt so far away, so alienated, so distanced from himself? That his previous life bears an uncanny resemblance to the dreadful wreck of the *Sagamor*?

"Are you okay?" asks one of the doctors.

The man's features are drawn. He must have worked all night long.

"Yes. Thank you."

"That cut on your chin. Let me see."

"It's nothing."

The doctor ignores him and dabs a liquid on his chin with cotton. It smarts.

"You were one of the last people off the ship, weren't you?" asks the doctor.

Nicolas nods.

"Not like the captain. He was the first to leave, I'm told." The doctor's voice is dry. "He'll be the shame of our country for years. Twenty people died last night and at least fifty passengers are still missing. He wanted to show off in front of the Gallo Nero, to bring the boat in as close as possible."

Another agitated reporter appears, flourishing a camera.

"Nicolas Kolt! Were you on board? Can you tell us what happened?"

Should he tell the reporter that he went up on that sinking ship and desperately tried to save an old lady, and failed? That the old lady's face will haunt him till the day he dies?

"No, I'm not Nicolas Kolt." He waves the man away.

"It's true, you do look like that writer," remarks the doctor. "My wife and girls loved that book. They loved the movie, too."

Nicolas does not reply. The cut on his chin stings.

Glancing up at the terrace, he sees a group of journalists setting up an interview with lights and a camera. He recognizes Lily, still wearing her crumpled silk and gauze dress. She speaks into a microphone, miming the climbing of a ladder with her hands. The reporters listen, enthralled.

Nicolas imagines the headlines. SAGAMOR DISASTER HEROINE: BRAVE HEIRESS SAVES THE LIVES OF THREE PEOPLE THE NIGHT OF HER SISTER'S WEDDING PARTY.

He looks back at the *Sagamor*. It is impossible not to look at it. Divers can be seen circling in motorboats, commencing the grisly chore of bringing bodies back. All those goods trapped within the great ship. He makes a mental list. Luggage, clothes, money, computers, cameras, books, letters, jewelry, souvenirs, everything that will be lost forever. The vast amount of food rotting away underwater, the enormous quantities of fuel, of oil, the pollution slowly seeping into the beautiful seabed.

"Are you sure you're okay?" the doctor asks again, peering at him. "Perhaps I should have a proper look at you."

Nicolas is led to a nearby tent, told to lie down on a stretcher. His blood pressure is taken; a light is shone down his throat, into his ears. Expert hands palpate his stomach, his chest. His bleeding hands and feet are bandaged.

Nicolas feels almost comfortable lying there, save for the wretchedness tearing at his heart. He can still glimpse the wreck in all its horror through the tent's open flap. There may be passengers alive in there, somehow, somewhere, stuck in air pockets, like survivors miraculously plucked from rubble days after earthquakes. He thinks of those waiting: those who have not yet heard from their loved ones, those who have not even heard the news, seen the unbelievable images on television, those who do not yet know that death will come knocking at their door, today, with a phone call.

Exhausted, Nicolas dozes off. When he opens his eyes, the sun is high in the sky. It is past noon. Outside the tent, the same activity ensues. Haggard passengers are parked here and there. Some eat sandwiches. Others cry. Others lie under parasols, huddled up in sleep.

Nicolas walks carefully on his bandaged feet to his room. It is perfectly tidy. His clothes have been unpacked. His toiletries arranged in the bathroom. The Hamilton Khaki watch is on the bedside table. White roses and a bowl of fresh grapes sit near the sofa. It is as if nothing had happened. But when he glances through the window, he sees the bloodcurdling mass of the ship. Crowds of people are still taking photographs. Policemen firmly order them away. He watches. The telephone rings. It's reception. He has messages. Several people have tried to reach him: Emma Duhamel, Malvina Voss, Alice Dor. He should call them. They are all anxious, because his mobile is not taking messages and they have seen the alarming images on the television. Instead of making phone calls, he takes his notebook and his father's Montblanc pen. The first and only word he writes in it is the name Natacha.

Nicolas goes back down to the terrace, the Moleskine in his

pocket. He finds he cannot turn away from the *Sagamor*. He is drawn to it, chillingly. The sight of it wounds his eyes, but he must look at it again and again.

A tap on his shoulder. It is Lily, wearing jeans and a T-shirt. Her face, devoid of makeup, is surprisingly pretty.

"There you are! Mr. Hero!" She hugs him, pressing her bony body to his. "I was so worried about you! I thought you were stuck on the boat! Did you save that last person?"

"No," he chokes.

Lily's hands fly to her mouth. "Why?"

His chest feels tight.

"She wouldn't come."

The unbearable vision of Natacha waiting for her death down in the rising water makes him shudder from head to toe.

"Shit, that's so sad," mutters Lily. She wraps her arms around him again. "I should have stayed with you. We could have pulled her out, the two of us."

He manages to say, "She was Russian. Her name was Natacha. She just wouldn't be saved."

"But why?"

"I don't know."

"You're crying," murmurs Lily. "Are you all right?"

The sadness is spurting from a closed and forgotten place, from an emotion he fought so hard to protect himself from. Over Lily's head, Nicolas looks out to the wreck. Natacha. Наташа. Her weary face turned up to his in the greenish light, the dignified beauty of it, the bravery of her last smile. What was Natacha's story? Was this her first time in Italy? Who was she with? Surely she hadn't been on this cruise alone. Why had they left her behind? Had she decided to let the water circle around her and pull her in because she was too tired to move? Or was there something else? A deeper, darker reason? Some other secret explanation that gave her no more incentive to live? Some final understanding that numbed her, forcing her to stay there, trapped, as death slowly inched its wet way up her old body? Natacha's final choice triggered questions deep within him, those very questions he had not wanted to look at for so long, and that Margaux Dansor had faced for him through her own destiny, not his.

"You're going to write about all this, aren't you?" Lily murmurs.

"Yes," he replies. "I am."

"What are you going to start with?"

He holds Lily tightly. Her embrace is a comforting, friendly one.

"Before I begin, the first thing I need to do is call Alice to tell her she has a book on the way. To tell her she has not lost me, that I'm still her author and that Dagmar Hunoldt talked mumbo jumbo about astrology and Epicure."

"Dagmar, you mean *the* Dagmar Hunoldt?" whispers Lily.

"I'm not even sure it was her. It doesn't matter."

Lily takes a step back and stares up at him. Again, he is touched by her natural beauty, the simple lines of her face.

"You've changed, Mr. Hero."

"You've changed, too. That stoned girl at the bar is miles away."

She hugs him again.

"What about your ex-girlfriend? The one you wouldn't talk about? Is she still in the picture?"

"No," Nicolas says unhesitatingly, watching small dinghies circle the wreck and divers shouting to one another in Italian. "She doesn't know it yet, but she will soon."

He does not mention the unborn baby. He knows his mind is made up. There will be no wedding. No future with Malvina, even if there is a child. The strength of that inner conviction sweeps through him with an unexpected force. He does not bring up Delphine, although he also knows he will want to talk to her as soon as he returns to Paris, and that he will do everything in his power to see her.

"Are you going to put me in your book?" Lily pleads. "You promised!"

"How could I not?"

"Will it take place at the Gallo Nero? What will it be called? Will we all be in it? Will it begin with the ship sinking, or end with it?"

"I can't tell you that. I haven't even started."

"But surely you already know! Surely you can tell me about the beginning!"

He smiles at her enthusiasm. She is like a child, heady with anticipation. He already knows his journey into writing this book will be far less simple than she imagines, far more foreboding, far darker than she can ever fathom.

Nicolas is aware he will need to venture back into that black well of suffering, into Natacha's secret pain, into his own failure in trying to save her. He will have to open the door to the silent torment he was faced with when confronted with Alexeï's death, with his father's death, with the dreadful finality of their watery graves, with the many unanswered questions. Saint Petersburg awaits. Back to the Koltchine family. Back to Pisareva Street, to the Fontanka, to Volkovo, with Lisaveta Sapounova by his side.

But now Natacha's story weaves its powerful strand into his personal tapestry, adding other colors, other textures. Now Nicolas can see the book clearly, as clearly as he saw the lit-up runway for *The Envelope*. The story is sketched out in front of him, like the long, dangling rope ladder leading to the *Sagamor*'s upper deck, like the distress rockets blooming white into the dark sky. To write the novel, Nicolas knows, he will have to dip his father's Montblanc pen into Russian ink.

Acknowledgments

In alphabetical order :
Elisabeth Barillé, my "Russian sister," for being my Saint Petersburg eyes before I got there.
Elena Boudnikova, for her help.
"Momo" Cohen-Solal, for the cigar details.
Abha Dawesar, for her feedback.
Julia Delbourg, for the khâgne information.
Dagmar Hunold, for kindly lending me her name (without the *t*).
Ksenia, my Russian teacher, for her patience.
Laure du Pavillon and Catherine Rousseau-Rambaud, my faithful first readers.

Last but not least:
My Russian family, Natalya, Anka, Volodia, and their children, for their welcome and for taking us on Tatoulya and Natacha's trail in Saint Petersburg.

The SMP team in N.Y.C.

And thank you above all:
My children, Louis and Charlotte, for their unfailing support.
My husband, Nicolas, who gave me the key to Manderley.